Extrasenso
in the African American Culture

Company of Prophets describes the variety of past and present expression of African American intuitivity. African Americans who possess defined extrasensory perception, spiritual awareness, and psychic ability discuss the nature of their gifts.

Represented in the 121 persons surveyed are a range of lifestyles, economic and educational backgrounds, philosophical outlooks, religious practices, and age groups. Exemplifying these are artists, teachers, housewives, children, ministers, activists, authors, and professional psychics. Harriet Tubman, Sojourner Truth, George Washington Carver, Mary Church Terrell, Howard Thurman, and Richmond Barthe are examples of the historical and contemporary persons included. In an anecdotal framework, their experiences are largely related via direct quotes from research sources or personal interview. The struggles they faced in growing up with special qualities, adjusting to their uniqueness, and handling the attendant hardships and privileges are entailed. The subjects discuss their efforts to use their psychic faculties to improve conditions in life for themselves, their families, and society.

Each chapter addresses a different attribute of intuitivity. The psychic faculties are explained and defined through the subjects' own descriptions. The reader is afforded an opportunity to assess and affirm parallel faculties in his or her own life, and also receives an overview of various facets of extrasensory perception in the context of the African American culture. The book educates additionally via metaphysical principles and philosophical concepts from the subjects' perspectives.

Company of Prophets features the author's prose-poetry reflective of her own psychic experiences. Several psychic teachers and the author briefly explore the significance of the ancient spiritual roots in African American culture. These roots reside in the mass consciousness of the black culture, and from their source exists a potential for generating a cleansing, and a major spiritual resurgence in the group consciousness of African Americans.

About the Author

One of seven children of African American parents who migrated north from Virginia in the 1930s, Joyce Elaine Noll grew up in East Harlem in New York City. She moved to the San Francisco Bay area in 1959 to complete undergraduate studies at San Francisco State University. In 1971, she received a Master's degree in social work at the University of California at Berkeley. As a social worker, she has counseled and provided varied supportive services through public agencies and hospitals.

Since undergoing a period of intense spiritual distress nearly a quarter of a century ago, Joyce has been consciously working on gaining spiritual insight and understanding. She is a student of religious and metaphysical disciplines and has received and given counseling in self-development, through which she has gained personal knowledge of psychic phenomena.

Joyce is married to an educator who is also a metaphysical teacher and writer. In addition to writing, counseling, and creating stone sculptures, Joyce manages an active family life (she has two daughters, a son, three stepdaughters, and four stepgrandchildren).

To Write to the Author

If you wish to contact the author or would like more information about this book, please write to the author in care of Llewellyn Worldwide and we will forward your request. Both the author and publisher appreciate hearing from you and learning of your enjoyment of this book and how it has helped you. Llewellyn Worldwide cannot guarantee that every letter written to the author can be answered, but all will be forwarded. Please write to:

Joyce Elaine Noll
c/o Llewellyn Worldwide
P.O. Box 64383-583, St. Paul, MN 55164-0383, U.S.A.

Please enclose a self-addressed, stamped envelope for reply, or $1.00 to cover costs.
If outside the U.S.A., enclose international postal reply coupon.

Free Catalog from Llewellyn

For more than 90 years Llewellyn has brought its readers knowledge in the fields of metaphysics and human potential. Learn about the newest books in spiritual guidance, natural healing, astrology, occult philosophy and more. Enjoy book reviews, new age articles, a calendar of events, plus current advertised products and services. To get your free copy of the *New Times*, send your name and address to:

The Llewellyn New Times
P.O. Box 64383-583, St. Paul, MN 55164-0383, U.S.A.

Company of Prophets

AFRICAN AMERICAN PSYCHICS, HEALERS & VISIONARIES

Joyce Elaine Noll

1991
Llewellyn Publications
St. Paul, Minnesota, U.S.A. 55164-0383

FIRST EDITION, 1991
Second Printing, 1992

Cover: *Touch Drawing* © 1991 Deborah Koff-Chapin

Library of Congress Cataloging-in-Publication Data
    Noll, Joyce Elaine, 1940-
        Company of prophets : African American psychics, healers
    and visionaries / by Joyce Elaine Noll. — 1st ed.
            p.   cm.
        Includes bibliographical references.
        ISBN 0-87542-583-6
        1. Afro-American psychics—United States—Biography.
    2. Afro-American healers—United States—Biography.
    3. Afro-American mediums—United States—Biography. I. Title.
    BF1026.N65 1991
    133.8'089'96073—dc20   91-26482
                                                                                            CIP

Llewellyn Publications
A Division of Llewellyn Worldwide, Ltd.
P.O. Box 64383, St. Paul, MN 55164-0383, U.S.A.

In memory of
Edith Harris Stancil and Emma T. Stancil,
my mother and grandmother,
whose love continues to sustain me.

ACKNOWLEDGMENTS

My grateful acknowledgment to the many individuals whose encouragement, guidance, and support helped in bringing *Company of Prophets* from an idea to an actuality.

I, especially, wish to thank the individuals I interviewed who generously shared information about their lives. Among these deserving specific mention are Peter Brown, Jr., Mother and Clarence Ellerbee, Cora Scarvers Keeton, Tureeda Mikell, Queen Ann Prince, and Henry Rucker, who gave much of their own time and energy toward the completion of this project.

Acknowledgments, too, go to those individuals who provided inroads to many who appear in this book and to valuable sources of research: Phyllis Bischoff, Ethnic Studies librarian at the University of California at Berkeley, Paul Coates of Black Classic Press, Betty Culpepper of the Library of Congress, Father Jay Matthews of the Catholic Diocese of Oakland, California.

I wish to include my sister, Addie Greer, for several valuable leads. Thanks to my children, Melissa, Rachel and Michael, who helped keep the inspiration alive. And to my husband, Ray, deep appreciation for his consultations and editing during the course of this project.

Contents

After that, thou shalt come to the hill of God ... and it shall come to pass, when thou art come thither to the city, that thou shalt meet a company of prophets coming down from the high place .... And the spirit of the Lord will come upon thee, and thou shalt prophesy with them, and shalt be turned into another man. And let it be, when these signs are come unto thee, that thou do as occasion serve thee; for God is with thee ....

And it was so, that, when he had turned his back to go from Samuel, God gave him another heart; and all those signs came to pass that day.

And when they came thither to the hill, behold, a company of prophets met him; and the Spirit of God came upon him ....

I Samuel, Chapter 10, Verses 5-10
The Old Testament

PREFACE

Four o'clock in the morning. The hour of God, but also a time of vulnerability. Along some routes, this is a favorite hour to clean buses. Roused from sleep, we stumbled down into the darkness. Half formed. So wispy our connections to our bodies, so in our own universes, that we were the dotted figures in childhood activity books. Lacking the proper lines to impinge as real.

My journey to gather material for this book was made mostly by bus. It was the way in which I could best afford to travel, and it was certainly the only direct passage to many places. I made four cross-country trips.

Bus-riding was familiar enough to me. As a child, I rode southbound buses from Harlem for more than a decade to visit my grandparents in Virginia. Once through the Holland Tunnel, manmade structures gave way to the wonder of the non-concrete, to flowing space at eye-level. It seemed to me, Space spread in all directions in an absoluteness. Blending in were stands of trees, cornfields, farm buildings and small towns, not violating Space with their presence.

My joy, too, was in feasting from what seemed a bottomless shoe box. Packed with a wonderful assortment of picnic goodies by my mother. And there was singing. Hour after hour, my two sisters, cousin, other young passengers and I sang the "hit tunes" of the day, with the driver and adult passengers indulging us at least most of the time. Those memories all had their part in strengthening my decision to travel by bus.

Pilgrims, as travelers used to be called, would often receive a benediction prior to their setting out. I always got a good sendoff from my husband and children. But in El Paso, on my third trip out, during midday rest stop, I crossed over to the convention center, inexplicably drawn to it.

Seizing, I thought, an opportunity to be apart from the chaotic current that mobilizes a bus station, I hurried toward the restroom, ostensibly to wash away road grime before doing a quick tour of the center's art gallery. A group of five women was already there in the ladies lounge, and I exchanged greetings with them. Upon learning of the nature of my trip and the subject matter of my intended book, they showed sudden spiritual excitement. They spontaneously formed a prayer circle with me; and there, in that improbable location for an appeal for divine intervention, the bathing and toileting facilities of a Texas convention center, I received their blessings and good wishes for a safe trip and a successful project. I left El Paso feeling restored, and well enough that I should: they were part of a southwestern Charismatic Catholic convention!

The bus and its stations usually served as my main hotel accommodations. I would draw as many interviews from a town as possible, and then rush for the evening bus. But after two or three nights of sleeping on buses, I needed a bed and full bathing facilities. I usually stayed in hostels, and they in their many regional variations proved to be secure places. College dormitories were greatly sought by me for lodging, but they were seldom available; most colleges seemed to have problems accommodating their own student bodies, let alone mine.

I was fortunate in being able to arrange for quarters at Fisk University, in the same building where the Jubilee Singers had lived. As the only person lodged on the top floor of that old building, I thought I might have an encounter with one or more of those esteemed, historical, although deceased, performers. But even my sleep was dreamless, and interrupted only by a coed coming upstairs to use the hall telephone.

The individuals whose stories I heard and read, during these travels and in my research, are adherents of many different religious faiths, belief systems, and practices. They have a variety of lifestyles, and come from diverse socio-economic and educational backgrounds. But in common, they have these characteristics: identity within the African American culture, native-born United States citizenship status, and substantial and definitive psychic abilities.

Very little information is available concerning this particular population, those United States-born African Americans having extrasensory perception. The existing data are scattered mostly through magazines and newspapers. This book is an effort to provide a more comprehensive and focused view.

My main intent in writing *Company of Prophets* is to provide overdue acknowledgment to a group of people who have essentially been ignored.

I began my search in the fall of 1983. With an Interstate USA bus pass, a few referrals and leads, I headed away from home and California. In my search, in addition to finding opportunities to interview contemporary individuals, I hoped to unearth historical material on that population as well. The material for this book was gathered from personal and telephone interviews, books, newspaper and magazine articles.

There were heartening occurrences during my travels. Conversations overheard in the most unconnected of places resulted in an enrichment of my store of information, and in one instance led to a significant interview. A book randomly pulled from a library shelf, on several occasions, presented a new personality, or provided the basis for a sketched image suddenly to become defined and locatable.

However, a number of disappointments are sorely remembered. I missed people whom I had traveled several days to see; our signals were misunderstood. There were also prospective interviewees who couldn't comprehend what I was doing, or feared for their privacy, and so declined interviewing. Fortunately, these were very few in number.

The warm reception, the hospitality, the encouragement and blessings bestowed upon me across the country by other African Americans in telling their stories to this stranger constitute the creation of a most singular lifetime experience. Not forgotten, either, is the generosity of resource people. A number of individuals around the country, both black and white, freely shared information, their own research materials, and sometimes their homes with me.

The range of testimonies includes those of psychic counselors, historical figures, religious recluses, artists, children, and people of varying professions and disciplines.

The individuals whom I interviewed all believed in a Supreme Spirit consciousness. Many followed traditional Western religions. Others studied the teachings of the East, and yet others belonged to

New Age religions and groups.

People of both religious and secular communities are presented here in a sequence of my own creation, without reference to any hierarchical evaluation, in terms of their station in life or state of being. This sequence is based solely upon carrying along a continuity of interest and description.

Following a necessity for some form of guidelines and parameters, I have omitted charismatic religious leaders, who may have or had psychic abilities; their inclusion would have opened too wide a range for the particular purposes of this book. There seems to be ample material on many of these individuals already in circulation, continuously being made available.

That an individual is mentioned more than once is not indicative that his or her abilities have greater quality or significance. Multiple inclusions reflect, rather, the person having a breadth and diversity of attributes which would be of interest to the general reader. Furthermore, the book is arranged, not by individual identities, but by *abilities*, under which system an individual may be presented in more than a few sections.

In terms of attitudes toward the material world held by people included in the book, I found a broad range of considerations regarding the acquisition and holding of worldly wealth. Some interviewed were quite intent upon creating a balance between the material and the spiritual. Others had little or no interest in the area of economics, beyond how to survive in the world and in physical body while they continued their work.

I had a set of questions, fairly basic ones, to use for the interviewing process. They were often answered before I could express them. Of specific interest to me was how individuals were using their gifts, such as whether they sought to realize goals through their supernormal powers, extending beyond desires for self-enhancement alone. Throughout interviews and research, I found that the desire to help others held strongly in this group. Many spoke of their struggles to articulate their gifts meaningfully into service for humankind. There were those, too, who believed they could not use their abilities for themselves at all, that their gifts would vanish if they were in any way to profit from them.

As general terms, "abilities," "gifts," "power," "talent," "spiritual gifts," and "psychic gifts," all refer to extrasensory perception qualities. They also allude to those invisible channels of thought and spirit by which human beings can exercise an apparent power to affect physical matter, time, and space and the minds of others. They are used interchangeably throughout this book.

The marked and deep intuitivity in the African American culture has long been generally known and implied through writings. Much of what has been written has concentrated on the mysticism and psychism of black people in Africa and the Caribbean. This book is one person's survey and view on the subject of U.S.-born blacks with advanced psychic abilities.

This writing is only intended as a descriptive, and not an all-inclusive, effort. I only interviewed a small percentage of this population, and I undoubtedly missed a number of people whom readers may believe should have been included. I sincerely regret such omissions.

I was fortunate in this project. Interviews and research were sometimes such intense being-to-being experiences that they affected my spiritual outlook profoundly. From these contacts, new realizations about myself and about existence surfaced in a greatly accelerated manner, leaving me breathless in their impacting clarity. Stirred from a long-held stance of wooden wondering and hesitation, I was inspired to move with greater resolution into fully immersing myself into living, as myself.

Company of Prophets is a compilation from the personal experiences of individuals exemplifying the ways that intuitivity and the power of spirit manifest through native-born African Americans.

I had wandered among my own people, to tap not the genetic roots, but the spiritual roots of the *collective spiritual consciousness* of my race; and as an unexpected consequence, I received healing through the power of that assembled and unified spirituality.

Joyce E. Noll
Oakland, California

July-August suns, Summer,
I touch, taste, smell, hear, see, command!
Part of All,
of the Indivisible Totality.
All of All, I am the Sole Reality.
Infinite,
untainted by Self-Doubt,
wholly whole.
I, the scrawny, dark-brown girl clad in yellow,
caterpillar-striped swimsuit,
sweaty-hot, restless, sand-gritty,
follow the Right-Hand Path to the Ocean,
propelled by cool winds at my elbows, knees,
inebriated with Sacred Curiosity.
My back to the world of the red-checkered tablecloth
anchored by the wicker hamper laden with fried chicken,
potato salad, watermelon pickles, cherries, punch and cookies.
Escaping my mother's vigilant eyes, I renounce Security and
distance myself from the Known.
The surf's vibration draws, soothes me.
The ocean explodes as we meet, and I am anointed.
The waves, though forbidden to snatch me seaward,
spray, sting, roll, strangle, suck me under.
Arising undaunted I use my swimsuit to gather treasures
beamed up from the Deep at my bidding.
I am Warrioress, I am Initiant!

CHAPTER ONE

Children with Power

In the lives of children who have advanced psychic abilities, there is a profound turning point of a kind. Sometime, when either fully or partially aware, they determine whether they can tolerate their unique abilities. They can resolve to sustain and use the gifts as best they can or, when the ability is seen as "diseased" by self or others, the child can resort to doing all manner of things to make the "disability" vanish.

A child, bent on being free of his or her attributes, removes an integral part of self, and in that way withdraws from vital aspects of psychic-spiritual existence. The effort to cancel the gift may subtract from normal senses as well, and will suppress the child's overall being.

In discussing the topic of supernormal abilities in childhood, in both interview and other settings, a number of individuals stated that when it became obvious to them as children that they had a psychic gift, they prayed to God to take it away. Or they fought the gift. Some of the reasons given were: they were frightened by the phenomena of the gift; it brought unbearable isolation from others; it ran against familial or peer belief systems; they feared the power it gave them, and the power the ability might wield back against them. It was often seen as mysteriously dangerous. In several cases, it was too difficult for the young person to gather the courage needed to maintain the co-existence and exercise of the ability in the face of even mild opposition.

Regarding the gift as harmful, the child would seek release and relief through his or her efforts to eradicate or abandon the gift.

Some prayed; others pretended it didn't exist; others ignored it; some disowned it.

In contrast, a psychic child may be quite aware of his or her life's mission connected with the possession of an extraphysical ability. At an early stage in childhood, such a being may confidently prepare for the actualization of the ability and the goal. That child would be immune to outside influences, standing his or her ground with enormous integrity.

With a child who has supernormal attributes there is always an attendant vulnerability from the conservative orientations of other people. The fragility of the child's own world of psychic realities is pitted against the monolinear physical perspectives of some adults who use adherence to material reality as a guise of absolute power, and those adults who are "all-knowing," and who effect a strict enforcement and obedience to their constricted belief systems. Such adults create an interpositioning of barriers to the child's recognition, acceptance, and utilization of his or her gifts.

The black psychic child's struggle to incorporate the Truth of his or her own expanded universe into life is further complicated by specific traces of contracting negative energy in the collective spiritual consciousness of society. Largely in the past, but even now, within the national collective consciousness, this negativity has been generated; it surfaces as inclinations to minimize, distort, or destroy self-confidence regarding the most ordinary of capabilities that any member of the African American culture might possess.

Such persisting consciousness, in a mental dimension, created by the collective negative energies of our nation in the course of its history, constitutes a stagnant repository of centuries-old prejudgmental and attitudinal programming of a racial nature. Although this negative influence lies unperceived from any body orientation, it can still fully impact upon the physical dimension. Reflexively, it activates a negative psychic programming, in most on an unconscious level, to oppose any African Americans—including children—exhibiting remarkable qualities. These energies of mental opposition and invalidation can be extremely subtle, but a child in the early stages of psychic revelation is sensitive to them as to any substantive, prevailing energies.

The African American psychic child's awareness thus becomes dispersed in trying to sort out and identify the many opposing factors in the basically materially oriented society in which he or she lives. Even more telling can be the opposition from closer in, common to all psychic children, that comes from the valued affinities of parents, family, friends, or from the religion which he or she inherited.

The effects created by these adversities can be reduced by the child's drawing upon the positive energies of the collective spiritual consciousness of the black race, which safeguards and balances group members who can resonate at its vibratory frequency. Imparted from the group soul to the consciousness of the child are the original group's African beliefs and acceptances of intuition, of supernormal qualities, and the range of psychic and mystical states of being. The race spirit affirms those qualities. It states out of its own traditions their ascendancy to any transplanted conditions or states, founded culturally or scientifically, imposed and arbitrarily placed by authorities in the material world.

Through that collective spiritual consciousness of the black race, tribute is imparted to those beings possessing spiritual or psychic gifts, no matter whether their bodies identify them as adult or as child.

Shortly before she first prophesied, Jenny Benson, then eight years old, was outside playing in the yard. All at once she ran indoors with a message for her grandmother.

" 'Mama,' I said, 'Aunt Mahalia is dead!'

"She said, 'Oh, my God, who told you?!'

"I said, 'Something told me.'

"She hauled off and hit me upside the head. Pow! 'What did you tell that lie for?' "

In a while, one of Jenny's cousins came by on a horse. As he approached, he called out to her grandmother, "Cousin Nance, I stopped by to tell you Aunt Mahalia is dead."

"My grandmother asked when, and it was just the time I told her."

But there was no apology forthcoming to the girl for delivering authenticated spirit-prompted messages, or for the blow that punctuated the prophesy. "They thought I was crazy. I had to be determined. My grandmother said I wasn't going to live long, I was too peculiar. I got a backhand lick for telling the truth. It didn't stop me!

"When I was born there was no such thing as birth control pills—not in the country of Mississippi. My mother was pregnant but one time, and that was with me. She prayed to God to close up her womb. I never stayed with my mother; but while she was with me, she said I was very peculiar. I stayed with my grandparents."

Though unappreciated by adults in those early years, she confides how her playmates waited eagerly to hear her pronouncements. "They would ask me questions, and I would say, 'Tonight, I am going to talk to the Lord. What He tells me, I am going to tell you.'" Her friends accepted Jenny's prophetic messages and always seemed satisfied with what she said.

She was but eight years old when the inward voice she hears told of her destiny. "The Lord told me I would be in Nashville, Tennessee, and of the good works I would do for him."

Three gifts have been realized since childhood by Jenny Benson Vaughn—the gifts of prophesy, preaching, and healing. Residing in Nashville, Tennessee, she is the minister of St. Teresa Holiness Science Church and holds ministerial positions in several churches in other states. Most of these churches she helped found.

Henry was bouncing in and out of his body after his tonsils were removed. It started as he came from under the anesthesia. Seeing his body from different locations in the hospital room, and being acutely aware that he was yet in another space—at distance from his body—caused the eight year old to feel alarmed and insecure. He tried to tell the nurse what was happening, but she didn't seem to hear him. That night he attempted to anchor himself by concentrating, but he would involuntarily relax and end up somewhere else in the room, again viewing his prostrate body. He battled all night but was unable to keep spirit, mind, and body in the same place.

The experience brought a marked change into the Southside Chicago boy's life. He now felt a depth of uncertainty and loss. That which had been real to him before, and in agreement with everybody else he knew, was undone. From then on he heard voices and saw pictures projected in his head. He was often the awed and unwilling receiver of the transmitted thoughts and emotions of others. People's faces changed as he looked at them; their past lives' facial features opened to his view. Even while he was in a schoolroom, he traveled out of his body in astral flight, to the detriment of his academic performance.

An inner voice emerged. He learned from the voice; but he was upset by its presence in his universe. Henry was ashamed and embarrassed about his newly extended perceptions. This facet of himself was further inhibited after he offered to help a disabled man, through his young healing gift, and was rejected. The man's wife firmly told Henry not to bother them with that "nonsense."

Concern over being singled out as a "kook" or classified as insane prompted Henry to keep his impressions contained, so that the boundaries of that inner world never flowed over into his social life. Persistently he monitored himself in this manner, thus succeeding at being a "normal person" during his childhood and into early manhood.

It took many years for Henry Rucker to openly accept his psychic talents. When he did, the inner voice instructed him around his primary gift, psychic healing, which in childhood he had repressed into a state of limbo.

"Between ten and twelve, I could tell in advance when something was going to happen. If I wanted someone to do something, I would send them a thought, or I would send a thought not to do something.

"At that time, I was a mean, hateful child. My energy was strong. I could project it to hurt a person and I knew I could," recalls Jessica Marshall.

Separated from her mother and native Louisiana at seven years old, she and her older sister were transported to Oakland to live with their father and his new wife. The move was traumatic for Jessica who changed from a good-natured child to a sullen one. "I was angry with my father and stepmother.

"I never got into fights. I could see things happening to friends and I would tell them, but they didn't like it. So I stopped telling them."

Jessica became a loner with only one or two friends. "I learned to play by myself. I couldn't take crowds for some reason or other. But I loved sports and was captain of a team. I had leadership abilities."

In this period the family moved to Los Angeles. Her father, whom she calls "adventuresome," presented his children with many creative challenges. "I was often plagued by being the only black. My father wanted us to be aware of everything. He wanted us to be around and familiar with different cultures and different religions. He wanted us to understand that people were only people regardless of color. That we are all one.

"My gift was a knowing, but I didn't know how I knew. I could always see something before it happened. I thought everyone could. I was fourteen when I found out that everyone couldn't."

For a year after she died, Bob's aunt appeared to him, from time to time, in his family's kitchen. He was then seven or eight. Another spirit, a guide, had come shortly after the death to help him.

"I missed a lot of unpleasant things by following what the Spirit told me," Bob now says, looking back.

The guide directed him not to go down certain streets, saving him from encounters with bullies and loose dogs. He became able to control dogs which dashed toward him. When they came within a hairsbreadth, they could advance no more, and he could walk away.

He was so well-oriented by the Spirit that he never got lost in all of his childhood meanderings; first through the streets of Memphis, and later through the streets of Chicago. That other children or adults could get lost mystified him.

Now an adult whose occupation is in sales, Bob Edwards lives in Los Angeles. His psychometric gift is strong. He picks up vibrations from an individual's possessions, and receives mental pictures of that individual's current circumstances. In his psychic work, he finds lost articles, animals, and people. He is assisted in his readings by his inner voice and a male spirit guide.

Almost fifty years later, Dorothy Hall still tells this story. She fervently insists even today that she knew nothing about the outcome of a prediction spoken through her teenage body, except that it was revealed through an inner voice and vision.

"There was a girl at school, Clara, a kind of fast kid. She used to pick at me all the time. Her desk was behind mine. One day she hit me on the shoulder.

" 'Dot, you know what? I'm going to a party tomorrow night. Me and my friends. And I know you wish you could go. I know you wish you could go, and I know you can't go because your mama don't let you go nowhere except to school and back home.'

"She was picking on me like that, trying to make me feel real bad. I just sat there and looked at her. All of a sudden I could see this blood coming out of her face. At the same time a voice was telling me:

" 'Tell her, don't go!'

"I had to say, 'Clara, don't go to the party!' "

At Dorothy's entreaty, Clara's tactics changed from razzing to railing. "You can't tell me what to do! And you sure ain't my mama!"

Impelled by the voice, Dorothy continued, "If you go to that party, I see you getting hurt." Unnerved, Clara laughed uneasily and walked away with her friends.

"That girl is crazy," Dorothy heard her say as they left the classroom.

Three days later, Dorothy's teacher sent her to the principal. A detective and police officer were there with him.

"The principal asked me what I had said to Clara on Friday and I told him." The confused and frightened thirteen year old struggled to tell why she said Clara shouldn't go. She was not yet familiar with the language pertaining to psychic phenomena, so all she could say is "something" told her to give the message.

Reproachfully, the principal disclosed that Clara was in the hospital. At the party, someone had cut her with a razor. The consensus among the adults was that Dorothy knew something about it. Denounced as uncooperative, Dorothy was suspended from school, only to be readmitted after the bishop of her church intervened. She remained a student for one more year, leaving when she reached the eighth grade.

"The bishop told them they'd better not expel me no more, and they didn't. But they would watch me in a peculiar way. I felt 'funny', so I quit and took a 'place on the job', staying in with white people."

Prophesying was Dorothy's strongest childhood gift. But relaying prophetic communication from the spirit world had caused her upsets prior to the incident at school, and would cause upsets in the future. Nevertheless, the Chicago girl was often moved to share spiritual pronouncements with others in her well-intentioned but blunt way.

At home there was a constant collision of wills between Dorothy and her mother over the girl's prophesying. Her mother, a member of the Methodist church, urged Dorothy to stop the "nonsense" through verbal and physical reprimand. Intent upon helping and despite harsh punishment, Dorothy continued to relay unwanted messages to the disapproving parent all through her childhood.

An only child, Dorothy was the survivor of a set of twin girls. In looking back on her share of childhood camaraderie she comments, "I mostly stayed to myself. I didn't have no sisters, no brothers, no nothing. I wanted to play with kids, but they didn't want to play with me. They acted 'funny' with me, so I just stayed to myself."

But one friendship from childhood she can recall—a secret one. Soon after she moved to a new home with her mother and stepfather, Dorothy met a white man.

"Every night at twelve o'clock this man would come through the back door and get me out of bed. He would be dressed in a tuxedo with a white shirt, black bow tie, and a tall black hat. He would take me by the hand to the backyard and set me in the swing my stepdaddy made for me. I would go with him because I thought he was human. He would talk to me. He told me he had a lot of money but not to tell nobody. I was about nine years old at the time and I said I wouldn't tell. He made me promise. I'm thinking he's human because he looks human. I didn't know he was a spirit. He told me the money was right beneath where I was swinging, in a tin box, and that it was for me and nobody else.

"My mother got up one night, and she had to go right by my room to get to the bathroom, and she missed me. I wasn't in the bed. I could hear her calling my name, but I couldn't answer.

"Finally when I come to myself, I said, 'Mama, I'm out here

with ... ' When I said 'with', I looked around and there wasn't a soul out there.

"So my mother took me in and beat me, because she thought I was just out in the backyard at three o'clock in the morning. Oh, how she whipped me.

" 'Mama, I wasn't out there by myself, the man was out there with me.' She sure enough whipped me then. So I had to tell her. I had to break my vow. So I told her about the money under the swing."

Dorothy's stepfather and a few friends dug under the swing to search for the money. They struck the box at the place pointed out by Dorothy, but as they reached for it, the surrounding earth collapsed and the box sank. A fear-inducing aura permeated the excavated area, disturbing Dorothy's stepfather so much that shortly thereafter he moved the family again.

Ordained in a Spiritual church at fourteen, with her gift being fully recognized, Dorothy prophesied from the pulpit. Of that period in her life, Dorothy observes, "I was at church more than at home."

The minister of a Spiritual church, counselor and healer, Dorothy Hall lives in Chicago where she was born.

Alpha, the first of nine children, was raised from "Day One" by her maternal grandmother, as she says it. Her mother was still in college, and the birth was a difficult one. Delivered prematurely, Alpha entered life with bronchitis, and a film of tissue, called a veil, covering her head.

Her grandmother was an influential force in her life whom Alpha studied closely. Although the older woman had not gone beyond the third grade in formal schooling, she worked intensely with her grandchild around studies. By five years old, Alpha could write a business letter, redone under her grandmother's tutelage, until a certain level of perfection was reached.

Heartened by the relationship she shared with her grandmother, the girl was inspired to seek out the companionship of elderly people. Then, too, she was a child who didn't care for games much at all because "they were win or lose," as she summarizes it.

Her psychic self seems to have always been active in childhood; but in growing up, she recalls tending to push back that aspect of herself. Although none of those early intuitive experiences stands out, she remembers that as a child sometimes her head would seem to open up with information flowing in, and that she would smell flowers in the most unlikely situations. There were also her abilities to see ghosts, and to smell death.

Alpha Omega, born in Aldrich, Alabama, is a long-time resident of New York City. She is a teacher, lecturer, and healer.

More than once when sickness kept him home from school, Lee felt himself being observed by the figure. In front of his bed, gazing upon him, with piercing and loving eyes, was a monk, resembling St. Francis.

Not frightened, the boy absorbed the love. He needed it. In his physical life, love was marked by its inadequacy. He was a lone child, raised by a mother who expressed her unknown guilt to him in anger and blows.

Lee was an adult when he described his unhappy childhood to Ruth Montgomery, who wrote of him in *Threshold to Tomorrow*. In the accounting, he spoke of his mother's physical and emotional abuse of him. She was protective, however, and provided well for his physical needs. Four half-siblings older than he, whom he never saw during childhood, were legally removed from her custody. She had abused them, too. His father, whom he saw on a few occasions, he never really got to know.

To others, Lee was a likable child, bright and talented, a self-taught musician who was playing the piano when he was three. He had learned on a toy piano. He practiced wherever he could, having no piano at home. In a visit to a rest home when he was twelve or thirteen, Lee practiced on the piano there. Soon heard was a scooting sound and in turning his head, he saw the elderly residents drag folding chairs near to listen to him. They flooded him with admiration, and he loved them back. During the years of grammar and junior high school, the boy regularly visited rest homes and convalescent hospitals—even after he obtained his own piano.

Ruth Montgomery's spirit guides call Lee a "Walk-in." "Walk-ins are idealistic but not perfected souls, who through spiritual growth in previous incarnations, have earned the right to take over unwanted bodies, if their overriding goal is to help mankind. The original occupants vacate the bodies because they no longer can maintain the physical spark of life, or because they are so dispirited that they earnestly wish to leave."[1]

Lee William Carnett, Jr. changed his name to Count Carnette in adulthood. He contends he is not aware of that transition taking place. But being a Walk-in explains to him much about that early period of his life.

After the revelation from Montgomery's guides, Carnette was told again that he was a Walk-in by a discarnate named Dr. Callaeo. In direct-voice channeled through Carnette himself, the being told of how the transition was made when Carnette was less than ten years old.

From Dr. Callaeo's reading, as reported in Montgomery's book: "It was one of the rare cases of a Walk-in entering the body of a child, but it was necessary, because the boy was on the verge of a nervous breakdown or suicide."

A concert pianist, composer, and vocalist who performs intuitively, having no professional training, Count Carnette resides in Seattle, Washington where he was born. Performing traditional music and a type of music he describes as "psychic," he tours the country giving recitals.

From material in one of his record albums the following quote is taken: "I plan to work earnestly and faithfully as a Worker of Light; a blessing to those who would let music speak to them. My conviction is that the heavenly vibrations flowing through this music have the power to heal the sick, put an end to wars, and once again bring about peace and harmony to our planet, Earth."[2]

The two children were playing "Ring-around-the-Rosie" when Louise saw them from her grandparents' verandah. They were about her age, seven years old. The girl was prettily attired in a white dress with ruffles to the tail; the boy's outfit was white, too. He wore a whole suit with a wide-collared shirt, Louise still recalls vividly.

She saw they were really having a good time, and she became

excited at the thought of joining their game. But her grandmother, stepping out of the house at Louise's call for permission to play, responded with a gentle but firm "no." Seating herself beside Louise, she drew her close.

"The children are not real," she explained.

She, herself, could not see them. She reminded her grandchild that seeing into the world of spirit was the young one's own special gift. Like her other gift, which was to know of things beforehand.

The two black children clad in finery, and seeming so full of happiness in their games on the adjacent cemetery green, were not the first discarnates Louise had seen. But they were certainly among the first to impact upon her so strongly. Long before she was seven, the spirit world opened to Louise. Her ability to predict had come earlier. "Forerunner" was a nickname given her by her grandfather, who was proud of her abilities.

Louise Washington is a licentiate minister and certified medium in the National Spiritualist Association of Churches. Her church, the Tucker Smith Memorial Spiritualist Church, is in Chicago. She grew up in Walterboro, South Carolina.

"It was a regular thing, that most of us kids would walk home to lunch, and there was always a train, boxcars, standing on the tracks near the school. We'd crawl under it or over it to get to our houses for lunch," remembers Calestine Williams of being a fifth grader.

"On this particular day, I was puzzled at strong feelings that the train meant danger. I warned everybody I could not to go near. Some of us did not go home at all for lunch, the feeling was so strong. Some of the kids were not convinced, though. The train began to move, and one boy was cut in two."

Without self-doubt, Calestine acted on these intuitive messages of danger.

Another incident involved a bridge which she and the rest of the neighborhood children either crossed or played on every day. It spanned a deep ditch where the water level would get high enough for someone to drown.

"One morning," she mentions, "a feeling began to bother me

that there was danger. I went to the store in the neighborhood and got some white wrapping paper and penciled in, 'Don't play on the bridge.' I posted the sign. That evening the bridge collapsed. No one was on it, but there were some dogs on it, and they ended up in the water."

Forming within Calestine, when she was but six, was a sensitivity about people and houses. Emanating from people she perceived an energy which clearly told her of their emotions and attitudes. Of houses and geographical areas, she could sense whether they would be good places in which to live.

At ten, hysterical, she told her mother and stepfather everything she felt about the house they planned to buy. It would not be a good home or good investment, she advised. But they didn't listen. The house became a place of terrible family conflict once they moved in. Its function for the family unit was finally destroyed when Calestine's stepfather declared himself sole owner of it and evicted the rest of the family.

Mostly burdened by her gift while growing up, the Mississippi-born psychic, who now lives in Memphis, Tennessee, says in those early years she played the comedienne to mask that she felt different.

The girl's mother, perplexed by her young child's unusual perception, often questioned the validity of what was sensed. But from her grandmother, Calestine received the strong reassuring message, "God is speaking to us through you."

Hurt by a blow to his head in a schoolyard accident, six-year-old Ron was transformed. Thereafter, he was subjected to small epileptic seizures. At first the attacks came daily, but their frequency lessened as he grew into his teens. Affected, he went inward, became meditative and a "loner," as he describes it.

But flung open was the door to a new world. Scenes unfolded to him as if he were watching television. At thirteen, in a vision, he saw the house he and his wife presently own. Initially, most of his visions were about himself, but gradually he began to see future information about family members.

Almost immediately following the accident, his dreams

changed. To the six year old, some of the contents of his new dreams were very strange; however, in time, many proved prophetic.

Visible to him when he looked at the sky were Indian chiefs riding across its expanse. Their presence was somehow very reassuring to the boy. At the phase of the full moon, while he watched the sky, he saw images of the future. Later in his life, he experienced these predictions as they were manifested.

A prime target for "bullies," Ron avoided them with his sensitivity. Through his body came a signal when a bully or other danger was near. His hair stood up on the back of his neck.

There was further acceleration of his awareness after he again was knocked unconscious in an accident at age twelve. He started experimenting with telepathy. He sent out thoughts of love and harmony. His parents became discordant with one another; wanting to keep the family together, he directed strong thoughts of love and reconciliation toward them. The relationship between his parents improved, as did their home life.

Ron was fourteen when he saw a "wolfman" movie with a Tarot card reader in it. "I felt I was shown about the cards because they are a deep well to relate from," he asserts.

Shortly after seeing the movie, he joined a metaphysical book club and secured books on the Tarot. In libraries and bookstores, he determined what he should read by running his hands along the shelves of books until he felt heat on his hands. The heat-generating book was selected.

With his mother Ron shared freely his precognitions, and she told of some of her own psychic experiences. However, the child never told anyone when he foresaw death. He felt intuitively that it was not the right thing to do. At school, he learned from experience that if he spoke of his visions there, he would be taken to the nurse's office.

In a reading, Ron was told he was an advanced and able psychic being, an Adept, in a past life. But at that time he had been overpowered by magicians of evil intent.

Using his gifts, Ron relates how he found Sandra, his second wife and soul mate, who early in her life became aware of her spiritual self. Together they are raising their child, and Sandra's child from a previous marriage, to know themselves as spiritual beings. Both children are gifted.

A resident of Los Angeles, Ron Bonner uses Tarot cards to give consultations. He emphasizes in his teachings how people can change their lives, and that obstacles can be overcome by the human will.

"When I was little I used to get death all the time. I asked God to take that gift from me.

"I never wanted to be a medium this lifetime. I never wanted to claim that kind of energy. But that is the kind of energy that I initially drew. When I would be on the Greyhound bus going to visit my father, especially on the turnpike, I would see people where there had been accidents. I'd see them walking and searching and looking. It was heavy. I realized after a while they weren't real. No one could see them except me."

Delilah Grayer's first awareness of her abilities came when she was around five years old. Until adulthood, she says, her powers were not productively used.

Encouraged to talk freely about her spiritual perceptions and prophetic dreams, the child enjoyed a secure home life. As the seventh female child in her family line to be psychic, she felt most harmoniously situated. Though she protested over her perception of death and her view of afterlife states being the dominating quality in the emergence of her abilities, Delilah reminds us there was also a lighter side.

"I had a dream that my mother surprised me at Christmas with a suit I really wanted. She didn't put it under the tree until later on Christmas Day. And that happened in reality! In the dream I wore the suit to school and a string was hanging down. I pulled the string and the suit fell apart. I totally forgot about the dream and wore the outfit to school. I was sitting in English class—I'll never forget it! I pulled the thread and the suit fell apart.

"I screamed, 'Oh God, just like in the dream!' "

With her gifted daughter, Bakara Oni, Delilah Grayer now lives in Shaker Heights, Ohio.

The mother and grandmother of Bakara Oni Lewis sat in

numbed silence. They had just learned that the child's great-aunt, Gladys, had been rushed to the hospital and was in the intensive care unit. Neither adult really noticed the little girl entering the room, but soon both were blown from solitude by the authority in the child's voice.

"That lady is so tired, she is so tired."

Taken aback, the child's mother, Delilah, asked, "What lady?"

Bakara Oni said she meant the lady in the hospital. She told her mother that they were cutting a hole in the lady, "Right here"—and the little girl pointed to her throat. "Mommy, she breathes like this." The two year old then did an imitation of a shrill-pitched, labored breathing. Lying down on the floor, she built to shriller tones, and then became softer and less and less audible.

Despite Delilah Grayer's abundant personal and professional familiarity with psychic phenomena, she could not control the panic she felt in watching her own daughter. As Delilah considered giving in to an impulse to leave the room, Bakara Oni commanded:

"Mommy, stand still, don't move—listen to me!" The child began singing a nursery rhyme, a favorite of Aunt Gladys.

She stopped singing suddenly and said, "Don't you see her flying up to the sky?"

The family learned that their relative died at approximately the time that Bakara Oni dramatized her ordeal; and that as part of the emergency treatment, the woman had undergone a tracheotomy.

In early childhood Bakara's talent was evident: to view into, and be inside spaces at a distance from her body. Her mother recalls one example of many, a time when they passed a house which her child remarked she had been in before, and that she knew what the house looked like. She described a room with a lot of people sitting around a table drinking and playing cards. None of this was apparent from the closed-up exterior. However, on their way back home, Delilah saw the exact scene described by Bakara through a door which had been opened.

During the same period, before her sixth birthday, Bakara Oni had clear memory of a brief past life, the details of which she shared unaltered with her mother many times. She named her brothers and sisters then, and described her toys. There had been a tragedy—a fire.

Since infancy, Bakara Oni has often been a calming influence on her mother during stressful times. While in the child's presence, the parent feels her worries diminishing.

Delilah perceives her daughter, now in middle childhood, as being less free. There are reduced instances of astral travel and diminishing evidence of the spontaneous side of her gifts. But her ability to predict remains unchanged. She often informs of events. There has been a trade, a surrendering of some psychic spontaneity and drama, for deeper insights of a spiritual nature.

The woods behind Augusta's house was inhabited by a number of beings not of the physical world, beings only visible to the child.

She discovered Indians, seemingly in another dimension, whom she loved to watch as they gathered and cooked herbs. They showed no concern in the least at the five year old's encroachment on their camp. Soon admitted among them, the child was taught to hunt herbs and prepare remedies to be used in healing. Augusta retained this information on herbs, and when she was a healer at eighteen she used it.

Beings she later recognized as angels spent hours singing and playing with her. The devas gave her a present of two Chinese dolls in a swing. And the dolls delighted her, although they were only spirit-world manifestations. On Christmas of that year, she was especially surprised by the gifts from her parents, the identical toys in real-world substance!

After she told her mother of the Indians, the angels, and the dolls, Augusta was shut off from the woods, and strictly forbidden to go there again.

The final sundering of Augusta from her woods in Slaughter, Mississippi came when her family moved to Stuttgart, Arkansas before she was six. Her companionship with beings of other dimensions ceased until she was twelve. At that age, more beings from the etheric world came to counsel her, and the way she was gifted became more defined. Among the extraphysical ways she perceived were by visions, prophetic dreams, and telepathy.

At eighteen, she began her spiritual work by preaching, and using her gifts of healing and prophesying in her life's mission, that of helping people improve their lives.

Born in Mississippi, Bishop Augusta Harris now lives in Little Rock, Arkansas, where she is a spiritual counselor and the founding pastor of Damascus Spiritual Church.

"I do not know when the visions began. Certainly I was not more than seven years old, but I remember the first coming very distinctly,"[3] recalled Zora Neale Hurston in her autobiography, *Dust Tracks on a Road*.

> My brother Joel and I had made a hen take an egg back and been caught as we turned the hen loose. We knew we were in for it and decided to scatter until things cooled off a bit ... There was some cool shade on the porch, so I sat down, and soon I was asleep in a strange way. Like clear-cut stereopticon slides, I saw twelve scenes flash before me, each one held until I had seen it well in every detail, and then be replaced by another. There was not continuity as in an average dream. Just disconnected scene after scene with blank spaces in between. I knew that they were all true, a preview of things to come, and my soul writhed in agony and shrunk away. But I knew that there was no shrinking. These things had to be. I did not wake up when the last one flickered and vanished, I merely sat up
> ...

Arising from the strange "sleep," Zora was sobered. The carefree child of a short time ago was gone forever. "I was weighed down with a power I did not want. I had knowledge before its time. I knew my fate. I knew that I would be an orphan and homeless. I knew that while I was still helpless, that the comforting circle of my family would be broken, and that I would have to wander cold and friendless until I had served my time."

The visions returned at random periods to haunt her at night. They were unaltered in detail except for the last picture. Zora never told anyone about the revelation, fearing she would be laughed at and thought of as different.

Born in Eatonville, Florida in 1901, Zora was nine years old when her first vision came to pass. At that time she, as one of the family's eight children, was orphaned by her mother's death.

> Oh, how I cried out to be just as everybody else! But the

voice said, "No." I must go where I was sent. The weight of the commandment laid heavy and made me moody at times ... I studied people all around me, searching for someone to fend it off. But I was told inside myself that there was no one. It gave me a feeling of terrible aloneness. I stood in a world of vanished communion with my kind, which is worse than if it had never been ...

Time was to prove the truth of my visions, for one by one they came to pass. As soon as one was fulfilled, it ceased to come.

William Edmondson had his first vision at thirteen or fourteen years old while working in the cornfields. This he described to his biographer, Edmund L. Fuller, for the book *Visions in Stone*.

I saw in the east world, I saw in the west world, I saw the flood. I ain't never read no books nor no Bible, and I saw the water come. It come over the rocks, covered up the rocks, and went over the mountains. God, He just showed me how.[4]

Born in Nashville, Tennessee, about 1883, William Edmondson was more than fifty years old when he began to sculpt in stone. His art is in the collections of museums and art galleries around the country.

Starting with a full moon phase, six-year-old June Juliet Gatlin "slept" continuously three or four days. Her worried parents, in an effort to break the sleep, forced her eyes open. But everything she saw in this state was in double image; and when she was stood up, her legs collapsed under her.

Undisturbed by the body's afflictions, June, the spiritual being, viewed the scene from a distance. From the ceiling she looked down at her body, aware of her external volition without it.

While in the hospital, with her physical self undergoing brain scans and series of tests, June willed herself spiritually about in astral travel. Even before she was three, she knew she lived in two worlds—of spirit and of flesh. By six years old, spiritual activity was increasing and would continue intensifying through her fourteenth year. During one hospitalization, a staff doctor following the case remarked to June's parents that her state was well-known in his native West Indies, where children with similar trance-like symptoms were called "moon children."

Spirit intelligences whom she calls "energies" came to teach her, early this lifetime, guiding her to experiences needed to expedite her evolvement in an existence as a being. Wandering through the aisles of libraries, she was guided to books crucial to her spiritual unfoldment which she identified by intuitive touch.

Past lives opened up, especially those spent in India. Untrained in India's religious practices, she spontaneously at thirteen assumed advanced meditative yoga positions. Later when led to books on yoga, the familiarity of the knowledge she attained in those lives long ago was integrated knowingly into her present life.

One of nine children, June was born in Akron, Ohio to devoted parents who provided their children with a comfortable and economically secure life. With her peers, she was a confident and natural leader, a nonconformist who believed in challenging authority and in testing the validity of rules at school and at church.

June was born with the gifts of prophecy and healing. Her childhood church, Church of God in Christ, co-founded by her grandfather, was the place where these early talents were affirmed. Members of the congregation, aware of June's healing presence, would crowd around her, seeking help. Unfamiliar with ways to handle the denseness of negative psychic energy generated by crowds, June, unknowingly, absorbed that energy and fainted. Her parents then took measures to protect their daughter from detrimental public exposure. Church members would line up to touch her and speak with her. They would testify to the physical, emotional, and spiritual benefits they received through June's contact with them.

By age nine, June discloses, she was already aware of her responsibilities and purpose for this life: to assist other African Americans in knowing spiritually who they are. She explains that African Americans have limited themselves by allowing others to dictate to them instead of following their own directions and using their own resources.

"I am here," she declares, "to awaken black people, to shock them out of inertia, out of accepting and not questioning."

The African American community in the small South Carolina town in the late Twenties and early Thirties had, for all intents and purposes, put the child up for trial, convinced she was a witch. Her presence and behavior instilled fear and hostility in many Bennetsville residents, as they did in her stepsisters and stepbrothers. The community's trial was called off when she triumphantly marched about with the Bible and a cross—both of which the residents finally agreed no witch would dare carry.

To reduce her other-worldly awareness, when she was five Estelle's parents took her to a root doctor. The treatment failed to work; she continued boldly and assertively to foretell and to experience in ways that confounded those about her. However, having psychic awareness himself, Estelle's father understood his daughter, though he was unable to protect her from his wife's severe beatings and the community's ridicule. Still he encouraged her to use her gifts, saying she had a mission from God.

Seeing death upon her only ally, timorously Estelle queried him. "Daddy, are you going to die and come back to scare me?" Three weeks after assuring his twelve year old that he had no such intentions, her father died. The girl's stepmother, who overheard their talk, predictably blamed the child for his death.

Like many children touched by wonderment, she innocently shared with others what she felt and saw: the sensation of being in the body of a bird she had seen perched in a tree, seeing the world through its eyes; the trees talking to her; angels singing. Sometimes, she would leave her body to travel, cutting loose from feeling unwanted. At the opening of church services, she knew already which ones among the congregation would be saved that day. Especially at night, Estelle would see ghosts wandering the countryside. Some would approach to attack her, but she called out to God, and like puffs of smoke, malevolent spirits vanished.

Barely seeing over the counter in the toy store, not knowing the name of what he wanted, five-year-old Chuck Wagner pointed, instead, to the item almost hidden away on the highest shelf. The Tarot cards handed to him were, on a physical level, totally unfamiliar to the boy; but instinctively he had been attracted to them. And he knew, at once, how to use them. While his child cohorts were playing with trucks, and mimicking a current hero, Hopalong Cassidy, Chuck was busy with the cards.

To discourage his cardplaying, Chuck's maternal grandmother, who raised him, took his Tarot deck away and burned it. A highly religious, strict fundamentalist, she saw the cards as instruments of the Devil.

Chuck's mother, who was very young when he was born, wanted to be a singer. She and her sisters were persistent in their attempts to get away from home and the South. They would sometimes jump boxcars in their eagerness to escape. When only five years old, Chuck, her only child, tried to persuade her not to go on one of these trips. "I told my mother if she waited, her dreams would come true," Chuck recalls. "I think everybody thought she would have a bad time and wouldn't do well, and maybe she would have to hitchhike home." After she had gone, he was still puzzled by the message from the cards. "I kept telling my grandmother that she would come back in a box. I didn't know she would come back dead in a coffin." After her daughter's death, Chuck's grandmother stopped objecting to his Tarot card readings. She had grown certain of his gift being God-given.

When he spread the cards, Chuck felt he was watching a movie. They came to life for him, conveying meaning he passed on to others. He was saying things he could not have been told previously. No one had previewed the information, or requested it. Although certain of what the cards revealed to him, the child did not know what he was doing. It seemed a game and unreal. At times, he thought people agreed with him and validated his pronouncements because they liked his grandmother and wished to keep on her good side.

Shortly after getting the cards, Chuck amazed the waitresses at his grandmother's restaurant with his readings. Patrons were asking for him, and strangers soon came in looking for him. His uncle gave him a little cash box, and on some days the five year old had as much in it as his grandmother had in the cafe's cash register. Those receiving readings had spontaneously and gratefully made donations to him. He was popular with both African American and white Kansas City residents.

So impressed was a minister from a nearby Missouri town that he convinced Chuck's grandmother to allow the boy to prophesy from his church's pulpit. Chuck became a minister at six years old and was licensed at seven. An ordained minister in the Holiness Church at twelve years old, he toured the South with the sponsoring minister, accompanied by his grandmother. Often the principal speaker in the tents and small churches where they held service, the child read his Tarot cards from the pulpit, frequently drawing large crowds.

"A lot of kids used to come to me for advice. I just told them, and it was always right. It was such a natural thing. It was no big deal," recollects Vera Sutton about her psychic counseling as a student in junior high and high school. "They would say, 'I have this problem and that problem.' And I would go from there. They knew it worked, so they came back. Other than that I was real quiet about my gift. I stayed to myself."

Vera was struck by the magnitude of her popularity as a counselor while in the ninth grade. "I thought, 'Why are they all coming to me about their boyfriends and problems?' "

"You sound like our mothers," she was told.

"I remember one girl saying that I always looked and acted more mature."

The youngest of ten children, Vera was born in Atlanta. She relates that she was raised in a very loving home environment by both parents. The young girl preferred being alone at home and at school. Shyness did not cause her to withdraw; she did so as a matter of choice, catering to an impelling need to meditate and explore her inner self. "I was always within myself for whatever ... I remember praying since I was three. When I was nine, my sister gave me my own personal Bible. I read it until the back came off ... I used to sit and meditate and be right in those places where Jesus Christ was. Holding His hand and going around with Him when He talked to people. I could see myself doing that."

In describing her childhood gift, Vera relates, "I remember being aware when I was very young, even as early as five years old ... of a natural knowing. It was not like a voice. I never heard anything.

I didn't close my eyes. It was just something that was a part of my consciousness, and I was so clear about it. It was not like reading faces or anything like that. It was self-knowing.

"I knew that I knew, and what I came up with was right. There was no struggle to it, it was natural, and clear, and without a big 'adoo'."

Pleased that he could elevate his body and his books into the air without any physical means, eight-year-old James often allowed himself that pleasure. "I would actually be suspended from the bed."

His spirit guide, warning "You are misusing your gift!", eventually taught the boy how to convert the energy he was using for amusement back into his body, to be used for something more practical, such as healing.

"I had a spirit that was charged to me when I was a child. The spirit looked like an Arabian man . . . . The little man told me that his brother was going to come, and when he would come there would always be trouble—very deep trouble," explains James Moye, who was seven when the spirit mentor entered his life.

James was fourteen when the being did arrive with another spirit—his twin brother. They had come to console and support him, but he was not aware why. It was soon after that James' mother died. "I was somewhere between six and seven that I remember seeing these people come from the cemetery. They would come and talk to me. These people would come like floating apparitions. They would appear to be on floats. I would always see the mist rising up. They would be talking at one time. I told my mother that I saw these people coming and they had to be dead, because they were all so pale.

"I was born with the gift . . . I was able to see so much at an early age." There was a telepathic tie with his mother, and the ability to see future events followed. At first, he only shared his prophetic insights with family members; but by the time he was nine, he was making predictions at church.

His message-giving was frowned upon by the church hierarchy and there was official effort made to suppress James' activities. "I chose to go underground, more or less. People would still want to know. They would ask me after service if I saw anything for them."

One woman, told by her doctor that she could never bear a child, asked then nine-year-old James to pray for her. "I prayed for her, and the child did come."

The older girl playfully whirled her sister by the heels; but when they closed in on a tree, their fun came to an abrupt end. Betty's head hit the tree solidly, and cracked open. This severe wound, like all the illnesses and mishaps of the family of eight children, was treated by their mother, using the ways of natural healing she learned from her mother out of their Caribbean past.

After recovering from the injury, seven-year-old Betty was astonished to find unprecedented and sudden attention given her by other children. This confused her, and she remembers thinking to herself: "I am just a child; why are they coming to me as if I were their mothers?" Children at school and in her Newark, New Jersey neighborhood were asking her questions and seeking solutions to problems in their lives. With ease she marveled she could answer them.

A young woman came into the hospital where the sixteen-year-old Betty worked as a tray server. Following a psychic impression, Betty asked the woman if she had four children. "She answered, 'Yes, but what business is it of yours?' I told her, 'I don't know, but don't go outside the way you came in because someone is waiting for you.'" Together they went to the exit to check out Betty's premonition. Peering outside, they saw a man crouching in the bushes with a switchblade knife. The woman thanked Betty for saving her life and left the hospital by another exit.

A native of New Jersey, Betty Comes, an evangelist and psychic counselor, has lived in Los Angeles since 1977.

Thrown from sleep by a loud explosion inside her body, Bennie at first thought somebody had hit her. No one else was awake. The twelve year old's discomfort grew as more internal sensation followed. She felt rapid bursts of energy within, and a bright light flashed through her mental space.

Even now she recalls vividly how loud the explosion was. To her at the time it was a mystery, and remained that way until she was told many years later that the startling and uncomfortable impressions she felt that night were caused by the opening of one of her chakras. Chakras, as explained to her, are psychic centers in the body through which spiritual energy flows. The rest of her chakras opened when she was twenty-nine years old, while giving birth to her son, Teddy. Soon after, she began hearing voices, and psychically seeing into the thoughts, emotions, and intentions of others in an intensified way.

With her five sisters and brothers, Bennie was placed in a Cincinnati orphanage by their parents who were unable to support them. She regards the move as predestination; she had to be sent away, since growing up under her mother's direction would have hindered her spiritually. At the orphanage, Bennie was popular with the staff. To amuse themselves they had her assess the age and weight of visitors. The accuracy of the seven year old astounded them, but they treated her performance as a game. None then ever recognized that the girl had a gift.

Born in Ohio, Bennie Holloway moved to California in 1962, where she is a psychic counselor. She tells of her spiritual purpose here on Earth, to help usher in the Golden Age of spirit on the planet.

Beatrice had a peculiar gift. When someone was going to die, she felt pushed away from that person. She would know, regardless of what was tried, that person could no longer be helped, and would die.

Her abilities came when she was eleven years old. She closed her eyes and saw images, and from these she predicted. Those events of the future she perceived happened as she described them, she states.

After her mother died, Beatrice was raised from age nine by a relative. Although other children were aggravated by her strange knowing and mannerisms, calling her names and shunning her, and although she was called "crazy" by her aunt who didn't understand her gifts, older relatives and neighbors accepted the girl. Feeling sustained, Beatrice hung around them, sharing the benefits of her special awareness.

A native of Charleston, South Carolina, Beatrice Washington still resides there. Trained through revelations from God, her spiritual work is done primarily through prayer. She is a healer and a prophet.

Wilda grasped the woman's shirttail, steadying herself. The adult was often an assuring support for the toddler to lean against. When she was older, Wilda saw the familiar figure once again—in the family photo album. She was amazed to learn the woman was her maternal grandmother—who had died four years before her birth!

From her bed, many times, she watched small animated shapes of energy advance menacingly toward her; but they never could pass through the circle of light surrounding her bed. Unintimidated by their presence, she felt pity for these discarnate beings, and an urge to change them through love. Habitually during childhood, an angel visited her. Protecting Wilda seemed the cherub's duty. The time Wilda's clothing was aflame after playing with fire, the angel appeared. The four year old was unharmed, although her clothing burned away to nothing.

A middle child with four sisters and five brothers, Wilda enjoyed her siblings' companionship. She and one of her brothers were in the same grade at school. One day while they were in class Wilda looked at him; she sensed a distancing between him and everybody else—a fading quality about him—as if he were less present. On a family outing, that same year, she noticed a halo-shaped light above her brother's head. Again, he seemed strangely faraway. This brother died by drowning two weeks later.

After his death he appeared to Wilda when she was intensely grieving over him. He patted her to soothe her grief, and she felt the warmth of his hand. Within a few weeks, he came to thirteen-year-old Wilda again. As they walked, he told her he was all right. He had comprehended he was eternal. Then Wilda perceived they were, in a nonphysical plane, "walking" across the sky together. After this meeting, her sadness lessened. She felt relief in her recognition soon afterwards that her brother left this dimension of his own free will.

Born in Arkansas, Wilda Mays is a resident of the San Francisco Bay area.

As a young slave, George had no means to get the pocket knife he craved. He prayed, prayer after prayer, that such a knife might be his. In what he called his first revelation, George Washington Carver had a dream. The next morning, the six-year-old boy excitedly rushed through the plantation fields in a knowing search. It was not long before he found what he was seeking—a watermelon from which protruded the type of knife for which he prayed. This scene of the watermelon with the pocket knife stuck into it was the exact vision he had perceived in his dream the night before. Carver considered that particular experience as being the earliest in the course of events which continued throughout his life. The commonality of these events was that desired knowledge, conditions, and objects came into existence in the physical universe as the results of his prayers.

That he had a high psychic sensitivity to the life energies of plants was quite evident by his middle childhood years. So confident and intuitively knowledgeable about botany was the frail and usually shy boy that he would advise adults with unhesitating authority on correct treatment for their ailing flora. The residents of the southwestern Missouri community of Diamond, where George spent his early years, accepted his natural wisdom. His own recalling of his faculty in childhood is noted in *George Washington Carver: In His Own Words* by Gary R. Kremer.

> And many are the tears I have shed because I would break the roots or flower ... off some of my pets while removing them from the ground, and strange to say all sorts of vegetation succeed to thrive under my touch until I was styled the plant doctor, and plants from all over the country would be brought to me for treatment. At this time I had never heard of botany and could scarcely read.[5]

Although George enjoyed being with other children, he was rather withdrawn around them. He was liveliest ministering to and playing with the life that generated from earth itself. His brother, Jim, in watching George gently tending roses, once asked what he was doing. The boy's reply was that he was "loving the flowers."

Before she was nine years old, for several years Elizabeth was totally blind. The lack of physical sight was partly offset by the emergence from within her of a new source of information. This information, she describes, consisted of pictures, but never a voice. She used these prophetic visions as they came. "As a child, I would sit on the sidewalk, and as people came along, they would stop and I would tell them what would happen that day."

Memphis-born and raised, Elizabeth Toles was three months old when her mother died of childbirth complications. The infant's care was taken over by an aunt, and later in childhood by a stepmother.

As a high school student, she felt her teachers were quite inadequate—"dumb." Elizabeth would read the first page of her book assignment and then "make up" the rest, and they never detected this. From her "made-up" material, she wrote reports and received A's; other students, however, didn't fare as well when they, on their own, used the making-up technique which she shared with them. They received F's. As exam days approached, without probing, Elizabeth spontaneously knew the details of the tests. Although she did not comprehend the true significance of what she was doing, Elizabeth remembers she consciously used these gifts all during the years of growing up. Elizabeth did not realize at the time that her gift enabled her to know a book's content after reading the first page.

"There's my green animal. Now, that animal, he's in the Garden of Eden ... God has him there but He hasn't put him on earth so man can see them,"[6] explained elderly artist Minnie Evans of a green creature in one of her paintings.

> Green is God's theme color .... He showed me that animal, I wasn't old enough to go to school. He was on that ring around the moon. There were three of them. One real large and a medium size and a small, and I was playing out in the

> street ... and the moon was back up here, shining, and it drew
> my attention.
>   Children said, "Minnie, what are you looking at?" I said,
> "I'm looking at those elephants." ... And they came an'
> looked up too and said, "We don't see no elephants." I
> thought everybody could see them .... One of the little chil-
> dren jumped up and hollered and fell down and laughed,
> said, "Minnie's crazy, she sees elephants going around the
> moon." But they was going round that circle. I haven't seen
> another circle as bright as that in all my life. It was just as
> bright as the moon.

On hearing the other children laughing at her daughter,
Minnie's mother summoned her home. "Let that child alone, leave
her alone," said a neighbor interrupting the mother's reprimanding.
"God has showed her something He hasn't showed to you or me or
nobody else."

In the documentary film of the painter's life, produced by Allie
Light and Irving Saraf, the artist declared that dreams never let her
rest much from childhood on. She was almost always tired in the
morning. At thirteen came another series of dreams.

> It was old men startled me. They wouldn't try to hurt
> me, but they would throw me up. There was five or six of
> them dressed up like the old prophets. They would catch me
> as soon as I dozed off to sleep .... They would take me, carry
> me down the street, push me down, some catch me, keep me
> from hitting the ground, throw me up, just laughing and go-
> ing on ... till I was just tormented, but they wouldn't try to
> hurt me. For three different times they had me down ... to the
> Soldiers' Cemetery. I have woke up more times in that ceme-
> tery.

Someone called Minnie's name all day long whenever she
stayed at her grandmother's house across the street from a cemetery.

> I said, "Listen, somebody's calling me." And every time
> (my grandmother) said, "Don't answer. Don't answer." She
> was afraid. She say, "You fixing to go to the bone yards." The
> cemetery she would call it.
>   She say, "If you hear them calling ... don't answer, just
> come and say, 'Mama, did you call me?' " ... I had to break
> myself off from answering, cause they called me so much ...
>   "Oh, what a miserable life I had, to be a child, I wasn't
> nothing but a child."

Born in North Carolina in 1883, Minnie Evans began painting and drawing in 1935. The animals going around the moon which she saw in that childhood vision are among the subjects of her art work.

"I was between twelve and thirteen, between thirteen and fourteen—I saw the very first airplane. I didn't know what it was. I was in such a awful fix. So much of dream. I dreamt those great big . . . I didn't know what to call 'em. I called on my mother, 'There's some big white . . . iron birds flying over our heads.' She said, 'What kind of crazy thing is that?' I didn't know, big iron birds and they're making a lot of funny . . . sound, flying over me . . . But they were flying over . . . and dropping fire. I was running along with the people. The street was . . . full of people, and they was howling and screaming, talking about this war." Since her mother didn't understand, Minnie went to her grandmother about the dream. "I said, 'Mama, what is it? What kind of thing is that?' She said, 'Minnie . . . something or other God has for you.' "

Later into the new century, when airplanes were invented and came into wide use in warfare, Minnie then recognized "what kind of thing" she had foreseen in her prophetic dream.

In a revelation when she was twelve, she was shown her gifts by the Lord; whether awake or asleep, she would have visions. Spirits would come to talk with her. She would sense and know the dispositions and thoughts of other people, and absorb their pains. She would receive empowerment to heal others through prayer.

Ionia admits she felt unready to be entrusted with the gifts. As one of twelve children being raised by a widowed father, too much of her was needed in physical-world living. Then, on an afternoon when she was quieter than usual, the Lord began to prepare her. Ionia tells that He gave her immediate understanding of the Bible. And when her father perceived her sharp comprehension, he assigned her to read the Bible to him every Sunday.

In adulthood, she has accepted her gifts. They are as she was shown in the revelation. She uses them to counsel, and to be of service in her community. A member of the Praise the Lord Foundation, she visits prisons where she lectures and teaches. She prays with the inmates and instructs them in the scriptures.

Born in Louisiana, Ionia White has lived in Richmond, California for almost three decades.

"I remember the first time I turned Queen of the Morning at Disneyland. The first time! I wanted to be the Queen and they came over. It was like I made them—had them do it because they just came over and made me go up there. I wanted to go and they picked me! Then I did it another time," confessed April King in 1985. "I had a dream about a queen that pulled a sword out of a stone and that was with Merlin. That was the night before we went to Disneyland. The next day I was Queen of the Morning."

Her mother has noticed that whenever people with cameras are around, April manages to get her picture taken. "Well, it's like I think that they will do it and I want them to—and then in a little while they turn the camera around and they do it," explains the little girl.

"April is accurate a lot of the time. Whenever she has a hunch, I definitely pay attention," remarks the mother, Lori King, who is herself a psychic, and hostess of a metaphysical radio program.

Even before the child was two years old, her mother was led to act on the young one's precognitions. For Lori, a particular incident of that period stands out. The family was then living in San Francisco, and Lori was still married to April's father. "April kept going to our front door and banging on it and saying, 'Mama, go see Granddad! Get car—go now!' I called my husband at work and told him that we were driving to Bakersfield. We got there, and within three days my father was in the hospital for bypass surgery! I felt if we hadn't been there to help him get to the hospital he might not have made it. April was really in touch with him, even though she didn't know him well at that point."

Since she was three months old, April has been reading cards. At thirteen months she acquired her first deck of regular playing cards for her own independent readings. Her technique was to examine the deck, pass her hands over each card, then select one or two cards, and point them towards a person in the room. She has read at psychic fairs with her mother. Through her accuracy she has gained her own small following. A crystal marble is a part of her readings.

When she looks in it, she sees pictures.

Described by her mother as an "open" child, April has been especially vulnerable to influences of negative spirit entities. The period between ages three and four was a critical time for her. To handle the psychic turmoil which threatened to encompass April, Lori took her to a spiritual teacher. They would have sessions with the teacher, Mishenanda; and at other times he would appear in spirit to help April handle the entities harassing her.

April's great-grandmother, a discarnate being, has been vigilantly present in her life. She appeared during the child's birth and shows up on occasion very visibly, manifesting as she appeared in life—a short, dark-complexioned woman of pure African lineage. She consistently is present when April is sick, and gives Lori instructions, and fusses at her about the care of the child. Aware of her paternal great-grandmother, April talks with her in dreams. At times, they astral-travel together.

"One time my mother was sick in the afternoon. I touched her and she felt better for a little while. The next day, I touched her and she was completely fine." By touching, April has helped her mother and several animals feel better.

Participating in a psychic fair at six years old, April sold aura drawings she created, her mother reports.

Born in May, 1980, April King lives with her mother in Bakersfield, California where she attends a Quaker school. In response to a question about what she thought she was here to do in her life, April replied, "To be a doctor, and to help people get well." She also thought of becoming an actress or a practicing psychic.

The mother-daughter relationship between Lori and April is older than the present lifetime. Once the child asked the mother, "Who is the mother and who is the daughter this time?"

CHAPTER TWO

The Medium's Way

The *National Spiritualist Reporter* (April, 1984) gives the following definition:

> A Medium is one whose organism is sensitive to
> vibrations from the spirit world, and through whose
> instrumentality, intelligences in that world are able to convey
> messages and produce the phenomena of Spiritualism.[1]

Until the middle of the 1980s the newsletter was published
monthly by the National Colored Spiritualist Association of the
United States of America. Organized in 1925, the Association continues to hold national conventions annually. Through its "Declaration
of Principles" the group imparts a philosophical profile.

1. We believe in Infinite Intelligence.
2. We believe that the Phenomena of nature, both physical
   and spiritual, are the expression of Infinite Intelligence.
3. We affirm that a correct understanding of such expression
   and living in accordance therewith constitute true
   religion.
4. We affirm that the existence and personal identity of the
   individual continues after the change called death.
5. We affirm that communication with the so-called dead is
   a fact, scientifically proven by the phenomena of
   Spiritualism.
6. We believe that the highest morality is contained in the
   Golden Rule: "Whatsoever ye would that others should

do unto you, do ye also unto them."
7. We affirm the moral responsibility of the individual, and that he makes his own happiness or unhappiness as he obeys or disobeys Nature's physical and spiritual laws.
8. We affirm that the doorway to reformation is never closed against any human soul here or hereafter.
9. We affirm that the precept of Prophesy contained in the Bible is a Divine attribute proven through mediumship.
10. We affirm man's spiritual gifts, and that they are confirmed by the works of Jesus Christ, the prophets and apostles as recorded in the Holy Bible.

The term "medium" became popularly associated with Spiritualism in the United States sometime during the last half of the nineteenth century. Modern Spiritualism began as a movement in the United States in 1843, following the mysterious rappings heard by Kate Margaret and Leah Fox in their Hydesville, New York home. The rappings were revealed to be signals from a deceased man. Through the use of a code, communication was established with the spirit.

The concept of mediumship has been broadened over the past two decades. "Channeling" is the contemporary and comprehensive term in this recent outgrowth of mediumship. The role of the channel approximates that of a medium but differs in that communication received through a channel may come from sources of consciousness other than those of earth discarnates; they may be from other dimensions, spiritual planes, or extraterrestrial beings. These spirits may have never had organic forms like those known upon Earth's gross physical plane of existence.

"When you unfold, you are supposed to have a spirit guide who corrects you in all conditions; a physical health guide to take care of your health and to help you in sickness; and a finance guide," asserts Chicago medium Louise Washington.

Louise's history with the National Association of Spiritualist Churches goes back more than half a century. The oldest person in the organization's Illinois chapter, she has been a featured speaker at national conventions for many years. She lectures, instructs, and demonstrates the principles of Spiritualism at the church she founded, Tucker Smith Memorial Spiritualist Temple.

"I am never alone. I talk with and see my guides all the time. I don't make a move without guidance." Her direct experience with the spirit world, progressing from childhood, has been eventful.

"I worked with the trumpet years ago when I was in class," explains Louise about an apparatus used in standard seances. Through it the sound volume of spirit-world communication is increased. It is a tool to facilitate communication between the two realms for the better understanding of seance attendees. "The trumpet is made of metal and shaped a little like a horn. In a class it is set on the table or floor. When the trumpet is charged—it will float. It is floated by the spirit world. It moves or floats to whomever the message is for."

Not long ago spirit-world doctors were with her while she underwent major surgery. On their advice, she demanded the operation as the way to rid her body of a major disease process which had been undetected by medical science before her guides intervened. Wide-awake during the entire operation, she listened to the spirit world. "I told the doctor where to cut," Louise confirms. Disease sites were found and removed where Louise had indicated.

"Disembodied intelligences call what I do 'inspirational writing', as opposed to automatic writing," says native Chicagoan Peter Brown, who became an ordained minister in the Spiritual church at eighteen years old. "There is a distinct difference. In automatic writing, you pick up a pen and wait. You take whatever you get. That is not necessarily good because there are intelligences that will play with you," he warns. "With inspirational writing, you begin each session with a prayer. You ask for divine guidance. Then you have specific questions which you present. And these are answered.

"I incorporated that into the ministry because they (the intelligences) told me that was the proper function. It is a modern day prophetic exercise. I moved it out of the realm of just psychic phenomena as such. It is a legitimate religious experience.

"In counseling, when people have problems, they want answers. They come to me, we pray about their problem. I present the question and we get the answers."

Peter was eighteen when a medium told him that spirit forces had been trying to get his attention for years through the form he called a cornucopia. This form is shaped similarly to the "trumpet" sometimes used in seances for communication between the spirit world and humans.

"In high school, I would doodle while sitting in classrooms, being bored most of the time. I would draw a cornucopia—the horn of plenty. Time after time, I would draw that thing," he laughs.

A week after the medium's reading, Peter got a sharp pain in his arm while writing. "My handwriting changed." Peter watched his hand write, "Hello!"

"I looked at it, thinking, 'What is this?' "

His hand wrote again. "I've come to teach you."

"I called the medium up and told him what was happening. He gave me a lot of instructions.

"For three and a half or four years, I sat every morning for more and more instructions and information which came from the other side," he recalls.

Over the many years since his first experience, Peter has had a succession of spirit teachers. "You graduate from one to another. They pass you along. I've had a time with that. I developed a rapport with the first one. His name is Hilarion. I decided I didn't want any changes. He had to really give me a going over. He said, 'You can't grow this way. I am supposed to be the starter, then I am supposed to pass you on.' " To be a channel through which other human beings can truly receive help, Peter has had to work on conquering his own mental aberrations. In this work toward spiritual maturation, he has been closely guided by the teachers.

"The channel through which the information comes has to be reconstructed, has to lose opinions, instead of being opinionated. One has to be willing to lose the ego.

"It takes some time to get over the things you know that are true, that really aren't true, plus deal with the flaws and weaknesses in your own personality. These are presented to you first. You have to overcome these," Peter says. "In that kind of catharsis, it may take you two to three years to overcome just one thing!"

Spirit-directed, she dispensed messages to individuals from the pulpit of her church, the Upper Room, in Chicago. In a state of ecstasy, she danced while prophesying. Strangers often swelled the congregation, anxious for insight into their lives.

Born in Arkansas in 1880, Mother Susie Booth had a church in Memphis, in her early adult years. However, most of her life was spent in Chicago where she was at one time a minister in Clarence Cobb's First Church of Deliverance. She was always prophesying. Day and night, her home filled with people coming for counseling. She kept up that pace until she was one hundred and three years old. A devout lady, she was forever praying, fasting, and dressing in white. God told her to wear everything white.

Long ago, God also told Mother Booth to design and sew gowns for church functions and not to charge much for them. She obeyed and called this activity her second mission. Her robes were recognized by choir groups throughout Chicago and her artistry proclaimed. She was far past her ninetieth year before she stopped sewing.

Of the things Mother Booth foretold, there were many. What she said came to pass. Even her own death, at the exact time she described, occurred as predicted!

A steady companion of Mother Booth for many years, Janie Lewis provides much of what is written here from her memories of the medium, who lived to be almost one hundred and six years old. Her spirit guides were powerful, Janie says. When these beings entered the house, energy drained from everyone's body. A person couldn't do anything until they left. Mother Booth's conversation with them could be heard. She worked with many different entities. Sometimes she was in a trance and sometimes not. One spirit guide seen by Janie was towering, and his presence felt immense. Excited that Janie accurately described him, Mother Booth cried out, "Yes, yes, that's him!"

Too tired to move from her chair one night to place the requested pillows under Mother Booth's feet, Janie in some agitation saw a pillow rise, then slide under the feet by itself. To calm her, the medium assured her softly: "Don't worry, Janie, it's my mother!"

Directed by an unknown force, he stopped playing. His hands returned to the keyboard again, now guided into playing a style of music unlike anything he had ever played.

"Who is there?" asked Count Carnette, telepathically, sensing an undeniable spirit presence which emanated serenity and love.

"I am Frederic Chopin," the entity responded.

As evidence of life after death, Chopin revealed he and other discarnate composers would return to give music to Count to share with the world.

"I thought I was going crazy," says Count, in speaking of his initial reaction. "I didn't know my true divine nature, then." To understand the phenomenon, he turned to psychologists, priests, and rabbis. It was not until he corresponded with Rosemary Brown in England that he began trusting his own intuition. A psychic herself, she began channeling music from the masters in 1964. What Count already knew within himself, she confirmed. His music was inspired. The masters were channeling their creativity through him. That first appearance by Chopin in 1974 marked the beginning of a series of pupil-teacher relationships which included Johannes Brahms, Franz Liszt, Sergei Rachmaninoff, Robert Schumann, and lesser-known composers.

In *Threshold To Tomorrow* by Ruth Montgomery, Count described interactions with individual composers.

> I have a tender regard for Liszt. I feel a special rapport with him and recognize him as a loving soul with great patience and understanding. His method of working (with me) is typical. I am given a short section of the piece, which I must memorize (because he does not know how to write it down). During each sitting I am again given more to memorize. Later I am told exactly where each segment fits into the work as a whole.[2]
>
> Robert Schumann's method differs somewhat from that of the other composers. When "To a Rose" was channeled, we worked nonstop from two a.m. until five a.m. At the end of three hours the entire piece was completely learned and memorized. Later he explained the music to me in detail, and said that it was dedicated to his wife, Clara. He said that in this piece it was his wish to show the many aspects of love: the joy, the sadness, and the intensity.

"Schumann was very formal and intimidating," the young musician recalls. "But, he was a wonderful teacher. He told me, 'You can often love a piano back into tune.' " The channeled composer worked only once with Count.

In Seattle, Washington, Count lived in a large old church where he was caretaker. It was there he created and received instructions from discarnate composers.

"I don't go into a trance when I play. I don't give up my body for any other being."

On the jacket of his record album, *Psychic Piano Music from the Masters*, Count further described the phenomena of his music. "I, myself, cannot take credit for these piano compositions and arrangements, and believe that I have been assisted by supernatural forces. It is my belief that those Masters and Teachers who work with me give me music to use for a variety of purposes. Some of the music can be used during meditation to soothe the mind and help guide it inward. Even physical healings could take place through the vibrations of this music."[3]

A New Age performer, Count tours the country in response to a growing demand for his recitals.

"I have not studied piano formally since I began to play at the age of three," he explained on the album jacket. "Not one page of music manuscript was consulted during the preparation of this recording, nor do I have the ability to notate any of the new music which I have received. Everything was prepared through what I call my psychic intuition. This process involves being as aware and as receptive as possible to each thing that is given. The music which comes to me does so with very little effort on my part. It simply flows."

In 1933, the same year she became a Spiritualist, Nellye Mae Taylor joined the National Colored Spiritualist Association of the United States of America. Experiences with racial discrimination in the churches of the National Spiritualist Association of the United States, both in Oklahoma and Kansas, led her to join the organization. In those days, she remarks, African Americans were welcomed at services in Spiritualist churches in the South but were not permitted to conduct service or give readings.

During the early years of her mediumship, she worked in African American Spiritualist churches in Tulsa and Kansas City with her husband, Horace, a minister and medium. A former student of his, she had attended his philosophy and development classes. "When I met him, he had been in the work twenty-five years. He was twice my age. I learned to be guided by the spirit and intuition and that helped me to help others," she remarks. For more than three decades she has been a resident of Phoenix, and pastor of the Taylor Memorial Interracial Spiritualist Church. Horace passed away during the 1950s.

Born in Tulsa, Oklahoma in 1910, Nellye Mae attended Western University and looked forward to a life as a foreign missionary. "But I knew I was lacking something spiritual and began to search."

At thirty-five, she became a billet reader. Blindfolded, she randomly picked out of a container a question someone put into one of the sealed envelopes collected from the congregation at church service. It was not through her physical senses that the inquirer's name and questions became known to her, as she held the selected unopened envelope, but through clairaudient communication with her spirit guide Great Eagle.

Years ago in Tulsa, Spirit once spoke loudly to her outdoors. "After visiting a sick person, I was walking home in the dark around two o'clock in the morning when I heard a voice say, 'Look up and look out!' I looked up and saw fire coming out of a house."

At the endangered home, an angry woman responded to her frantic knocking. In reactive disbelief, the woman repudiated Nellye Mae's warning and ordered her to leave.

"Instead, I snatched the screen door open, broke the glass, reached in and unlocked the door!"

As the hysterical woman advanced with a gun, Nellye Mae held her ground and talked with the children who huddled in a room nearby. One child, coaxed by her, went outside and saw the flames. Certain that the family was now mindful of the danger, Nellye Mae hurried off to call the fire department. The fire, located in the rear of the house, was caused by faulty electrical wiring, the apologetic woman later told her.

About an experience with an apported object, Nellye Mae Taylor explains, "Spirit brought the tape recorder from Miami to Phoenix." In spite of a thorough search by the Miami hotel management and herself, the tape recorder she had placed on the bed in her hotel room before going to a meeting could not be found. After it had been missing for more than a year, it reappeared in the living-room of her home!

Eddie Cabral aligns with three entities to create what he describes as a "triangular energy." One spirit, an ancient Egyptian teacher-deity, rises from repose on a bier within a golden-walled tomb to communicate. The second entity, called Korondu, is a lion; and the third being, a shiny black panther or jaguar, is named Niema. In teaching and healing, Eddie uses this triangle of energy.

"I will not speak with any entity that is not illumined. Illumination is a space wherein negativity cannot exist," he explains. In a semi-trance, he reads for individuals. "Two African gods open me as strongly as I need to be for the situation."

Born in Rochester, Massachusetts, Eddie has been in California since 1981. In the Los Angeles area where he resides, he is the assistant minister of a church. Each month, one hundred miles away in Bakersfield, he co-hosts a psychic radio program.

Also a visual artist, Eddie works primarily with oil colors. He has done paintings which were, several years later, revealing in prophetic ways. While creating on an aesthetic level, he contacts a dimension of transcendent intelligences who have never known physical existence. "I channel a lot of my work," he explains.

Writing songs and plays and acting round out Eddie's major activities. A goal he has in working with audiences is to "stimulate the Truth within each person" through his creations. He expresses an interest in seeing a spiritual reformation within the entertainment and media fields. He wants to see a shift from destructive themes in plays and movies to constructive ones. Toward that objective, he has been channeling good information to the core of that group consciousness which can produce the needed change.

"I do the work of God when I do something artistic. I know the power behind the work is a power far greater than me."

"In Macon, Georgia, a colored girl, who was an excellent physical medium, frequently exhibited the feat of thrusting her hand amongst the blazing pine logs, and removing it after some sixty seconds without the least injury. She always insisted, however, that she would only perform this feat when 'Cousin Joe,' whom she called her guardian spirit, was present and bid her do it."[4] Reported in the *Christian Spiritualist*, a periodical of 1860, were the activities of two individuals described as physical mediums. Under the direction of Spirit, they gained ability to place their bodies in burning flames for prolonged periods without being harmed. These were manifestations of a phenomenon called "fire immunity."

> At New Orleans, Louisiana, a negro by the name of Tom Jenkins was well known for his power of resisting fire, under what he called the " 'fluence of Big Ben," a boatman, formerly on the Mississippi River, and who, since the day of his death by drowning, had come and made what Tom called "magic" for him. On one occasion . . . (Tom) became entranced, took off his shoes and stockings, rolled up his pantaloons to his knees, and entered the pine wood fire, literally standing in it as it blazed upon the hearth, long enough to repeat in a solemn and impressive manner the 23rd, 24th, and 25th verses of the third chapter of Daniel.

After completing a painting, artist Reginald Arthur found he had painted a man of East Indian descent, with careful detailing of sideburns and mustache. It was not a face he had ever seen, or a type he felt inclined to paint.

In following another impulse to paint, not long after that, he surprised himself by producing the same picture. Giving no special meaning to the duplication, he sold one painting and gave away the other. At an unplanned reading with a psychic, several years later, Reginald was told that an entity was present. From the description given by the psychic, Reginald realized he was meeting the man in his two paintings! It was the being's third attempt to contact him, the psychic explained. The spirit, Auriel, in wanting to work with Reginald, influenced him to do the paintings; and in a final effort to communicate, led him to the reading.

Of that relationship, initiated over twenty years ago, the artist remarks, "Auriel became my spiritual teacher and guide after that meeting."

For a while Reginald gave messages in Spiritualist churches, from information received from Auriel in words and pictures. With his guide and Tarot cards he presently gives consultations to individuals in New York City.

A performing artist who has a Master's degree in theatre arts, he sings, dances, and acts in off-Broadway productions. Teaching theatre methods to young African Americans in a way which would increase their psychic perception is a future project of his.

"You ask God to strip you of your self, set your mind blank so the spirit of the Lord can command you ... Sometimes nothing happens, but other times the Lord or other spirit forces desire to speak through you and prophecy occurs."[5] In this way Lydia Gilford described her mediumship to Michael Smith, author of *Spirit World*.

The minister of the Infant Jesus of Prague Spiritual Church in New Orleans, Gilford has lived in that city all of her life. Raised a Catholic, she was twenty-one when her mother took her to a Spiritual minister for counseling. Later she joined a Spiritual church, and in 1966 she founded her own church. "You could vent the spirit forces. When you feel like dancing, you dance. When you feel like shouting, you shout. When you feel the visitation of the spirit, you do whatever you feel like doing and it's all right ... it's better felt than told," she said, conveying her deep affinity for the Spiritual church.

"The Spiritual churches have all the same saints as the Catholic churches, but have added a few more, like Black Hawk, and Sitting Bull—who were praying Indians—and others. We go to Black Hawk for peace and justice."

The information communicated by Gilford while in the trance state is not remembered by her afterwards. But people return to let her know the messages helped them. Believing the individual is responsible for making his or her own decisions in life, she explained, "If it doesn't come from within, it just doesn't work."

Through his mediumship, Joseph Calloway has prevented physical accidents, costly production delays, and has assisted fellow crew members in solving personal problems on the set. "Spirit has been working with me to open doors," he says. Spirit friends, guides, and teachers come to him through the "law of attraction," guiding his spiritual development and his creativity. Sometimes in creative endeavors, such as script-writing, set-lighting, and conceiving camera movement, spiritual knowledge has spontaneously been imparted to him.

Joseph is a free-lance director of photography in the Hollywood film community. His first job was with *Lady Sings the Blues*. "I didn't understand it until late, but I know I wouldn't have received the opportunity to work on the film if Spirit had not intervened directly on my behalf. My great-uncle, who was Billie Holiday's publicist, and the lady herself, were both influencing forces."

Joseph has worked around the country on projects such as *Pee-wee's Playhouse* and *The Five Heartbeats*. He recently co-produced *The Gifted*, a science fiction thriller about the supernatural.

"There was strong influence from Spirit," he notes of a pilot series, *Worlds Beyond*, which he worked on in the fall of 1986, an experience he considers unique to his film career. Working out of Lilydale, New York, he was executive producer and director of five 30-minute videos on Spiritualism, including mediumship and healing, sponsored by the National Association of Spiritualist Churches. He tells of exceptional mediums who greatly contributed to the film's smooth production flow. Problems tended to dissipate as quickly as they arose, and an unusual harmony thrived among the entire crew, both Spiritualist and non-Spiritualist.

Joseph received a Spirit message through a medium which said, "You will be lucky for those with whom you come in contact." He has been instrumental in assisting several aspiring directors to launch their film careers.

Since he was sixteen years old, Joseph has attended the National Association of Spiritualist Churches of which he is now a member, a certified medium, and a former board member of the California State Spiritualist Association. A certified clairsentient with psychometric abilities, he lectures, teaches, and has read billets at church services nationally.

Although a mental medium, Joseph experienced physical mediumship phenomena during his high school years. A photography and art major, he often developed his own film late at night. While developing several prints from the same negative, he discovered spirit-like faces, unidentifiable but distinct. These individuals had been nowhere in visible range when he took the picture and did not even appear on the negative.

Joseph says of his mediumship, "God works for man through man. We give back to God by what we give our fellow man. I attempt to give out the highest and best so I may receive from the infinite the highest and best."

"Al Benson was as good a medium as there was anywhere," remembers psychic advisor, Alvin Lock. "He was a real trance medium. I worked with him from 1962 through 1967."

"If he told me that door would fly open at 10:00 p.m.—you could bet it would do that. He was just that much in tune."

Now deceased, Benson, whose real name was Arthur B. Leaner, was once a top Chicago disc jockey known as the "Old Swingmaster." He was active as a medium in Chicago during the 1950s and 1960s.

A medium and healer, Coleman Hill was bishop of a Spiritual church in Bakersfield, California in the 1940s and 1950s.

"Bishop Hill could stop storms and calm rivers that were overflowing," recalls Arizona psychic Frank Gipson. "He knew my name and told me what I had been through before I ever talked to him." Impressed with Hill's clairvoyance, his mediumship abilities in diagnosing and healing, and his psychic rapport with animals, Gipson became his student in the early 1950s.

Sally Wales was already reading when she and Clarence Cobb, a Chicago psychic and Spiritualist, decided to study together around 1935. She sought to expand the potentials of her gift.

"My mother was always psychic," says her daughter, Odessa Payne. "She got her messages from Spirit. She would look at people and read them from Spirit. At times, she used cards."

Born in Point Peter, Georgia, Wales' religious upbringing was in the Baptist church; later, she changed over to the Spiritualist church. In Chicago, about 1937, she set up her own storefront Spiritualist church and delivered messages.

On the effects of having had a gifted and well-known mother, Payne remarks, "My mother never probed into my life. She gave me suggestions. She was a very happy person. She made people quite happy. She would talk with them and help them."

While living in the Shaker community of Watervliet, New York, Rebecca Jackson received news of spirit "rappings," the phenomena which signaled the start of American Spiritualism. Her impressions of the event and her personal experiences with mediumship appear in *Gifts of Power*, edited by Jean Humez.

> In the year 1850, March 15, a pamphlet was put into my hand, which gave an account of the spirits visiting the inhabitants of the West with strange knockings, and of their communications to the people, through the alphabet, by which they have been able to make known to the people that God has sent them to help the inhabitants of the world. While giving attention to these things, I had a clear view of God's dealing with me, from July in the year 1830 to the year 1850, that I was greatly astonished at His mercy to a worm of the dust like me ... Through the aid of departed spirits, I have been able to tell many things before they took place ... For all these years I have been under the tuition of invisible Spirits, who communicate to me from day to day the will of God concerning me and concerning various events that have taken place, and those transpiring now and those that yet will occur in the earth. But this communication to me has been in words as clear and distinct as though a person was conversing with me. By this means I have been able to tell people's thoughts, and to tell them words they have spoken many miles distant from me. And also to tell them things they would do a year beforehand, when they had no thought of ever doing such things.[6]

After participating in a seance on August 1, 1854, Jackson determined to form a "circle" at home. With her close companion, Rebecca Perot, she sat intent upon contact with evolved spirits. "I felt that the foundation must be laid in strength and in power, in order for me to work under God for the good of souls. Therefore I desired higher spirits than those of my natural kindred, for it was the latter that I was called to help."

Soon known to Jackson was that Perot's attention was fixed upon a lower vibratory level. "I asked her if she felt any gift to desire any spirits. . . . She replied, 'My mother.' Then I told her how needful it was for us to have higher spirits at the commencement, to give us right knowledge of so great a work. She agreed with me."

At one seance, in deep distress, the spirit of Jackson's deceased husband, Samuel, entered. A prayer offered on his behalf immediately brought spirit-world assistance to him through her brother, Joseph Cox, also deceased.

> When my brother came running, to help him into liberty, it overcame him. For he well remembered the deep sorrow, shame, and tribulation of soul he had caused my brother to feel by his cruel persecution of me. And he supposed he would be the last one to come to his aid. But instead of that, he, with me, was the first. He, out of the body, and I, in the body. He soon learned that it requires mediums out of the body and mediums in the body to help souls into the way of salvation. He saw many souls, with me, waiting to help. And that I was ready to lead him to a place in the spirit world, where he could be taught the work of "progression."

Mother Estelle Ellerbee often hears beings crying for help, and sees them walking "between the earth." Feeling their anguish, she prays for and with these earth-bound spirits. In many shapes and energy densities they appear to her. As lights, vapor, energy patterns, materialized heads and hands, and in the projected bodies of their former life identities, they come. Spirits of the living, temporarily detached from their bodies, meet with her as well. There are temperature and vibratory changes in the room where disembodied spirits are speaking to and through her. These changes are sensed by her son, Clarence, and other observers. Both psychics and non-psychics. Visual phenomena are seen around her—flashing lights, electrical streaks, and non-physical human-like forms.

An evangelist, Mother Ellerbee founded the Miracle Chapel Deliverance Church in New York City where she lived for many years. Now she holds prayer meetings in her home in East Orange, New Jersey, and is frequently a guest speaker at church conventions. At the close of one church service, a woman from France came forward. A visitor to the United States, she had been referred to the church by a friend. Having a message conveyed to her by Mother Ellerbee was strengthening, the woman said. As a result, she knew she could face the crisis she was in. The message from Spirit that day had been spoken in French, a language totally unfamiliar to Mother Ellerbee!

Arriving home from a party around four o'clock in the morning, Jesse James Jr. had an urge to make breakfast. "While the bacon was cooking, I decided to lay down and take a short nap. And of course, the bacon burned. In the meantime, the house had filled with smoke.

"I had an entity who came and in warning shook the bed for me. When I awakened the whole bed was shaking, and there was no one in the room but me.

"That proved to me that there are those around us who watch out for us. Some may call them guardian angels, some may call them spirit guides. I know I have a bunch! They really look after me."

Jesse was newly into Spiritualism when this happened. His spirit rescuer, Dr. Joe Davis, became his first guide. They met through dream state. His Indian guide, Tomahawk, came one year later. "I felt I needed to change my life and it just came about. I happened to go to a Spiritualist church and enjoyed the service. The minister 'opened the doors' for me. I stayed with her church for a couple of years. Then I went on to another church and studied with a development class for one month—and my psychic ability just opened," Jesse remembers.

"Basically I am a clairvoyant. A clairvoyant speaker and healer. I am a medium more than a psychic. I do psychometry, billet reading, a lot of counseling, and fairs in churches." A licentiate minister in the National Association of Spiritualist Churches, he has been in the work for almost a quarter of a century. In his hometown, Gary, Indiana, he is the president of a Spiritualist church. He teaches classes in mediumship development, metaphysics, psychic unfold-ment, and co-directs weekly seances at the church. An inspirational speaker, lecturing for civic groups and at universities, Jesse was one of the first African Americans to lecture and give readings at Camp Chesterfield. Located in Indiana, it is one of the oldest Spiritualist camps in the United States.

"To be of service," he explains as his purpose in life. "To me, service is the greatest religion. There is no religion greater than serv-ice. I believe that should be the path of everybody."

Jesse has had experiences with physical manifestations by spirit. "I have had apports. I was in the beauty salon where I work when three kernels of corn were apported to me. Five women were present in the room, and we were just talking when the Indian corn just dropped right in front of me. I knew what it was after it hap-pened, but I was so startled because I wasn't expecting it. I was so pleased. It was my Indian spirit guide telling me I would be well blessed on my spiritual path."

A flow of teachings from spirit-world masters are communi-cated through her in accordance to seasons. Rose Anderson, an inde-pendent Spiritualist, is a teaching medium. Although frequently in and out of trance during class, she never allows herself to be com-pletely taken over. Nor does she leave her students undirected, ob-serves long-time student, Roena Rand.

In the Oriental season, the group benefits from the teachings of a spirit who is an Asian master; and during the healing period, an entity who is a healing teacher works with them. Intensive medita-tive exercise is a part of the class process. After the weekly meeting, students return to class, in astral body, twice a week, at 10:00 p.m. to continue their instructions.

Only a few saw the visitor, but at one session the entire class heard the bells and felt the energy radiating from its presence, Roena recalls. It was an angel, who had arrived to assist the group.

After he had studied with Anderson for some time, Joseph Calloway astral-traveled to a West Coast church while his physical self was in Chicago. A member of the West Coast church told of having seen him. He advised her on a serious matter within the church organization. Joseph claims this ability resulted from his meditation exercises.

One Lenten season, Anderson directed the group back to the time when Jesus made His entrance into Jerusalem. Guiding the class from spectatorship into being a part of the Jerusalem crowd, she led them to experience the city's dust, and to feel the vibrational waves of emotion there. Despite its varying levels of awareness, the whole class time-traveled with her, perceiving sound, color, smell, and sensations.

Anderson, a retired Chicago school teacher, began her spiritual teaching mission under the tutelage of Clarence Cobb. In addition to conducting spiritual unfoldment classes, lecturing, and giving workshops at secondary schools and universities, she is a civil service administrative assistant in Chicago.

Surveying the natural resources of Britain by psychic impression, Ivan St. John placed his hands on the map at locations named by his friend, Peter.

"I went on and said whatever came to my mind. To me it was not the most interesting kind of thing to be doing. At some point, I dozed off . . . bored. I woke up. I sort of jumped and said, 'I'm sorry I dozed off!'

"Peter said, 'This is the good stuff. Why didn't you tell me you were a trance medium?' " Spread on the table were voluminous notes Peter had taken while Ivan "slept."

"My first reaction was that he was joking. Soon I became very suspicious. One of the reasons I had such a reaction is that up to that time I had regarded mediums, for the most part, as a little strange and rather hokey—to tell the truth.

"When I did lectures, occasionally, or talked to people about my psychic abilities, before this, I always said it was straight ESP. I had nothing to do with spirits. I used pure psychism and none of that stuff.

"I looked at (Peter's notes) and thought, 'This is all interesting. I wonder what's up and what he is up to?' I didn't think I could have been asleep long enough for him to write those notes. There were answers to some of the questions he was concerned about and there seemed to be some information about lost civilizations. I thought, 'This is really strange even if this is the 1960s in San Francisco.' "

Enthusiastic about the trance information, Peter convinced Ivan to have another session a few days later. "I didn't know what I was doing. I didn't believe very much was happening. I closed my eyes and sat and sat. I opened my eyes and said, 'This is stupid.'

"Maybe this will make you feel comfortable. Maybe you are self-conscious," said Peter as he blindfolded Ivan.

"I found myself going into this slow breathing and I nodded off again, and I woke up. I thought, 'This is silly.' "

"This is terrific!" said Peter. He had more notes on Britain's natural resources, and on lost civilizations.

Intent upon putting an end to Peter's game, Ivan talked him into doing another session the same evening—one they would record on tape. "I woke up, took off the blindfold, looked at the tape. A lot of it was used." A deeper-toned version of his own voice was heard by Ivan as he played the tape.

"You aren't kidding," Peter said. "This is new to you, isn't it?"

"It seemed like I was listening or repeating things someone was telling me," explains Ivan. "I kept saying, 'They're showing me such and such. Then I said, 'He wants to introduce himself.' In a trance, I described this person talking to me."

The lost civilization of Atlantis was among the topics which the etheric-world entity discussed with Ivan.

"I had a complete mixture of emotions. I was intrigued. I was very 'turned off'. It scared me. I wanted to hear more.

"It seemed so 'cornball' at that time. Something claiming to be somebody out there, or possibly another part of me that was talking. It took me years, personally, to come to the conclusion that it was another personality and not a secondary personality."

Following the experience, Ivan began a series of "sittings." A small seance group formed. The personality of the etheric-world teacher, Tony, grew more distinctive. "It took me a while to come to a conclusion that this was a discarnate. I began questioning what was coming through. One of the things I had to learn was that whomever it was, he seemed to have work to do, and that my role

was that of a medium. I didn't have to like everything that came
through.

"One of the things I have had to learn is when people get angry
with Tony, which happens on occasion, they are angry with Tony,
not with me. I will not let people take it out on me, nor do I resent
them. I will explain what I think he means since I have some idea
about what he has been saying over the years.

"The teacher and I went through probably everything people
go through in any other relationship. In the early days, he would
many times say, 'I can't get this through because the medium is consciously blocking me,' or 'The medium is unconsciously coloring the
information,' or 'The medium is biased against this particular topic.'
Over a period of time, he gave information about himself. . . . We ne-
gotiated terms of work."

The contract Ivan made with Tony covers twenty-five years.
There was a time Ivan felt overburdened by their work. It absorbed
all of his time, he complained to the entity. In response, the entity
said, "Have you ever thought about this fact: whenever you book a
reading, a lecture or a class, I show up. And you have not consulted
me once ahead of time?"

"It made me look at how I was dealing with other people. How
I was taking other people for granted," says Ivan.

"A great deal of teaching is done in the trance work. Occasionally, some healing meditation is done. The trance work has brought
about the end of some physical conditions, but I wouldn't say I am a
healer. Healing is one of the incidental things which happens," reflects Ivan.

"Through trance we have done psychic photography. A case of
projecting images on film that was in sealed containers. We have all
the years of documentation of that. Occasionally, in a trance, I did
what is called sealed-letter reading where people write things on paper, seal it, and without opening the letter, I would psychometrize it.
I would do that as a sort of 'warm up' before I did the trance work. I
stopped doing that years ago."

Classes and workshops based on Tony's teachings have been
given by Ivan. Some people have attended these events for the past
twelve to eighteen years.

In teaching, the channeled being emphasizes he is not saying
anything new. The teachings are old, but he is putting them into new
terms. "He doesn't make himself infallible. He makes it very clear

that he doesn't know everything, which was a shock to some people. Somehow, people get this idea when you get someone on the pipeline like that they know everything."

Out of the seance group rose a natural policy on how to regard the entity's communication. "If the information seemed to have some validity, let's deal with it. It was a growth thing for everyone.

"I feel that a very important thing to do is to check the information. I tell people who come to the meetings, 'This is my belief, you don't have to believe it.'

"I have worked more intensely than ever since the arrival of Tony. Simply because I have been put in a position to learn a great deal about myself through his teachings. He has taught me to work hard and to dedicate my life to my work. I don't think I have had as much fun or laughed as much. But, on the other hand, he has taught me that you can be a spiritual person without being 'sour grapes'. Before I thought if you got into one of these things, you didn't have fun and you were just religious.

"He has taught me that no matter what your spiritual path is, you are not going to be exempt from daily problems. It doesn't surprise me if I get ill, or if something in the house breaks, or someone 'rips off' something. That doesn't have anything to do with my spiritual interior status.

"What Tony has taught me is how to gear my reactions to those things. That a continuous process of dealing with, confronting, and interacting with oneself is growing."

Ivan grew up in St. Louis, Missouri, traveled, spent three years in New York City developing "survival skills" before he moved to San Francisco in 1966. He was the owner of a metaphysical bookstore, "The Philosopher's Stone," in that city.

"I was a natural psychic before I became a medium. But that was mostly premonitions, either conscious or in dream state. Occasionally, I would just perceive things about people, sometimes I would say things without thinking. It would be something that amused someone or gave spontaneous insight into a person. People would either react in positive ways or react in negative ways depending on the information.

"As far back as I can remember, it was just one of those things. I can't think of any first time. When it happened it was very natural. Gradually, it was brought to my attention that most people—most children—didn't do that.

"Sometimes we would go somewhere and my mother would say, 'If you see anything, keep your mouth shut!' "

In a difficult period, a few years after he became a medium, Ivan was home one day, feeling hopeless. The effect of being financially and emotionally drained engulfed him. He was unable to reach to friends for help since his temperament had alienated them—he felt. "I began to have this feeling someone was watching or looking at me. I turned—there he was! I thought, 'Well, you've done it! You've snapped!' "

"Do you recognize me?" a familiar voice asked. In the bright afternoon sun, Tony, the entity, appeared as solid as any embodied person. Immediately Ivan spouted off his frustrations. They talked about their work, the barriers between them, and ended by reaffirming their agreement to work together. Asking for his teacher's blessings, Ivan knelt and closed his eyes.

"He put his hand on my head, and I felt like I was going to die. It seemed like volts and volts of electricity went through my body. I could feel his hand and gradually I could feel it fade. When I opened my eyes, he was gone. I just started crying, and laughing and dancing around at the same time.

"Then I sat there and thought, 'Well, I guess I'll just have to get to work, won't I!' "

CHAPTER THREE

Ascetics, Ecstatics, and Seekers

On a plain, everywhere, sea anemone-like animals inverted in hollows in the earth, filling and coloring the pits with their bodies of purple and black parachute silk.

In that wide expanse, she walked, meeting only one person, a plumpish woman with gray-brown skin, who looked East Indian.

Since there were no walls, the walker's stomach uneasiness emanated greatly, and the woman answered to it:

"Look to Paris for this residue carried from your past life there."

The walker's mind fixed upon that thought, and discomfort vanished.

She was, then, stirred to speak; but the ache in her throat, from something pondered too long, slid out as a deep sigh.

Her weighted thought ("I want to be on my spiritual path") was an entreatment and a long wail. When cast over the distance between them, that thought, too, was absorbed by the woman.

"All you need to do is say it," the woman said to inspire her.

But when the walker tried, that inmost energy, drawn upon to form conviction, constricted in her throat from the fears of sacrifices she might have to make. Yet steadily in her heart, assured of birth, Truth grew.

Desiring spiritual understanding, he began to search whole-heartedly when he was about forty. His route was through reading metaphysical and religious books, and taking occasional classes. In this pursuit, the framework of what had previously been Walter's normal life fell away.

In his gradually altered life, connection with the spirit world was made through dreams; Walter's father appeared and spoke with him. His sleep was marked, further, by dreams of intuition. Soon he realized he could separate from his body; and he was covering appreciable distances before returning to it.

While still in his early forties, there came an occasion when Walter would perceive a small beam of intense light when he closed his eyes in a meditative way and asked questions. His awakening spiritual faculties are described in his book *Divine Light Meditation*, written in the 1980s.

> This light was unlike any light that I had ever seen. My eyes were closed so I realized that the light was within me. It was not with my physical eyes that I was seeing this light; it was with my consciousness that I perceived this light. No sooner had the light appeared than it disappeared, and before me was a scene. In the scene was a person sitting at a table, and they spoke the answer to my question.[1]

Communication between Walter and the "Divine Light" continued with his being counseled and guided by it.

Drawn to Eastern philosophy, his study of meditation, yoga, and Eastern teachings mostly came, again, from books. The great teachings of the East, he found, all had one thing in common: "The common denominator is that God is within each and everyone." Perceiving meditation as the way to "become one with the God within," Walter meditated more often.

> I was in my middle fifties, and I had been practicing meditation and beginning to experience uncontrolled bodily movements while I sat in meditation. When in meditation I would be given guidance.... The inner voice would speak loudly and clearly with my voice....
> One day as I sat in my chair to meditate, I was rocked back and forth and eventually lifted up into the air a distance of about one or two feet. I was surprised that this could happen, but I sat down and did it again. The inner voice then told me that it was lifting me.

In this same span of time, the inner voice named Walter a master, revealing to him, "A master is one through whom God freely expresses."

> I have been asked, "How do you manage to levitate?" . . .
> I will share my secret with you. I of myself cannot levitate. It is God, the Divine Light within me, that levitates me. When I sit to levitate, I talk with the Divine Light, and it tells me that it is going to levitate me, and it does so. . . .
> Levitation is not a form of entertainment. Levitation is done for the purpose of God demonstrating his presence. In levitation God is saying, "I am present, and I can defy the laws of gravity and physics to prove my presence."

In teaching meditation and imparting spiritual knowledge, Master Thomas conveys his certainty that "When we live in harmony with God within, our life is fulfilled and enjoyed.

"There will be no peace on Earth until we, each, find peace within ourselves," he explains.

Born in Chicago, May, 1925, Walter Nathaniel Thomas Jr. founded the Divine Light Temple in that city in 1975. The Temple, initially called the Center For Seeking, was settled at its current location in 1980. Master Thomas wrote of a providential event in securing it in his book *Spiritual Meditation*, in which he refers to himself in the third person.

> It never entered the consciousness of the Center For Seeking members that the temple would not be constructed. The year was 1980, a time when real estate transactions were grinding to a halt due to the sky-rocketing interest rates. Master Thomas . . . was paying the mortgage on a 12 (unit) apartment building which was barely profitable. He came to the decision that the property must be sold. One day while meditating in his closet, he was lifted up into the air and screamed out, "You will sell the building today." Approximately two hours later, he received a long distance telephone call from Washington, D.C. The lady . . . had heard that Master Thomas wanted to sell his building, and she was able and willing to pay cash for the purchase . . . with this infusion of money the completion of the CFS Healing Temple was made possible. . . [2]

"I cried mightily to God to make me holy!"[3] wrote Rebecca Jackson. Aspiring to spiritual clearness following a conversion experience in 1830, she began the practices of fasting, continual prayer, celibacy, and other activities of self-denial. "I prayed to God to give me a strong mind that I might be able to serve Him with all my days, with all my heart, soul, mind, and strength." This she recorded in her journal, which is presented in the book *Gifts of Power: The Writings of Rebecca Jackson, Black Visionary, Shaker Eldress*, edited by Jean McMahon Humez.

"I saw clear that nothing short of a strong mind would fit me for this journey, and prayed the Lord to show me all things that He would have me do, both spiritual and temporal."

Of the way she acquired knowledge, Rebecca declared, "It pleased God in His love and mercy to teach me in dreams and visions and revelation and gifts. Herein my faith was often put to the test."

Thwarted by illiteracy in her intense desire to read the Bible, Rebecca was also disappointed over her brother's laxity about teaching her to read and write. While she was feeling disheartened about his unresponsiveness, she began receiving messages.

"And these words were spoken in my heart, 'Be faithful, and the time shall come when you can write....' "

On a later day, another communication was given. "This word was spoken in my mind, 'Who learned the first man on earth?' 'Why, God.' 'He is unchangeable, and if He learned the first man to read, He can learn you.' I ... picked up my Bible ... opened it, kneeled down with it pressed to my breast, prayed earnestly to Almighty God if it was consisting to His holy will, to learn me to read His holy word. And when I looked on the word, I began to read. And when I found I was reading, I was frightened—then I could not read one word. I closed my eyes again in prayer and then opened my eyes, began to read. So I done, until I read the chapter."

Rebecca went to her husband, Samuel, to tell him of her newly received gift.

> ...."I can read the Bible." "Woman, you are agoing crazy!" "Praise the God of heaven and of earth, I can read His holy word!" Down I sat and read through ... So Samuel praised the Lord with me....

In her spiritual quest, Rebecca was led to examine her thoughts and beliefs. And one of the beliefs she pondered was, "those who had done me wrong ... I had never forgiven them and I never intended to unless they came to me and asked my pardon for the wrong which they had done me. Nor did I believe that it was required of me at the hand of the Lord."

> In those days of my fasting and praying, I was under continual instruction.... I was told I must never speak of anybody's faults, but pray for them. I must never let the sun go down and I feeling hard at anyone that had done anything to me, however cruel or unjust. I must go and pray for them till I felt sorry for them and loved them as though they had done nothing. Then I might pray for myself. For my prayers could not be heard for my own soul, until I loved and prayed for all my enemies.

In preparing to leave for a meeting which, earlier, Samuel had agreed to attend, Rebecca was suddenly opposed by him.

> ... It was cloudy at breakfast. He looked at me. "Rebecca, you ain't agoing." I said nothing. He said, "You are a strange woman." I then said, "No." And as soon as I said "No," these words were spoken to me: "Whom do you serve, God or man?" I got right up and went to my place of prayer ... and prayed to Almighty God to teach me at all times what He would have me do. And these words were spoken. "Ask what you will. It shall be given." "Lord, stop the rain till I get there." So I kept in prayer. It was said, "Your prayers are heard. See? It don't rain."
> I should have said, while at table it began to rain hard, and then I said I should not go. So now it was done raining ... I began to get ready. Samuel placed himself in the door.... He said, "You ain't agoing."
> I came by him with these words, "Farewell, don't think hard of me—I must go. And when I got out the spirit of the Lord was upon me ... and the journey was light, though ... I was in poor health....
> ... my brother saw me, but he thought it impossible.... He then began to call to me.... When he got to me, he said, "Where did thee come from?" "Why, from home." "How did thee get here?" "I walked." He was like one lost in his mind. He knew that when he went out the door, I had yet to dress. And when I was well, I could not keep time with him in his common gait of walk. "Sister, I want to ask thee something. Didn't thee go upstairs to pray to the Lord to stop the rain?"

"Yes." "I thought so." "And it won't rain until I get there." ...
"And Samuel will come also." "No, Sister, he will not." ...
When I got about a stonethrow from the meeting, it began to
rain. If my brother had not forced me aside to his friend's
house, I should have got to the place before it rained—though
I did not get wet. So, as my brother was to hold this meeting,
when he got a little way in his subject, Samuel came in. It affected my brother so he could hardly collect himself.

Through a vision, while awake, Rebecca saw a woman she was
to emulate. "In this great struggle of fasting, praying, and crying to
God to know His will concerning me from day to day, all at once I
saw a woman step before me.... And it was spoken in my heart,
'This is the way I want you to walk and to dress and when you are as
you ought to be, you will look like this woman and be like her.' So I
was strengthened, and my soul much comforted. I soon found that
she was sent from God to teach me the way of truth and lead me into
the way of holiness and in God's own appointed time I would over-
take her."

In 1836 Rebecca visited a Shaker community for the first time,
and was reminded of the vision.

... the Shakers was dressed like the woman I followed
three years who showed me how to walk through the world
without looking right or left. She walked straightforward, and
so did the Shakers. I had never seen anybody before that
looked like her, and I never saw any people before that I loved
as I loved this people ...

Among the realizations which Rebecca shared about her
dreams were these: "I fell asleep and dreamt this dream ... there was
angels in the room. I was under great power, and I had presents
given to me by the angels.... And I woke and found my hearing and
understanding and knowledge of spiritual things increased."

... A white man took me by my right hand and led me ...
where sat a square table. On it lay a book open. And he said to
me, "Thou shall be instructed in this book, from Genesis to
Revelations."

In so describing a dream which occurred in January of 1836,
Rebecca was then shown two other books by the man, and each was
in a different place in the room. At the site of the second book, he told

her: "Yea, thou shall be instructed from the beginning of creation to the end of time." And at the third, he said: "I will instruct thee—yea, thou shall be instructed from the beginning of all things to the end of all things. Yea, thou shall be well instructed. I will instruct."

> He was dressed all in light drab.... His countenance was serene and solemn and divine....
> And then I awoke, and I saw him as plain as I did in my dream. And after that he taught me daily. And when I would be reading and come to a hard word, I would see him standing by my side and he would teach me the word right. And often, when I would be in meditation and looking into things which was hard to understand, I would find him by me, teaching and giving me understanding.... And oh, his labor and care which he had with me often caused me to weep bitterly, when I would see my great ignorance and the great trouble he had to make me understand eternal things....

Concerning her spiritual tasks, Rebecca said: "The Lord has called me to call sinners to repentance, and on my obedience to that call depends my eternal salvation...."

Among the abilities by which she was fortified for that mission were preaching with power, prophesying, and controlling the weather and people. On one occasion while working with a group, she noted, "Nothing appeared to be hid from my spiritual eyes, whether of thought, deed or word, whether I was absent or present ... the Lord laid open their hearts from their childhood up to that time...."

"I have learned obedience by the things I have suffered, and it is sweet to my soul," Rebecca affirmed.

As she performed her spiritual tasks and devotional activities in obedience to the will of God, she realized "flowings of the spirit of God" in her soul: joy, love, and "flowing of the spirit of peace."

With disobedience to these came anguish, grief, confusion, illness, cloudiness, and darkness.

Expressing her unwavering commitment to the path she had chosen, Rebecca wrote, "When I saw God, heard His voice, and understood what His will was concerning me, I lost sight of my brother, husband, and all of my people by nature, for I would not displease God to gratify my self in anything, no, nor any other person on earth...."

Rebecca Cox Jackson, an ecstatic, was born in freedom in 1795, in the area of Philadelphia, Pennsylvania.

They were startled that day in 1955 when she brought the application home. And in the wake of their disquietude, dreams churned, and their minds shaped protests that rolled straight off their tongues.

That she had always wanted to be a nun, and had often reminded them, did not diminish the shock. It was hard for her parents to look over and see a postulant's desire in their very social child. Of their three, she was the one who really enjoyed people and was given to diversion. Her promises to pursue her goal declarations brought from her mother a standard, light teasing reply: "Until the next telephone call!"

Barbara Jean La Rochester, a native of Brooklyn, New York, soon after joined the apostolic order of the Sisters of Nazareth in Philadelphia, Pennsylvania when she was twenty-two. And the substance of her former identity was subjugated by spiritual discipline and the practice of spiritual devotion.

Yet, her new life, by way of her duties, fully immersed her in the physical world. Barbara found an abundance of earthly communication in teaching and childcare, work she loved. And she traveled, throughout the city and its adjoining localities, in service.

"I was drawn toward prayer and solitude in the midst of all the activities.... "

In 1972, Barbara decided to join the Carmelite Order in Baltimore, Maryland. As a Carmelite nun she would have virtually no contact with the outer world. Cloister is only broken in the Order for habitual food and clothing shopping, school, and infrequent workshops for "nourishment of spiritual life." This change unsettled her family again and it was a struggle to gain their understanding.

Barbara's work is currently the activity of vocal and mental prayer, the role of a Carmelite nun. "I feel I have been gifted with a tremendous gift, and I am about sharing it. I know that I am called to love, and that I experience that love more than others."

Additional tasks for her at the monastery are the instructing of others in prayer, and the giving of spiritual direction. She acknowledges the latter as an innate ability. Her good-listener attributes date back to her adolescent years when schoolmates sought her advice.

In her life of self-sacrifice and incessant prayer, Barbara speaks of "dry points" but of no regrets. "I do the best I can from day to day." Sometimes in prayer, she "gets caught up in the Lord." She explains, "I know when I experience the Lord, that is real. I have experienced that the Lord is with me."

Tracing his sudden awakening as a sculptor, William Edmondson told author Edmund L. Fuller that God spoke to him from the head of the bed like a "natural man. He talked so loud He woke me up. He told me He had something for me."[4]

The message was clarified in the following week: "I was out in the driveway with some old pieces of stone when I heard a voice telling me to pick up my tools and start to work on a tombstone. I looked up in the sky and right there in the noon daylight He hung a tombstone out for me to make."

"Edmondson became totally immersed in his love for his 'heavenly daddy', as he called his God," observed Fuller in his book, *Visions in Stone.*

At one time, the artist told Fuller, "I knowed it was God telling me what to do. God was telling me to cut figures. First He told me to make tombstones; then He told me to cut figures. He gave me them two things."

God gave commands which Edmondson obeyed, even if the sculptor's faith would occasionally waver. "The Lord told me to cut something once and I said to myself I didn't believe I could. He talked right back to me: 'Yes you can,' He told me.

"It's wonderful," said Edmondson, "when God gives you something—you've got it for good, and yet you ain't got it. You got to do it and work for it. God keeps me so busy He won't let me stop to eat sometimes. It ain't got much style. God don't want much style. But He gives you wisdom and speeds you along."

Edmondson's career as a sculptor was more than fifteen years long. His first work was in the carving of tombstones which he gave away or sold. Later, his yard, as described by Fuller, "became filled with 'miracles' that were not tombstones: preachers, women, doves, turtles, angels, rabbits, rams, horses, and other 'critters' and 'miracles' that often defy identification as well as imagination."

What he saw or heard from the Lord provided most of the subject matter for his creations. He said that his ideas came also from the things he saw in the sky; "... you can't see them, but I can see them." Sometimes people made suggestions—like his sister, Sarah, who asked why he didn't have angels. He began carving them after that.

The material which Edmondson used for sculpting was limestone. God had said to him, "Will, cut that stone ... and it better be limestone, too." His stone was from construction and demolition projects. It had all been used previously for other purposes. His tools were the type used by handymen. His instructions in stonecarving were the divine commands he received.

He never participated in any kind of formal education. The artist was well into his fifties when he started carving. His stepniece, Mary Brown, recalled that he took on the work in either 1931 or 1932. "I think things just came to him. About this stonecutting, he got up one morning and just said he was going to cut some stone. A voice spoke to him just like that Martin Luther King (Jr.) said up on that mountain. He said he wasn't going to work anymore, just get my hammer and my chisel and cut away on some stones.... "

During his lifetime, Edmondson had worked at many jobs—a railroad hand, hospital janitor and orderly, shoemaker, servant, and gardener.

In working with stone, Edmondson perceived himself as "just doing the Lord's work. I didn't know I was no artist till them folks come told me I was."

He reflected on his creative ability, too, and said: "This here stone and all those out there in the yard come from God. It's the work of Jesus speaking His mind in my mind. I must be one of His disciples. These here is miracles I can do. Can't nobody do these but me. I can't help carving. I just does it. It's like when you're leaving here, you're going home. Well, I know I'm going to carve. Jesus has planted the seed of carving in me."

Approximately five years after Edmondson began sculpting, he was recognized by the art world. During his lifetime there were museum exhibits, public acclaim as well as sales. As a "modern primitive" artist, he was honored with a one-man show at the New York Museum of Modern Art—the first African American artist to receive that recognition. Despite these activities, he did not have broad public recognition as an artist in his lifetime. However, in recent years, there has been a revival of interest in his work.

Edmondson was employed for a while under the 1930's Works Projects Administration Federal Art Project. This involvement pleased him very much. "Wouldn't that jolt you now? All the WPA and fine folk spreading this Lord's work around so children can learn wisdom. Wisdom, that's what the Lord give me at birth, but I didn't know it till He came and told me about it."

Born in Nashville, Tennessee around 1883, Edmondson was one of George and Jane Edmondson's six children. Both parents had been slaves.

Clarence Ellerbee's brother-in-law unexpectedly was called upon to speak a few words before the congregation. A stutterer, he faced the gathering, ill at ease and uninspired.

Suddenly, from where she sat among the people, Mother Estelle Ellerbee jumped up, extending her hands to him. The power flowed from her body to his. He then gave a stirring sermon, though he was neither prepared nor trained. He did not once stutter; and he never hesitated, as he spoke with power.

Later, he said, as her energy touched him, it rushed right through him. His mind was cleared and he felt great calm. When the words came through him, he knew he controlled them. He felt heartened, and very much reassured of his own worth.

There are others to whom Mother Ellerbee has transferred the Spirit of God, as she describes it, enabling them to speak with authority, sing with intensity, or help in healing. She stretches out her hands toward them or catches their hands in hers, affirms Clarence, her son.

When Clarence's young coworker met Mother Ellerbee, the Spirit of God jumped in her, and she gave him a message. Catching the young man's hands, she transferred power to him, telling him to take it to his mother who was ill, as it would help to heal her. The young man was stunned that energy was penetrating his body. He followed the instructions, and noticed later his mother was better.

One evening, in 1968, while Clarence was in Georgia, doing his basic training in the Army, he talked with his mother by telephone. She asked him to speak to the men in the barracks about God that evening. Flashing through his mind were thoughts about the potential difficulties in such an effort, differences among the men, their ethnic backgrounds, cultural and religious beliefs. He felt reticent. He would need also his commanding officer's permission.

She sent the Spirit of God through the telephone, and it imparted courage to him, and his mind was flooded with inspiration. In this state, Clarence spoke to the captain who simply answered, "What took you so long?" He made the men get out of bed to listen to Clarence. They were all attentive and respectful. Some asked questions, some requested to be taught how to pray, or to understand the Bible.

With the rest of his company, Clarence soon afterwards received an order to go to Vietnam; but Mother Ellerbee said, "You are not going." So he told her again he had official orders to go, but she repeated, he would not go. There was the Power of God flowing from her through the telephone as they talked, Clarence recalls. On the night before departure, his C.O. told him, "You are not going to Vietnam. You are staying here in Georgia for the next seventeen months." All of the other men in the company were sent to Vietnam.

Mother Ellerbee has visions of Jesus. Once He said to her, pointing to a statue of the Virgin Mary, "Go to my mother." The Virgin Mary has been a guide to her, giving her messages, and instructing her use of the rosaries, although Mother Ellerbee is Pentecostal. She has seen John the Baptist, angels come and sing to her, and she sometimes travels to the "Other Side."

Mother Ellerbee has been called a major prophet. At prayer services she uses her gift of foreknowledge, picking up on the minds of people to help them resolve problems in their lives. When she is with people in a service, and the visions happen, some have felt the atmosphere growing warmer, a change in the vibratory rate of the space, and a sense of upliftment. When she sees death entering individuals, she prays, and sometimes death loosens up and the person has more time.

A speaker in tongues, she also does interpretation in tongues. In other ecstatic moments, she has spoken different languages, such as French, Hebrew, and the language of ancient Egypt—all later verified.

Mother Ellerbee's gift of healing has always been strong; so is her desire to be of service through this gift. She has worked with people with afflictions that are physical, emotional, and spiritual in nature. Many have been healed or have improved. A ten-year-old boy, whom she foresaw as doing God's work later in his life, suffered from epilepsy, with two or three seizures a month. After she laid hands on him, his physician began lowering the strength of his medication at each visit, since he was having no seizures at all. Considerable time has now passed since he has had a seizure of any magnitude.

In her preaching, prophesying, and healing, Mother Ellerbee is fulfilling her promise to God that she would serve after she was cured of a terminal illness in 1964.

Although material means must be employed in the production of music, music is actually spiritual in nature, and its message is addressed to the soul. I became aware of this truth long ago, together with the other truth that goes hand in hand with it. That is that the voice of inspiration is the voice of God, and the soul of man must first hear it before its message may be transferred to the intellect. Anyone who wishes to hear the voice of inspiration clearly must be in accord with its possessor, and he may attain this accord through prayer.[5]

Mississippi-born composer William Grant Still went on to convey his thoughts on serving God.

"Music shouldn't only appeal to the vanity of the person who writes it," he maintained. "It should serve others just as religion serves mankind, by helping people to live better lives and by giving them—even if only for an instant—a glimpse of real inspiration."

These insights are expressed in the book, *William Grant Still and the Fusion of Cultures in American Music*, edited by Robert Bartlett Haas.

While in his twenties, Still made a promise to use whatever talent God had given him in His service. He then perceived that the way for him to serve God best was through using his talents in music to serve all people.

"Billy's constant prayer had been that God would make it possible for the music he had written to be heard and that the music, in turn, would bless all who heard it," recalled the composer's wife,

Verna Arvey, in her book *In One Lifetime*.[6]

Early in his career, Still determined that his musical individuality was important to his task here on earth. He must have an integrity about, and fidelity to, his own musical personality, even when it meant opposition and economic hardship, and the delaying of his spiritual goal.

The book edited by Haas reflects Still's belief that every composer should strive to manifest his own personality in music.

> There is a tendency in all the arts toward the new, the sensational, the cerebral, rather than the beautiful and the worthwhile. It is important to have the new, sensational products, but it's important to have beauty too. How can we afford to emphasize one more than the other? ... [7]
>
> Anyone who underestimates the great value of differences would do well to remember that life would indeed be dull without variety. Progress would be impossible if all thought alike. It follows, then, that everyone should work toward variety, each individual expressing himself, particularly if he has decided to enter the creative field. He should begin by analyzing himself and his capabilities, in order to learn whether he is really doing—or will be doing—what he really wants to do.

That Still felt supported by spiritual forces in his work, and in his decision to be himself, is revealed by Arvey in her book. In 1926, he wrote of a dream which conveyed this support to him.

"I beheld a host of angels. They approached me like a mighty cloud and sang a song of overwhelming beauty; one that I have been unable to remember though I am a musician, and usually retain with ease any melody that appeals to me. As the angels sang, I broke into tears and awoke to find myself sobbing with joy."[8] In speaking of the dream later, he said the angels in it were black.

Arvey told of other dream-like incidents. "He saw an owl who talked to him and the time later when he was lying on a bed, half-asleep and half-awake, and saw a faceless being clothed in white entering the room. The Being told him to get up and when he did so, he looked back and saw himself still lying on the bed. The Being showed him wonderful symbols, such as lush green foliage, crystal clear water, and then explained the meaning of each symbol." From this experience, Still was almost overpowered by a feeling of exaltation.

"Having consciously allied himself with God and with His constructive forces on earth, these experiences indicated to Still that he had chosen the right course, so he went ahead with confidence. On his subsequent scores, he inscribed: 'With humble thanks to God, the Source of inspiration,' " his former wife related.

There were dreams in which the composer was encouraged by their prophetic content. In one instance he dreamed of his grandmother. "She seemed to be trying to impress on his consciousness the words, 'Watch February 5th,' " Arvey recalled. The dream so impressed Still that he greatly anticipated that day's arrival. However the day came and passed uneventfully. "A few days later, he received a letter written and mailed in New York on February 5th, inviting him to compose the theme music for the (1939) Fair."

Still knew the manifestation of answered prayer. As recorded by Arvey, "His prayers were answered in a most remarkable way. There came a time when, at the major performances, there would seem to be a spiritual bond between the music and the audiences. It seemed to be a living, tangible thing. Billy, conducting, felt it. When sometimes I played the piano part, I felt it. The audiences certainly felt it, for often there would be a hushed silence, and a huge ovation, of a different quality than we had known before."

William Grant Still was born in Woodville, Mississippi in 1895. Regarded as the Dean of American Negro Composers, he was the first African American to write a symphony which was performed, and the first to have an opera produced by a major American company. Also among his achievements, he was the first African American to conduct a major symphony orchestra in the United States. As a composer of serious music in America, he is considered to be among the finest.

"She said she never ventured only where God sent her."[9] This was the guiding principle of her successful mission in leading slaves north to their freedom, as explained by Harriet Tubman to Thomas Garrett, a Quaker supporter.

" 'Twan't me, 'twas de Lord!'" Tubman exclaimed another time. It was an expression of her total reliance upon God to bring her safely through the perilous trips to and from the South with fugitives from slavery.

She had often said to Garrett that she "talked with God and He talked with her everyday of her life."

Recorded in Sarah Bradford's book, *Harriet Tubman: The Moses of Her People*, are the remarks of some of the supporters and witnesses of Tubman's activities on how they knew of her faith in God. Bradford described Tubman's prayer as "the prayer of faith," and made note of the former slave's confident expectation of help whenever she prayed. That she had escaped cleverly designed traps, or that incredible physical obstacles were removed from the route to freedom did not amaze her, and neither did the sudden availability of provisions, monies, and supporters along the way. Her faith in God allowed for all these things to occur. For as she told Bradford, "when she felt a need, she simply told God of it, and trusted Him to set the matter right."

She spoke to Garrett of one trip in which there were changes in the route. "She said that God told her to stop, which she did; and then (she) asked Him what she must do. He told her to leave the road, and turn to the left; she obeyed and soon came to a small stream of tide water; there was no boat, no bridge; she again inquired of her Guide what she was to do. She was told to go through. It was cold, in the month of March; but having confidence in her Guide, she went in; the water came up to her armpits; the men refused to follow till they saw her safe on the opposite shore."

After wading through a second stream, the party came upon a cabin, and the inhabitants provided them with housing and comfort for that night. Later Tubman and the escapees learned that the masters of the men had set a trap along their route and offered a large reward for the capture of their slaves. That ensnarement had been avoided through the change in plans.

Garrett recalled another occasion when Tubman came to his store. He had not seen her for three months.

> I said, "Harriet, I am glad to see thee! I suppose thee wants a pair of new shoes." Her reply was, "I want more than that." I, in jest, said, "I have always been liberal with thee, and wish to be; but I am not rich, and cannot afford to give much." Her reply was: "God tells me you have money for me." I asked her if God never deceived her. She said, "No!" "Well! how much does thee want?' After studying a moment, she said: "About twenty-three dollars." I then gave her twenty-four

dollars and some odd cents, the net proceeds of five pounds sterling received through Eliza Wigham, of Scotland, for her.... That was the first money ever received by me for her. Some twelve months later, she called on me again, and said that God told her that I had some money for her ... I had, a few days previous received ... one pound ten shillings from England for her.

Through the voice she knew as the voice of God, and through visions, dreams, and forewarnings, Tubman was led where to go or what to avoid. A vision which came to her one night in 1860 caused her great joy.

She rose singing, "My people are free! My people are free!" She came down to breakfast singing the words in sort of ecstasy. She could not eat. The dream or vision filled her whole soul, and physical needs were forgotten.

Her host, Reverend Henry Garnett, told her that his grandchildren might see the day of emancipation, but neither he nor she would. She insisted then that they would see it soon, and repeated: "My people are free!" Three years later, while others celebrated the news of the Emancipation Proclamation, Tubman's composure about the event was observed. She responded to inquiries with: "I had my jubilee three years ago. I rejoiced all I could den; I can't rejoice no more."

Of the more than three hundred people she conducted to freedom, none was ever recaptured while under her supervision.

Born on a plantation in Maryland in 1820, Tubman appropriated her freedom in 1849.

Delivered from thoughts of race, religion, or creed, from the moment of her birth she loved all human beings. "I was born with the Holy Spirit," claims Beatrice Hardaman, a native of Montgomery County, Alabama. Born in 1906, one of eight children, God first spoke to her through a chestnut rosebud when she was very young. "When I was a child I used to travel with my mother. Tie my hands on to her apron strings. She would take me when she didn't take any of the others."

At sixteen, she decided she had to do what God wanted her to do. "I've had to suffer in order for God to reveal to me what he wanted. You can't take a gift, just pull that gift, and do it yourself. You've got to suffer; and when you suffer you know what that gift is, and it means so much to you." Over the years, she married, had a son, and taught school. When her grandchildren came, she helped in raising them.

She counsels, "God will take something that a person doesn't want." She helps in physical and spiritual healing. "If a person has the power to be healed, he can be healed in a special moment."

"I meditate, and there is the power of Almighty God. Then He talks to me."

Beatrice resides in Birmingham, Alabama. She is a counselor, healer, and an active community worker. Embracing people of all ages who come to her in need, she says with commitment, "I've got so many children. All of them are my children."

Jean Toomer, born in 1894, was a writer of fiction, poetry, and metaphysical compositions. His dedication in life was to spiritual evolvement, his own and in assisting others in their spiritual evolvement. He saw human suffering as stemming from the disharmony within each person, an imbalance within, and the individual's identification with a "false self."

He felt inner harmony could be achieved; and in that state of higher consciousness, knowing one's true identity, one could transcend earthly existence and thereby assume one's proper relationship with God and the whole universe.

In *The Wayward and the Seeking: A Collection of Writings by Jean Toomer*, edited by Darwin Turner, he developed this idea.

> Because of my personal experience, my ups and downs, my I-am-I states, and my I-am-nothing states, I was fairly well convinced that in man there was a curious duality—an "I," a something that was not I; an inner being, an outer personality. I was further convinced that the inner being was the real thing, that the outer personality was the false thing, that the "I" was the source of life, that the personality was the sack of poison. The question was—how to bring man together into an integrated complete whole. My answer was—increasing the "I" while at the same time eliminating the personality.[10]

In his autobiographical work, *Exile into Being,* and the notes of March 12, 1939, Toomer further defined the "inner being." Referring to it as "essence," he described it as that "which is undying, which has lived before and will live again, which passes in and out of life but never passes out of existence."[11]

Perceiving one of the difficulties which the spiritual being might have in trying to maintain its true identity while living in a body on earth, Toomer wrote of his own personal intuition. "Before entering the womb I prayed, 'Lord, may I remember who I am.' My birth-cry, correctly interpreted, meant 'I have forgotten.' "[12]

Toomer had an experience in 1926 during which he realized a higher state of consciousness. He, the spiritual being, achieved separation from the physical body, and was emancipated for a time from the influences of earth. A description of the occurrence is given in *The Lives of Jean Toomer: A Hunger for Wholeness* by Cynthia Earl Kerman and Richard Eldridge.

> One evening on the platform of the Sixty-sixth Street El station in New York ... Toomer suddenly had a feeling of inner movement, as if some other power had taken over within him. Gradually, something like a soft light seemed to unfold from just behind and inside his body and to shape itself into a new body, a new form enveloping his physical body. "This was no extension of my personal self, no expansion of my ordinary awareness. I awoke to a dimensionally higher consciousness. Another being, a radically different being, became present and manifesting." ... He still felt identified with his everyday self, but he could clearly see both as if from outside. But the next step was a shift of identification—a change in location but without movement.... "... I was being freed from my ego-prison. I was going to a strange incredible place where I belonged." ... His ordinary self, with its feelings, desires, and confusions, had disappeared for the duration of the experience. Yet within his new larger consciousness, his awareness of sensations and use of faculties remained....[13]
>
> His body ... seemed small and removed from him, no longer identified with the "I" ... His being towered above the platform and the streets: "I saw the dark earth, and it seemed remote, far down and removed from the center of the universe, a small globe on the outskirts.... Not only was I not of that world, I could not feel myself even to be within its boundaries." Somehow, feeling that he was an intrinsic part of the extended universe, he also could closely observe the people walking mechanically over the earth's surface ... as if

they were robots. He then felt cut off even from his own body, as if he had died: "It seems I was in the illimitable reservoir of life before it is poured into moulds..."

Toomer was in that state of consciousness for about two weeks.

He found the teachings and techniques of George Gurdjieff compatible with his own philosophy on the attaining of higher states of consciousness. Introduced in 1923 to Gurdjieff's philosophical system called the Fourth Way, Toomer became a teacher of the system after studying in New York, and then with Gurdjieff in Europe in 1924. Using the system, he led groups at different times in his life.

According to Toomer, "We do not exist so as to live this life to the full; we live this life so as to exist to the full, so as to Be."[14]

"These are some of the Lord's doings, and they are marvelous,"[15] declared Amanda Smith in *An Autobiography, Amanda Smith*.

> In 1855 I was very ill. Everything was done for me that could be done.... One day my father said to me, "Amanda, my child, you know the doctors say you must die; they can do no more for you, and now my child you must pray."
>
> O, I did not want to pray, I was so tired and wanted to sleep.... In the afternoon of the next day after the doctor had given me up, I fell asleep ... or I seemed to go into a kind of trance or vision, and I saw on the foot of my bed a most beautiful angel. It stood on one foot, with wings spread looking me in the face and motioning me with the hand; it said "Go back," three times....
>
> Then, it seemed, I went to a great Camp Meeting and there seemed to be thousands of people, and I was to preach and the platform I had to stand on was up high above the people.... How I got on it I don't know, but I was on this platform with a large Bible opened and I was preaching.... I suppose I was in this vision about two hours. When I came out of it I was decidedly better.
>
> One of the first things I discovered after I came into the blessed light and experience of full salvation was a steady and appropriating faith that I never realized before. I always believed the Bible and all the promises, but I did not seem to

have the power to appropriate the promises to my soul's need; but after the light broke in and my darkness had fled, power was given me not only to believe the promises, but to appropriate them. . . .

I would read the promises . . . I took hold of them and wrapped them round me and walked up and down in possession of the land. All things are yours, and ye are Christ's and Christ is God's. . . .

The Reverend Mrs. Amanda Smith spent her lifetime in evangelical preaching and religious teaching in an era when women found no easy acceptance in this calling.

One night . . . I had a good religious paper in my hand, which had a good sermon in it and some experiences. I said I will take this and give it to someone. . . . On the boat a nice looking lad sat just opposite me, and as I looked at him the Spirit said, "Give him that paper." I got up and handed it to him. He took it and threw it underneath the bench. . . . I lifted my heart in prayer and said, "Now, Lord, if there is anything in that paper that Thou dost want that young man to know, make him pick it up. Lord, don't let him go out, make him pick up that paper." I continued to pray, and we were nearing the shore. I saw the fellow was very restless. O, how I did beg the Lord to make him pick it up. I felt it had a word for him. Just as the boat struck the dock, he stooped down and picked up the paper and put it in his pocket and ran away. Just then the grand old text came: "If ye shall ask anything in My name, I will do it."

As the Lord led, I followed, and one day as I was praying and asking Him to teach me what to do I was impressed that I was to leave New York and go out . . . He gave me these words: "Go, and I will go with you." I said, "Lord, I am willing to go, but tell me where to go and I will obey Thee"; and clear and plain the word came, "Salem!" I said, "Salem! why, Lord, I don't know anybody in Salem. O, Lord, do help me, and if this is Thy voice speaking to me, make it plain where I shall go." And again it came, "Salem."

. . . O, how I was tested to the very core in every way. My rent was five dollars a month, and I wanted to pay two months before I went. I prayed and asked the Lord to help me to do this. It was wonderful how He did. I needed a pair of shoes. I told the Lord I was willing to go with the shoes I had if He wanted me to, but they were broken in the sole, and I said: " . . . if it is Thy will to get the shoes, either give me some work to do, or put it in the heart of somebody to give me the money to get the shoes." And these words came from God to my heart: "If thou canst believe; all things are possible to him that believeth." And I said, "Lord, the shoes are mine."... I claimed them by faith ... O, how true that blessed promise—"What things so ever ye desire when ye pray, believe that ye receive them and ye shall have them."

... We had a good prayer and testimony meeting ... I told them the Lord had told me I was to go to Salem, and I was going, and I had only come to say, "How do you do and good-bye."... As dear old Father Brummell passed out he said, "Good-bye, Sister Smith." He shook my hand and put something in it. I thanked him and put it in my pocket, and went home.... I put my hand in my pocket and took it out; there was one two dollar bill and three one dollar bills.... It was the first time I had that much money given me in my life.... Just then a voice whispered, "You know you prayed about your shoes."

"O," I shouted, "Yes, Lord, I remember now. Praise the Lord!"

And I began to trust Him for temporal as well as spiritual blessings as I had never done before. And, oh, how faithful was my Lord. How He has blessed me, and all the little I have done for Him.

... Then darkness came over me, and the joy and peace all seemed to be gone. I did not know what ailed me. So I set apart Friday to fast and pray, and find out the cause of this darkness.... I took my Bible and knelt down to pray. And I said: "Oh! Lord, show me what is the matter. Why is this darkness in my mind? O! Lord, make it clear to me." And the Spirit seemed to say to me very distinctly, "Read." And I opened my Bible, and my eyes lighted on these words: "Perfect love casteth out fear. He that feareth has not been made perfect in love." Then I said: "Lord, if I am not, I will be now." Then I saw what was the matter. Fear! And I said: "Oh! Lord, take all the man-fearing spirit out of me. I thank Thee for what Thou hast done for me, but deliver me from fear. Take all the woman-fearing fear spirit out of me, and give me complete victory over this fear." And, thank the Lord, He did it. There was no especial manifestation, but there was a deep consciousness in my heart that what I had asked the Lord to do, He had done, and I praised Him ...

At various times, uneasy that Amanda might want to be ordained, men at church gatherings prepared to oppose her. "The thought of ordination had never once entered my mind, for I had received my ordination from Him, Who said, 'Ye have not chosen

Me, but I have chosen you and ordained you, that you might go and bring forth fruit, and that your fruit might remain.' "

Having been invited to preach by a minister in Salem, she stood in the pulpit for the first time, asserting her ordination by the Lord.

> ... The church was packed and crowded. I began my talk from the chapter given, with great trembling. I had gone on but a little ways when I felt the spirit of the Lord come upon me mightily. Oh! how He helped me. My soul was free.... When I asked for persons to come to the altar, it was filled in a little while from the gallery and all parts of the house.
>
> A revival broke out.... It went from the colored people to the white people.... The whole lower floor would be covered with seekers—old men, young men, old women, young women, boys and girls.... How He put His Seal on this first work to encourage my heart and establish my faith, that He indeed had chosen and ordained and sent me ...
>
> And I said, "Praise the Lord. Is there anything too hard for God?"
>
> We were off to our open boats again to Monrovia. Out all night. Oh, how good the Lord is. A storm overtakes us and threatens us heavily. As I looked up to my Father, God, and called on Him to help us, He answered me speedily, and in a little while the wind seemed to subside and the clouds passed away....
>
> While I was praying ... I was led to pray, "Oh, Lord, put it into somebody's heart to build a railroad through this part of the country, so it will not be so hard for those who are isolated to get the things they so often need."
>
> ... When I arose they laughed at me, and said, "You think we will have a railroad?"
>
> "Yes," I said, "God will do it. You will see."
>
> And it did come to pass in less than two years, after, that the East Indian Railroad Company put a railroad right through that section of the country....
>
> Eight years I was in Africa ... I was pretty well scorched with fever, and as the days and nights went on, and nothing cool to drink, and no appetite to eat anything I could eat, I craved what I could not get ...
>
> So one night I prayed nearly all night, and asked the Lord to take all desire out of me for everything I could not get, and help me to like and relish just what I could get.... I fell asleep, and woke ... and every bit of desire for mutton chop, and rolls, and hard butter, and fresh cream was gone, and I was as free from the desire as if I had never had it.

Evangelist and singer, Amanda Berry Smith was born in January, 1837 in Maryland to slave parents, Samuel and Miriam Berry. She, her mother, and five siblings were eventually purchased by her father who earned enough money to free himself and them. Reverend Smith began her evangelistic work in October, 1870. In 1873 she traveled to England, and continued to India; and in 1882, went on to Africa. She returned to the United States in 1890.

"Draw or die!" said a voice in a vision.[16]

On Good Friday, 1935, Minnie Evans, then fifty-two years old, started drawing. She recalled: "I never did nothing so hard and as terrible as that in all my life. For hours I worked." From that day on, Minnie affixed her dreams and visions into the physical universe with crayons, pencils, watercolors, and oil paints. Religious and mystical themes were vividly presented through her drawings and paintings.

Among the things her son George discussed with film makers Irving Saraf and Allie Light, in 1980, was his father's reaction to his mother's art.

" 'Minnie's crazy,' her son recalled him saying. 'She's going crazy doing those things she's doing now.' And he used to try and take it away from her. I used to tell Pop, 'Leave her alone, let her go ahead and paint.' "

Minnie confided in George, "This stuff I'm doing right now, I have dreams of the thing, and I feel God gave me this mission to do this."

Minnie contended she was trained by teachers whom she described as "not of the physical world. I'm without a teacher, a worldly teacher ... God has sent me a teacher, an angel to stand by me ... (he) directs me what to do. Time for me to paint a picture, and I be tired. I say, 'I'm gonna rest up a couple of days.' He won't let me, come there and grab my feet and shake me, beat me on the feet. Scared me so bad one night I jumped out of bed and looked, thought some of the children had come in there. Nobody in the room, no one."

"Sometime I just make a picture: it's wrong, I got to erase it out. Who tells me that picture's wrong? God tells me. Oh, I have erased one or two pictures completely out and put 'em down and wait till the next day to start working on 'em. Well, I paint, I just go until I just get nearly crazy, say, 'What on earth this picture be?' And I keep putting down something till after awhile they say, 'That's right.' Then I looks at the patterns again, then I got through with the picture, then He tells me I did right . . . I have a very peculiar picture He likes."

When some of her first paintings fell apart because of age, Minnie was worried and didn't know what to do. "The angels spoke to me: 'Paste them on a board.' I said, 'Thank you. Thank you.' I had the boards . . . I had the glue . . . I got up the next morning and started to pasting them . . . and they're very pretty."

In an earlier interview, she had said to film makers Allie and Irving, "I thank God for the gift. I told my mother, 'God had this planned out for me before you received me in the womb; God had that planned and was passed on to me. Just like that, God has a plan for you."

Minnie Evans was born in Pender County, North Carolina, on December 1, 1892. She spent most of her life in Wilmington, North Carolina. Her first art exhibit was in 1961. Since then her work has been shown at major museums and galleries in the United States, and has been exhibited in Europe.

Zilpha Elaw was born to free parents in Pennsylvania around 1790. After her mother's death, her father placed her with a Quaker family when she was twelve years old, and there she remained until she was eighteen.

She began to attend Methodist meetings at fourteen, and at eighteen joined the Methodist Society. While part of a camp meeting in 1817, she had an experience which she said was either a trance or ecstasy. This she described in her book, *Memoirs of the Life, Religious Experience, Ministerial Travels and Labours of Mrs. Zilpha Elaw, an American Female of Colour.*

> Whether I was in the body, or whether I was out of the body, on that auspicious day, I cannot say; but this I do know, that at the conclusion of a most powerful sermon delivered by one of the ministers from the platform, and while the congre-

gation were in prayer, I became so overpowered with the presence of God, that I sank down upon the ground, and laid there for a considerable time; and while I was thus prostrate on the earth, my spirit seemed to ascend, up into the clear circle of the sun's disc; and, surrounded and engulphed in the glorious effulgence of his rays, I distinctly heard a voice speak unto me, which said, "Now thou art sanctified; and I will show thee what thou must do." I saw no personal appearance while in this stupendous elevation, but I discerned bodies of resplendent light; nor did I appear to be in this world at all, but immensely far above those spreading trees, beneath whose shade and verdant bowers I was then reclined....[17]

Before the meeting at this camp closed, it was revealed to me by the Holy Spirit that ... I must employ myself in visiting families, and in speaking personally to the members thereof, of the salvation and eternal interests of their souls; visit the sick; and attend upon other of the errands and services of the Lord....

Later in her life came Zilpha's awareness of extraphysical communication. "I have been lost in astonishment at the perception of a voice, which either externally or internally, has spoken to me, and revealed to my understanding many surprising and precious truths. I have often started at having my solitary, contemplative silence thus broken; and looked around me as if with the view of discovering or recognizing the ethereal attendant who so kindly ministered to me ... not indeed, with the slightest alarm, though with much wonder; for I enjoyed so intimate and heavenly an intercourse with God, that I was assured He had sent an angel to instruct me in such of His holy mysteries as were otherwise beyond my comprehension. Such communications were most gratifying and delightful to me."

In 1819, while uncertain about her recovery from a serious illness, Zilpha received a message:

About twelve o'clock at night, when all was hushed to silence, a human figure in appearance, came and stood by my bedside, and addressed these words to me, 'Be of good cheer, for thou shalt yet see another camp-meeting; and at that meeting thou shalt know the will of God concerning thee." I then put forth my hand to touch it, and discovered that it was not really a human being, but a supernatural appearance. I was not in the least alarmed, for the room was filled with the glory of God....

At that camp meeting Zilpha said she heard "the same identical voice which had spoken to me on the bed of sickness many months before ... and (it) said, 'Now thou knowest the will of God concerning thee; thou must preach the gospel; and thou must travel far and wide.' "

By following the directions of voices of "invisible and heavenly personages sent from God," along with visions, dreams, and impressions, she continued to realize and expand her spiritual course. And through certain manifestations she knew when her actions were self-directed rather than God-willed. Once when confronted with obstacles which seemed insurmountable, she disowned her commission to preach, reducing it to imagination:

> ... And in prayer I said to my heavenly master, in reference to my ministry, "Now I know I am mistaken: and I am not going out at all."
>
> I had no sooner uttered these words, than a dreadful and chilling gloom instantaneously fluttered over and covered my mind; the Spirit of the Lord fled out of my sight, and left me in total darkness—such darkness as was truly felt; so awful a sensation I never felt before or since. I had quenched the Spirit, and became like a tormented demon. I knew not what to do, for I had lost my spiritual enjoyments; my tongue was also silence, so that I was unable (to) speak to God ... I had no power whatsoever to preach....

The confirmatory evidence of the validity of her spiritual course was soon manifested.

> I sat in thoughtful meditation on the varied goodness of God towards me; and looking upwards, the Lord opened my eyes, and I distinctly saw five angels hovering above and engaged in the praises of God; the raptures of my soul were too awful and ecstatic on that occasion for human description: the sensual world are unacquainted with the overwhelming fascinations which thrill through every instinct of the spiritual mind under the complacent manifestation of ethereal intelligences and their enchanting influences. I concluded that this wonderful manifestation was a token for good, and a proof that the Lord was well pleased with the course I had taken.

She was sent deeply into the interior of slave-holding states to preach for extended periods. Sometimes she preached to slave and slave-holder in the same assemblage. "Blessed for ever be the Lord, who sent me out to preach his gospel even in these regions of wickedness. He preserved me in my going out and my coming in; so that the production of the documents of my freedom was not once demanded during my sojourn on the soil of slavery."

Her first message regarding travel abroad came in 1828.

> Suddenly the Spirit came upon me, and a voice addressed me, saying, "Be of good cheer, and be faithful; I will yet bring thee to England and thou shalt see London, that great city, and declare my name there."

The second message of her destined trip to England came as part of a vision in 1837, and she embarked for England in 1840. There, as predicted by the Spirit, she preached, traveling to different regions of England to speak.

> Ere this work meets the eye of the public, I shall have sojourned in England five years.... I thank God He has given me some spiritual children in every place wherein I have laboured.

Thomas Glover entered the Abbey of Our Lady of Gethesemani on December 9, 1949 and assumed the habit of a Trappist monk. He took a new name, Brother Josue. He stopped running from himself. Feeling he owed God everything, with this move Glover sacrificed his music as a gift to Him.

Glover had known some success as a jazz musician, playing the tenor saxophone with the King Kolax big band from 1943 through 1946. He did solo performances and wrote some of the band arrangements. He had dreams of being great and famous.

But in the Kentucky monastery, his life became one of silence. Speech was replaced by sign language, and the outside world could not invade by radio, television, newspaper, or magazine. His days were defined by prayer, meditation, manual labor, and theological study.

When Marc Crawford of *Ebony* magazine interviewed Brother Josue in October, 1960 it was the first time in a decade that the monk had spoken with anyone from the outside world.

> Though it seems curious, I do not remember ever asking
> for anything but what I got it. And I always received it as an
> answer to my prayers.[18]

When sold as a slave for the second time during childhood, and removed from brutal mistreatment, Sojourner Truth, living in the first half of the 1800's, had no doubt that the event was an answer to her repeated prayer. She had appealed to God to help her father get her a new and better place.

It was her custom, she claimed, to talk with God everyday. When she was about thirty years old, Sojourner spoke with Him about her master's deceit. Her owner had withdrawn his promise to give her freedom, but she was planning to leave, as described in her book, *Narrative of Sojourner Truth: A Bondswoman of Olden Time.*

> "Now," says I, "I want to git away; but the trouble's jest here; ef I try to git away in the night, I can't see; an' ef I try to git away in the day-time, they'll see me an' be after me."
> Then the Lord said to me, "Git up two or three hours afore daylight, an' start off."
> An' say I, "Thank'ee Lord! that's a good thought."
> So up I got about three o'clock in the mornin' an' I started an' traveled pretty fast ... then I begun to think I didn't know nothin' where to go. So I kneeled down, and says I.
> "Well, Lord you've started me out, an' now please to show me where to go."
> "Then the Lord made a house appear to me, an' he said to me that I was to walk on till I saw that house, an' go in an' ask the people to take me in. An' I traveled all day, an' didn't come to the house till late at night; but when I saw it, sure enough, I went in, an' I told the folks that the Lord sent me; an' they was Quakers, an' real kind they was to me.

Sojourner had been working for these people for a few months when one morning she told her employers that her old master, Dumont, would come that day, and that she was to go home with him. Surprised by her pronouncement, Sojourner's employers asked her how she knew. She replied her feelings told her he would come. Before night, Dumont arrived.

On that same day, when Sojourner's employers bought her

services from her master, and he left without her, Sojourner gained a
new awareness of God through a vision.

> Jest as I was goin' out to get into the wagon, I met God!
> an' says I, "O God, I didn't know as you was so great!" An' I
> turned right round an' come into the house, an' set down in
> my room; for 'twas God all around me. I could feel it burnin',
> burnin', burnin' all around me, an' goin' through me; an' I saw
> I was so wicked, it seemed as ef it would burn me up. An' I
> said, "O somebody, somebody, stand between God an' me!
> for it burns me!" Then ... I felt as it were somethin' like an am-
> berill (umbrella) that came between me an' the light, an' I felt
> it was somebody—somebody that stood between me an' God;
> an' it felt cool, like a shade; an' says I, "Who's this that stands
> between me an' God?" ... I begun to feel t'was somebody that
> loved me; an' I tried to know him ... An' when I said, "I know
> you ... " the light came; an' when I said, "I don't know you ...
> " it went jes' like the sun in a pail o' water. An' finally some-
> thin' spoke out in me an' said, "This is Jesus!" An' I spoke out
> with all my might, an' says I, "This is Jesus! Glory be to God!"
> An' the whole world grew bright, an' the trees they waved an'
> waved in glory, an' every little bit o' stone on the ground
> shone like glass: and I shouted an' said, "Praise to the Lord!"
> An' I begun to feel sech a love in my soul as I never felt be-
> fore—love to all creatures. An' then, all of a sudden, it
> stopped, an' I said, "Dar's de white folks that have abused
> you, an' beat you, an' abused your people—think of them!"
> But then there came another rush of love through my soul, an'
> I cried out loud—"Lord, Lord, I can love even de white folks!"

Sojourner explained that when she had the experience she
"hadn't heerd no preachin'—been to no meetin'. Nobody hadn't
told me. I'd kind o' heerd of Jesus, but thought he was like Gineral
Lafayette, or some o' them."

One year after obtaining her freedom, Sojourner moved to New
York City. In 1843 she left that city, directed by the Spirit, which, she
said, told her to go east and preach. It was at this time she changed
her name from Isabella.

> An' the Lord gave me "Sojourner," because I was to
> travel up an' down the land, showin' the people their sins, an'
> bein' a sign unto them ... The Lord gave me Truth, because I
> was to declare the truth to the people.

With deep spiritual conviction, Sojourner Truth committed her life to working for moral and social reform as an abolitionist and advocate of women's rights.

A nurse with whom James Hampton shared a car pool was among those he invited to see his work, which he created in a garage, going there after his swing-shift job to toil through the early morning hours. So wrote Toby Thompson, reporter for the *Washington Post Magazine*, in an August 1981 description of Hampton's life.

Hampton rented the garage in 1950 in which to do his project which he entitled, "The Throne of the Third Heaven of the Nations Millenium General Assembly."

In recalling her visits to see his art, nurse Otelia Whitehead said, "I felt the presence of some unknown force. I returned to visit Mr. Hampton a dozen occasions. No one could sit on the Throne, but he would permit you to approach it on your knees. I knelt before the Mercy Seat and it was like praying before a great altar."[19]

Later, some people remembered him wandering the street of his neighborhood in Washington, D.C., picking up discarded objects. He was seen bringing home old furniture from junk dealers. All these pieces he collected for his work.

He had visions which were actually visitations. Through them Moses, the Virgin Mary, and Adam appeared to him. God and they oversaw his work, he declared.

He kept record of the visitations. "This is true that on October 2, 1946, the great Virgin Mary and the Star of Bethlehem appeared over the nation's capital." His last known written observance about a vision stated, "This design is proof of the Virgin Mary descending into Heaven, November 2, 1950. It is also spoken of by Pope Pius XII."[20]

James Hampton was born in 1909 in South Carolina, and he moved to live with his brother in Washington, D.C. when he was nineteen years old.

He worked on his project, which he considered his life, for fourteen years, dying before he completed it. The National Museum of American Art acquired "Throne" in 1964. The work has been loaned to various museums throughout the country.

Every sincere desire of the heart is true prayer and when this desire, or prayer, is formulated and given, the Principle (or an answer to prayer I prefer to say God), is immediately providing us with every step necessary to the perfect expression of this desire, or prayer; and our failure to receive these directions is due to ignorance or lack of faith, which causes our mind to become disturbed with doubts, fears, our reasoning mind arguing that it cannot be done.[21]

Garland Anderson, playwright, metaphysical lecturer, and author of *From Newsboy and Bellhop to Playwright*, spent most of his early life in San Francisco. In that city, over a period of fifteen years, he worked in various hotels as a bellhop; and was so employed when he wrote the play *Appearances* in 1925.

When the desire came to me to write a play my first reaction was "how absurd, with only four years schooling and no training, how could I ever hope to write a play." These and many other negative thoughts arose in my mind ... It dawned upon me that to suppress a desire to do something worth while in life could be likened to the outer shell of an acorn after it was planted ... saying to that inner stir of life ... "What are you stirring around for, surely you don't expect to become a big oak tree, why, you are only the inside of a mere acorn, how could you ever expect to realize such a big desire?" God would never have given the acorn the desire to become a big oak tree without equipping it with the power for the full realization of this desire, and much less would He give man (created in His own image and likeness) the power to desire to do something big in life without equipping him with the power for the full realization of the desire.

With this idea firmly fixed in mind, it took three months to completely clear my consciousness of all the doubts, worries, and fear—the disturbances which prevented a poised state of mind, necessary to receive the answer, which was always there but unable to manifest due to these disturbances. The minute I believed I had received, however, the ideas flowed normally and naturally; and while it took three months for me to clear my consciousness, it only took three weeks to write the play, which is positive proof that the fulfillment comes with the desire, when the mind is poised in faith.

The question might arise here, How did you know the

technique of dramatic writing having never learned? And my answer is, of myself (intellectually) I knew nothing about technique but with faith in the presence of the principle of success (of God Within) I knew all about it.

Anderson's play opened on Broadway on October 13, 1925 and ran for three weeks. He was the first African American to have a play produced on Broadway.

He later produced *Appearances* in Los Angeles, where it ran for five weeks, and in March, 1930 the play opened in London.

"Go preach, tell it to the world!"[22] a voice told Gertrude Morgan when she was thirty-seven years old.

Born in 1900 in Columbus, Georgia, she moved to New Orleans in 1939 and became a street-preacher. In addition to preaching, she sang, played her guitar and tambourines, raising money for the orphanage which she started with two other women. Jane Livingston and John Beardsley wrote of her life in their book *Black Folk Art in America*.

Directed in 1957 through another vision, Sister Gertrude began dressing in white, a sign she had become "the bride of the Father and the Christ."

"I did my missionary work in the Black Robe around eighteen years, teaching holiness and righteousness. That great work was so dear, He has taken me out of the Black Robe and crowned me out in white."

In the 1960s, Sister Gertrude received another message: "The Lord told me to leave the streets, give up music, and find a new way to speak the gospel."[23]

She took up drawing and painting as a means to depict thoughts about her mission with God, and especially about the book of Revelations. There have since been national exhibitions of Sister Gertrude Morgan's art.

Howard Thurman sensed all beings and all life as joined into a single consciousness. "Life is One."[24] That creation had unity was a reality to him. He was aware of a matrix of all spirit, of which each living thing was a part, with each part containing the attributes of the whole—God.

Thurman, theologian and educator, wrote of many spiritual observations. Memories of certain childhood experiences early in this century nurtured and validated Thurman's perception. These experiences were undoubtedly the seeding grounds of his theology.

> As a child I was accustomed to spend many hours alone in my rowboat, fishing along the river, when there was no sound save the lapping of the waves against the boat. There were times when it seemed as if the earth and the river and the sky and I were one beat of the same pulse. It was a time of watching and waiting for what I did not know—yet I always knew. There would come a moment when beyond the single pulse beat there was a sense of Presence which seemed always to speak to me. My response to the sense of Presence always had the quality of personal communion. There was no voice. There was no image. There was no vision. There was God.[25]
>
> There is a unity that binds all living things into a single whole.... Sometimes there is a moment of complete and utter identity with the pain of a loved one; all the intensity and anguish are felt.[26]

Such a moment was known to Thurman concerning his sister, Henrietta. "One morning as I opened the office windows, I had an overwhelming impulse to pray. As I prayed, the picture of Henrietta lying in bed with her eyes closed in suffering came to my mind. Soon I was praying for her, and I began to weep. Moments later, a messenger knocked on the door and handed me a telegram. It was from Mama telling me to come home at once, Henrietta was dying. By the time I arrived, she was dead."[27]

Here, Thurman described that phenomenon in his own life, which he defined as the grace of God.

> Some years ago I was crossing the United States by the southern route. I had been advised to stop at San Antonio to see the Alamo. So, when the train stopped at noon for a half hour, I got off to look around. If I found myself interested, I could stay till the next train. At first, I thought I would not stay, but just as the conductor announced that the train was

ready to go, in a split second I changed my mind. I ran into the car, took my topcoat and bag, and jumped off the slowly moving train, much to the consternation of the conductor. I caught the midnight train. The next day when the train to which I had transferred approached Yuma, Arizona, it slowed. Just off the track ahead were two huge engines just like two monsters that had been in a life-and-death struggle, and some fifteen or twenty steel cars twisted and turned over. Their sides had been cut open by acetylene torches so that the dead could be removed. That was the train that I had suddenly jumped off, several hours before.[28]

Howard Thurman was born in Daytona Beach, Florida in 1900. After completing his undergraduate studies at Morehouse College in Atlanta, Georgia, he went to Rochester Divinity School in New York to do his graduate studies in theology. In 1926, he served his first full-time pastorate at Mount Zion Baptist Church in Oberlin, Ohio. During his ministerial career, he was dean of Rankin Chapel at Howard University and dean of the chapel at Boston University. In San Francisco, he was co-founder and minister of The Church of the Fellowship of All People, whose membership is committed to sharing worship in a way that transcends racial, cultural, and social distinctions.

> The imprisoned self seems to slip outside its boundaries and the ebb and flow of life is keenly felt. One becomes an indistinguishable part of a single rhythm, a single pulse. . . . And yet there always remains the hard core of the self, blending and withdrawing, giving and pulling back, accepting and rejoicing, yielding and unyielding—what may this be but the pulsing of the unity that binds all living things in a single whole—the God of life extending Himself in the manifold glories of His creation?[29]

In a vision, when she was twelve, Elizabeth was told to "Call the people to repentance!" only years after the nation was founded.

> The presence of the Lord overshadowed me, and I was filled with sweetness and joy. . . . In this way I continued for

about a year; many times while my hands were at my work, my spirit was carried away to spiritual things.[30]

Between her conversion experience and her forty-second year, the time when she fully engaged her vocation, Elizabeth had other visions. "I was often carried to distant lands and shown places where I should have to travel and deliver the Lord's message. Years afterwards, I found myself visiting those towns and countries that I had seen in the light as I sat at home at my sewing—places of which I had never heard."

Born a slave in Maryland in 1766, Elizabeth was eleven when she was separated from her parents, sisters and brothers. Her master hired her out to another farmer and later sold her. She obtained her freedom when she was thirty years old.

Her autobiography, *Elizabeth, a Colored Minister of the Gospel, Born in Slavery*, was recorded when she was ninety-seven years old.

My entire being is strengthened daily through the trust I have in the teachings, the deeds, the philosophy of Jesus Christ.[31]

I am a part of a great, true, wonderful, sterling ideal, which has real presence within me and helps to keep me aware. This awareness is a fresh and flowing stream that goes with me, even as the bloodstream circulates to give me the breath of life. The breath of spiritual life and the breath of physical life are one for me, and when I speak or think or act I have done so from this empowering presence which quickens my flesh and assures me that I have thought or spoken or acted in truth.

Mary McLeod Bethune, educator and social and political organizer, was born in 1875. She was the fifteenth child of former slaves.

It seems to me that every experience I have possesses meaning and significance. I can see the focus of that which happens to me upon the screen of my life and can understand that the messages are coming in to me, and they will be prepared to go out from me as I seek to guide and lead and develop people who need my help. Because of my rich experiences and because of my ability to meld these experiences into meaningful human truths, I am possessed of a greater faith, and can hold that faith for all people.

Among her accomplishments were the founding of the Bethune-Cookman College in Daytona, Florida, and the organizing of the National Council of Negro Women. She had been an advisor to four presidents.

Herein dwells the still small voice to which my spiritual self is attuned. I find, also, that I am equally sensitive to any outside obstructions that would mar this harmony or destroy this fortress. These inspirational vibrations are known to me as my inner voice. Therefore, as I come face to face with tremendous problems and issues, I am geared immediately to these spiritual vibrations and they never fail me. The response is satisfying, though the demand may call for great courage and sacrifice.

This power of faith which is my spiritual strength is so intimately a part of my mental and emotional life that I find integration and harmony ever present within me ... and my happiness within is a fortress against doubt and fear and uncertainty.

To answer author Glenn Clark on how a clay with a color called "the lost purple of Egypt" was discovered, George Washington Carver said:

"I talked with God one morning and He led me to it. And when I had brought my friends and we had dug it up, they wanted to dig farther, but I said, 'No need to dig farther. This is all there is. God told me.' And sure enough there was no more."[32]

Most widely known for his research with the peanut plant and the development of multiple products from it, Carver was an agricultural scientist and educator.

In Clark's book, *The Man Who Talks with the Flowers*, is described an informal gathering in 1935 at Tuskegee Institute where spiritual views were shared. Carver told the group, including Clark, of his relationship with God, and of his belief in divine revelation.

"There is literally nothing that I ever wanted to do that I asked the blessed Creator to help me to do, that I have not been able to accomplish."

He told them of his practice of getting up at four o'clock every morning, going to the woods and talking with God. He explained, God "gives me my orders for the day. Alone there with things I love most I gather specimens and study the great lessons Nature is so eager to teach us all. When people are still asleep I hear God best and learn my plan.... I never grope for methods. The method is revealed the moment I am inspired to create something new.... After my morning's talk with God I go into my laboratory and begin to carry out His wishes for the day."

George Washington Carver was born in slavery in Marion Township, Missouri. He was never certain about his birthdate, although he generally estimated it as "about 1865."

Documented are Carver's recognition of his having prophetic insight, and his interest and utilization of telepathy as a means of communication. Individuals felt strong healing emanations when Carver prayed.

Manifested to Carver on his first day at Tuskegee Institute, through the phenomenon of a vision, was how the land surrounding the school would look in the future. The details of this prophetic glimpse are given by Linda O. McMurry in her book, *George Washington Carver: Scientist and Symbol.*

> While listening to the principal, he gazed out the window and suddenly saw the barren clay and dismal poverty of central Alabama transformed into rolling green hills dotted with neatly painted farm houses and enjoying obvious prosperity. He knew that somehow he was to play a major role in the transformation.[33]

Mentioned in McMurry's book is the seven-year correspondence between Glenn Clark and Carver. Prior to their first meeting in 1935, the two had "corresponded and set times to pray together...." They knew of each other through a mutual friend. After meeting, the two "continued to pray together across the miles that separated them, claiming a spiritual communion that allowed them to communicate telepathically."

John Sutton, who did his postgraduate work at Tuskegee under Carver's supervision, regarded his life as greatly influenced by Carver. McMurry writes, "Sutton felt so close to Carver that he believed the professor communicated with him telepathically while he was in Russia, giving him the solution to a difficult research problem."

His strong belief that his life should be committed to being one of service overrode Carver's desire for a career as an artist, and led him to align himself with the goals which Booker T. Washington expressed for Tuskegee Institute. "It has always been the one ideal of my life to be of the greatest good to the greatest number of 'my people' possible, and to this end I have been preparing myself for these many years; feeling as I do that this line of education is the key to unlock the golden door of freedom to our people."

Through a regression technique she met herself one hundred years earlier.

Repulsed, her brown-skinned, small female-bodied self drew back, from the old identity's large white maleness, protesting.

"That's not me!" she cried, trying to tear him from her heart. "I am a meditator and a mediator!"

But the newly surfaced thick-necked roughcast cowboy, a mercurial-tempered grudger, remained rooted.

His ruthless force in acting solely for his own gain pulsated in her in a strong and unexpended current.

Wasn't she forever transmuting that same brutish urge into penitent acts? The giving of self to others in delusive sweetness?

Those acts were part of the unwholesomeness amassing in her in heavy frozen rivers. Congealing her inner life.

This goal she held to: "Be helpful to all." Sometimes undermining her own integrity to keep it.

Commanded by her search for Truth, she looked again into that image of her former life. Disturbing as he was, she knew him well!

Amending activity followed the inspection. Impenetrable feeling and compacted thought softened, broke up. A weightiness moved off, leaving her in fluidic expansiveness, lighter than ever.

Other incarnations were uncovered, but none caused as great a shift in her perspective as the cowboy.

CHAPTER FOUR

And Some Are Old Souls

The doctrine of reincarnation is a non-Western way in which the spiritual issues of the immortality of the soul, individual spiritual progress, and personal salvation are addressed. According to basic reincarnation theory, many lifetimes are lived by the individual soul in unending succession. Once a cycle of birth-through-death is completed, the soul assumes another body, most often close to the time of birth. With that physical form begins yet another period of existence. But periods of rest between incarnations also occur.

The individual soul, which has experienced many incarnations, and whose spiritual development and knowledge have increased significantly with each lifetime, is known as an "old soul." Although there is usually no memory of past lives on a conscious level, the soul is always in the process of evaluating its past experiences, and using them as valued tools for gaining enlightenment in the present life, as part of the course of its spiritual evolvement.

Memories of past lives are transmitted into the present life in many ways. Dreams and visions exemplify these. Pre-existence knowledge may also become available through sudden insight, deja vu, intense spiritual discipline, soul-mate meetings, past life regression therapy, and readings by mediums and channels.

Dreams and Visions
Every soul is compelled to regain spiritual wholeness. But the life pattern and belief system to which it has subscribed in any one

lifetime may distract from or block that purpose. In the effort to restore its integrity, the soul may use certain imagery to remind itself.

Contact with a past life through dream or vision state allows the soul to liberate and reintegrate estranged self-truth. Fragments of self are regained which have been encapsulated in the many identities the soul has assumed over numerous lifetimes. The past life revealed will often contain information regarding disabilities and imperceptions which the soul is struggling to resolve in the current life.

Sudden Insight

A spontaneous awareness of a specific past life, or that one has had previous lives, that arises suddenly in one's consciousness. It contains no doubt; there is a strong and compelling certainty that this was a former life.

Deja vu

As related to past life memories, deja vu refers to having a strong sense of recognition that one has previously known a person or has been in a location once before. In those situations, the person is in contact with a soul or location known in a previous existence.

Spiritual Discipline

Those techniques, exercises, and practical studies undertaken by individuals striving to contact and develop their spiritual selves. Revelations about previous incarnations may be brought about through the seeker's intense mental, emotional, and physical efforts to overcome the barriers which separate him or her from the spiritual aspect of self. Discovering one has lived before may occur at any time during concentrated spiritual training.

Soul Mate Meetings

The reunion of two beings who have an uncompleted past life relationship, or who made an agreement to be together in a present or future life.

Past Life Regression Therapy

Many techniques exist which enable the interested to contact and re-live their past lives. Depending upon which method is employed, a person may be completely aware, or in varying stages of awareness, during the process. Among the ways to uncover past life material are through hypnosis, forms of counseling, special massages, and rituals. Some of the methods are ancient, and have their bases in religious or esoteric schools.

Those undergoing therapy are usually directed through the experience by a trained person; although, sometimes advanced seekers work independently to unveil their own past lives. Past life regression therapy is considered to be, by many, a means of spiritual cleansing.

Past Life Readings

The soul generates an energy field which surrounds the physical body. This field is the primary source of information in past life readings. All significant experiences which the soul has undergone over lifetimes is condensed in it. Additionally, the energy field contains the soul's projections and visualizations for the future. Energy field information taking the form of images, thought, and impression is available to the gifted reader.

Under an extended definition of old souls in this chapter is included those individuals who have a strong measure of certainty about the existence of past lives; readers who discerned the existence of past lives in others; and individuals who hold assured beliefs about past lives and who have intuitivity on the subject of past lives.

"I am who I am. I was before I came to this body."

Sculptor Richmond Barthe perceives among his former incarnations those lifetimes he spent as an artist. "The first time I tried portrait sculpture instead of painting, it was classic. You don't start with classic. You have to work up to classic. I have never done anything that was amateurish or primitive. My work has always been classic. And that convinces me that what mediums have said to me is true. Three of them told me the same thing. That I was a very old soul. They told me the different countries I have lived in."

Barthe's reputation as an artist was well established by the 1920s. Now a resident of Pasadena, California, he was born in Bay St.

Louis, Mississippi in 1901.

"My mother had five children, but I always felt that the only person in the house that I was related to was my mother. I wasn't related to anyone else. I feel we had known each other before. I have never said that. I didn't want my brothers and sisters to know it. She (a medium) told me and that's the way I felt."

In the 1930s a writer asked Barthe to make a Christmas gift for her husband. She wanted a portrait of his friend, entertainer Jimmy Daniels, sculpted in white marble.

"This was back during the Depression, and everybody was out of money in those days. I felt I had to take the job.

"I accepted the commission without telling her I didn't know how to carve. I had never tried it! Now, don't tell me that's a first attempt!" The artist points to a photograph of the bust of Jimmy Daniels. "Where did I get that technique? I had to bring it here with me. This is my first and only portrait in marble. You have to have a hammer and chisel chipping away. I was turning corners as if I really knew what I was doing."

Barthe's work is in art museums, galleries, public buildings, and private collections around the world.

"I was born at the right time. Just at the time that I did two heads, I had just finished them when something happened in Chicago that had never happened any place else in the world up to that time.

"The white people on Michigan Boulevard were going to celebrate a Negro and Art Week. Who ever heard of such a thing? They went around Chicago, picking up every sketch, every drawing, every line, every etching, every water color, painting, done by Negroes, to exhibit. There was not one sculpture.

"They heard about those two heads that I had done. I said, 'I'm not a sculpture student, I'm a painting student!' " But the committee member told Barthe, "These are beautiful!" and they were included in the collection.

The Chicago Institute of Art had this big exhibition. They had the Jubilee Singers, artists, poets, and everybody. There were speeches by Alain Locke, Langston Hughes, Countee Cullen, and James Weldon Johnson.

"What did I do in another lifetime to deserve this? I believe you have to reap what you sow. If that is true, then, I must have done some sowing the last time because this time I started reaping as soon as I got here. It is as if everything had been planned."

"I feel it is my duty to teach reincarnation," says London Wildwind. "God told me to teach it. I have had to force it on people sometimes.

"People will tell me, 'I don't want to hear about the past.' I say, 'How are you going to know about the present if you don't know a little bit about the past?' "

A new young parent, upset over her mother's dislike for the infant granddaughter, turned to London. "I channeled information. In channeling, I contacted her mother, and her mother said she didn't like the baby girl because the baby girl shocked her. I channeled in that the baby was her father who had reincarnated. She said she couldn't accept him in that form—as a 'her'. And that it was competing with her to have a new daughter in the family.

"And then I went into the future and saw that in three to five years, the grandmother seemed to be accepting the baby more but not now."

The young parent, unfamiliar with past lives, needed help in understanding the concept.

"It really takes a long time to give people the whole principle of reincarnation. You literally have to take the time out and really teach it.

"A lot of the female black clients who come to see me have been goddesses," discloses London. "They had powers in their past lives in Egypt."

Not all of his clients immediately open up to the idea of reincarnation. "They will not accept it until a year or two later, or until I find the right book for them to read—like Edgar Cayce. They come around eventually to the karmic."

Concerning those who are strongly opposed to working with past lives, London comments, "When they come for a reading, now, I cut out a lot that is spiritual and give them what they want—which is still spiritual, but it's more like what is happening now. It would be more spiritual if I could give them the karma with that. But they are not ready for it. I have learned not to give people what they are not ready for."

London was born in Stockton, California, but has spent much time in the San Francisco Bay area, where he attended college. He writes poetry, composes music, and plans to make a film. His interest in metaphysics goes back to when he was twenty and decided to develop his intuitivity by reading books in the field.

Aura and chakra readings, spiritual healing meditations, Tarot, numerology, and I Ching are methods he uses in his present work with individuals and groups. Assisting individuals in uncovering the skills they had in former lives is one of the objectives of London's counseling. These untapped resources, which can give strength and direction to the present life, he calls "roots."

"One woman came to me and I gave her a life reading. As I looked into her past lives, I said, 'Over and over, you always worked with fabric, and you always dyed. You wove rugs and things like that. Do you think you might like to do that in this life?' She said, 'I don't know.'

"The woman called me a month later. She told me she got two books out of the library on batik. She started doing batik, and people started buying her work. She brought one over for me which had a big piano note on it.

"She adapted that quickly from her roots. I found them. But I can't always find them.

"Sometimes they don't really listen to the root thing that they have to do to get money. They keep trying other things—like trying to win money.

"I do think that people who do spiritual counseling can give people those roots they need."

"Lady Sante Mira Bai was a writer and singer. Crops grew when she sang . . . She had a deep love of God . . . She hated the caste system," says June Gatlin of a past incarnation in India revealed to her during the 1970s.

In 1980, an East Indian spiritual teacher acknowledged that life by calling June "Mira Bai" when he first met her.

An ability of Lady Sante Mira Bai carried over into this lifetime: people have experienced healing through June's singing. She is a vocal entertainer who sings styles from gospel to jazz. She has performed on stages with the Staple Singers, Otis Redding, and The Temptations. Her creative abilities include writing poetry and fiction.

A spiritual advisor, June says she "reads human energies as others read books." She has prophesied since childhood. She was still a child when she recognized that her present life was only one in a series of innumerable existences. She extracted skills from her collective memories. Locations and circumstances of many of her previous identities became evident early in her current life. "Queen" was the nickname given young June, the oldest of nine children, because of her regal mien. She was aware that in a past existence courtly attendants had waited on her. "I have had picture flashes of many lifetimes in Africa, India, and Egypt.

"I have strong feeling toward the French. I was an illegitimate daughter of Louis XV and a black woman. I was hidden away in a convent. I have feelings of being a nun and knowledge of being in a convent." In the United States, an earlier lifetime was also uncovered. Born into slavery, she later escaped and helped others gain freedom. The name June was known by in that earlier life was Harriet Tubman.

"I saw this person's picture in the paper and I just knew that I knew him. Every time his picture was in the paper, I would turn to it and sit and look at it, thinking, 'I know this person!' One day, he walked in my store," says Catherine Wilson.

"I don't even know how to describe how it was when he walked in. We talked. He came back the next day. He asked me if I liked fish, I said, 'Yes.' He went out and bought a fish for me to fix, so I invited him to the house to have dinner."

Catherine dreamed about him a couple of nights later. "He and I, we were together many, many years ago. It was in the very olden times—way back. It seemed we were in a wagon train, traveling together.

"There were old men with us, playing the type of music he plays that most people can't identify with. Black people, especially, can't identify with it. They were playing the music and he was listening.

"I was there. And for some unknown reason, I just know I died of childbirth under that wagon. And here we meet up again in another life!"

He had no awareness of that life seen by her in that dream state, but sensed they had been together before. "We are very close, it is something high and spiritual," he told Catherine.

He could be as far away as Canada, but if she wanted to talk with him, he would call. "I would concentrate for maybe fifteen minutes. All I had to do is just put it out there. In the next few seconds, the phone would ring. 'Hello, what do you want?' Just like that! That only happened to me with one person."

Catherine, a widow and mother of five children, put an end to their relationship. He moved to Canada, and she went on raising her children and expanding her import business in the San Francisco Bay area.

"He wanted us to marry, but I wouldn't marry him. He wanted children. I was young enough for children at that time. But I didn't want any more children.

"It was one of the hardest things in my life to do was to send him on his way. I felt it was something I had to do for him, also. Because he needed to grow."

Using self-hypnosis and the help of another past life counselor, Cora Keeton went back to a past incarnation in prehistoric times. "It was very cold. There was ice, and I was always having to hunt," she says about the life spent in mountain wilderness. "I was a man."

Cora traces her instinctive liking for mountains to that existence. The hunter had loved the terrain despite its harshness. "I feel I have lived many lives . . . After coming out of each experience, I have felt it was a part of my life. It has meaning and purpose."

Cora co-founded the Crenshaw Metaphysics Institute in Los Angeles through which she works with people in their spiritual development. Past life therapy is used by her to enable individuals to find direction in life. Her technique utilizes principles of meditation, visualization, and "white light bathing." She "soul travels" with individuals to their former incarnations.

"I went out of the body. I saw myself in a group. I saw candles,"

Cora says of another of her experiences. She was in a different time and place. Clad in an orange robe, she was one among other priests, chanting. She came back to the present with new awareness of an earlier life in a Buddhist monastery. For a period she remembered how to chant. This experience spontaneously began while she attended a Buddhist ceremony—a religion unfamiliar to her. A knowledgeable acquaintance corroborated the details of her experience and urged her to resume the advanced path she had been on in Buddhism.

In a cycle of existence reached through past life regression therapy, Cora went back several hundred years, entering at the point of her death. "I was a blind apple peddler. I fell down a well and broke my back. I remember coming up out of the well without my body."

"All I know is that I did something. It's been recorded in history and there is a statue or something," responds Tureeda Mikell to a query about her former lives.

"But it doesn't matter because that was in the past and I have to be concerned about my growth in the present. So it doesn't really matter what I did, it's just necessary that I learned—no matter how little or great or whatever."

Tureeda, poet, healer, and psychic counselor of the San Francisco Bay area, receives information about her own past existences intuitively. "The information just comes. I can go back. I did one on Atlantis and when I came back my palms were sweating, and my voice was shaking. I went way back."

In tracing with others through their incarnations, she uses spiritual readings and "light-travel therapy."

"It depends on the person ... If they can look. When people come for a session, I may have to go back to a past life. Something that is very pertinent. It is not like someone calls to say, 'I would like a past life reading.' If they want that, we can focus on that, but it is not separate from the reading."

She began writing poetry in recent years and much of the poetry comes from her inner voice. The theme in two of her poems, "Dark Sun Child" and "Trees," is reincarnation.

"Have you heard of neurolinguistic programming?" she asks.

"It's like neurolinguistic physics or reading the body. Looking at the whole body as a geological light structure.... It is like a certain energy light may be out and you reconnect it.... It is dimensions of healing.

"There are people who tend to be living life working out things that they took on at another level or another structure, that are somehow inflections or reflections of what they did before."

Tureeda's counseling activities began in 1978. On occasion, she speaks of metaphysical and cultural topics on radio. She conducts classes, seminars, and astrological readings.

"I met an astrologer who did my chart. He said our charts were very similar and he tried to get me to deal with him. When I was with him, I felt like I was talking to myself. When I was around him, I felt like I had nothing to say to him. I began to lose a lot of weight. When we sat down to eat, I would sometimes get nauseated. Yet I felt like I was supposed to be with him.

"It ended when I had a reading done. It turned out he was a guru with me in a past life. I broke that contract. I had to realize that I had moved on."

A stately woman in a chariot rolled through Mother Estelle Ellerbee's front room in New York City. The scene formed and animated every now and then, waking old Egyptian memories in Mother Ellerbee. She had been there—one day, in a time long gone—when the procession actually passed. A spectator in the crowds pushing forward for a glance at the regal woman.

With her son, Clarence, then a schoolboy, in this life Mother Ellerbee searched through encyclopedias. Knowing a modern depiction of the woman was somewhere, she continued on her course until she found Queen Nefertiti. That was the woman in the chariot!

Years ago, through a vision, she was transported back to Salem, Massachusetts. She saw herself in a horsedrawn cart, a prisoner accused of witchery being led to trial in the year 1692. She emerged from the vision distressed about the false accusation which brought on her death. "Most witches were really spiritually gifted people!" protests Mother Ellerbee.

Fourteen times, she "died and came back" during one of her

trances. Sometimes when preaching or speaking she will detail what she saw and heard in those fourteen past lifetimes. She lived in the very early days of civilization. She remembers Israel, Pakistan, and Moslem nations.

While traveling, Mother Ellerbee "feels out" things in places, realizing she once lived there. She and Clarence went to old Jerusalem in 1982. There she pointed out spots familiar to her. Her burial site was found. A Jewish girl in that lifetime, she died young.

She spontaneously speaks languages unfamiliar to her in this lifetime, being understood by the indigenous people. The spiritually gifted, in several locations, recognize her as one returning home to her people.

"I have been an executioner, a prostitute, a love goddess," she reveals. "This is just a body. I may come as an ape, a bird, or from another race."

While holding her newborn granddaughter, Mother Ellerbee received a message from the Lord. "This is your baby from another time." Cold chills broke out all over her. In a past life, she and Clarence were together. Even her adopted daughter has reunited with her from another time.

"I came from God. I have lived many times.

"I'm part of everybody, every nation, and everything."

Award-winning entertainer Hayward Coleman returned to an old home on his first trip to Egypt. "When I got to the pyramids, I began to realize I had been there before. There was no personality, or name, or anything about the life I led. It was more of an awareness of who I was. Flashes that I had lived there." A few years later, in a psychic reading, he was told he had been a scribe during Pharoah's reign.

"Before I went to Europe, I had flashes of streets and alleys there." He confirmed the existence of these spontaneously remembered past life environs during his stay in Europe.

"Basically, I went to France to study with Marcel Marceau. My girlfriend went to study with Jean Louis Barraut who was the Olivier of France.

"It was her sudden death from asphyxiation from gas while

taking a bath on a cold winter day that made me begin to wonder about the possibility of energy never being destroyed, even though it passes from physical life."

His awareness heightened through his reading of metaphysical books and clairaudient contacts with his deceased girlfriend, Leila. "It was Leila who brought me in contact with what I call my spiritual teacher." This was not the first time that Leila had assumed a role in expediting his spiritual progress.

"My most recent life in India—I feel strongly towards that life. I was in a monastery as a boy monk. One day I saw a guru." Hayward recognized the being as his spiritual teacher. At once he left the monastery to accelerate his progress on his spiritual path with that advanced teacher, who in this life was Leila.

Eleanor Walker's consciousness opened up while she listened to a metaphysical radio broadcast in her Washington, D.C. home. Suddenly she realized she had lived before. That day she received impressions of her own past existences and some of her family's, too.

After metaphysical counseling and training, more information about her past lives became available to her. "In 1970 I joined a metaphysical organization, and that is where I started developing. I was in the organization for seven years. A foundation was laid and I began to realize the abilities I have."

"I was to know that I could go into past lives and receive impressions for other people and myself.

"I am clairvoyant, clairaudient, and a metaphysical teacher.

"I believe in reincarnation. In one of my past lives I was a Scandinavian male, a fighter. I have been a fighter more than once.

"I never realized why I don't like to fight now. I don't like to see fights. I don't like boxing. I didn't realize until I started going to school that I've outgrown fighting. I don't need to do it anymore."

"I have been here many lifetimes. This is my final lifetime here.

"I worked on my development in other lifetimes. It is my destiny."

Bennie Holloway picks up the thoughts, emotions, and intentions of others. Aware of her gifts since age twelve, she began using them after her move to the San Francisco Bay area in 1962. She does personal counseling and has participated in programs on psychic awareness on radio, television, and at schools. "I have given talks to classes, telling them about past lives. I enjoy helping young folks to have better understanding.

"My son, Marty, is a Master.

"My children are all very connected to me. My oldest son knows he has been with me before. I didn't help him in that life," she says.

Bennie perceives having lived in Atlantis.

"I know I was at the Mystery School with Christ. I was at the Round Table with King Arthur."

Born into a Presbyterian family, and raised as a Baptist in an orphanage, she was perplexed for a long time by her strong affinity for the Catholic Church with which she had no experience. The confusion was cleared through past life revelation. She became aware of having lived in a monastery where her identity was that of a priest and writer.

Before she leaves her present life, Bennie hopes to have made the spiritual progress needed to free her of the cycle of birth and death. She would then only incarnate for specific purposes.

Bennie notes it has become increasingly more difficult for her to stay within the body. She spends most of her time in the nonphysical world—on the astral plane. "I want to become a Master before I leave the Earth plane. I want to take on bodies only when I want to."

"Liszt told me I was one of his students in Weimar, Germany," imparts concert pianist Count Carnette, a self-taught musician and channel for the spirits of famous deceased composers.

The Guides of writer Ruth Montgomery tell that Count has had many incarnations as a musician. During the reign of Louis XIV, he was a concert harpsichordist and composer to the royal court.

This lifetime he suffered as a battered child. "I knew I was being tortured. I actually thought of a torture chamber. What did I know of torture chambers at that young age? A recollection of a past life?"[1]

In his last four or five past lives, the Guides reveal, Count was a white man.

In *Threshold to Tomorrow*, he said, "When I sing Negro spirituals I am totally black, but otherwise I never think of race, and I'm always momentarily startled when someone remarks on my Negro heritage. I know without a doubt that I agreed to don this physical body as a symbol of the white and black—the yin and yang.

"Just as my work is concerned with universal love, so I needed a body that would serve as a subtle reminder of it."

"The so-called talents I have, I think everybody has. It is called intuition and renamed psychic ability.... We are born with it." While growing up, Patty Ballard often perceived what people were thinking, good or bad, through the vibrations around them.

"I have always been interested in metaphysics. I took psychic development classes and realized that all my life I had been seeing in my mind's eye, clairvoyantly. I found I was good, and it surprised me. But being a practitioner of Science of the Mind, now I can look back and see what was happening.

"When you are developing psychically, you are getting closer to source, which is God.

"I found the closer I got to the source, the more I became attuned with the Universe and the more I was able to use these intuitive or psychic abilities."

She was born in Ft. Worth, Texas to a military family which thought psychism a mystery and dismissed it. Her family moved frequently. She spent a lot of time alone, reading.

"I started out using psychometry—which would be a piece of jewelry on somebody. I would hold it in my hands. What would happen is that pictures would come, and then I would ask questions to make sure those pictures were interpreted right."

Patty's direction is in teaching and lecturing. She co-hosts a cable television program in Los Angeles. "I started by reading at psychic fairs. And some of my first ones were past life experiences.

"It was really interesting to find that whenever I was reading these people the various things that had happened in past life experiences, they were going through in this life. It was like a lesson learned for them in this life. I am always surprised about the things that come out.

"The energy within the each of us is so untapped, we don't know the amount of power that each of us has. Imagine if the whole world got together and used that power for good."

"I do believe there are people who are lucky enough to continue a previous incarnation. Stevie Wonder, to be so gifted and to play so many instruments at an early age, had to learn it somewhere. The pattern was in his subconscious. It didn't develop. I think the mind is a collection of pictures of things we have experienced, and nothing is ever forgotten."

Chuck Wagner, New York Tarot master and astrologer, at five years old, began reading playing cards spontaneously. "I do believe I had to be familiar with them in some previous lifetime to even manage them. As soon as I got them, I started reading them."

CHAPTER FIVE

Gifted in Physical Healing

The people in this chapter use superphysical means in helping others recover from sicknesses which have afflicted their bodies.

Spiritual healing is done traditionally by the laying on of hands, and practitioners of that ancient technique are included here along with individuals who use prayer and other forms of spiritual intercession as means to effect actual physical changes, improving the health of the human body.

Healers assisting in the curing of mental, emotional, and spiritual ailments are presented elsewhere in this book.

"See that drawing on the wall? That was done by a tumor!" When he tells of one case history, Peter Brown, psychic and healer who works out of Chicago, adds that amusing note. "The woman in this case had gone to the doctor and the doctor told her she had a tumor that needed to be removed. She was seen by five physicians successively. Each said it was a tumor. But one did a sonogram.

"Finally they said it was a baby *and* a tumor! The tumor was blocking the birth canal so the baby would not come out. They were going to have to do a caesarian section.

"During that whole period of time Spirit was saying, 'No, it's a baby. It's a boy, it has a mark on its forehead and the name it's to be given is Monasa.'

"I sent her to a physician I knew. He examined her. I told her,

'Don't tell him anything that I told you.'

"He said to her, 'Has anyone done a pregnancy test?'

'No!' He did the rabbit test. He called me the next day. 'She's pregnant!'

"I said, 'I knew that!'

"She had a baby. She had a normal delivery after about an hour of labor. She had a boy, he had a mark on his forehead and they named him Monasa. He was the one that drew that picture on my wall."

James Ford was once church secretary at the Cathedral Temple of Divine Love where Peter has his ministry.

"I met James years ago when we were teenagers and then in our lives, he went one way, I went another. I was on WSBC radio station one weekend on a six o'clock broadcast which I had every Sunday morning. I got a phone call off the air. It was him.

"He had been at the County Hospital and was over at Hyde Park at the 'Y'. Would I please come and see him? I said I would and I did.

"He weighed all of sixty pounds. He was skin and bones. The story was he had had too much to drink one night and went home to his father's house. He went into the bathroom and took what he thought was mouthwash. It turned out to be an acid. He drank it and it burned him all the way down to the belly. They had to take out most of his stomach because it was so badly burned and make a new one.

"He had a hole right above his navel, the size of a half dollar. It wouldn't close or heal. Basically because he didn't have any reserves. The food he ate, the little quantity was just enough to maintain the body. He didn't have anything to grow on. They were having problems with that wound! They couldn't get it to close.

"So one night, we were talking about it. He asked, 'Would you ask the Lord about it?' So I did." Through inspirational writing, Peter drew a picture which showed how he and a few selected individuals could help close Ford's wound.

"They told me to put my left hand on the back of the neck and the right hand over the hole. It was nine o'clock at night. In ten minutes they (Spirit) would close it.

"When They said, 'Go!' both my arms locked. I don't know if you have ever stuck your finger in a light socket and got a shock. That's how it felt. Try that for 10 minutes. I couldn't get loose from him. When they said the time was up, I was released from him.

"So we sat down and were talking about how it felt and that he felt an electrical tingling all over. And then we looked and the hole had closed down to about the size of an eraser. And it was draining.

"He said, 'Oh no, this can't be!' We were looking at it, and when he said it can't be, it stopped closing! And it stayed that little hole and that was okay. We took him to the hospital and with a couple of stitches, it was closed.

"After that he started picking up weight. He was a marvelous secretary."

One of Peter's goals is the creation of a seven-pointed, star-shaped building, which would implement programs utilizing the information received from Spirit through his inspirational writing. The seven units to be housed in the facility are concerned with healing, communication, childcare, residential care for the elderly, a library, a school and a hospital unit. "Spirit has given me information on how to help children to develop. What you can do to reverse illnesses using music, using color, using all of the sciences and arts that people know about. They have given treatises on dietary principles, food combinations, even the kinds of fabrics one ought to wear or not wear."

Peter relates in another case history a healing accomplished by telephone. "I got a phone call from a lady who asked me if I would read for her daughter. Her daughter was an adult who was having epileptic seizures. They had been to one of the renowned clinics in this country as well as to the hospital at the University and they were not able to find the cause of these seizures.

"So the woman discussed with her physicians that some years before I had read for her and her mother and told them the things they needed to look for. They were successful. So she was saying to one doctor, 'Let's try him and see what will happen.'

"They called. The woman said to me, 'We will leave Peoria tonight about 9:00 and we'll be there (Chicago) about 4 or 5 o'clock in the morning if you'll see us.'

"I said, 'No, you don't need to do that because there is no time, there is no space. I am where you are. You are where I am. We are all in one world and we can do this!'

"I just needed the girl's name and she gave me the name and I did the reading.

"The reading said that talc was the cause of these episodes. That talc and talcum powder. The mother then made a list of products that had talc in them. She came up with 41 products like rice which is polished with it." With the isolation of talc as the triggering agent for the seizures, Spirit advised that the daughter receive a minimal dose of a certain medication and after that course of treatment the illness would reverse itself and she would be "okay." Her condition improved as Spirit indicated.

A pregnant woman came to Peter in desperation before following through with a therapeutic abortion which was medically recommended. Extensive testing showed that the fetus she was carrying was severely damaged and most likely dying. In the reading the woman was given a list of strict instructions to which she must conform. She was to have her mattress turned every day. She had to wear a green dress with polka dots on it, and wear shoes only made of leather. Daily walks were to be taken by her regardless of weather conditions. Dietary changes were prescribed by Spirit which included that she eat a piece of bacon daily. What was stressed above all was that she should eat a bowl of plain oatmeal every single day.

During the routing for hospital admission the fetus' condition was noted as improved and the abortion cancelled. A normal course of pregnancy progressed with the woman adhering to the instructions of Spirit. After an RH factor problem was discovered by her physician, she asked Peter to do another reading. The physician said the infant would need a blood transfusion immediately after birth. "They (Spirit) said, 'No blood transfusion. The baby is going to be perfectly normal and that's that!'

"When she delivered, they tested the baby and there wasn't a thing wrong with the blood.

"But the thing about that child," says Peter of the girl, who was 13 or 14 years old in 1985, "she can sit down and eat a box of oatmeal raw and she loves it.

"There was something in the combination of oatmeal, bacon, leather shoes, walking in the out-of-doors and some other things that turned the woman's whole system around."

A nineteenth-century faith healer, Henry Adams is primarily known for his leadership in a grassroots organization formed of

Louisiana freedmen. This group advocated massive black migration from the South to regions where blacks might realize economic betterment. Adams campaigned for emigration to Liberia as well.

He joined the Army after emancipation in 1865, serving in the 25th and 39th infantries.

In the *Dictionary of American Negro Biography*, Neel Irvin Painter wrote: " ... that (healing) gift, together with his enterprising independence, assured him economic self-sufficiency, even before his emancipation in 1865."[1]

Born in Georgia in 1843, Adams grew up in Louisiana where his family moved when he was seven years old. He began practicing faith healing in childhood and was active as a healer into the 1870s. It was noted by Painter that faith healing "reinforced his public influence."

"We had gone to the Jai-alai to play. I saw this man, we'd seen him before, we'd talked in passing. I saw this night he had a pair of crutches. I pulled him aside.

"I said, 'I've got something to tell you, I can tell you something that will cure.' I said, 'You have a fractured bone in three places.'

"He said, 'How did you know?' I said, 'That's what the Spirit said. You go to a botannica or herb store or health food store and get these herbs. Put them together and make a tea. In three days time, you'll come off the crutches.

"In three days time, the man was walking without the crutches."

The ancient African Spiritual resources of the Yoruban priest belong to James Moye. Primary to his priestly ministrations is his work as a healer. Through prayer, consecrations, cowrie-shell divination, sword and the obeah stick, he works with the African gods. Of the people contacting Moye from around the country, most want help with body problems. Spirit directs the Yoruban priest-herbalist in selecting plants which have healing properties for individualized treatment. His herbs, collected from around the world, come mostly from Nigeria.

Physical, emotional, and spiritual afflictions are brought to him by individuals in person or by telephone. A parent reported her young son suffered a severe abrasive injury in a fall from his bicycle. He was treated by a doctor; but on visiting the home the following day, Moye observed the boy's great discomfort and created a salve for him of ingredients specified by Spirit to soothe the wound. The parent watched in awe as the injury changed. Rapidly it improved, and in less than a week there was only a faint reminder of the accident.

Moye was working with a waitress who burned her leg while at work. He was in the restaurant when it happened. She later came to his cottage by car. In the process of treating her, he chanted a Yoruban prayer. "I'm going to tell you something," he instructed the woman with the burn. "You have to be very careful with your leg. You have difficulty sometime with circulation, is that true?"

She said, "Right!"

"The ankles are also weak," he continued, "you need shoes with arches and heels. You have to be careful because if you don't, you may have problems later with varicose veins. The female side of your family has trouble with varicose veins."

The waitress murmured, "My grandmother and mother do."

"Spirit says for you to take a lemon and mop the leg down with it." He chanted again. "Coconut butter and lemon! That's what Spirit says!" he exclaimed.

"Do you have trouble with your knee? You bent your knee in an accident?"

"Years ago," the waitress said. "I busted a hole straight through it when I was nine years old."

All through the healing ceremony Moye talks with the one being treated. Informing of what Spirit advises on the condition and what the remedy might be.

"One of your children has been having trouble with the ear. A little boy!"

"That's my baby!" said the waitress in surprise. "You have never seen him!"

Moye chanted and then said, "I can cure your son's ear. Bring him one evening. I will fix up something for him for his ear."

The waitress commented that she felt a drawing sensation in her burn. That she felt relieved.

"This was a historical illness," recalls John, another patient. "It went back a few years. I had pernicious anemia. The body's ability to make red blood cells was impaired. You have to receive vitamin

B-12 shots each and every month. That's the only way you can live. Moye managed through some kind of way to get me out of the shots, and of course my doctor insisted that this could not happen. Pernicious anemia is not curable. It is only treatable with the B-12 shots."

"When John went to the hospital," Moye adds, "the doctor did a thorough examination only to find that John's records said he was supposed to have pernicious anemia. But the pernicious anemia was nullified. They couldn't find any trace of it. They found he had diabetes instead. That was the trade off.

"I said, 'I can work on this, take it from you and give you something else. I can take the third thing from you. In the final analysis you won't have to worry about the sickness. You'll have problems with the doctor. The doctor will be looking at you with 'fish eye'."

Moye makes himself available to those in need. His main residence is a small cottage in Tallahassee, Florida. He also has a place in New Jersey where many of his relatives live.

"I have a deluge of many people coming from many different places. The majority of problems of late are problems of dealing with health. I have worked with people who have had terminal cancer. That the doctors have given up to die. I went to see such a lady. About four weeks after I had been there, no trace of cancer. In working with the Orisha (African Gods), many things are possible."

"I am dealing with the light in life that comes through the darkness. I am an instrument of God." June Gatlin is a singer and spiritual healer who lives in Los Angeles. "I want to move and inspire people. I have done that while singing gospel. People have gotten healed through my voice.

"When I sing, people hearing me who have ailments, physical pain, or mental problems, have felt healing sensations."

She performed for the Jesse Jackson presidential campaign in 1984; Muammar Qaddafi's representatives were there. They said to her, "Your voice, there is power in your voice!" and invited her to Libya.

In Mikall's Club in New York in 1981, she gave a performance that was heavily attended by entertainment industry people. Miles Davis was in the audience. After the show he spoke to her. "That voice, I'd be pleased to play for you anytime."

After concerts, people tell her how her singing sent healing vibrations through their bodies and minds.

"When I am singing in church, in the power of my voice they feel healing energy reaching the soul and spirit." June perceives that each individual is a distinct system of energies. The energies are visible to her. While working on an individual through spiritual contact or laying on of hands, she becomes aware of how that person's energies were aligned in the original and optimum state. At the same time, she sees how the pattern has become altered as the result of physical, emotional, or spiritual suffering. She may perceive the details of the trauma. Observable to her are the energy distortions caused by pain. How the original smooth lines of energy go into jagged misalignment with stress. "I deal with the Power that generates the mental energy for people to create. I go to the Source: God with the Holy Spirit.

"I align energy. I work at realigning joints, straightening and reconditioning cells.

"I realign energy, recharge and restructure that energy." Two case histories she shares are of women who had long-term infertility problems. Both conceived and successfully became parents after June adjusted their energy systems. Persons with physical illnesses have responded well to realignment. "If I call God, He changes the person from within.

"I have prayed not to have to leave until I could do something about the suffering and pain."

"Polly Ostrander scalded her hand with a pot of boiling coffee, came into me and said, 'I have scalded my hand,' and I saw it looked like scarlet. I was told to pass my hand over it three times and then kneel down and pray. I did. And she kneeled also. And when I rose, she praised the Lord.

"Her hand was restored white as her other."[2] This healing, performed in 1843 by religious leader Rebecca Cox Jackson, is recorded in her autobiography, *Gifts of Power*, edited by Jean M. Humez.

Communicating with her through inner voice, Spirit provided Jackson with her methods of healing. "There was an old woman that was blind. . . . She heard a woman was to speak—she desired to hear her. One of her friends led her to the place where I was put up and when I saw her, I was sitting in prayer and I had such a sense of pity for her. And in it I was moved to go and lay my hand on her head in love. I got up and went, and as soon as I done it, I was commanded to sing, hold my right hand on her head, my left one on her left shoulder . . .

"So while I sung with my hands upon her, she received sight . . . I did not know that God was going to give her sight by my hands, but knowed that He gave me the sense of pity that I had, and told me to do all that I had done."

Born in the late eighteenth century, a free person, Rebecca Jackson's spiritual awakening occurred at the age of thirty-five. Taught through dreams, visions, and revelation, instructions from Spirit became integrated into her daily life.

Through spiritual perception, Jackson was led to the home of a sick man. She was accompanied by her husband, Samuel. "So when I knowed what I came for I said, 'Let us pray.' The man, in five minutes' time, would be laying on the floor, then on the chair, then upstairs, groaning, crying. He appeared to be in the greatest agony I ever saw anybody in. I clearly saw that prayer could do him no good, yet I knowed I was sent there to pray. It was said to me, 'Ask what you will and it shall be given.'

"Lord, rebuke his pains.' And at that word he kneeled. When I closed, and rose upon my feet, he said, 'God bless you. You have cured me. I have no pain. I am well as I ever was. Three weeks I have been just as I was when you came in, and have had no sleep.' . . . All this time he was talking, his wife, her mother, his children, Samuel was crying and praising God."

Jackson recounted a personal experience. "Recovering from a long fit of sickness . . . at one time I thought my eyes would burst in my head, they were so painful, I expected never to see again. And when I viewed the work I had yet to do in time, which work I could not do without my sight, it seemed as if I would go out of my right mind—I then prostrated my soul, body, mind and spirit before God and Holy Mother Wisdom in prayer. Yea, I cried in the bitterness of my spirit to that God who hears the ravens cry.

"And my prayer was answered . . . 'And if you are faithful, you shall be restored again to comfortable health, and have your sight also, to do the work which I gave you to do on earth.'

"In a few days after, I received a healing gift, and my eyes were healed."

"I was saved, sanctified. I was baptized with the gifts of the Holy Ghost at ten years old, and the Lord used me to his glory."[3]

Archbishop Bessie S. Johnson, as quoted in *Spirit World*, was born in Baton Rouge, Louisiana in 1893. She is regarded as the oldest and most revered living leader in the Spiritual Church in New Orleans.

A contemporary of Mother Catherine Seals, she became a divine worker during the many years she worked closely with Leaf Anderson, the founder of the First Spiritual Church South in New Orleans in 1920. Anderson, who was half black and half Mohawk Indian, had been an opera singer and church leader in Chicago before her move to New Orleans. Anderson taught her students the concept of "spirit returning," that discarnates come back to guide the living.

"It's like when you hear an inner voice telling you what to do," explained Archbishop Johnson to *Spirit World* author Michael Smith. "That's one of your spirit guides. You should listen to what your spirit guides tell you."

"It was Leaf Anderson," continued Archbishop Johnson, "that told me I was gifted, and that I was born under John the Revelator, a beautiful guide and teacher. I preach through him.

"Every medium does not prophesy. I was given the gift of prophecy in Biloxi, Mississippi. I was by a (water) hydrant, and I heard a voice. That night we had a meeting in Biloxi. When I went into the grounds I began to prophesy to a lumberman that his daughter was going to walk again. And she did walk ... Then I became a divine worker under Leaf Anderson."

Archbishop Johnson spent her childhood in New Orleans. At the age of ten she was healed of blindness by a Sanctified man.

"The gift of prophecy is something which comes to you through the divine spirit force," she told Smith. "I can get in spirit and the spirit will tell me who you are, what you come from, and whether your intentions are good ... A lot of people come to be healed and they are healed, if they come in good faith. Sometimes a

body is just naturally sick and the doctors just can't reach the condition. But God can reach all complaints. By my faith in Him, by my
confidence, my being instructed through the divine spirit of God,
and these people having faith, they are healed. I have stayed right
here in my house and people call me on the phone, and I ask them to
get a glass of water, with faith believing; I say the prayer over the
phone, they drink the water, and they are healed."

"She says she does no healing herself; it is all done through her,
as a medium, by the divine spirit force. She also speaks in tongues at
times. She then interprets what has been spoken so that people can
be 'edified'," Smith reported. "She has no particular method, but
heals 'however the spirit tells me to heal.' "

"When God speaks out the spirit to me, my mouth just flies
open and a beautiful song rattles out of my throat into the atmosphere for the people to hear." Fannie Bell Chapman is a God-in-
spired singer who creates songs while she is in the dream-state. "I
sang at the University of Mississippi in concert. There were about
500 in the house.

"I was born September 6, 1909. Born in Amen, Mississippi."

The visions and her love of singing started in childhood. She
sang traditional Baptist hymns at Sunday school. The visions were
intense and frequent enough to impress her that she was dreaming
during their duration. Most often the themes in the visions were of
sick people. At fourteen she visited the sick in their home, singing,
praying, and healing. All was preparation for the religious mission
to which she would so deeply dedicate her adult life.

"My mouth flied open, just like a mockingbird, and I went to
singing, 'God spoke in His Holiness.' " Fannie Bell asked her daughter to accompany her on the piano to fully bring out this song since
she felt too nervous to write the words down. Their collaboration
marked the beginning of her family's sharing in the creation of her
music. A song would come to her; she would hum it; the words
would come; she began to sing it. Then she would call in the family
to do the background. And out of that the "family of songsters" was
created, and her mission shaped.

"Visions followed me up so closely from on up until now that I had to try and see whether they were the handworks of God." One late evening Fannie Bell received a sign. She sat on her porch, her attention drawn to the beauty in clouds which were rising. Through prayer she appealed to God to flash the "pillar of clouds" with lightning if He wanted her to go out to pray and help people through the visions, as so many years ago she had been instructed to do. After she prayed, an airplane passed close to the clouds, illuminating them. This Fannie Bell rejected as false because the airplane was manmade and not a divine work. She resumed praying until she received her sign.

"That pillar was so prettily flashed. It just went on down until you could just see a little cloud, and He flashed that lightning. Ever since then I've been working, praying, and going to people's houses and having prayer meeting here in my house." The prayer group travelled around its community in Centreville, and into New Orleans, visiting homes, hospitals, and churches.

She confides about the manner in which her visions come. "Some of them come to me while I am awake. But most of them come to me no sooner than when I lay down. Then they shake me and go to talking to me. I'd get real sleepy. I'd go and lay down. No sooner than I lay down the visions would come to me."

She speaks in tongues and is sometimes possessed by the Holy Ghost.

When she was growing up a preacher helped her to understand the visions. "I'd always take my visions to Brother Montgomery and he would interpret them. I couldn't learn from God. I had to come in at the door.

"When a vision came to me, it showed me sick people. It showed me what to do to them when I got to them. Lots of them I healed; some of them, you know, I didn't heal. You just don't heal all of them.

"Sometimes when my hands would get to working over the body over the person, my hands would just fly like that. They would go right on in wherever the disease was. Visions showed me what to do. I'd do it and they'd get along pretty good. Some of them a lot better. I went to their homes.

"My husband was the first person I healed," Fannie Bell says in recalling early healing activities as an adult. "He had been to every doctor he knowed. He came round and I told him to sit under here with the Bible, talk to Jesus, and see what Jesus had to say about it. I told him it was nothing I could do." Her husband improved, and thereafter she went for many years praying and singing.

Fannie Bell was in Natchez visiting when she got so sleepy she couldn't keep her eyes open. "I told the lady, this is a vision on me now and I've got to lay down . . . Just as I lay down He spoke to me . . . 'Call your house now and tell them to treat the house like it was when you are there. If they don't treat it like it was when you were there, some of them are coming right back over here.' "

Fannie Bell made the call and hurried home. "By the time I got here, got out of the car, they were bringing one of my grandchildren out of the door. I said, 'O Lord, what's the matter?'

"My daughter said, 'This child is sick. I've got to carry him to the hospital I've got to rush him to Centreville.'

" 'No, Baby, don't rush him to Centreville, you've got to take this child to Natchez.' "

She took him to Centreville anyway, and the doctor told her to take him to Natchez as quickly as possible.

"The vision told me that she was going to be brought to Natchez."

Fannie Bell uses her hands and the Bible in her healing work. Her hands possess "healing power straight from the Holy Ghost." She gives prayer services to the hospitalized, and when she goes into the home of a person regarded as incurable by doctors, she uses laying on of hands.

During the project to record her singing at the Center for Southern Folklore, she spoke of her healing work to William Ferris and Judy Peiser. "Yeah, my hands do a heap of touching in my work. The Lord give me the power to cut all disease from the body. These fingers of mine cut the disease fine as cat hairs![4]

"So when I works people over, I works them from the top of their head to the end of their feets. I pass my hands over the body and I kinda squeeze all the temperature of hurt out—turn it loose and let it go. Then my fingers find where the misery is. My hand go to beating fast as electricity, just be hitting all over the body, untwisting and unloading disease and throw it out to the atmosphere. When my hand finds where the trouble is in the body, it don't go no further. It be beating like a sewing machine. That hand get to whopping and pulling and mangling the disease, until it find out whatever aches and pains is in the body. And when the fingers have cut the disease, it is gone, just gone!

"That is the way my hand works with the Lord."

Fannie Bell is the mother of ten children. She has thirty grand-children. A talent for singing is there in the group, but none of the children so far has manifested a gift for healing or experienced visions. The family has lived in the Centreville, Mississippi area for fifty years.

"I have done a great job in my life. I don't want to make up anything false. What I see is true," Fannie Bell summarizes.

"The good spirit is in me 'cause God wanted me to have it. I have healing hands,"[5] explained Lillian Chatman in an interview for the *Arizona Daily Star* in the late 1970s.

"I'm an old woman, I wish I could heal forever..."

Chatman was five when first she knew of this "good spirit" within. "It remains alive and well within my broken body," she said shortly before her death in 1984.

After Chatman's repeated success at relieving an employer's headaches in her earlier years, that employer, recognizing a power in Chatman's hands, sponsored her training as a masseuse. Chatman worked in bath houses in Texas, and later in New Mexico, assuaging physical pain by her touch.

In the 1940s she moved to Bakersfield, California. There, under the tutelage of Bishop Coleman Hill of the International Constitutional Spiritual Church, she developed her ability to heal into a helping tool she used for more than forty years.

"The Bishop read my mother the first time she came through his door," says her son, Frank Gipson. "He said she was a born healer, a seer, a reader, and a Mother. He said she needed papers."

Frank recalls the constant flow of people requesting help with physical, emotional, and spiritual problems. They arrived at his mother's home at all hours. She turned no one away. She placed her hands on the area of distress; with prayer she directed the pain away from the body. Her large eyes were intensely penetrating as she worked.

Mother Chatman, who was born in Crockett, Texas in 1903, ascribed her powers to the good spirit dwelling in her which had been willed there by God. People came from parts of Arizona, California, and Mexico seeking her help. Members of the medical school faculty at the University of Arizona studied her gift in healing.

In Tucson, Chatman founded a Spiritual church. In addition to healing, she taught.

Besides performing laying on of hands, she transmitted healing energies through prayer. Incense and water were part of her process. Her voice was also a strong instrument. She often worked by telephone. There was the case of the woman calling from California who had a chronic problem with nose-bleeding. The bleeding stopped at Mother Chatman's command, given over the telephone.

John, her husband, regarding her work as important, had routed unending streams of people through their home in a manner that bespoke his love and respect for what she did. Chatman once said she couldn't explain her gift. "It just works," she said. "The people keep coming."

"Sickness passed through my mother's hands and left from people. She would perspire when she touched them," explains her son. "She had a paralyzing stroke in 1975. Before then she was working around the clock," Frank remembers. "Healing was something she loved. It was her mission. Even when she was paralyzed."

It was said that white people were hunting her father with guns and bloodhounds. She got a gun and went to stop them. In the middle of her pursuit, a voice called her name and bade her to look up.

"Go home and minister to God's people."

On returning home Ma Sue picked up the Bible and easily read it. Until that time she had been illiterate.

Ma Sue Atcherson lived most of her life in La Grange, Georgia. The eldest of thirteen children, she raised her sisters and brothers. Their parents died sometime shortly after the Civil War.

Accounts are that she was around forty years old when she began healing and teaching, practices which she continued until her death at the age of 101 or 104 years old.

Stipes McWhorter lives in Carrolton, Georgia. He was a student at West Georgia College, and in constant physical pain, when he met Ma Sue in 1970. "A seven-ton truck ran over me three-and-a-half years before I met her. She rubbed my right knee and said a few sacred words. The pain became bearable after my first visit to her and has been at that level since that time.

"Ma Sue taught me telepathically. Three times over ten days, I would wake up knowing things I had no way to know. When I had an idea, I would wake up with the whole concept." Stipes knew it was she who had helped him.

"She had a young-old face, and it looked that way for many, many years."

A woman was in a terrible auto accident. Three physicians treated her, but eight or nine months after the accident all the glass still had not been removed from her hand. Her pain was so intense, she could no longer work as a typist.

Stipes met the woman's husband during that eight- or nine-month period. "I said, 'I know of a psychic connected with the College.' They drove to La Grange to see Ma Sue.

"That lady was not old but she had aged with pain. She had wrinkles and a frown from pain. When she returned from La Grange, her skin was smooth.

"Piece by piece the glass worked its way out over eight to ten weeks. I witnessed it."

Lori Ethel Squires was also among the West Georgia College parapsychology students studying with Ma Sue in 1970. Lori befriended and stayed in close touch with the elderly healer until she left the area in 1976.

"Ma Sue was 102 when I first met her ... She never went to school. Ma Sue told me, 'I can read anything.' " Lori took textbooks to her from West Georgia College and Ma Sue read them like an educated person.

"She was busy healing. Her yard would be full of Rolls Royces, limousines, people from all over the United States. People sent her letters every day. There was money all over her house," Lori remembers.

"When I came, Ma Sue told her daughter, 'Jessie, let that little teacher in. I've been watching her in the fire.'

"She lived in a little bitty black shack. She didn't want to move." Ma Sue seemed unconcerned about physical possessions and money. She continued to live in the same small, rundown shack even after she could afford a better situation.

"She outlived all of her sisters and brothers. . . . She did a range

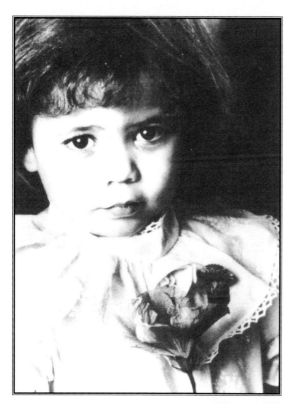

April King
Chapters 1 & 9

Reverend Nellye Mae Taylor
Chapters 1 & 2

*Above: Bakara Oni
Chapters 1 & 9*

*Right: Alpha Omega
Chapters 1 & 5*

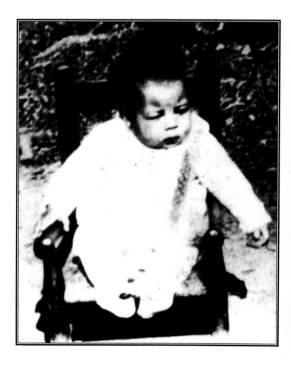

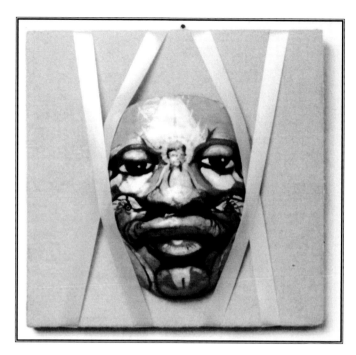

Art by Eddie Cabral
Chapter 2

Mother Susie Booth
(center figure, seated)
Chapter 2

Minnie Evans
Chapters 1 & 3

Painting by Minnie Evans

Painting by Minnie Evans
Chapters 1 & 3

Painting by Minnie Evans

June Juliet Gatlin
Chapters 1, 4, 5 & 7

Alpha Omega
Chapters 1 & 5

Chuck Wagner
Chapters 1, 4 & 8

*Above: Richmond Barthe
Chapters 4, 5, 7 & 10*

*Right: Sculpture by Richmond Barthe
"Pregnant Madonna"*

Fannie Bell Chapman
Chapter 5

Reverend Peter Brown
Chapters 1, 2, 5 & 6

*Hayward Coleman
Chapters 4, 6, 7 & 9*

Reverend Mary Bivens
Chapters 8 & 9

Mary Bivens and associate

Left: Henry Rucker
Chapters 1, 5, 6, 8 & 10

Below: Henry Rucker
(2nd row, 3rd from right)

Luisah Teish
Chapters 7, 8, 9 & 10

Queen Ann Prince
Chapter 10

James "Son" Thomas
Chapter 10

Reverend Estelle Ellerbee
Chapters 2, 3, 4, 6 & 7

Soyini Grayer
Chapters 1, 7, 9 & 10

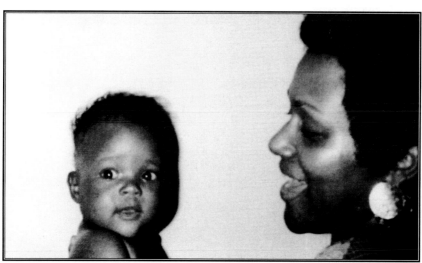

Soyini Grayer and daughter, Bakara Oni

Betty Comes
Chapters 1 & 5

Master Walter Thomas (Chapter 3) and Joyce Noll

of healings including drug healings. She worked on every kind of disease. She would ask about the problem. She opened her Bible to Psalm 23, and lay her hand on it. She did not touch people. She would hold out her hand to them and quote the Scripture.

"I think she traveled out of her body a lot," Lori concludes.

Some faculty members and students in the Parapsychology Department at West Georgia College participated in making a film titled *Psychics, Saints, and Scientists*. Ma Sue and witnesses to her healing abilities are presented in it.

Janie Veal, a parapsychologist, was a graduate student at West Georgia College who met Ma Sue in the early 1970s. "Ma Sue didn't give readings. She was a woman who healed the heart as well as the body," Janie observes. "There was a presence about her. She was fragile looking, very slender, with not much hair. She wore it braided. Her skin was medium brown. Her eyes were alert. She had beautiful hands. She would rub olive oil on your hands and arms. She would almost croon and would talk about the things that were deepest in your heart.

"Ma Sue always had her Bible. She talked in a sing-song voice. 'What is on your heart?' she would say. She had you write down what bothered you. She put it inside her Bible." Janie pauses, reflecting. "The time I spent with her was a magical time. She was an extremely religious person. Extremely gifted. She gave a person a wonderful feeling."

Sculptor Richmond Barthe has a photographic memory. He needs only to study a person's features briefly, then he can go home and reproduce his observations with preciseness in clay. "I study the face on the subway, street or stage or some place like that, I go home, I sleep all night, I get up the next morning, I get my armatures ready, and I get my clay. Then I move back to last night and copy what I see, a mental picture."

Barthe's basic schooling ended with the seventh grade. He received no art training before his admission to the Chicago Institute of Art, where he studied from 1924 through 1928. His admission to the Art Institute was arranged by a Catholic priest who recognized Barthe's remarkable artistic talent after viewing a painting of the head of Christ which the youth had done.

At one point in his career, Barthe conceived of creating a sculpture of the Virgin Mary, and was making plans to that effect. He proposed to replicate her in a condition of pregnancy. "I wanted a very beautiful, young, Jewish face of a girl. I had a Jewish friend. I decided I was going to use her as a model. I knew her height and everything. When I finished it, I called Sondra.

" 'I have a surprise for you. I've just finished doing a figure of you as the pregnant Virgin Mary.'

"She was anxious to see it. She said, 'Wait until I tell Otto!'

"Sondra and Otto, her husband, had been wanting more than anything in the world to have a child. But they couldn't have one. This had been going on for fifteen or sixteen years. Sondra came over and was thrilled with the pregnant figure. I got the very likeness of her plus the spiritual aspect.

"A month or so later, Sondra called me. She said, 'Have I news for you! I really am pregnant!'

"She had a girl. She called her Eve. Eve is grown now. If Sondra had not seen herself life-size pregnant, I'm sure she would never had had this child."

"Oh! Lord, I will never take another bit of medicine while I live without you tell me to!"[6] vowed Amanda Smith in surrendering the state of her physical health to the Will of God. "I got up and threw out all my medicines—I had a few simple remedies in the house—and for a year and eight months I never touched anything. Oh! What wonderful lessons the Lord taught me at that time," she wrote in the *An Autobiography, Amanda Smith* in the late nineteenth century.

Spirit whispered to Amanda in a voice as clear and distinct as a person, warning her of risks to her health as she went about her daily living. "I would hear the Spirit whisper ... 'You are sitting in a draught.' Often I have looked around to see if there was not really a person speaking ...

> I would feel a pain in my back, or neck, or somewhere. Then I would at once look up to God and say, "Now, Lord teach me the lesson you want I should learn; and then do please relieve me of this pain." ... Sometimes He would bless

me so ... But the Lord knew how to teach me, praised be His name. So at the expiration of a year and eight months ... I took a severe cold.

I never thought of medicine. The Lord was my physician, and had done everything I asked for myself and my child for a year and eight months, so of course He would now. So I prayed as aforetime, but still grew worse. Oh! how dreadfully ill I was. But I held on. Oh! how I did cry to God for deliverance. For three days and nights I could not lie down, my cough was so bad. I had a raging fever. My head ached, and every bone in my body ached. I still grew worse, until the morning of the fourth day. I tried to get my clothes on, but could not stand up long enough.

Oh! what shall I do ... Oh! how I cried and prayed. Oh! Lord ... What have I done? Thou didst always heal me when I asked Thee, and now Thou seest I can hardly hold my head up, I am so sick ... Now, Lord, I will just be quiet till Thou dost speak to me and tell me what I have done, and why Thou dost not heal me as Thou usest to do.

So I waited a few minutes; I don't know how long; then it seemed as though the Lord Jesus in person stood by me; such a peaceful hush came all over me, and He seemed to say ... "Now, if you knew the Lord wanted you to take medicine would you be willing?"

"No, Lord, you always have healed me without medicine, and why not now? What have I done?"

Then it seemed just as though a person spoke and said, "No, no, but if you knew it was God's will, would you be willing?" I said, "No, Lord; you can heal me without medicine, and I don't want to take it."

Then the patient, gentle voice said the third time, "If you knew it was God's will for you to take medicine would you be willing to do God's will?"

Oh! how I cried. I saw it, but I said, "No, Lord, I don't like medicine; but Thou canst conquer my will. I don't want to live with my will in opposition to Thy will. Thou must conquer."

It seemed wonderfully sweet to die to my own will, and sink into God. So just then it came to me to use a simple remedy that I had used a thousand times before, and in twenty-four hours I was as well as ever. I never got over a cold like that before in my life in so short a time; a cold like that would always be a three weeks' siege.

"I've been healing since I was a girl." Although no specific incidents come to mind from that period of her healing, Mother Brown remains inspired when she recalls the "joy of that day I received Christ when I was a small girl.

"The Lord told me to wear white a long time ago. He told me to get rid of all my other clothes and wear these." She points to her long white dress and cap.

A respected healer in Durham, North Carolina's African American community, Mother Brown, now in her eighties, works in two ways: laying on of hands, and praying for healing over distance. She has helped many who were troubled by a wide range of physical and emotional ills.

The only child left in a family of seven, she experienced fully the offerings of severe living in her times. She is well acquainted with plowing fields, chopping wood, and picking cotton.

For more than thirty years she has followed the divine directive to wear white, and in that same time she has held weekly church meetings in her home. She frequently bursts into song, praising the Lord, and is carried away into ecstatic moods.

While in her late seventies, Mother Brown became the instrument for her own healing. "I woke up with real strong pains in my arm. I heard a voice, the voice of the Lord that said to me I was having a stroke."

"Get out of bed and jump three times!" His voice commanded. With great effort she followed the instructions. The pain lessened, then with the completion of the exercise, vanished.

Prior to one parishioner joining her church, healer Bishop Butler had come upon him in his makeshift residence at the city dump. He suffered from blood poisoning caused by an injury which had left both legs extremely swollen and putrefied. He turned down medical care because treatment was to be the amputation of both legs.

"I asked the Lord what I could do for his legs and he told me what to do."[7]

Bishop Butler is the minister of the Beauty of Holiness Church of the Lord God in Creation, a Spiritual church in New Orleans. The example of her work with this man is presented by author Michael Smith in his book *Spirit World*.

She returned to the dump to ask Frank Gilbert if he believed the Lord would heal his legs. The sick man replied that he did. "Then I brought him to my house. I anointed his legs with hot oils and prayed over it. Then one of his legs popped open like a hot potato and a kind of steam came out. I got two basins full of corruption out of that leg.

"My husband got frightened and ran out of the house to a neighbor. He thought I was going to be arrested for practicing medicine ... So we took Mr. Gilbert to a doctor ... The doctor gave him a shot and said to keep on doing what we had been doing. Then the legs began to heal up."

Frank Gilbert attested to this healing, verifying all that Bishop Butler had said.

"My gift was great until I found God, then it became greater. I realized after I was saved how to use my gift with greater consciousness. I prayed to God to let me go as far as possible with my gift." Betty Comes is a healer and psychic who in the course of her career has given readings to movie stars. These celebrities include Eartha Kitt, Freda Payne, Fred Williamson, and Vince Edwards.

She has an ability to see through people's bodies, with x-ray vision, as they sit before her. She can detect in the body the sites where an individual had operations even many years earlier. People with afflictions may be in Betty's presence or at a distance while she transmits healing energies to them. "I am able to detect physical illness. I can diagnose what part of the body the illness is in," she informs.

While attending a party in 1979, Betty became aware that entertainer Lola Falana, who was also present, had an acute physical problem. "I took her aside to tell her what I saw." The tumors seen by Betty had already been surmised by the celebrity's physicians. "I told her to go ahead with the surgery, she would be all right." Later in a medical follow-up, fifteen tumors were found in Falana's stomach. "I worked with her after the operation, and she was able to move about and do exercises very soon afterwards, which surprised her doctors.

"I only use trance if someone has a serious illness. I only do that if it is an emergency.

"I am able to relieve a person of pain by taking the pain into myself, and I get rid of the sickness by praying." The most disquieting part of her work is in the transferring of illness from her clients into her own body; but as she reads selected verses of the Psalms, the negative energy disperses.

In the dream state, Betty has full-blown, vivid, and clear visions which often come true within a short time. She is conscious of continuously working in activities of the spiritual realm.

She notes that her gifts make men reluctant in seeking her company—that people in general tend to be uneasy around her. "I no longer long for the things of the earth, I am not into the needs of the material body.

"I am a loner. I stay with God."

"When I was in kindergarten, my mother said, 'When you were a baby I gave you to God.'

"It kind of plagued me all my life. I had it always in the back of my mind that she said, 'I gave you to God and you are going to have to work for God.' " So contemplates Henry Rucker, psychic healer, in looking back at the possible genesis of his healing ability.

In March, 1976 Paul Neimark, a *Sepia Magazine* reporter, wrote about Rucker's gifts. "Several leading professionals witnessed this happening when they were with Henry on the West Coast recently. A woman in a store had acted rudely toward Rucker and instead of taking offense, he looked 'inside' her.[8]

" 'I can sometimes look at people and not see the coat or tie or dress that they wear, but see through to the skin, or even to their organs,' Rucker says. 'If an area is inflamed or infected, I see it as a brighter red.'

"In this case, Rucker saw that the woman's heart was bothering her—but that there was nothing wrong with it. 'You've been experiencing an irregular heartbeat,' he told her. 'But that's only because of some problem with a loved one. It gives you pain in your chest, but your heart is physically healthy, though you are very worried about it. Because of that, you're making that situation worse with the loved one. Your husband, I think. And you're not acting like you usually do toward people like me. Because you are actually a very kind individual.'

"The woman's eyes opened wide. She didn't say a word.

"Rucker went on. 'In just a moment the pain will be gone. And you're going to your doctor next Monday, I think it is.' The woman nodded silently. 'He will also tell you that there is nothing wrong. Then you'll decide to go to the real source of pain in your heart. And you'll make it right.'

"Now the woman could speak. She told Rucker, and those with him, that everything he said had been 100 per cent correct!"

Rucker works with Norman Shealy, M.D., director of the Pain and Health Rehabilitation Center in La Crosse, Wisconsin. The neurosurgeon, who has an interest in exploring the possible use of psychics in medicine, contacted Rucker after he learned of his psychic healing reputation. The physician had a personal reading from Rucker and began sending patients to him. Several other psychics and Rucker participated in a series of experiments concerning patient diagnoses administered by Shealy. Rucker was found to be correct 80% of the time. He joined Shealy's clinic staff as a psychic medical diagnostic consultant and in that role he works with and accompanies physicians on their rounds. Other clinics and hospitals in Wisconsin, Ohio, and Texas later acquired his services.

In the *Everett Herald*, August 11, 1979, reporter Clara Phillips noted: "At the pain facility Rucker helps patients 'eliminate pain, not tolerate it.'[9]

"Attitude is the most important aspect of physical, emotional and spiritual well-being, he says. Pain, he maintains, is guilt turned inward. He teaches people to free themselves of guilt and to love themselves. After all, he says, when you love yourself, you're loving God.

"Rucker also claims diagnostic and healing powers. He says he sees through clothing and skin into people's vital organs to discover tumors or infections, being correct four out of five times. Because he isn't licensed, he collaborates only with doctors, indicating to them which tests to run to verify his diagnosis. He also diagnoses from photos doctors send him.

"Rucker's healing technique is 'a little different' from faith healing.

"Rucker calls his ability 'magnetic healing', and he never

touches a person.

"Healing energies from his hands can project out to cut away a malignant growth or sew up a rupture in a person across the room, he says, explaining that he works on the energy field enveloping that person.

" 'There are many people in the world who heal without knives, anesthesia or prescriptions,' maintains Rucker. 'I think every human being heals someone at sometime or other.' "

"How does this psychic healing actually work?" Dane Headley, a friend and college newspaper reporter, asked Rucker.

Rucker responded, "The healing takes place on several levels. I've learned that various energies come out of my hands that have healing powers. I can project heat across the room. I have done this before with you, so it's not a proving type thing. I can take the energy and seal a rupture, for example, a hernia. I can pull it back together with that energy and knit, sew, and stitch. I can cut and sever with power like that of a laser beam."

Modern People, February 8, 1976, records that Rucker walked up to a stranger, a woman in a supermarket, who looked ill.

> "Are you all right?" he asked.[10]
>
> "Just a little dizzy," she answered.
>
> "You have a pain in your abdomen," Rucker said suddenly. "You've also felt dizzy like this every morning for several days. Your mother died of a blood disease last year, and you're so afraid that you have it. But you don't. You're in perfect health. The reason you feel faint and have that slight pain is that you're pregnant with the child you've always wanted—even though the doctor said you'd never have a baby."
>
> The woman looked at Rucker in astonishment. "How can—how could you know all that?"
>
> "I just know," said Rucker. "And now the pain will be gone, now that you understand it. Feel it going ... going. Is it gone?"
>
> The woman felt her middle. "Yes ... there's no pain left. And I don't feel as dizzy ... "
>
> Being able to relieve pain comes from two things, according to Rucker. "First, I'm able to tune in on what their pain is because I'm psychic. And that makes a person trust me."
>
> But second, the article continues, Rucker seems to understand pain, or at least has a new idea about it.... "Physical pain is at least 90 per cent guilt, or something like guilt," he

says. "Yes, we all get sick. But I've seen people punishing themselves by getting sick. And I've also seen people punishing themselves by feeling as much pain as they can once they are ill."

For his book, *Psychic City: Chicago*, Brad Steiger interviewed Rucker regarding the African dialects which the healer and his associates have used in their healing work.

"The particular dialect we use is not important,"[11] Rucker explained. "We use these dialects in our healing work, because we can control powers which are not known by ordinary individuals. We use them to change the vibrations in a place. By intoning certain vibrations, I can change people's entire concepts. By chanting, I could change vibrations in this room so that a person wouldn't want to walk through the door. I don't do demonstrations like that just to show off or to prove a point, however."

An article on Rucker in the *Globe*, July 21, 1981, elaborates. Dr. James McNeil, treasurer of the American Holistic Medicine Association, said that Rucker performs his diagnoses and healings by "working with the patient's energy field. He can manipulate people's electromagnetic fields by influencing their thoughts."[12]

One of Rucker's more spectacular healings involved a young child who had suffered a severe skull injury in an automobile accident. Dr. Shealy reported, "There was a hole in the skull that wouldn't heal or grow back together. Henry began working with the child and the bone began to heal."

About the beginnings of his work in healing, Henry recalls, "They asked me to lecture as a healer. Meanwhile I had been doing healings, and I had stacks of books where people sent me pictures for healing. They began to call me from all over the world. 'Would you come over to do this here?' After I went to the Philippines with the Philippine healers, people asked me to lecture on it, and then I would do healings on my own. Then the group came over here and we worked together. So I was known as a healer.

"So much has happened in 20 years," Henry goes on. "Dr. Norman Shealy came, and I gave him a reading, and he wouldn't leave. He stayed for two or three hours. He asked me to come up to his clinic to diagnose his patients. I've worked with him in the clinic since 1972. I function as a counselor, a pastoral and psychological counselor.

"My wife and I went to Egypt. I did healing there. They would line up and tell me about their complaints like a doctor. They've got my picture up in a lot of stores there. I was in Aswan, Cairo, and Karnak.

"I'm not a Jesse Jackson or a Martin Luther King. God has not put me on that path. Whatever I do for my race would have to be by example. I really try to organize programs—they all fall through. I really try to be more aware of my black brothers and sisters," assures Henry.

"I reject no man. When people come to me for healings, I don't consider their race. I've healed people from South Africa. When patients come to be healed, I don't pick them. I don't know what my mission is. We won't know until I'm dead. I live from day to day."

Recalling again his mother's having "given him to God" at an early age, Henry concludes, "I do not feel basically that I am the one who does the healing. God does the healing. I can't tell you why, but maybe God chose me as one of the channels."

Alpha Omega had a series of dreams in 1978. Many nights of that year she dreamed of being taught in the same classroom setting. The dreaming roused an unappeasable interest in reading which led her to read a great diversity of books.

"I had dropped out of regular school in the ninth grade. It had been boring.

"I have never had idols nor have I worshipped people. But I have always been enamoured of someone with a fine mind, and when I was growing up I often sought out elderly people."

The dream state classroom held her attention with themes dwelling mostly on the cause-and-effect relationships in diseases from spiritual sources. She began keeping a notebook, for the insights would even come during waking hours.

"My interest has always been in dealing with feelings and what makes up the human person.

"I suddenly couldn't read enough. The books were all saying the same thing. I was being led to the religious context in all the books.

"Then I began to write. For an entire year I wrote. In 1979 through 1981 the writings continued. I carried the notebook to record about disease, its cause and effect.

"I was going through many changes in my feelings. I began to experience more love. It was almost to the point of being painful ... I began to get the realization that I should stop doubting. I felt I was being prepared for understanding.

"A person reaches a point in seeking and becomes sensitive to everything outside himself. Crisis provides the path to evolvement. This occurred with me. I had reached a point where nothing was right. I was living on the outside and life was leading nowhere."

To gain understanding, she attended psychic meetings. At one a reader said healing power radiated from Alpha's energy field. The energy would turn harmfully inward if not utilized, the psychic warned. The reader, who held meetings in her own home, invited Alpha to the next one. A room full of people was already gathered when Alpha arrived, waiting for her to work on them. Although she protested, she soon found herself working among those lined up for help with natural certainty, moving her hands over their heads. One woman, complaining of a chronic thyroid problem, told Alpha that her condition improved after that session. Several other people with physical ailments spoke of the healing benefits they felt after her work.

With the new-found ability came an extremely uncomfortable side-effect. It seemed that the pains, emotions, and spiritual blocks, suffered by the people she had treated, amassed in Alpha's body and auric space. She absorbed the negative energy from their old and current ills and experienced aching and malaise. Discouraged, she resorted to intense prayer and meditation for guidance in handling the side-effects. "I had to get closer to God. I started meditating and reading the Bible. I prayed that if I was to be the vehicle to help others that God would give me more knowledge."

A new manifestation appeared when she resumed her work. Whenever she gave treatments, she belched. The aching and discomfort dissipated as she belched, and eventually the discomforts ceased. Belching, she learned, allowed energy, which had previously accumulated in her, to be released. She could actually feel the energy pulling away from the organs of her body through the process. Those receiving treatment also began belching with beneficial effects.

"My biggest battle as not to become a big ego, as I was getting much attention. I had to work at understanding I was just a vehicle that other forces were working through. Many people have been so gifted."

As Alpha worked on people, she gradually realized she was dealing with energy fields. Revealed to her was that each individual had a timing system which she could audibly perceive. There were distinct sounds and voices in each one's psychic space. She often picked up the impressions of relatives and friends as she worked on a person. Their ailments and problems were there, as influences on the sick one. She heard harps and singing from one person; these she successfully recorded on tape. There was also the time she was able to control the flow of blood from someone injured. And among the treated, one of them gained psychic abilities as Alpha worked on her.

"I have gone back with people to their basic personalities and the creative areas of their minds. I began to pick up energy near the beginning of time."

Alpha Omega lives in New York City. Through teaching and lecturing she encourages individuals to move towards higher states of consciousness and realizing spiritual potential. She continues to receive insight on how she is to work. "Nothing is beyond our knowledge," she affirms.

She recorded psychic sounds as part of her treatment procedure. It became evident that when she touched a person's body, the sounds from his or her energy field could be transmitted to tape and thereby be perceptible to others as well. She plans to use this information to further understand spiritual energy. "If I can bring to the world in sound and in sight what energy really is and what we are composed of—I'll be satisfied. When people can see that we are not just one entity but many, we can begin to understand."

"Jennie Benson," the Lord said, "You are going to heal."

She was a teenager when Reverend F. A. Jones, an evangelist, went to her home to talk with her. "The Lord told me to tell you, Jennie, that you can't do like other girls. That you were born for a purpose and he wants to use you."

During her young teen years, Jennie moved to Jackson from her home in rural Mississippi, then on to Memphis. Her next move was to Pittsburgh, Pennsylvania, where she fell ill and was hospitalized.

"I'll never forget my chart number, D3925. One day the doctor came in to pick up my chart and said, 'I don't know what's keeping you here. A strong constitution? You are dead but you haven't quit breathing!' " She wasn't even well the day she was discharged from the hospital. On the way home the Lord spoke to her.

"You're going to heal my sick and you're going to prophesy my name. When you promise me all these things, I will let you up."

"The Lord let me up and I started preaching. When I first started out I was fourteen. "There is something about you when God calls you; you can study all you want, but when you get up to speak, it all goes except what God wants you to say," she states.

At eighteen she moved to Cleveland, prompted by a divine directive to heal alcoholics and drug addicts. "When I moved to Cleveland, I had thirty-five dollars in my pocket and no friends there. I was in Cleveland about three months and I was already conducting a service. God moves so!"

Jennie's mother would go miles to hear Georgiana, her adopted daughter, sing; but she refused to go hear Jennie preach. The adopted daughter had a health problem. "She would eat and food would come back up. She would break out in large perspiration.

"God came to my mother in her sleep one night and said, 'I'm going to heal your daughter, Georgiana, but I'm going to heal her through your daughter, Jennie.' "

On the designated Sunday night, Jennie's sister attended service. "Call your sister up," the Lord told Jennie, "I'm going to heal her now."

"As she walked up, I said, 'In the name of Jesus Christ, be thou healed.' She fell on the floor, and she hasn't been sick since that day! God knows all this is true; I wouldn't have said that if it weren't true."

Jennie Benson Vaughn founded the St. Teresa Holiness Science Church in Nashville in 1979 with her husband, Frank, also a minister. It was not the first church she had set up. Several years earlier, she had established a church in Cleveland, Ohio. She is known for helping those lacking economic resources in the community.

In healing she stretches out her hands or touches the troubled person, saying, "Be healed in the name of Jesus Christ!" Jennie affirms with determination, "I will continue to heal the sick. We give the needy clothing and give them food when they come by and ask for it.

"Over the last ten or twelve years I don't pay attention to what people say. All I know is what God says. That's what counts!"

The graceful exactness of Tureeda's hand motions trace back to an old, old science. Its origin is Egyptian. She is aware of a deity working through her. An inner voice instructs her how to work with each person. Dietary information, included in readings, flows from both her intuitive and technical knowledge.

Tureeda Mikell works to reclaim physical health. Through the agency of her hands, healing starts, then accelerates. The energy an individual has absorbed from the world dissolves as she moves her hands over and near the body. Assisting people in contacting and aligning with their higher selves, she enables mending between the physical and the spiritual, and the restoration of well-being.

Recently Tureeda learned that the instinctively developed hand movements she has used for years in her spiritual and physical healing work are known as "mudras." The information was conveyed to her by an Indian yogi observer. Constituting a sign language in Hindu and Buddhist religious traditions, mudras are mystical poses of the hand or hands used in worship, yoga and inconography. States of awareness and psychic energy levels are influenced by them.

"I prayed one morning when I was going through a lot of stuff about what it was I was doing. This old man called right after I had done this strong prayer. He said, 'What you have is so old that you can't go around and try to chuck it down everybody's throat. What you're going to have to have is patience. Something just told me to call and tell you that.'"

A native Californian, Tureeda lives in the San Francisco Bay area.

"I played nurse when I was a child. My parents always wanted me to play the piano, and I played classical piano for seventeen years. But in college, science became my major and music, my minor."

Tureeda has taken different roles in healing. At five her abilities were already evident. Her first young effort brought family members relief from pain and tension through massage. She saw colors radiating from people; and there was, too, the sound of inner voices which at times seemed a host of varied instruments offering comfort and counseling to the little girl. Although Tureeda's mother accepted her daughter's hands to soothe an arthritic condition, she firmly discouraged the child's talk of colors and disembodied voices. The psychic aspect of her daughter's personality the mother tried to arrest by pushing her toward aesthetic activities where she showed talent, such as with piano, ballet, and violin.

While working in hospitals after completing nursing school, Tureeda perceived traditional medical technology did not allow for the physical/spiritual healing process needed by the sick. She sensed that the suppression and removal of diseased body parts did not lead to a stable recovery. She realized her spiritual self was extending into the patients' spaces, blending with them, as she worked to assist them. Telepathic exchanges occurred between her and patients with their emotions and pains being absorbed by her.

"I became a nurse when I was 21. I walked in this man's room and felt his medication on my body. He was getting medication in his right eye and I could feel it in my left. I was mirroring people, and that got to be a bit deep. I could wheel people from surgery and feel their missing parts ... When you remove a part that is diseased, it does not cure the situation. If they have had one operation, they have to have several. They have to keep removing parts which have been affected. That made me realize, too, how ignorant people are in their understanding of what medicine is.

"The intuitive had been happening for years. I didn't know I was doing it. People told me.

"A friend once said, 'You—psychic thing, you!'

"It turned out that I was actually reading him. I didn't know what he was talking about. I was just being me."

She concludes, "You cannot deal with this world unless you know who you are."

Medical procedures, she saw, physically smothered or severed the patient's signals of distress from the diseased areas. But the signals still flashed on a spiritual level—unheeded. Tureeda came to regard these as "missing information." She laid aside her career in nursing when she concluded that she could not use traditional medicine as a means to assist in healing. Its techniques did not align with her perception that both the physical and spiritual had to be addressed for healing to take place.

"I use my hands and my hands basically tell a story. I clear the energy people have absorbed from the world and put them in touch with their higher being. That's the physical thing I do. That's the mending that takes place between their body and spirit.

"My sister almost had a hysterectomy at 21. I told her what to do. Her doctor said she was probably too scarred to have a child. She was pregnant two months later. She had a Scorpio son. I've done this with two women whom doctors told they were not going to have babies. They both had Scorpio boys.

"These are things which have always made me realize that there is something greater at work. I know that I am a catalyst and a tool. There is something greater. I cannot plan this. I am not responsible. I am the instrument. My head is in no way big. I know I am the instrument. I tell people this when I do readings."

At twenty-six, Tureeda began a search for greater understanding on how to use her healing gift. Buddhism and metaphysical training advanced her awareness, providing orientation. The gifts already present became stronger and defined. Through voice, vision, and the healing power in her hands, she established her way to help.

"It is indeed an old science. I have seen things numerically, astrologically, physiologically, anatomically that relate to what Truth is."

Tureeda does not confine her service to healing. She is a poet, a spiritual reader, and an astrologer. At local colleges she talks on spiritual healing and psychic ability within the African American culture. She reads her poetry in the elementary schools to arouse within African American children, especially, an interest in becoming aware of themselves, and in learning to be harmonious within the self. She has found that many African American children do not like their skin color.

After one presentation, Tureeda received from one child a letter which read, "Thank you for telling me I am love."

CHAPTER SIX

Expelling Negative Spirits

That they were to wait ... was all that could be remembered by most of the tenants of the human edifice (this one was a black woman's body).

Any one of these spirit occupants could will itself over a short distance beyond the body's aura. But a journey was never long before the entity was impelled to return. Not bonded to the body, but to each other (soul to soul) in secrecy and mystery so deep they had simply forgotten how they had become a compulsive congregation of spiritual beings, moving from one incarnation to another, attached to each other as if they were one.

Each time they incarnated, it was much like bees in setting up a new hive. One (it was always the same spirit) would take a position around the head and eyes. It moved in a freer manner, floating in and out around the body, radiating its presence. When it communicated with the other spirits (telepathically as they all did) what it said was taken as command, because its energy flowed stronger.

Amnesia covered them all except for the higher sentient spirit. But even it was not complete or near perfect in its knowing. It only partly comprehended its own identity and half-knew a vagueness of the secret which kept it bound to the other spirits.

But sentient it was indeed, in the company of the insensible, the half-awakened, and the lethargic.

All spiritual beings, embodied and disembodied, when in positive energy states, are naturally inclined to be of friendly disposition and helpful toward other spiritual beings. The endowments of spiritual beings include qualities such as flowingness, lightness, illumination, harmony, and potentials of certainty, complete awareness, and total understanding.

Inversely, a spiritual being can become blocked from its natural state of spirit brotherhood by conflict, in various forms of negative energy characterized by disagreement, misconception, and misinterpretation, that lie for ages unresolved. The records and images of discordant times accumulate in the individual's space in the form of harmful energy. Over the ages, such a spirit's boundaries become thickened, clouded, and constricted.

Spiritual beings naturally abstain from creating confusion, contention, and destruction; but a being, unable to repair these negative conditions, may be moved to act out the negative energy in its space, in deeds of hostility and harm toward other spiritual beings. When an entity performs more negative actions than positive ones, it is on a path of *devolvement*. At any point, when negativity is the dominant creation of a being, that spirit, for the time, is a negative spirit.

The majority of earthbound spirits are not negative entities, but a negative minority does exist among them. Some of the circumstances which keep disembodied beings in the physical realm are excessive desire for sensation, continuing desire to own material things, disorientation, lack of knowledge, and unresolved matters from recent lifetimes—especially injurious acts to others.

It has been said that negativity can only be expressed in the physical realm and in a few of the levels of the astral realms; and that no spiritual being engaged in negativity can locate above these vibratory levels because of the entity's denseness.

This chapter describes the psychics who are skilled in dispelling the presence and influences of disembodied negative spirits that are harassing, influencing, and obsessing positively directed human beings.

Hayward Coleman, a Southern California mime who incorporates yoga into his performances, shares an experience he underwent as part of his spiritual development. At one point his etheric body was invaded by a lower astral being. This entity for a while deceived Hayward by pretending to be his spiritual teacher.

"So I found myself going to the bars and drinking wine which I never do. So here I am drinking wine ... and I begin to suspect this voice. Then the voice confessed and said he was a soldier in the French Army and was killed. He just wanted to be my friend, but he always needed to drink some wine. And by using my body he would be able to drink and enjoy the wine.

"You see, when people die, it doesn't make any difference. Nothing is eliminated. They still have the same desire, the same cravings. In Buddhism they teach you to eliminate the desires and the cravings in this life so that you can be a greater being and go on to greater levels or states of consciousness," Hayward advises.

"A lot of the beings who pass on still have the same desires to smoke a cigar, or whatever. They find vehicles to realize this, and I had become one of those vehicles unknowingly. Once I became cognizant of that fact—the entity did leave.

Hayward recognizes "this was something I had to go through. It was like an initiation period to be able to understand all the different astral levels."

"I went to a house not long ago where pictures were falling off the wall, dishes off the kitchen table, when no one was anywhere near. It was obviously some form of spirit which had been let loose by some hostile member of the house.[1]

"When people have strong negative feelings that they can't express ... ghosts appear," remarked Henry Rucker of Chicago who founded the Psychic Research Foundation in that city in 1969. He told a reporter from *Modern People* that he had gone to many houses to remove ghosts.

He visited the home with the mysterious occurrences to find that recently the parents had sent an older son away from the house to a military school. "The younger brother felt abandoned, and as a result he was releasing these evil forces through a ghost. Ghosts are always activated by some person who has a lot of negative feelings, and doesn't know what to do with them.

"Once I was able to talk with the boy," Rucker said, "things were okay and dishes stopped flying off the table."

In an article in *Sepia Magazine* Rucker described one of his "ghostbreaking" activities which occurred in California. At the request of a woman whose home was under an attack by earthbound entities, he traveled from Chicago to Los Angeles. The besiegement had terrified the divorced woman, her fourteen-year-old daughter, eleven-year-old son, and two other relatives. The ghosts' deeds, observed by Rucker, included smashing objects against walls from considerable distances, dislodging pictures from walls with such force they would break on the floor, and creating in the house gusts of wind which blew the drapes wildly about.

Rucker explained how the situation was created and resolved. "What you must understand about ghostbreaking is that individuals in the house itself are often their (ghosts') power source. In this case I discovered that it was the eleven-year-old boy. He was intensely hostile about his parents' divorce, and was activating these spirits because of it.[2]

"I was able to disperse the negative forces in the house by dealing with the boy's own negative feelings. He had been having 'dreams', for example, that he was not a Negro, but a Japanese. And also, an Indian witch doctor. When he told his mother this, he met with even more resistance.

"But when he told me, it was a different story. I've seen some evidence of reincarnation, and what this boy was calling up might have been the past lives where he had these powers. We talked, and he recognized me from one of his past lives. We got along fine, and the boy's hostility abated. And with it, the spirits dispersed."

Henry Rucker teaches classes in self-awareness development and psychic sciences. He has lectured and given classes and workshops throughout the United States at colleges, corporate organizations, and conventions. He travels abroad to do healings and lecturing.

For Rucker, psychic abilities are not inherited traits. However, he recognizes the characteristics of a healer in his oldest son. On occasion when he was young, his son, who can perceive deceased persons, would accompany Rucker on ghost-hunting rounds. As a team they worked to rid houses of negative forces. Sometimes the child performed exorcisms without assistance. Rucker considers this son, now an adult, to possess the same quality and range of psychic talent he has.

"In the name of Jesus, come out!" With this cry, Mother Ellerbee, evangelist and spiritual counselor, commands negative spirits who are obsessing her parishioners. "Some demons would say, 'We are not coming out!' " she says. Then the struggle intensifies, with the person's body rolling and thrashing around on the floor, and spitting out foam and pus. But the entity eventually flees at Mother Ellerbee's constant prayerful cries to God in her battle with it.

"Other demons use strategies," Mother Ellerbee continues. "They pretend they are angels of light. Some say, 'I'm fine!' " But the evangelist senses that the demon is still there, acting deceitfully, speaking as if it were the parishioner. "You lying demon!" Mother Ellerbee charges, and resumes her prayer in the exorcism process. She indicates that these spirits have intelligence, but it is used for evil. Mother Ellerbee perceives when a sickness is caused or aggravated by demon possession. She summons these demons out, identifying the illness with them. After a negative spirit's exit, pain and the symptoms of the illness leave. She works with medical doctors who believe in the power of spiritual prayer in the healing process.

At one meeting, a visiting woman, darkened by despondency and confusion, improved almost immediately after Mother Ellerbee laid hands on her. She almost glowed as she told the group how much better she felt. But before the gathering was over, a young girl across the room slipped from her chair to the floor, and lay there with her eyes rolled back. Discerning the sameness about the body's vibrations, Mother Ellerbee sensed the demon had transferred. Before dislodging the spirit again, Mother Ellerbee had all the spiritually vulnerable ushered from the room, and handed Bibles to others. The transferring spirit was finally exorcised.

In his work with Mother Ellerbee, her son, Clarence, often sees the effects of negative forces removed. In church settings, and prayer meetings, usually two or three spiritually strong and consecrated people stand around Mother Ellerbee while she lays her hands on people to command demons to come out in the name of Jesus. The ministrations may last five minutes or as long as five hours.

"The door for demon spirits to enter," Clarence relates, "is often opened by hatred, resentment, jealousy, fear, and the effects that drugs and alcohol have on the self. The deliberate use of rituals for evil intent, and other negative emotions and negative conditions, are also factors.

"There would be a definite change in the face and the voice and the eyes of the victim," Clarence says. "After exorcism, a look of peace comes into the eyes. With heavy demonic presence there is fog or darkness. But when it is cleared up, you can see light, and the person has a cleaner look. People would become free and healed of their emotions and bad habits."

Mother Ellerbee speaks of battles with evil presences even as a child, and of times she dispelled them by herself through calling upon the help of God. "My success in the physical world is the result of battles won in the spiritual world," she declares. "The moment you decide to give your life to God, negative forces will start to rail against you. The stronger I became was a direct result of overcoming dark forces."

"I can do an exorcism without seeing the person."

Near the beginning of their talk, Cora Keeton let the parents know she did not need to travel to Mississippi to work with their son; the problem would resolve through long-distance consultations. The boy's personality had changed, they told Cora in their call to Los Angeles. Described by them was a shift in the thirteen year old's personality which had been extreme and sudden. His good nature had given way to moodiness and unrestrained fury. School life became disordered; he blocked communication with everyone. In wild discharges of anger, he threatened family members and others with knives and other weapons. Not knowing what else to do, his parents finally had him admitted to a psychiatric hospital.

But they still were concerned about his recovery, and contacted Cora.

Remotely investigating the boy's psychic condition, Cora detected his space was contaminated by something that vibrated differently and lower. Its emanations were satanic. Through pervading the energy surrounding each parent, Cora perceived how the entity had been drawn to the group. It was through the mother! A storehouse of hostility and anger, she fed and activated the entity. The obsession entered the boy because he was the most vulnerable person in the family.

After a series of consultations, there was improvement in the conditions of the mother and son. The woman began dealing with her negative attitudes, and as a result the entity's power supply was appreciably diminished—eventually disappearing altogether.

When the boy was to be released from the hospital, Cora perceived where the negative spirit entered his auric space. Psychically she repaired the area, and strengthened his field so the entity could not return.

Born in Texas and raised in Los Angeles, Cora Keeton has a doctorate in metaphysics.

"I am doing more exorcisms since the veil between the visible and invisible is thinning. More souls are lighted up."

In another incident, not long ago, Cora returned home from Missouri, accompanied by two entities occupying a girl's body. She saw them both, the overwhelmed and the aggressor. The girl had become obsessed while channeling. Her body was taken over by a spiritually undeveloped female entity. Once the invading spirit gained control, its instability of personality and behavior led to the girl being placed in a psychiatric institution. After Cora caused the intruder to leave, as part of the recovery process she taught the former victim how to protect herself against future invasions and attacks. In addition, Cora gave the girl lessons in metaphysics, and trained her, expanding the abilities she had. Already the young person astral projected at will and communicated telepathically with animals.

"More earthbound souls are contacting me of late," Cora reveals. "I use my guides. There are three who have been with me a long time, and others come to help."

People troubled by malevolent spirits were coming to Jessica Marshall. This evil aspect of her clients' problems made her uneasy. Though she wanted to help, she was unsure for her own well-being, and uncertain of the future influences of negative spirit entities upon her.

It was about ten years ago that Jessica, metaphysical counselor and teacher, confronting this dilemma, thought seriously of abandoning her work. In the course of making a decision, she spoke to a great-aunt, a psychic experienced in working with candles, oils, and herbs to change energy and its influences on people. Her great-aunt's only response was that Jessica should pray to God to release her from her psychic gifts. Letting go of her gifts did not seem the right action to Jessica. While meditating, she confirmed her abilities were tools given her to help others. Hadn't she already used them for that reason? And now she would not allow negative entities to block her way of helping. She felt from this realization a renewal in commitment to her work. She further came to understand that her own spiritual growth was dependent upon her willingness to confront and overcome negative energy in any of its manifestations.

Jessica, a resident of Los Angeles, is co-founder of the Crenshaw Metaphysical Institute. In the tradition of her great-aunt, she sometimes uses oils, candles, and incense in exorcisms and other facets of her work.

"I can't very well counsel a person if I have no reality on what they are experiencing," she summarizes. "I know my experiencing these negative entities is for my own growth. In metaphysics, you never stop growing. You must learn to work at different levels."

"When this thing would happen to him, he would fly through the air 13 to 20 feet!" Peter Brown recalls. "He was possessed—literally possessed."

Peter James Brown, Jr. is pastor of Cathedral Temple of Divine Love in Chicago, and a psychic counselor. He indicates that Spirit gives him instruction on how to exorcise entities from possessed people.

"I got involved with this man when he stepped on some glass.

Only thirty minutes had lapsed but the wound looked as though it had been made a week or two before."

Peter had been called by a physician at the institution where the "flying" man was being observed. The doctor was unable to accept such phenomena. "It just couldn't be—it didn't fit anything!" The doctor advised the man's mother to find someone in the psychic field, so Peter was contacted.

"He could be sitting in a chair and talking normally, when all of a sudden—bingo!—it would be on. And just as suddenly as it came, it would go away," describes Peter.

Peter's guides through spirit writing revealed that the man was possessed; he had epilepsy, and there was deep conflict between him and members of his family. "That form of epilepsy behaves in such a way that if you were not observing it, you would not see it. It was an outgrowth of the spiritual kind of war going on within him." A course of treatment was developed, with the new information, which addressed both the physical and spiritual aspects and the conditions abated.

"I will tell you about a girl who had sixteen entities in her, and they tried to make her disembowel herself. She would come to church the first Sunday of the month. We usually had communion then. I could talk about anything other than the blood of Jesus Christ. If I talked about the blood of Jesus Christ, she would go off. She would scream like you've never heard except in a horror movie. Then she would be out of it for two or three days."

Peter took on this girl's case. Spirit gave instructions on how to oust the entities. In the process, Peter engaged in conversation with a being who was apparently the group's spokesperson.

" 'I'm not going anywhere!'

"I said, 'You have to!'

" 'No, I don't. I don't have to!'

"I asked, 'Why?'

" 'We're here by invitation. She likes us. She lets us in and we're going to stay.'

"I said, 'No, you can't do that.'

" 'Yes, we can!'

"They were talking through her. She had a lovely voice. But when this happened, her voice would drop about four octaves and it sounded just like a man was talking through her."

Following the instructions given by his disembodied

teacher-guides (through spirit writing) Peter forced the negative entities to withdraw from the girl. She stabilized after counseling, medical treatment, and dietary changes. She even went back to school and became a registered nurse. She has been doing very well for the past twelve or thirteen years; but she can't drink alcohol, or watch much television, for it was her indulgences in those activities that lured the negative spirits to her.

In the Cathedral Temple's brochure Peter explains, "All psychic phenomena has its roots in the Bible, and that Jesus demonstrated all its facets during his earth life and in addition said to his followers, 'These things that I do ye shall do and even greater.' "

CHAPTER SEVEN

Astral Projection

World-sated, setting her sails for enlightenment, she prayed.

But her thoughts were sucked up by low, astral-plane energies streaming through where she first opened the porthole to the spirit realm.

In waves, they wracked her.

Through the resulting dregs of darkness, on rough currents of unceasing and tormented sleep, she drifted.

In its redemptive roots, an ancient tree, dream-borne, reaching far beyond earthbound shores, capsized her wayward barge.

Set loose, water-cleaned, in new life she awakened.

. . . A paper-thin image of herself rose, floating out of the carcass, and rested itself somewhere above the stark white ceiling.[1]

Her perception changed, and she viewed the world from the eye of the image. The image watched quietly as the body adopted a grayish hue; the eyes grew cloudy; and the lips sealed themselves one to the other.

The chest no longer heaved up and down with the breath of life, and the heart ceased to pound out the terrifying drum rhythms . . .

From her view on the ceiling, the image saw the figure of a young girl come and touch the body, trying to arouse it, but receiving no answer, assumed it to be in deep sleep ...

Without warning, a voice—quite her own, yet more lovely—rose from the breast of the carcass and spoke, saying, "Get back in yo' body, Girl, you have work to do!"

No sooner had the command been given than a thin blue light appeared, streaming between body and soul. It flowed painlessly until they were one again, and the chest began to ebb and flow with a fresh spring air.

This excerpt, "Needy Winter," a story from her book *Jambalaya*, Luisah Teish explains is based on an actual occurrence she experienced herself.

"It happened a lot when I was a child," the author confides. "I used to think I was 'spacing out', daydreaming! As a youngster I had to be well-grounded because I was in a large family. I had a lot of responsibility. When my quiet time came, I would go sit in a closet or lay up on the roof. I know now that I did a lot of out-of-body travel, but I didn't know what to call it—at that time. They (my parents) just saw it as—well, she's seeing some spirits.

"I have a friendlier relationship with it now," says Luisah. "Traveling out and meeting other energies on other levels. I have better control of it. Things don't have to get dire before I can do it ... I can do it on decision, but that decision is not just left-brain. The urge to do it comes on. The urge is based on the need to do it. I recognize that the urge is there, and I surrender to the urge. Cooperate with the urge and I can do it.

"You lay down on your bed—you tense, and relax your muscles," Luisah goes on. "You give up fear of what you're going to meet out there. You make an attempt to direct where you are going to go. You make sure you stay corded to Earth so you don't get out there and get too comfortable. And you can deliberately go. There are other times, however, when I don't have all that forethought, and I lay down to go to sleep and I feel myself flying, or riding my magical bicycle, or being on a roller coaster, and I go somewhere."

Luisah speaks of an astral visit made to a gathering at her childhood home. "A couple of years ago, I had this dream of myself riding this magical bicycle, and I went home to my mother's house. When I went there some kind of reunion was going on. I could walk around and see people. In my dream, I came back here and didn't think anything of it, except—well, I went (in spirit) to Mama's house. The next day or so my mother called me and said that an aunt of mine whom I hadn't seen in twenty years had been there visiting, and she kept asking for me. Without knowing it—I was trying to answer her call."

Looking back at what she calls her "regenerating out-of-body experience," Luisah attributes it to a ceremony in which she participated. "There was the giving-away of my possessions. There was the releasing of all my relationships. The abandoning of all my hopes and expectations. And I truly believe that it is that ceremony which caused me to have the out-of-body experience, rather than dying. Rather than just getting violently ill.

"I am interested in people recognizing that the spirit is layered, and that when it is time for an old layer to come off—when it is time for the snake to shed her skin—we feel a death coming on. But it is not necessarily a physical death. The blindness of materiality made me think that I was supposed to take myself out physically," she explains. "In another culture, in another time, I would have had an elder that I could go to and say: 'Life is perfectly rotten, I don't fit in, I can't handle it.'

"They would have had rituals to symbolically take me through that death, and let me feel and experience it, and then they would have been present for the rebirthing!"

"My spirit is leaving!" Clarence's mother used to announce to her children. She would retire to bed for as long as a week, on occasion, in out-of-body states, after such statements. Clarence Ellerbee remembers friends and neighbors saying they saw and talked with her on the streets. But at the time of those sightings, Clarence knew his mother's physical body was home, in bed, in a trance.

When the Spirit is with her, Mother Estelle Ellerbee moves outside the body. A speaker-in-tongues, evangelist and healer, she is often enveloped in rapture consciousness. She leaves to Clarence, her son, companion, and co-pastor, the management of most of her temporal affairs. He has been her assistant and her communicator since he was seventeen years old. He knew even as a small child that his life's work was in spiritual work with his mother.

Clarence observes that his mother's body becomes set and cold after she leaves it. Sometimes he fears she might not return to it, but hesitates to call her back, not wanting to disturb her work. In an effort to quell his fears, Mother Ellerbee told him to use his intuition, get the help of another psychic, but never to call the paramedics.

"My mother told me when she and my father first married he didn't know she was psychic," narrates Clarence. "He was a little 'devilish' and kept seeing other women." Once his mother, unembodied, went where his father was with another woman. She saw the street location, the house number, the details of the residence, and her husband with his friend. She astounded her husband by giving him a complete description of his clandestine outing when he returned home.

"Twenty-five years ago our family had just moved to Brooklyn. We didn't know anyone in the apartment complex yet, and no one knew my mother was psychic," Clarence remembers. "The cries of a woman in the apartment next door could be heard, one night. She was being beaten. As this occurred, Mother Ellerbee went into a trance state. The cries abruptly ended, and silence followed. "The day after, this neighbor came to our door," Clarence recalls. The awestricken woman told Mother Ellerbee that she saw her appear all of a sudden, in the turmoil of the beating. Mother Ellerbee then stood behind the woman's husband and prevented a further blow. She went on to say she felt waves of warmth from Mother Ellerbee's presence during that visit. In later years, this woman took up missionary work.

A particular night, in the 1960s, Mother Ellerbee was in the South with her son doing revivals, preaching from the pulpit. While she was preaching and healing, a friend, Reverend Morris in Mt. Kisco, New York, felt a presence in his room. Opening his eyes he saw Mother Ellerbee. Later, he told the Ellerbee family that a calming energy, a warmth emanated from her etheric body. Up to that time, Reverend Morris had been frustrated in writing a book, finally having to stop production on it. He claims that from her astral visit, Mother Ellerbee inspired him to resume his writing, and complete his work.

"I became interested in the import business when I couldn't find an African dress. Eventually I owned three African import stores in San Francisco, Berkeley and Vallejo."

Catherine Wilson, an herbalist and healer, works out of the San

Francisco Bay area.

"I found myself astral traveling when I was in the store," Catherine recounts. "I would visit places in Africa. I knew the languages and the land. Africans who visited the store were surprised that I knew their language and their customs." The places where she traveled were familiar, though she had never visited them in this life. She felt a deep affinity for the continent. At her store, among the goods and artifacts of African nations, she seemed to be drawn out of her body. But the out-of-body travels to Africa ceased once she left her import business.

An astral traveler from her twenties, these projections into remote physical spaces were not new to her. "I have been told by any number of mediums that I didn't come into my body until I was around the age of twelve. That is why I don't recall much of my childhood," she confirms.

"I have always as a child dreamed I had out-of-body experiences all along. I knew I wasn't in my body when I was little—that I was out."

Carolyn Marcus, an astrologer, social worker, and college instructor, teaches at Morgan State College in Baltimore.

"I could see all these things happening and being so real for no reasons. The feeling, the color, the sound, more intense than in real life. So I started writing down all my dreams. Some, I think, have been visions because I am right there. I go into a sweat and my eyes are open. It's just an intuitive kind of feeling that I know this is not just another dream. Something tells me that. It is kind of indescribable because it is a feeling. It's hard to talk about. I've tried to write some down. Just describing my feelings and the impact some of these experiences have had on me, I cannot come up with the words!

"When I have a dream that is very powerful to me, I write it down, I reflect on it and I ask myself: What am I supposed to do with this? I might not know the meaning of it for a week or two, maybe a month, maybe a year.

"But I never forget. And then things start happening and then I can piece things together. Sometimes the dream is in symbols and I say, Oh, that's what I'm supposed to do! That's what that meant!"

Carolyn comments she tends to choose companions and activities that are spiritually oriented. She seldom attends professional conferences unless they are about non-traditional ways to work with people. "I would rather be around people who can teach me more, who are up.

"In 1981 I began to take a serious look at Christianity. I decided to read the Bible from page one. While I was doing that I was having heavy dreams or visions. They really made an impact on me. I can relate to the Bible, the teachings and the principles involved. They can be used. I have respect for it.

"I don't have much respect for organized religion. A lot of churches that I have come in contact with I would call 'Christian country clubs'. I know now I do not need a church to go where I'm going to end up anyway."

Through a metaphysical organization Carolyn undertook studies on astral travel, finding they taught what she was naturally doing. "I've been interacting and learning some things that I cannot ignore. I know that I have to share all this information that's coming to me. If I hold it in, I know I will suffer—my health or whatever. This kind of information was not meant to be kept to oneself. It was meant to be shared with people for a universal kind of cause. I have felt myself become more universal, and to me that is very significant. Because it was like I was a different person."

When asked how astrology and metaphysics have affected her relationships with people, Carolyn responds: "It has enhanced in some cases, and in other cases it has been, 'How could she be serious about that!' They will put it on my personality. They would say, 'You know Carolyn has always been way out!' They knew I was willing to try things that other people wouldn't be willing to try.

"The older I get and more spiritual I become, the less need I have for those kinds of roots. I can look back, and I don't say it is a waste of time. I learned a lot of things, and I apparently had to go through all that I did go through to get where I am now," she reflects.

"When I was young I did astral travel naturally, in a dream state. But then I was afraid I was going to die or be unable to get back into my body. As a child, I knew if I couldn't get back into my body, I would be dead.

"I've learned since that has happened. I know I'm not alone. I know that God is always there and will protect me. I know that all I have to do is call on the Lord, and I'm delivered from whatever danger there is. That has happened to me thousands of times in dreams.

"All I would have to say is, 'Jesus, Lord!' And I am delivered! I don't care what was coming at me, to do to me whatever. I always remember to think on the Lord.

"I know from experience all you have to do is call—that's all you have to do."

In 1831 Rebecca Cox Jackson thought she was dying. The following observations of the experience she later recorded in her journal.

> Now, when my spirit left my body I was as sensible of it as I would be now to go out of this house and come in it again. All my senses and feeling and understanding was in my spirit. I found my body was no more than a chair to me, or any other piece of thing.[2]

Jackson, a preacher, a Shaker eldress and founder of an African American Shaker community in Philadelphia, further noted:

> After encouraging Samuel to be faithful, then taking leave of him in prayer, I left, passing out at my feet. I went directly west, I turned neither to the right nor to the left. I passed through all substance—nothing impeded my way. I went a straight course, came down to a river. It run north and south. I stood on the bank. I then thought, "Here is Jordan—here I have got to suffer." I found, when I came out of the body it was with all ease and without any suffering, so I now found I had this suffering to go through.
>
> As I stood on the bank looking across, I saw a large mountain, a path which went up from this river on to the top of this mountain. It was very narrow. I saw travelers going up this path. Some was further up the path than others (for two could not walk in it abreast). They all walked as if they were tired.
>
> On the south side of this mountain was a great deal of ice in great flakes. In the midst of it was a man with a boat, atrying to get it out. I thought he was the one that had taken them over and he was acoming for me. I seen his eyes were fastening upon me. And while I thus thought, I heard a voice from above say, "You must go around the Mediterranean first." This voice sounded over my right shoulder. It was a man's

voice. I turned to go down this Jordan, which was south—I thought that was the way to the Mediterranean—but I was turned right around the way from whence I came and returned home.

I reentered my body. Samuel was weeping over me and said, "You have been dead some time." I spoke to him and then left as before. This I did three times, saw all and heard all, as at the first, spoke each time.

Then I passed out at my chest, going right through the ceiling and the roof. About twelve feet above the roof there was a cluster of angels on a cloud. They took me up a great height in the air, gave me much instruction, brought me back to the same place. Then I returned to the house, reentered my body, spoke to Samuel and he to me. This I done three times. The last time, when I returned, I found Samuel in prayer, crying to God in the bitterness of his spirit to only spare me a little longer.

I went three times to this Jordan, three times into the air with these angels. This made six times I left the body. These were all new scenes to me. (Thus it pleased God to show me the difference between the man and the mold ...)

These are excerpts from journals Rebecca Jackson kept throughout her life. The autobiographical materials have been compiled and edited by Jean Humez into the book *Gifts of Power: The Writings of Rebecca Jackson, Black Visionary, Shaker Eldress.*

"I was cooking dinner in the kitchen. I began to hear this vibration in my head. Then I felt this pull on my chin; my chin was pulled toward the light bulb on the wall. All of a sudden I became hypnotized by the light bulb. I was pulled out of my body. I looked down and saw myself with big, bulgy eyes, holding on to the dish rag. I was drawn further and further out of my body, up to the ceiling. And then I was passing through space at incredible speeds."

Hayward Coleman, Los Angeles entertainer, speaks of an astral projection experienced while he lived in Paris. "I got closer and closer to this disc and as I drew close—the more of a melting feeling I had. I thought, 'Oh God, I'm not worthy enough to be close to Thee.'

"And the vibration that pulled me out of my body began to vibrate in a way of saying, 'This is how I want you to be every moment of your life.'

"Then I found myself released. I found myself back in the room—up on the ceiling. I was slowly lowered back into my body. I was afraid because at first I thought I was dead and I would never get back into my body.

"I thought, 'This is how I am dying.'

"When I was released and back into my body, I dropped everything and started crying. I could see auras around everything. I could see atoms of the curtains ... Vibrant colors. My body was glowing. That was the beginning."

Delilah Grayer was uneasy, stopped by what her daughter, Bakara Oni, said a few minutes earlier. The five-year-old child had softly intoned: "Mommy, someone is so sick." As was her habit, the child repeated some of the phrase—"so sick." It didn't make sense, then, but within a week, Delilah, who had no idea it was she who was ill, had to be hospitalized.

Under intensive treatment, which required blood transfusions, Delilah used visualization concepts to accelerate healing. At one point of her self-healing work, she became aware of her astral body coming out, unlocking. "My higher self moved out from my head, first, and feet, last. I began to walk on top of myself. As I walked, I walked on my forehead, nose, chest, all the way down. I bent over and lifted up my stomach, my insides, and put them back." She then went back into her body with the realization she was healed.

Professionally trained in social work and clinical psychology, Delilah combines these skills with her psychic gifts to give consultations through her social-psychic consulting practice in Cleveland, Ohio.

"I began dancing on top of the world ... I was traveling all over the world! To Nigeria, Haiti, places I had visited."

She astrally met with a friend, Edna, who had died five months earlier. "I went and visited her, but it was like being in a tunnel. I saw her. She was tall, and was in an armored dress. It was like of mail, really heavy.

"I said, 'Edna, Oh, Edna! I really like talking to you. You came to the hospital. Now I'm with you and I feel so peaceful. I don't know if I want to go back.'

"She told me I had to go back. She kept staying, 'Stay back!' And she moved away from me."

In further contemplating the experience, Delilah remarks it was the first time she didn't fear death. "I was in that state of consciousness where I could feel I could have a choice."

During her astral travel, Delilah reconfirmed her spiritual direction. "My mission in this life and my lesson is: To let go, and let God. And that is exactly why I am healed, because I let go, and let God."

"Good Lord, man! You're two-thirds in the spirit world!"

"A medium once told me that. I think my mother would have agreed with her. When I was young, I would go into trances, completely forgetting what I was supposed to be doing.

"I didn't discover what it was until I was in my forties. I found myself outside of my body. I've seen this body. I've always been a dreamer. I didn't realize what was happening. I thought my mind was just outside.

"When I was young, I also investigated all religions, including the Far Eastern ones which impressed me a great deal."

Richmond Barthe relates he has viewed with certainty his body while outside of it. He got up too quickly once, feeling weak. He looked back, seeing he had left his body behind. He lay down again, rising slowly this time with his body.

An artist of the Harlem Renaissance period, Barthe has received national and international recognition for his work. He has done hundreds of sculptures since 1927 when he first began his work. He has been called the Creole Michelangelo and compared with Rodin. In East Pasadena where he lives, a street has been named in his honor.

Barthe came back from one of his out-of-body travels with the insight needed to complete a sculpture of Christ. "This statue is six feet tall," he indicates. "It is looking right through you. It makes some people uncomfortable. I thought it was the best thing I'd ever done by far, but there was something disturbing about it. I couldn't figure out what it was. I checked it. I couldn't find anything wrong. So I decided, 'I've done the best I can. I can't find out what is wrong with it.'

"So then I think, 'I shall have to ask for help.' I went to my bedroom, sat on my bed, took my shoes, belt, and collar off. I didn't want anything to physically attract me. I meditated on my problem, and asked for help.

"Soon every bodily sensation disappeared. My only consciousness was right here," he describes, pointing to his third-eye area. "The rest of my body just disappeared, as far as feeling went. Suddenly I found myself floating out of my forehead. I went up through the ceiling, through the clouds. I was going up again, now swinging to the right, now swinging to the left. I found myself way out in the outer stratosphere. It was better than flying because I didn't have to wave my arms. I was just relaxed and floating up like a toy balloon, being let out with hundreds of miles of thread.

"I don't know how long I was up there. Suddenly I landed with a thud. I found myself sitting on my bed on 8th Avenue. I came out of the room, I'd forgotten why I went in. I heated my dinner, sat down, ate it, but forgot to taste it. I was trying to hang on to the feeling of floating up there in outer space. I finished dinner, went into the kitchen to wash the plates.

"I was looking at the wall when suddenly I saw my Christ figure. The right hand was out like this," Barthe gestures. "The right arm was wrong. That wasn't the Christ I was doing. I wasn't doing the religious symbol, I was doing the man! As I had seen him. Not the religious symbol—that was tacked on hundreds of years later!

"That was what was annoying me—I couldn't see it! So I lowered his hand and now he is looking right at you. And I called it, 'Come Unto Me.' "

While the statue was still in his studio, Barthe had another experience with this work. An elderly woman came to commission him to do a plaque for her church. "She asked if she could see what was under the sheet. I removed the blanket, and she looked directly into his eyes and he was looking at her. That woman's attention never left his eyes, never looked at his face, hands, his feet, or anything. She never saw the rest of him. She was locked into those eyes as if she had been hypnotized. I sat on the model's stand, smoking, watching her face. Gradually her eyes filled with water, tears ran down. I don't think she was conscious of them, she didn't wipe them away. Finally she took a deep breath. She wiped her face.

"She said, 'Mr. Barthe, I want to thank you for what you have done for me this morning.'

"I said, 'What is that?'

"She said, 'Yesterday, when I made the appointment, I was feeling fine. I went to bed last night feeling fine. This morning when I woke up—I was so depressed. I could hardly get out of bed. I thought of calling you and canceling the engagement, but I thought it wouldn't be fair to you. I forced myself to come. When I got here I had to pull myself up by the bannister. I felt as if there was a heavy, heavy load upon my shoulders. Mr. Barthe, the load has been lifted, and I feel light and happy. Thank you very much.' "

Barthe reflects, "She was cured by just looking into the eyes of a piece of clay. Her faith did it—I didn't!

"The body is the house you live in," Barthe summarizes his astral plane experiences.

It was as if, from a position slightly above and behind my head, I were observing my body and its movements in a way that turned a spotlight on my body and made the most familiar things seem new and incredibly strange.[3]

In the publication *The Lives of Jean Toomer: A Hunger For Wholeness*, Cynthia Earl Kerman and Richard Eldridge have presented Jean Toomer's perception of himself rising above his body, viewing it from the outside, as it continued, apparently on its own, to walk and communicate.

An early disciple and teacher in the George Gurdjieff Movement, an applied philosophical system, author Jean Toomer brought the teachings of the Russian philosopher and author to Harlem during the Renaissance period. Toomer basically followed a life-long commitment to spiritual development for himself and to the sharing of knowledge with others, such as his experiences in being on other planes of existence.

His recognition of being separate from the body also is conveyed in the autobiographical work, *Exile into Being*.

It was as though an enormous weight had lifted, and (the) body was light and free. I am sure the weight of latent fear and insecurity, the weight of active ego-drivers and mental ambitions, had lifted. I know that me and I were lifting from the body, and to whatever extent I had been imprisoned in it, the body was relieved to be rid of its prisoner. It was as though a life-long strain had been departed, and (the) body was pliant.[4]

"I had such a strong sense to leave my body that I had to sit down. It was around 1971, and I was at the table with my son. He held on to my hands. Otherwise I might have stayed out there. He was holding on to my hands as I flew out fast."

As an informed and comparatively relaxed explorer in spirit form since childhood, June Gatlin now knows not to sleep on her back unless she wishes to "go out."

"At six through fourteen years old, I had outstanding astral travels. But now I am in more control when I fly." The singer and spiritual healer says there is sometimes the sense of rushing as she leaves her body. On her journeys she has looked through the eyes of an eagle, and is aware of having flown through time. "I have flown back to Egypt, and to the future. I have learned it (time) is all the same," she informs. She reflects that in its purest form the separation from the body brings a feeling of well-being. Not unsimilar to one's experience in the death process—of releasing from all worldly attachments. While separate from the body, she witnesses the presence of negativity, in the form of degenerate spirits, who inhabit the bodies of persons who exit impulsively, and leave their bodies unprotected. June has gained a sense of command over her astral travels. She prepares her body prior to moving out of it, and maintains an attachment during her absence. She describes her state of being in her astral travels as "a peaceful, wonderful existing!"

"I experienced going out of my body as a beam of light. I was light shooting through the cosmos. Then I became afraid because I wasn't sure I could come back to my body."

San Francisco Bay area resident Arisika Razak is a midwife, healer, and teacher of spiritual dance.

Arisika expresses her spirituality as evolving out of multi-cultural bases. One of these is Native American religious concepts and practices; another is out of African sacred traditions. A third stems from Wicca, a religion centered around female deities.

"Dreams are important in my life. I have a habit now, when I dream about people, I call them. I do want to know if something is up," she relates.

"I once had a dream that was a clear, clear dream. I came out of the dream with a clear message that I should try for midwivery school. I realized that all my connections were about things I did with my hands and my body. That's where my greatest skills and communications were. The dream told me that my fulfillment was around that.

"I didn't at first consider myself a healer. I remember going once to a congress and a woman came up to me.

" 'You're a healer, what are you doing with it?' she inquired.

" 'I am a midwife,' I replied. I hadn't considered my midwivery as healing because I don't consider birth sickness.

"Now I do think of myself as a healer, but I think of myself as a peacemaker, and a bridge between the races at some level, and starting to pull together peace.

"Part of who I am, part of being able to take up a world cosmology, is that I grew up in Harlem. My second mother was a Japanese woman. It was her family that I lived with when I was fifteen and sixteen. I am someone who has had people who are not black as significant others in my life ever since I was a child. I think that has kept me more open than other people."

She blesses some of the babies of the drug-addicted women giving birth in the clinic setting in which she works. She believes that if she doesn't say a blessing for some of the babies, no one would during the whole pregnancy—not even the mothers. From her viewpoint, every child is supposed to come in wanted. Many of the women Arisika sees do not consider birth as a spiritual event. The births happen in the middle of much turmoil. "The birth is happening when the woman is trying desperately to knit together the threads of her life, and it is real, real difficult."

Sometimes Arisika gets someone who wants a spiritual birth. She remarks how much she loves doing births that way, infrequent as they are. She does not impose her own spiritual beliefs on pregnant women. But she teaches relaxation techniques. "I try to encourage them to bring their spiritual beliefs to the birth of their child.

"I do believe we are light—energy. When we die we go back to being that pure energy," affirms Arisika.

CHAPTER EIGHT
By Way of Rites

Her body split while she meditated on Him.

"Elohim ... Elohim ... Elohim ... "

The right separated from the left. Each half compelled toward an opposing vector.

"Elohim ... Elohim ... Elohim ... "

Then came new orientation:

Her right eye, directed, took the lead whenever she was to spiritually see or read.

And she began to hear etheric-world sounds, first, through her left ear.

"Elohim ... Elohim ... Elohim ... "

Her heart burst while she meditated to surrender. Red and spherical, the twelve heart drops dispersed.

They were drawn together again, to be absolved, then absorbed into the projected stream of her returning.

"Elohim ... Elohim ... Elohim ... "

"It is a very revealing thing to be involved in Tarot. It is not just a device by which we divinate and tell fortunes. There's a spiritual and philosophical aspect of the Tarot that is fantastic! These very cards are symbolic in finding one's true inner self." So asserted Henry Rucker of Chicago in an interview with his friend, Dane Headley, in the early 1970s.

Presently a lecturer and teacher in spiritual development, Henry describes his earlier work with Tarot and palmistry.

"One day I said, 'How about it, God? Can I quit?'

"I just walked up and quit the post office and the Board of Education and never looked back. That was 1968.

"I had been working for the post office, and I had a reputation: He never does any work! All my supervisors and coworkers would always come and pull me out of a work section for counseling.

" 'What do you see about my kid?'

"Coworkers would complain and not want me for their coworker. If people were going to come up and ask about their families, I reflected, if I was going to do all this—why should I stay here in this place that I really hate?"

Henry took college courses, but these brought him no satisfaction. He had a strong urge to utilize his intuitive abilities. "But I was afraid to go out and say, 'I see this about you.' I needed a hook!"

In 1954, a book on palmistry caught his attention. "I learned palmistry and I've become an expert, they say," Henry recounts. "That started me on that particular path. There was a need to be seen in a different light. My first wife was a brilliant girl, a chemistry and economics major—heavy, heavy, heavy! She played the cello, piano, organ, and was into photography.

"We used to have people come over. Malcolm X, John Ali were good friends, though I was not a Muslim. We had discussion groups. I'm not academic. Reading is not my thing. They read and they were talking about Marcel Proust, Joyce, Jean Paul Sartre, etc. I felt inadequate.

"I said, 'I need something for myself: everybody is an expert!' Henry explains how, using palmistry at gatherings, he began reading people. "If a person throws his hand up, I take a mental picture of it and I've got it. I became the center of attention. Whereas I did not try to keep up with them academically, I had my own little thing, so I had a lot of attention.

"People would say, 'What do you see about this? Tell me about myself.'

"From '54 on I started to use that as my 'life-of-the-party', my 'thing'. No one competed with me and everybody wanted to know what I was into. Everybody wants to be recognized. After that point I was never the one who would sit back. My wife said I began to dominate the conversation!"

Henry first taught palmistry, then Tarot. Teaching people how to meditate on Tarot followed. And then he began teaching psychic development, and lecturing as a palmist and as a psychic. "It's not just the Tarot," Henry concluded in his talk with Headley. "Philosophically, yes, these cards mean something; but more important, the symbolism has a fantastic effect on the subconscious. It has a way of bringing the personality in tune with the higher-self through the agency and the vehicle of the subconscious."

Sue Avent's experience with the Ouija board was short-lived. Her older sister brought it home, and after a brief interlude, her mother threw it out. But not before Sue heard voices and picked up spirits through the board. In that context, she met her guides. She was seventeen. "Before I used the Ouija board I didn't have a singing voice. The guides work through me when I sing."

Sue has meditated since she was twelve. Even then, she felt she had lived more than one lifetime.

Her childhood home is Ohio. She has recently settled in Ithaca, New York. She studied metaphysics and received a doctorate.

She works with guides. One named Bruce writes through her. While looking at a person, she receives pictures. "I pick up what the person has created for himself." Sue can see what a person is doing who is geographically miles away from her. And she has created mental illusions which another has viewed. Sue counsels and teaches through the Tarot cards, automatic writing, and direct psychic readings. She is also a practitioner of magic. She describes as one of her objectives, "I want to help people to realize that the source of happiness comes from within, and that they can create it for themselves."

Kenneth Dickkerson writes, "Many times people ask me if they can use the I Ching cubes for gambling on numbers, horses, or whatever. I tell them you can use it for that purpose, but it does not guarantee you will win. These tools (I Ching, Tarot cards, astrology, etc.) were not given to mankind for the purpose of gambling. In a sense, they take the gamble out of a situation when used properly. This is ancient wisdom, given to humanity to help us make right decisions in the way we live our lives."

Kenneth is a New York City astrologer and Kirlian photographer who teaches divination techniques to individuals and groups. He is the inventor of the I Ching cubes and Astro Stones which are divination tools.

"I use Tarot cards and astrology. I wouldn't consider myself an expert in any of those—because as you use them you find out there is so much more. I will probably be a student of those things as long as I am on this planet."

In his early twenties, Kenneth became very depressed about society. Reading a book on "cosmic consciousness" changed him. "It gave me hope. I knew the world was not going to be destroyed."

He became involved in spiritual groups. He gathered more information from the Rosicrucians on cosmic consciousness, and he read about reincarnation. "In reading books from all different groups, I felt like I already knew this information. It reminded me of something I had somehow forgotten."

Kenneth tells of when "I started my own business. A picture frame shop. I had training in art work. I painted. But in 1973, I decided I had had it with the art, and cut it out. I started to get more in this present line.

"A girlfriend said, 'Why did you stop painting?'

"I said, 'I know I'm not supposed to be painting. I knew it in my guts.'

"She said, 'Did you ask I Ching?'

"I said I didn't have to because I knew it in my guts. She insisted I ask the I Ching. The I Ching agreed.

"My goal is to turn people on to an ancient line, to teach people how to read for themselves."

When Alvin Lock studies a ball of natural crystal, he sees images and scenes which are significant to the person receiving the reading. Water in a glass, Tarot cards, and palmistry are other means by which he becomes attuned to the energies around the person.

"People don't realize it wouldn't do any good if they couldn't change whatever you tell them. And many times you tell them something and it is very important, and they change it! That's the only reason you tell them. If there was a deep pit over there, and the person knows it, he can go around it. Why fall in it! That's the only reason messages do any good."

Born in Valley Mills, Texas, Alvin resides in Jacksonville, Florida. He gives personal consultations, workshops, and lectures on psychic and spiritual development throughout the country.

In his late teens, he became aware of his inner knowing of Truth. He shared it with friends, and the things he told them often happened as he said.

Alvin believes "The One Mind, the Universal Mind, you tune in to it. All things are there."

At his birth, both Pepe and his mother were pronounced dead; but they were removed from the morgue at his aunt's insistence. She knew well this tendency among her relatives to go into deathlike states. This was not the first time that some of them had to be rescued. Pepe's mother recalled seeing the whole drama from outside of her body, and aiding in the rescue of herself and baby.

Born in Texas, Pepe Washington remembers that even before he learned to talk, well before two, that discarnate beings came to visit him. Sometimes there were voices which no embodied person around could hear except him. His grandfather, a Pakistani, encouraged Pepe's psychic growth in adolescence by teaching him yoga.

Pepe's main activities and interests are in teaching, in preparing people for the New Age. He has appeared on television and radio programs. These are some of the ways through which Pepe Washington of Los Angeles counsels, instructs, and predicts: African cowrie shells, psychometry, tea leaves, sand, playing cards, telepathic transmissions, candle flame, auras, water, colors, runes, and spirit contact.

Independently, and as a member of a private police agency, he works with law enforcement agencies in solving murders, and in the search for missing persons, especially children.

Pepe served in the Vietnam War. During combat, he experienced increasing anxiety centering around his inability to see an enemy who might approach at night. His solution was to will himself night vision! Even now he can still read in complete darkness.

She went searching to understand her gift better. Born with the veil, she had heard voices and seen visions since childhood. She had been told by a Spiritualist she was going to do the work.

In Haiti, where she first traveled, there were no clues for her. Then on a second trip to Brazil, Mary Bivens sat at a table with Portuguese Spiritualists. A translator was there who asked everyone to do what they could do. She prayed. When Mary was through praying, they told her she was ready for the work, and to go home and do the work. "I do mine through prayer. I work through prayers," Mother Mary Bivens affirms.

"I was strictly working with the Spirit. Whatever the Spirit led me to do, I did. Wherever the Spirit told me to go, I went. The way I work, I work with the Spirit, and the guides. There is a guide for everything. I worked with the hills, the mountains, the rivers, the lakes, the oceans, the canals, the railroads, and the road crossings. I had to go to these places. I went as far as Colombia, South America, up in the mountains. Just wherever the Spirit would lead me to go, that's what I did. I did everything I had to do. I had rituals. I went through rituals and everything."

A man deep in litigation came to her for help. Discerning his innocence, she agreed. The night the man's case went before the jury for a verdict, he called Mary from court. "They are in there cursing, banging, and going on. I'm frightened!"

Mary said okay and then she went into her prayer room. "I got down on my knees and began to pray and cry out to God. 'What is it I'm not doing? Show me what I have to do!' "

Spirit said, "You have to get in your car and go down to the jailhouse." Up to that point, Mary had not gone there.

"When I got there I said, 'What am I to do now?' And Spirit said, 'Just stand right here and pray.'

"I stood there and prayed. I wasn't there thirty minutes when I looked up and saw the cameras flashing, and people running. He saw me, he ran to me and said, 'God is so good! We did it, I'm a free man!' "

Mary grows herbs in her backyard for use in cleansing baths and rituals. Spirit directs her in making remedies for the spiritually and physically sick.

"I thank God for what He has done for me."

Young professional people in Miami, where she resides, turn to her with their troubles. Some come wanting to know more about Christ and to join her prayer band. These individuals have worked with Mother Mary Bivens in community projects, such as helping youth to obtain jobs. She has participated with medical school staff at the University of Florida as a consultant on indigenous healing. She visits hospitals and prays for the sick. "Even if they don't get a physical healing, they get a mental healing. If you learn to live with your sickness, you can survive."

Henry Dutton's son and namesake describes his deceased father as an individual who had "deep instinct and good intuition."

A native of Louisiana, the elder Dutton gave up plans for a career in medicine to pursue his interest in palmistry. A counselor whose method was palmistry based, Dutton gave consultations for more than thirty-five years out of his office in Chicago.

"My father had good ability at knowing," his son looks back. "He could see things and tell of them way ahead of time."

Paschal Beverly Randolph, a physician and philosopher, received his final Initiation in the Supreme Grand Dome of the Order in Paris in June, 1850. On that same occasion, he was given the absolute right to establish the Rose Cross Lodge in America.

Randolph wrote *Ravalette: The Rosicrucian's Story*, published in 1861. Although labeled fiction, it is a mystical treatise. As such, it is a repository of his beliefs and experiences.

> I had already become a Rosicrucian, had passed through
> five degrees, had visited the Orient and was about to go again,
> had learned many dark and solemn mysteries, had instructed

in several degrees of magic, knew all about the Elixir of Life, the power of Will, the art of reading others' destinies, of constructing and using magic mirrors, and how to discover mines of precious metal ... [1]

We proclaim the Omnipotence of Will! and we declare practically, and by our own achievements demonstrate, the will of man to be a supreme and all-conquering force when once fairly brought into play, but this power is only negatively strong when exerted for merely selfish or personal ends; when or wherever it is called into action for good ends, nothing can withstand its force. Goodness is Power; wherefore we take the best of care to cultivate the normal Will, and thus render it a mighty and powerful engine for Positive Good. You cannot deceive a true Rosicrucian, for he soon learns how to read you through and through, as if you were a man of glass ... The Temple teaches its acolytes how to rebuild this regal faculty of the human Soul—the Will; how to strengthen, purify, expand and intensify it.

Paschal Beverly Randolph was born in New York City on October 8, 1825.

For seventy years, James Spurgeon Jordan practiced "herb doctoring supplemented with conjure work" in Maney's Neck Township, North Carolina, where, born in 1871, he spent his entire life.

Written by F. Roy Johnson, *The Fabled Doctor Jim Jordan*, provides a description of how Jordan's uncle, Allen Vaughan, a conjure man, taught him around 1890 to "read the cards and mix up herbs to control the spirits."

Jordan's cousin, Josephine Minton, known for her skills as a midwife, herb doctor, and conjure woman, taught him patient diagnosis, the effective administering of herbs, and how to read palms. From his mother, whose knowledge about herbs was regarded extraordinary, he first learned of plants and their remedies.

By 1906, neighbors were calling Jordan a root doctor, and telling of his "strange powers," his sister, Jennie Mae, was to recollect later. A nephew, in remembering the early days of Jordan's practice, recalled how he would search for a certain root or medicine to help a patient. In some instances, the root doctor would have the patient wait while he "would go into the woods, stay an hour or more; come out, stop in the field, and look into the sky in a study about fifteen minutes."[2]

In the community, he was known to have a "frank and objective manner in personal and business matters." He was considered "accommodating and helpful to others; fair and liberal in business." As his reputation grew, people came considerable distances for his advice and treatment. It was said of Jordan that he could "cast off spells, get you out of trouble, find things, perform magic, and treat with medicine."

Years ago, Lloyd Strayhorn went to an astrologer who said his chart indicated he had died! Lloyd immediately knew to what he was referring. At ten years old, while hiding during a game of "Ring-A-Levio," he thought, 'Wouldn't it be great to light a fire cracker and put in the gas tank of the car nearby!' Every time I lighted it—it went out. When I finally lighted it, one of the bigger boys came around, so I just ran off."

About ten years later, but before the astrological reading, Lloyd awoke in a cold sweat over the incident. He realized what he had almost done. "It's in things like that I realize that there is Somebody out there, watching over the kid. I said to myself, 'This is my second life.' "

Born and raised in Harlem, Lloyd's strong affinity for that community is conveyed in his firm statement that he has no plans ever to leave it.

"When I was real tiny, five or six," he recalls, "I had a dream I was over the table and I could see myself, my parents and my sister. I was up in the air near the ceiling looking down at us.

"I have a better understanding of the Universe and the Creation through this study (occult sciences) than from going to theological school," he concludes.

From 1979, Lloyd has had a syndicated column as a numerologist with 120 newspapers. He has hosted a radio show in New York City since 1981. His first book on numerology was published in 1980.

The faith which imbued his life as an altar boy and later as a student at Virginia Union University, a theological seminary, continues to inspire him. At one time he thought of becoming a minister, but then his life took a different direction.

Introduced to numerology in 1969, Lloyd recognized it as the compatible means through which he could express what he wanted to do in his life. "I want to understand people and to help people understand themselves," he affirms.

James Black was considered by many of his colleagues one of the foremost practitioners of astrology—a master.

He was self-educated in the field. In 1973 he was seventy-seven years old with thirty students under his instruction. He had been casting and interpreting charts for over forty years. His remaining goal was to convey the holiness of astrology to African Americans.

The Chicago astrologer refused to counsel some people. If he sensed an individual could not confront information on weakness, loss, or damage that showed up in his or her chart, he would give no further sessions to that person.

Black taught that the dedicated astrologer is characterized by willingness to be of service. Helping people is more important to the earnest astrologer than monetary profit.

Some years ago, Don Tanney Hill's aunt made him aware of his intuitivity. A perceiver herself, she encouraged him to learn more of this aspect in himself.

Of childhood, Don says, "I do recall having conversations with people who weren't necessarily there—physically there. Information was given to me on how to do something. I didn't hear them or see them. I was just aware of the information. I would get an imprint on how to do it."

For three years he took classes in self-awareness, learned psychometry, photoanalysis, the Tarot cards, and how to do straight psychic readings. "My interest came through in healing. Every time I do the reading, I feel I'm doing a healing, a psychic healing. A person has come away from the reading with a little bit more knowledge as to the control of their own destiny. Because that is basically what we are doing," explains the parapsychologist.

Don counsels exceptional children. "As you get in touch with the year 2000, more and more New Age children come up. Some of the children may have been considered 'abnormal' by parents and by the structure. Abnormal in the sense that they don't read well, may not hear, and are treated below normal. I find that many of the young people would have a slight difficulty with their peer group. They don't communicate quite as well because they are individuals who visualize a lot. They are dealing on an intuitive level and a telepathic level. And they are being given information by the Universe.

"They are very unnerved—a lot!—because they are not in contact with the people who understand them, communicate with them on the correct level, or on a telepathic level. These young people are extremely sensitive. Their skin, their sense of smell, their eyesight, their hearing are sensitive. Usually their environment, whatever it is, is bombarding them with pollution. Noise pollution, sight pollution. Emotionally they become extremely uncomfortable, and they wander around on the edge all the time. Some have to be given drugs to calm down.

"I see some of them and view that they are that type. They ask questions of myself and other readers who are sensitive to them, that they wouldn't ask people around them normally. Or the reader might draw out of them the questions they would like to ask. They find some comfort in the fact that people are aware that they are different. But not negatively different. That they are more gifted, more creative, more artistic and more telepathic."

Don explains some of the ways in which he works with these children. "I do a lot of ESP testing which gives them an idea of what areas of intuitive level they are dealing with more easily, or with more difficulty. I also give them practice sessions they can deal with on their own to increase their abilities if they want to. I give them reading material they could pursue. Generally I work with individuals between the ages of three up. But six is probably the minimum as far as teaching—generally between six and twenty."

Another population which Don counsels consists of individuals who have had contact with aliens and UFOs. "There is a young man whom I have read for who feels that he has been contacted by UFOs, by aliens. He has a completely different energy around him. I have seen different people all over the East Coast, and he falls into the category of persons I would say who have been affected by an alien energy. His aura is altogether different. There are some who have the same auras but they are from different geographical areas. Most of them are aware of some change. A lot of them are not aware of their past below a certain age. A lot of them have blanked out a certain time. They look different. Their intelligence level is extremely high. They are dealing with visualization or telepathy. They seem to have the ability to read minds. Many of them are attracted to the star constellation, Orion. Many of them are sensitive to the variations in energy as they drive down a road."

In commenting on his work, Don said, "One of the aspects of reading is that as you are of service to people, you spiritually are advancing. Once you become a parapsychologist, you become the non-reality, and the reality becomes non-reality. Reality for you is dealing with the psychic and with spirituality. The average life becomes non-reality."

A resident of Rochester, New York, Don Tanney Hill was born in the state of Massachusetts. A psychic consultant, healer, and nutritionist, he gives consultations and workshops around the East Coast.

"The Tarot makes the person aware of his potential, rather than fortunetelling so much," proclaims Tarot reader Chuck Wagner.

"I don't think it is like fatalism. A lot of people are afraid of (the cards) because of bad news, death, and all that. I don't think that is the purpose of a Tarot reading. The reading is to give a person hope and make him aware of what skills he has to solve his problems on this plane of action."

Chuck remarks that he was not always sure himself what the cards were saying, "but whatever they are saying it is always accurate." He has been reading cards since he was five years old, when spontaneously, he understood how to read them.

"In the Tarot you can go right to the problem. Then, of course, the burden is what are you going to do about anything. I don't think you really have to do anything. Life goes on forever. You have many lifetimes to get it together. If you can make progress this lifetime, it is good."

Chuck emphasizes the message behind the Tarot is basically, you are okay! If you are miserable, that's exactly where you have to be. Then you can start working your way out of it. Life is a place where you learn. There is no power in the universe that can improve a situation to the way you think, except you.

"The Tarot gives a glimpse of people's subconscious. You can see what is going on inside of them, which they may not be aware of, until they hear me verbalizing it.

"They realize they have some control because the cards are making them to be aware of this control that they heretofore gave to someone else—a teacher, their mother, whoever was the picture of authority. I think that is the main thing people learn, they become what they think about. Thoughts are like seeds. We produce that seed, whether good or bad.

"Great singers sing their songs with such great feelings," Chuck adds, "they are planting that seed. A friend who is a singer refuses to do negative songs. They now have to be a statement of what she wants."

Licensed and ordained a minister in childhood, Chuck used to read for people through the church. "I got this information from the cards. I said they would not go to heaven and lean on Jesus unless they reached it in this plane."

After that, the church said the devil really had him. But his grandmother, who never understood her grandson's card reading ability, validated his view: it made good sense to her!

He reflects, "I didn't think there was a capricious God who would have one baby born deaf and blind and another well. I thought it was because in life there was something to be learned. One had to learn here on this plane of action. God had nothing to do with it except to provide the space for that learning to take place."

Chuck has lived in New York City for many years. Besides giving private readings, he teaches Tarot card reading. He is occasionally featured on television and radio, and has had cable television programs.

Chuck clearly states, "Young people are our salvation." He encourages them to "believe in themselves and dream big dreams, and not to be afraid to express love."

"I heal with water," writer Luisah Teish asserts in reply to questions on her work as a healer. "I heal primarily with water. The other elements are always there—Earth, Air, and Fire. The Earth is the herbs, the fire is the candles, the air is the incense and the spoken word. Put all that together and the strongest element is a cleansing bath.

"People tell me that my voice is healing, that I have a knack for saying what goes right to the heart of their concern. In the storytelling—the tales themselves are healing in that a real transformation takes place."

Luisah Teish is an ordained Yoruba priestess of the African goddess Oshun. Born in New Orleans, she moved to the San Francisco Bay area in 1971.

"The other priestly work that I do besides divining—and I do a lot of divining—is that I have been blessed with an energy that is good for bringing people of diverse backgrounds together in large public rituals. That is healing in the sense that one temporarily loses self-consciousness. You are not lying in your own pain. You are lifted, relieved of the feeling of isolation and alienation. And learn how to mingle your energies with others in a healing way."

Luisah tells of an experience which happened a few years ago. A woman with spinal meningitis couldn't get proper treatment. She was bounced around among medical facilities. Found on a doorstep, she was brought to Luisah's home.

"It is not that I individually did so much for her, but somehow the kindred that I have helped. I'm a family member with people who have a number of healing skills. When I put out the call that I had somebody sick here, a number of people responded with various skills, and we together were able to get her on her feet. That's the way it is a lot of time. Somehow I see myself as the matrix of the healing circle.

"Most of the time when I do a cleansing bath for somebody, I do not do it by myself. I really feel that almost any condition is made better by the one who is down being touched by three people who are concerned about that person's well-being. I don't think you have to have a knowledge of herbs or really have the knowledge of water healing. If somebody is sick, and there are three other people who care about that person, and who will put their hands on that person, their intention will make her or him measurably better. Other things may be needed to make the person well, but basically there is that transference of energy.

"I do believe in contagious consciousness," Luisah concludes, "with people far, far away whom you cannot reach through material means, and who cannot experience you directly, you have to teach them in the form of energy and thought transference. It is good learning for you and the other person."

At night, a vague but discernible mist appeared as a barrier to the child's room shortly after his father had moved out of the home. His mother, who noticed it, felt uneasy as she entered her son's space, as was her habit, to cover and kiss him as he slept.

Over a few weeks' time, she sensed a presence building that in its final construct seemed both formidable and benign. Stationed beside the not quite two year old's door floated a silvery, vaporous form that radiated watchfulness, regularly perceived by her on her nightly rounds.

To protect her child, late one night she decided to confront the presence. At the door, the wispy sentinel, with luminous spear upraised, intended her retreat; and she was forced back. Then in dream-filled sleep she was borne away, captivated till morning.

Through the imprints of those dreams, she was told of that which stood watch over her son: it was neither guardian angel nor evil one. She learned that her child, with close ties to his father cut, had reached an insecure point in the brief span of his present incarnation. He was turning to a former self for succor.

The mother was shown the spot in the boy's auric space from which he had vacuumed the essence of one of his stronger identities from another dimension to stand vigil over his small, powerless body.

She came to realize that this protective entity was endowed with life by him. Its presence would not manifest during the day. But at night, the consciousness that dwelled in the fully solid, little brown body, lying abed in nursery-print pajamas, was creating an earlier existence. Of etheric matter, but intense and consecrated in his loving vigil, was the Roman officer, who stood in full military dress, brightness emitting from his helmet, from his reflecting chestplate, and from his weapon.

Awakened from her dreaming, she withdrew from fear. Imbued with new maternal confidence, she saw the singleness of purpose that blended the two, the child and the centurion, into an integrated wholeness.

It was all about healing; her son was healing himself.

Physical existence settled, the hard edges of life's changes softened, the apparition gradually faded from its assigned post. Hardly a month then passed—and the soldier quit his station forever.

CHAPTER NINE
Legacy of Second Sight

The Veil

The presence of certain body markings, delivery conditions, or planetary signs and changes at the time of birth have been considered, in cultures around the world and down the ages, as physical indications that the newborn child has entered life with unusual powers. The veil, or the caul, is probably the best known of the physical natal signs. It is a strong thin tissue which on occasion completely caps a baby's head or face at birth. The medical term is "amnion," that inmost membrane filled with fluid which surrounds the fetus before birth. Also called the "bag of waters." Sometimes a child is born totally enclosed in the unbroken bag. Often associated with the veil are the abilities to see spirits and to prophesy. Expressions such as "two-headed" and "nine-headed" refer to individuals possessing psychic gifts.

Theologian Howard Thurman wrote in his autobiography, *With Head and Heart*, of being born with special signs.

> One day, how early in my life I do not recall, I discovered a little scar tissue in the center of both ear lobes. When I asked about it, I was told that my ears had been pierced when I was a baby. I was told that at the time of my birth my eyes were covered by a film. This meant, according to the custom, that I was gifted with "second sight"—a clairvoyance, the peculiar en-

dowment of one who could "tell" the future. No parent wanted a child so endowed. It spelled danger and grief. If the ears were pierced, however, the power of the gift would be dissipated.[1]

"I heard my daddy say I was born with 'nine heads.' "

Fannie Bell Chapman of Centreville, Mississippi is a healer and gospel singer. She is known as a visionary.

"He said I wasn't like none of the others," Fannie remarks, whose visions began in childhood. "He said when I was born I looked more intelligent and was more upright."

Mother Mary Bivens, a spiritual healer, had visions as a child, and in her youth was told by a Spiritualist that she would do the same work.

"My mother went to Spiritual meetings frequently. She was training me while I was in her stomach. I was almost born at one of those meetings.

"I was born with a veil over my face. This is what they tell black people who are born with the gift."

"I was born without the aid of doctors," reports James Moye. "I was born with purple and white 'beads' around my neck, and a veil over my face."

James is a Florida-based Yoruban priest and herbalist.

"My mother was a Spiritualist; her father and her mother before her were Spiritualists. My paternal grandfather was also a Spiritualist. From my father's side, it was what they called Obeah man, a man who works with magic."

"My mother told me I was born with the veil," states June Gatlin, spiritual healer, singer, and poet, who grew up on Moon Street in Akron, Ohio.

From Chicago astrologer James Black she learned that at the time of her birth all the ancient planets were in their signs of rulership. He used the Bible to do her chart the ancient way, and conveyed to her she held the key to the Lion of Judah.

"He said he had never seen a chart like mine in his seventy years!"

They recognized each other instantly when they met. "I have been looking for you," he said to her. "I know you. You are the one to make the circle."

Ella Eaton, metaphysical counselor, and former New York Metropolitan Opera House singer, was delivered by midwives in the family home in North Carolina.

"I was born with the caul," she confides.

"My grandparents and my mother at the time were very aware of another dimension."

Louise Washington's grandmother told her, "I don't want you to forget this—this is your veil."

"I have seen the veil I was born in," Louise confirms. "My grandmother gave it to me when I was a child. It was shaped like a cured, hard piece of meat. It was big, and like wood."

A minister, and long-time member of the National Spiritualist Association of Churches, Louise has a church on the Southside of Chicago.

Her mediumistic abilities have been strongly evident from childhood. "I tied the veil with a string," Louise explains. "I played with it a long time. When my grandmother felt the time was over for me to be playing with it, she took it away. I don't know what she did with it.

"I carried my dolls around in my veil," she shares. "They fit inside it fine!"

The Legacies

Psychic energy grows bounteously in some families. These favored groups may produce one or more sensitives in each generation. The family may regard the presence of psychic power within its circle as signs of blessings or curses, based on the store of experiences gathered in the family group-mind over generations. Family history, with a preponderance of stored positive energy impressions, inclines the group toward acceptance, tolerance, nurturance; but with overriding negative energy storage come negligence, or nullification of the influences of its gifted members.

Each gifted relative has his or her own way to express the reservoir of family power dwelling within. The talents apportioned among the generations of parents and offspring may vary greatly or resonate deeply with sameness. To one family member through inheritance may come clear-hearing, and another may be gifted with dreams and visions. Some psychic characteristics may continue to appear strongly and predictably through the generations, sometimes evident distinctly in a single family member.

Being raised in a family where the elements of psychic energy are strong in the bloodline is, of course, extremely beneficial to the gifted person. Shared certainty about the extradimensionality of the universe is a strengthening force, proven many times as various family members utilize their gifts. With group encouragement and support, the psychic individual is freer to define, claim, and develop his or her gift. Greater inner stability is gained through being able to communicate to others who understand and share a history in common about something as subtle and intangible as spirit and its manifestations.

Among those interviewed, strong appreciation keynoted the relationship which the psychics shared with their psychic kin. This special kinship was mostly enjoyed. Comments came from parents about the pleasures of watching their children's intuitivity emerge and mature. Communicated, too, was the sense that family sentiency grew in strength at a child's magnification of a psychic trait that was already rooted within the group. Parents spoke of the measures they had taken to prepare their young children for their encounters with a largely disbelieving society. Overall, their interests were in helping their children to participate in the general culture, without compromising their awareness or shutting off their gifts. Members of families with several generations of active psychics seemed more confident about direction for themselves and their children. They were familiar with some of the ways used by outsiders to diminish or destroy uncommon perception and power.

A few adults felt they had always been a part of the psychic force within their families; however, they resisted picking up their own gifts until late in life, although they had been appraised as "special" by psychic relatives, early in their childhood. There were disappointed psychic parents who were disillusioned that the strong power which their offspring had as child sensitives was only being used in superficial ways in adulthood. Several people worried about very capable relatives misdirecting their gifts by working toward egocentric or destructive goals. As one might presume, there were non-psychic factions in some families which pruned off what they considered as the "hoodoo" sides of the tree.

To the core of the family which fully appreciates its psychic members, which encourages their varied expressions of psychic ability, is accrued an intense concentration of Truth, gained through group observations and experience. Through firsthand knowledge, the family has learned that it is not bound to earth as commonly accepted. Not locked into agreed-upon limitations. A united group, it experiences the transcending of physical boundaries.

Every family projects a spiritual force created by the energies of individual family members. It is the combined consciousness of all generations, the psychic joining of ancestors and current family members. This force, the family spirit, is an influence for perpetually welding the group into a singleness and unity. When the accumulated thoughts and activities of family individuals are primarily composed of, and dwelling in, negative energy, and in lesser states of awareness, then these types of energies animate the family spirit. In turn, the family spirit may exert greater negative influence within the group, even to affecting individuals. Confusion, disunity, and destructive behavior would be strongly manifested.

When most family members recognize themselves as crucial increments of the total group knowledge, and main tributaries to the family spiritual awareness, the family spiritual force grows vital, and this wisdom is followed by the spiritual elevation of individuals and the whole group. Creativity, harmony, and service would be among the positive energy manifestations flourishing in such states of group-being. This principle pertains to all groups. It does not matter whether the group is small or large. For example, a business, over a period of time, builds a group-spirit generated out of the concepts, attitudes, and intentions of its members. It especially perpetuates and reflects the belief systems of its founder. The business is also influenced by held-over traumatic effects from some of the group's more ruinous and catastrophic experiences in time. This principle of group-spirit, on a much larger scale, applies to nations, and even to ethnic and cultural groupings.

One morning an admonishment felled the plan which Delilah and her cousins had made to visit a nearby aunt. Their great-grandmother abruptly ordained that no one was to leave the house that day. The restive teenagers worked on the elder to reconsider: the very light snow meant nothing. Finally in the early afternoon she bent to the badgering group's will. They left despite her exhortations. "Don't go! You are going to have an accident!"

"I'll never forget this. We were like, 'Yeah! Right! Tell us about it!'

"We all got in the car and went to my aunt's. But on the way back, the hill we were on was the steepest hill in Pittsburgh. At the end of the hill, the brakes went out.

"I was holding my cousin's baby, and I jumped out of the car with the baby. All of us jumped out. The car went right into a row of houses.

"Then I started respecting and seeing all along my grandmother was telling us things. What we should, what we shouldn't do, who would come in the house that was okay, and who wasn't. These are the kinds of unorthodox tools which were basically part of our life style."

Delilah Grayer and her daughter, Bakara Oni Lewis, come from a line of women seers. In growing up in a household often shared by six generations of the family, Delilah was witness to events affirming that in the group of family women there harbored an intense form of insight. Her mother, grandmother, as well as her great-grandmother who raised her, bear its elements.

Delilah, a psychic consultant, lives in Cleveland, Ohio. At five years old, her psychic talent was evident; and her daughter, Bakara Oni, was yet a toddler when she showed prescience.

Delilah was 36 years old when her daughter was born. Shortly after the child was conceived, the women in the family were aware that the newcomer would be a girl—and gifted.

Actress Cicely Tyson observed she always had an ability to "see things," to foretell certain events before they happened, and to know sometimes in advance what people were going to say to her. At times, she senses what a friend might be doing at a given moment. Earlier in her life, her gift was somewhat frightening to her, but she has since accepted it.

Tyson discussed these psychic attributes in a January, 1979 article in *Ebony*. She noted that her psychic characteristics were shared by her mother. Had she listened to her mother years back, Tyson said, she would not have the large scar on her arm.

When she was young, each child in the family had chores to do. Hers included washing all the windows in their Bronx "railroad" apartment—a task she enjoyed. One morning she was strictly admonished by her mother not to wash the windows, to absolutely stay away from glass that day.

After their mother left for work, Tyson and her sister started playing. A chase from room to room ensued. With Tyson quickly gaining on her, the sister slammed the French doors to escape. Tyson's arm went through the glass, cutting her severely. A neighbor took her to the hospital.

Upon returning home, Tyson's mother regarded her bandaged child and said almost nothing to her about the incident. Tyson said she later realized her mother had foreseen the injury and had prepared herself to accept whatever happened. Other occurrences also demonstrated her mother's gift, she commented.

"Out of the ten children in my childhood family, all of us are psychic, including the boys. I'm the only one in the family that actually uses the gift. Nobody else uses theirs."

Raised in the Methodist church, Vera, her sisters, and her brothers were also familiar with the Spiritual churches of Atlanta. Their mother often invited spiritual people to the family home, where she participated in the organizing of some of the Spiritual churches. Vera says none in the circle of friends would give readings to her mother because her own resources at revelation were so strong.

"She was a born seer. We kids couldn't get away with anything!"

Atlanta, where she was born, is still home to Vera Sutton. She leaves it for brief periods to give workshops and group readings in places like New York, Pennsylvania, California, and Alaska. She teaches metaphysics and meditation. Astrology, palmistry, numerology, and the Tarot are some of the methods she uses to perceive psychic information. But most of the time Vera obtains information by the natural knowing about things, a talent she has had since childhood.

"My mother never restricted me from saying what I felt about people. That allowed me to always say what I saw. Children have a direct influx into the infinite. All they see is what is. They don't see any of the other stuff. That's why they are so accurate about whether they like this person, or why they are such good judges of character. That's where it comes from. She never restricted me.

"Most parents would say, 'That's not nice.' It allowed me my own spiritual information.

"My mother didn't push the devil. My mother said you're your own devil. I've discovered down through the years that that is the truth of the matter. So she was real wise in what she taught, and any information that she gave."

Vera's own children, three in number, made predictions while very young. Her daughter had psychic astuteness about the weather; and her middle child, a son, clear-speaking even at one-and-a-half years, perceived his mother's spiritual progress as she moved along in her meditational and unfoldment studies. He called his observations of her changes "blessings." This child also made predictions by objects which had numerical symbology, delighting his mother's number-oriented clients. He tapped his way into his potential for dream clairvoyance at an early age. In assessing her youngest child, affectionately called "Pumpkin," Vera saw his ability to detect and understand the emotions of others. At five, he was reading some of her clients. He, like his brother, "dreamed true."

"Children handle spiritual psychicness that way because of this direct in-tuneness they have with the infinite. They don't see it as a big deal because they said it would rain and it rained. As we grow into adulthood, then that's when people stifle their own naturalness about being able to be intuitive. I believe everybody is psychic to whatever degree it is, and we all use it in different ways. Men, too—they use theirs in their work. The constant practicing over and over again is just like practicing meditation.

"I believe my gift and talent is all about making sure people become self aware," Vera emphasizes. "That the lost key to life, or happiness, or wholeness, is self awareness. So I teach it, all forms of it."

"Part of my roots are Indian. My mother was half-white and half-Indian. My mother was like my guru, basically because she was that kind of spiritual person. I consider that I inherit my spirituality or my psychic abilities from my mother."

Hayward Coleman is a mime and physical comedian who performs internationally.

"My mother was psychic, because of her Indian abilities, or that type of consciousness. She was a sensitive woman. She, herself, had seen spirits many times. It was normal for her people to know this, and to have this knowledge. To be able to see spirits and communicate with their ancestors."

In girlhood, she had once reported a presence in their home to her own mother. From the child's description, her mother identified the apparition as a former occupant of their cabin, who had died before the girl was born.

Hayward remembers an incident from his boyhood. His mother, sensing something burning at three o'clock in the morning, woke him up to check on it. She refused to let him return to bed after he investigated their building where he neither found nor smelled anything unusual. Under her direction, he checked outside their area, and then finally went to look in a neighboring apartment. Peering through the window, Hayward caught sight of a sleeping man. And in that same instant a flame shot up from the mattress. By rapping on the window, Hayward was able to alert the neighbor, who put out the fire.

"From that moment on I began to become aware, and tune in to my mother, and began to understand her sensitivities."

In adolescence, Hayward's psychic awareness found expression through visions. His abilities became more available in young adulthood, manifesting through mediumship, telepathic communication, and astral travel. He, like his mother, has an ability to see spirits.

In childhood Luisah watched her mother "like a hawk."

"My mother did things that she took for granted," she looks back. "She took for granted certain things she knows about planting. The way she would interpret dreams. Healing a pig. Making a way out of no way. Mother said she wasn't much of an altar mother like her sister, but once in a while she would do a little work with the saints on somebody's behalf."

Luisah Teish, author, healer, teacher, and priestess, speaks of how her life has been influenced by her mother's intuitivity.

In *Jambalaya: The Natural Woman's Book*, Luisah writes of a time she was in bed with severe respiratory problems and fever, an incident illustrating the intense spiritual interconnection between the author and her mother. "I was too sick to heal myself (I thought) and too stubborn to die. I remember asking the question, 'What would Mama do if her child was this sick?' I asked the question and drifted into near-delirious sleep.[2]

"Some time passed; then I got up. As my feet hit the floor, I noticed varicose veins in my legs (which I do not have), and my muscles were not sore. I stood up and felt my hips much larger than they are (laugh, girls!). It seemed as if I were wearing my mother's body."

Perceiving as if she were her mother, Luisah prepared a range of remedies. She became herself upon returning to bed, almost too weak to use the preparations. Her "mother" tended to Luisah until daybreak. The illness dispelled in sleep.

Luisah comments, "This cannot be called an egun (spirit) experience, because my mother is still in her body. Maybe she sensed that I was in distress and projected her intelligence to my aid.

"In our household," Luisah recalls, "the one thing that was real clear, was Mama's pointed finger. And that is still an accurate oracle. If Mama points her finger at you and says something—this will come to pass. When we were little and she would do this, we would scatter!"

The following is excerpted from *Jambalaya*:

> Late one evening I was standing on the corner enjoying the liquor store light and eavesdropping when my mother called me to come inside. I responded, "In- a-minute, Moma." She squinted her eyes and said, "All right, 'In-A-Minute', mark my word, you gon' come running yo' behind in here!" I thought to sabotage the 12-foot journey by walking slowly, dragging my feet, when suddenly out of nowhere a creepy, buzzing, flying thing crash-landed in my flat bosom. I screamed, ripping at my clothes and ran into the house. My mother reached into my T-shirt and pulled out a crushed locust. She threw the thing out the window and as she scrubbed my chest with a soapy towel, she looked at me, smiled, and said, "Child, you'se a mess, yeah cher, wid yo' cheeky self."

"As a child, I watched my mother predict accurately. Just on a limb. 'Child, I tell you, this is what's going to happen with that.' Boom! and it happened just the way she said!"

Sandra Barry Bonner first knew she was psychic at ten years old. Severely upset, she had gone to bed, midday. "I opened my eyes and saw three people at the foot of my bed. They were just standing there. I rubbed my eyes, expecting them to vanish—to go away—but they didn't!"

Sandra explains nowadays she gets impressions from shaking hands, and personal belongings. She calls herself a prophetic dreamer. She "sees" things. She dreamed about her present husband, Ron, about four weeks before they met. Ron Bonner, also psychic, about that time was using Tarot cards, and saw a Leo coming into his life!

A child sensitive, Sandra did not try to sort out what was happening to her until she was well into her teens. At sixteen she studied astrology. She experimented with witches' spells. Frightened during one exploration, she avoided all psychic activities for a couple of years.

"I began picking up things on people. I would have prophetic dreams," she continues. Sometimes she told her mother, who has similar gifts. Her father always had an interest in psychic things. She soon began looking for information on her abilities again.

Sandra, who is a school teacher, grew up in Los Angeles. At twenty-two, while working on her Masters in education, she began meditating and doing readings. Soon she joined a group which inspired her to work on psychic development. "I feel I'm a better psychic reader than I am a school teacher, though I feel I'm a very good teacher!" Sandra reflects. Besides her psychic and teaching abilities, she is a skilled musician.

She teaches junior high school, but during most of her career, she has taught the first through fifth grades. Her student population is mostly comprised of African American and Hispanic, lower-income children. "In my classes I include meditation and relaxation techniques. Visualization and positive affirmation are part of my lesson plans. This is to help raise these children's low self-esteem. They need a lot of love."

Sandra's oldest daughter, Jamilla, is psychic. "She dreams very well!" the mother declares. Jamilla learned about psychometry from her stepfather, Ron.

When Jamilla was around two years old and still working on learning to pronounce words, she and her mother witnessed a serious traffic accident. They were at the scene when one of the seriously injured victims was being taken to the hospital.

Jamilla viewed the state of the person's body and his psychic being and then confidently and authoritatively announced to her mother: "He'll yive!"

"I come from a very psychic family," says astrologer Kenneth Dickkerson, a New York City resident who also does psychic Kirilian photography readings.

"My mother could astrally project at will. There were all kinds of ghost stories in my family. I was familiar with that. But as far as astrology, Tarot readings—I had never really heard of those things. My mother introduced them to me.

"All that time, I had no real awareness of my own psychic ability," Ken admits. "I realize now that I used it a lot and didn't know what I was using.

"When I first heard of the astrology thing, I thought it was ridiculous. Someone telling you things about the time you were born. I thought it was somewhat of a ripoff. I decided I would like to investigate it and see what it was and expose it. My uncle told me about this astrologer who lived in the same neighborhood, and who blew my mind.

"By the time this astrologer was finished, I felt I was walking nine inches off the ground. He told me things about myself that I didn't know were true but which made sense. He told me that my life was very close to my chart. I have to admit that after hearing that—it turned me really on to it. I immediately felt I would like to learn how to do this."

In 1975, his mother again prompted him. Calling from California, she told him about the Kirilian camera his father had constructed. The photographs were unusual, she said. In addition to getting pictures of the aura which surrounds the fingertips, the photographs contained faces, astrological symbols, numbers, past-life personalities, and sometimes spirit guides.

Ken commented on his reaction to his mother's news in Lloyd Strayhorn's column in the *Amsterdam News*, September, 1982.

"To say the least, on hearing this, goose bumps started popping out all over my body. She definitely piqued my interest. And so to make a long story short, I constructed a camera and became a Kirilian photographer. I now enjoy working in this field.[3]

"I have even done readings on my daughters!" Ken smiles.

"When I was five, I had a beautiful black cocker spaniel, Beauty, and I could talk to her," London Wildwind reminisces. "She would be asleep, and I remember thinking, 'I wish Beauty would come over so I could rub her.' She would open up her eyes, and walk over and sit by me. She used to do that many times. I didn't think about it until later on—that I had telepathy."

London's mother, Ellen, was psychically gifted. "She was the one who had those kinds of abilities in the family. She used to see ghosts—she called them 'haints'—walking around the house. She told my brother and me about them."

London's conscious efforts to develop his intuitivity began at 20. Influenced by a metaphysical book, he tested his potential to astral travel, finding he could exit his body quickly. After that, psychic experiences were spontaneous. Pots rattled when he looked at them. He saw spirits. They talked to him. He says his real psychic gift came through while talking to friends by telephone.

"I'd just be talking with someone, and I'd say, 'I feel it is going to happen this way.' And it would occur as I said. It was all very natural. It would come just out of the top of my head."

Personal consultations and metaphysical study groups are two of the techniques London uses in working with people out of his San Francisco office. He describes one of the aims for working with people: "I prepare people for new stages of life."

"My mother died when I was twenty-one. She began to slowly communicate with me. I did get messages from her.

"Her sister had also died, and she communicated with me very, very clearly. I remember her coming in and saying, 'Take care of my children.' I saw her face. It was an emotional plea. She was there and knew they really needed help."

London was meditating once when his deceased grandfather appeared. The spirit signified it had been trying to get in touch for two years. Etheric glasses were propped in front of London's eyes. His grandfather's message was that they were to give him a "long range view." The action showed that the being's humor had endured. During his lifetime, the former old man had visions, saw ghosts, and told his grandson of much of it in a light and inspiring way. He was the third member of the family to make a post-life appearance to London.

"My long-range goals are probably to make films. There are some films I want to make, especially one film for black people.

"I'm for mixing everybody together. Our family is a mixed family, Cherokee, Choctaw, Irish, Welsh, French, and Creole. I don't have any prejudices against anyone. I really don't identify with a black cause other than getting people out of being prejudiced against black people.

"I was born with the veil on my eyes," comments London. "My mother said my eyes were green for three days, and the doctor had to put a solution on them to take the veil off."

"I didn't pay any attention to my mother's psychic ability until I was in college. I remember her tuning into things about people far away, and then having whatever she said about somebody manifesting," states Latifu Munirah, a college instructor and social worker. "She told me she used to read cards when she was growing up and was quite good at it. She would read ordinary playing cards. I think after my brother and I came, she stopped reading them. I sent her a book and a deck. Nothing! To some extent, she is scared of her powers and she won't develop them."

While forming a new life, after separating from her husband, Latifu was helped to know that like her mother she also was a reader. Strong, too, was her self-knowledge of her healing, and spiritual-teacher potentials. In 1980, she began developing these potentials.

Latifu's mother was the first to know of her only daughter's pregnancy. She predicted to her child that the baby would be a girl. Awed by the remark drawn from her mother's dream state, which later proved true, Latifu felt in touch with the depth of her mother's giftedness.

Of Frank Gipson's four children, a daughter in childhood "saw" and told him of her contact with unembodied beings. Even then, the signs of the healing faculty were with her, he contends. She has never acknowledged her gifts. But he watches her merge them into her techniques in nursing.

According to Frank, his late mother, well-known southwestern faith healer Lillian Chatman, received her gift from her mother. The force of these group traits remained animated and expressed later in the son, Frank, who was teamed up with his mother to do healing missions. "My grandmother was a healer," he states. "She told my mother that someday she would be like her."

Dream-state communication is strong between his deceased mother and Frank, who continues his own healing and counseling practices.

Of his daughter's abilities, though yet by her to be recognized,

Frank declares, "I know she is chosen."

During critical periods in his family life while he was growing up, Allen Young's mother received significant information through prophetic dreams.

"She didn't know anything about astrology. She didn't know anything about Tarot cards," Allen relates.

"She seemed to have dreams at key times which kind of blew the family away. She knew when her mother was going to die. She said it. She knew when my father was going to have a heart attack. She said it."

Allen confides, "She knew certain things about family members from time to time. She knew when my stepbrother was in serious trouble with the law. She knew about inheriting money. She didn't have a lot of dreams, but enough so that when we were kids, she seemed to have dreams which consistently said something."

Allen is an astrologer and the founder of the San Francisco Aquarian Institute.

"I hear voices clearly and sometimes receive strong visual impressions," says Geri Glass, a clairaudient and psychic consultant practicing in Los Angeles. "The first time I predicted to a friend, I was 10 or 11 years old. We were seriously talking and I tuned into her. I didn't know exactly what I was doing. I could see, and I heard a voice."

Geri explains the psychic activities in her family as being hushed. "One of my aunts used roots and washes for healings. On my father's side, they practiced something which was hidden. I never knew.

"After my mother was murdered, I had conversations with her," Geri recalls. "Sometimes in dreams. Some were so real! In one, she recited a poem to me. She told me it was beautiful where she was. The next day, I saw her at the top of the stairs. She told me not to seek revenge for her murder.

"After that experience, I was able to let her go."

Born in 1910 to a Shawnee American Indian woman who was "very psychic," Nellye Taylor reflects on events at the first of this century. "My mother didn't use her gift like I've used mine. She would prophesy from time to time. But her mother stopped her. She, too, was a Shawnee Indian. She thought it was witchcraft."

"My mother was a Quaker. When she was young, the government sent her to Hampton Institute in Virginia for schooling."

"I was born a medium. At the time I was growing up, Spiritualism was not that well known."

Nellye was popular, other children liked her to tell about their futures; but adults cautioned her against prophesying. She predicted the weather, and could tell when a person was lying.

A resident of Phoenix and member of the Spiritualist church since 1933, Nellye is a medium, working with her guide, Great Eagle.

"She came around just as I woke up this morning," April says brightly of her great-great-grandmother, Vinnie Strong. "One time she took me to a place when I was asleep. To a place where there are green people and everything was green!"

Vinnie Strong has become a spirit guardian for her young great-great-granddaughter April. Although Vinnie died long before April's birth in 1980, she still communicates with the child and her mother, Lori King, through dreams, and occasional apparitional appearances. She returns, giving advice and remedies when April has physical or emotional upsets.

The discarnate elder coached and chided Lori, during her pregnancy with April, about proper activities and nutrition. As Lori indicates, she has remained a dominant and respected influence in their lives from the spirit dimension.

April kicked in time to music before she was born. As an infant she would consistently wake up five minutes before her father was due home. She sent pictures when she was hungry, and gave psychic information by touching playing cards before she could talk.

"Vinnie Strong had African royal blood when she came here.

She came to the States, free," Lori informs.

"She always turns up when April is sick to tell me what to do. She shows up a lot. I know sometimes in dreams she takes April places. I feel pretty safe about it."

From her side of the family, Lori, who is white, traces her psychic heritage to her great-grandmother, who was a reader in New Orleans. "I've been hearing voices and seeing spirits and having premonitions as long as I can remember," Lori says. "That's always been there. It's definitely an inherited trait. It comes from my father's side of the family. April has it from both families. April and I are fortunate in that nobody closed us off."

Lillian Washington, a woman in her sixties, has visions day and night.

She has lived on James Island, South Carolina all her life. She says the real Bess of George Gershwin's opera *Porgy and Bess* lives on the island, too, and looks very good in her old age.

Lillian is a singer, and a member of the island's St. James Presbyterian Church choir. The quality of the choir is such that it routinely goes on tour.

There is a young woman, on the same island, who sees into the ethereal realm. Twenty-six angels, each representing a different country on Earth, have communicated with her since she was in her teens. This young woman is Lillian's granddaughter.

" 'Pears like my heart go flutter, flutter, and den dey may say 'Peace, Peace!' as much as dey likes, I know its gwine to be war!"

This description is found in the biography *Harriet Tubman: The Moses of Her People*, by Sarah Bradford. "She says she always knows when there is danger near her—she does not know how, exactly."[4]

Harriet Tubman's psychic endowment was varied and rich. In helping slaves to escape she made use of her powers.

Her father could always predict the weather, and he foretold the Mexican war, she asserted. Some of her intense attributes were founded on the premonitive power which she said was inherited from her father.

CHAPTER TEN

Diversities of Gifts

Varied Talents

"It's hard to explain about a vision. It's not anything you can touch, of course, but you know it's there. It's about the only thing that is real to you while it's going on. I guess it comes closer to being like a dream than anything else, but it's not exactly like that, neither," expressed C.C. White in his autobiography, *No Quittin' Sense*.[1]

A lifelong resident of Texas, White, a preacher, was born in 1885. He remembered being inspired to preach at three years old.

" ... I got me some sticks. I tied rags around some to make skirts for girls, and left some just plain for boys. Then I stuck them in the ground and preached them a sermon ... I told them to repent of their sins, just like I'd heard the preacher say. And I sang them 'Old Mourner' till I got tired. Then I dug me a hole and poured some water in it and baptized them."

White's first visionary experience was in 1925. A vision in 1928 prompted his move to Jacksonville where he founded a church, and built God's Little Storehouse.

"I told Marthy (his wife), 'I been preaching, Bring your tithes to the storehouse! and I ain't got no storehouse. I think what I need to do is put me up something out here, a building people can see and touch, so they'll know there is a storehouse, and so I'll have a place to keep the tithes they bring.'

" ... And from that first day on, ain't never been a time I ain't had a little something in there to give God's hungry folks."

His congregation and community people brought donations of food, clothing, and money to the storehouse to help the needy.

"When God gives you a vision your whole body kind of soaks up the message, like a biscuit soaks up red-eye gravy," continued White in his book, co-authored with Ada Morehouse Holland. "And sometimes you can hear the message as well as feel it. And sometimes you can see it. But generally can't none of the people around you see it or hear it. Leastwise, none of the people around me ever did."

"Fear not, gather my children!" Mary Thomas saw Christ, in a vision, walking steadily up a mountain. When He reached the top, He spoke those words.

Mary is the founder and executive director of the Serene Community Homes, Incorporated in Sacramento, California, an organization serving the needs of handicapped children. The non-profit organization consists of three twenty-four-hour residential treatment facilities, and a private special education school. Service is provided to developmentally disabled children, emotionally disturbed children, and children with learning disabilities.

One evening, earlier in her life, Mary volunteered to help in the fund-raising activities of a church; her mission began unfolding in a series of unusual events. She felt compelled to get up after only a few hours of sleep that night. And over a period of seven days, she experienced a shifting in her consciousness. She was influenced in that inward remaking to anoint her own head with oil she blessed, then to cleanse herself with water. The first day she performed the ritual three times, each time repeating the same pronouncement: "In the name of the Father, the Son, and the Holy Spirit.

"I saw a configuration of the Father beckoning to me, beckoning to me and looking at his Son. What was going through my mind very strongly was, 'This is my Beloved Son, believe in Him.' "

Mary's family remained around her over the seven-day transitional period, but no one questioned her or seemed to regard her behavior as strange. She had a sense of being totally accepted by them.

"A golden key was dropped in my hand. I could actually feel my hand sting from it. I saw a woman and a huge body of water, the most beautiful water I have ever seen. This woman was standing at the edge of that water. Her shoes were off her feet. They were black brogans, and they were beside her. She had her hair parted in the middle, and it was taken back. She was slender, and her dress had a Peter Pan collar. This woman looked at me. Her eyes followed me until she had my full attention. She just drew me in with her eyes.

"She said, 'You have it, you know, now do it!' "

The woman she had seen in that vision, Mary later discovered, was Ellen White, founder of Seventh Day Adventism.

"Then I looked and saw another woman coming toward me. She had a bandana on her head. I looked and I said, 'That's me!' I was coming toward myself!"

Seven signs were shown to Mary in her first experiencing of visions. "On my brochure today, there is one sign that I remember, and I know one day all the others will come back. It is all coming together."

Mary actually began her work with handicapped children after talking with a neighbor, the foster parent of several young developmentally disabled children. During their conversation, Mary experienced a strong realization that this was the work she was to do. "I could hardly wait to get up the next morning to go to the agency. I told (the licensing social worker), 'I want to work with children who have problems, the children who really need my services. I want the most handicapped children that you have.' "

In the process of that spiritual reformative period, Mary received psychic information on nutrition which proved beneficial later to the children placed with her.

Mary was born in Durham, North Carolina. She earned a doctorate in the field of nutrition in 1983. Her work with children began in New Jersey. In 1974, she moved to Sacramento.

She continues to receive knowledge and intercession through visions. She reminisces about an occasion of being guided from taking a premature action in the sequence of establishing her work. "I went in and lay down. I heard this crunch, crunch, like somebody walking on sand. Then I saw this clear white sand and still heard the crunch, crunch. I was not asleep. I knew it was either Christ or an angel who said, 'I am with you. Would you go out before you are ready? Wait until you are ready.' "

Before going in to apply for her first foster parent license, Mary had randomly read from the Bible which she had spontaneously picked up. "I just opened it up. It opened up to the part where Peter had asked Christ, 'Who has sinned that this man be born blind, the parents or the grandparents?'

"Christ's answer was, 'None. That this be the will of my Father that his goodness will be manifested.' I closed the Bible.

"And that is still my philosophy with these homes and my agency today, that these handicapped children are like this because if we do our jobs, then the manifestation of Christ will come through and bring them into balance."

Urged by an inner voice, Memelle Wilson prayed for her husband. The voice directed her to specific Bible passages.

"I fell into a mixing machine," Memelle's husband said later, when he came home from work. With no immediate way to control the machine, the rest of the crew stood around in helpless dread over his imminent mutilation. But, miraculously, the machine switched off. The accident was happening, Memelle found out, at the precise time she was urged to pray.

Inner voice instructions first came when she was eight or nine years old. The onset of visions arrived in the same time. Perceiving in those ways was thought normal in her family. Memelle's mother had visions, and her grandmother, prophetic dreams. The two often and very naturally communicated with each other by thought.

"Things don't work out well when I don't follow the inner voice," she explains.

A bright light appeared to Memelle while she was doing yoga and meditational exercises. It stayed around the first time, following her throughout the house. Now, when she is very upset, the light returns, creating a calming influence.

Perceptive individuals have acknowledged Memelle's help in reversing the course of illness after she prayed for their healing. She also influences the weather.

Aware of some of her own past lives, Memelle says her mother has reincarnated as one of the grandchildren.

Memelle grew up in Shreveport, Louisiana. She devotes herself to creating constructive thought. "I have associated myself with positive thinkers," she says. She formed her ideal of the positive thinker from her grandmother and mother.

She taught many years in "rough" schools as a substitute

teacher in the San Francisco Bay area, where she lives. One class, with a reputation of rowdiness, responded dramatically after she meditated for peace. The students became so well-behaved that the principal, disbelieving what he saw, kept checking in!

"You have always been a beautiful sister. You are very special. Don't worry. I am happy. This is the end of physical life."[2]

Those words were given clearly to Calestine Williams by her brother, Benjamin Perry, in a dream while she lay in bed.

"Oh, no!" she moaned aloud, and began crying.

"What's wrong?" Calestine's daughter inquired anxiously, having entered the bedroom.

"Benjamin has died."

"No, Mommy, you were asleep."

The phone rang and her daughter answered. She was shocked by the call. Slowly, she put down the phone.

"Mother, you were right. This is your mother and your brother *has* died."

One of her many psychic experiences, this particular incident was related by Calestine in the *Commercial Appeal* in April, 1979.

Born in Mississippi, she is now a resident of Memphis, Tennessee and an administrator in the field of public health.

Obvious by the time she was six, Calestine's psychic gifts are wide-ranged. She sees the future and the past, and sends and receives thought messages. Through the emanations from energy, she knows the thoughts, emotions, attitudes, and conditions of people, objects, and geographical areas.

Calestine has been a frequent guest lecturer on the subject of her abilities at Memphis State University. She also appears on television.

"I work by telephone or in person," she says. "I have the person talk for a while, and as the energies come through I give a message. I can sense things about an area, the feeling about a house."

In counseling she works to raise individuals' awareness of themselves, and to assist them in bringing out their own abilities. "I try to motivate people to listen to the Self. My own growth is in working with people, seeing them change, seeing them coming into self-awareness."

A startling message came to Calestine about her father whom she had not seen for three decades. From rumor, she knew he might be living somewhere in Beaufort, South Carolina. But this news of him came flowing strongly and clearly through her innerspace, by-passing all physical barriers to communicate about his condition. Through what she calls "vibes," Calestine saw her father in a room, near death, with sores covering his body. By bus, she left home in Memphis to search for him in Beaufort. In tracing him, she was guided by the vibes, which intensified as she approached his home. There she found him in the condition she perceived through the energies.

Her father cried over how she had located him. Vibes also told Calestine her father would recover despite medical opinion that he was terminally ill. She brought him home, tended him, and his health improved.

Dr. Everett L. Sutter, a psychologist at Memphis State University, invites Calestine to visit some of his classes in parapsychology and share the podium. "She has been a tremendous asset to the class," he stated. "She is excellent as a person of precognition abilities and relates beautifully to the students."

The article in the *Commercial Appeal* goes on to describe another incident in which Calestine demonstrated her gift. A student reported, "We'd never seen each other until I went to a class of Dr. Sutter's. In an informal moment afterward, she told me, 'You are pregnant (which was obvious), but you are not married (which was not supposed to be obvious). I was, like in shock. I didn't know her at all, but she was 100 per cent accurate!"

Johnnie saw her husband becoming more spirit than physical. She said to their daughter, "We are losing Daddy." He passed with suddenness in 1977, and she thought she would go insane from the loss and the subsequent effects.

The day he left, he manifested to his sister-in-law. In his easy-going style, the apparition said, "Good-bye, black gal!"

The first year of his death, he came home every night. Johnnie could feel him getting into bed; and in the morning, there was the smell of coffee as he always made it.

"I didn't want to let him go."

"Everything is going to turn out all right," his spirit telepathically informed Johnnie, worried about a business transaction. Her anxiety abated with hearing the physical vibration of his voice.

The time came, though, when he stood in spirit form before her as though he were alive again, well-groomed, smiling, and light. "I am happy, I won't be back."

"I kept screaming for him," Johnnie recalls. He became angry over her reaction. His emotion jarred her, so she released him for both their sakes. "We were very close. He was out-going, a free-spirit, and religious. He taught me so much about life."

They had been married more than thirty years. Johnnie's husband would say to her, "Hey girl, you're unusual!" He was the first to really recognize she had gifts, and told her God sent him to take care of her.

Long-time resident of Los Angeles, Johnnie Page was born in Birmingham, Alabama. In addition to doing individual counseling, she teaches classes in metaphysics and has hosted radio programs.

She made predictions as a child. Those early signs of her gifts were mostly buried by parental hushes and rejections. Her mother ascribed Johnnie's gifts to "listening to grown-ups' business."

"I used to dream a lot. I used to get visions through dreams," Johnnie reveals. "I was gifted in knowing who was going to be President. I could tell. Eisenhower was my first experience. It came in a vision, in which this little newspaper boy was screaming and hollering, 'Eisenhower, President of the United States!' "

Johnnie told someone at work the next day who said, "You've got to be crazy! Nobody would elect a fighting man for President. This man knows nothing but war!"

"I don't care. Spirit told me last night!" Johnnie's co-worker laughed and walked off.

The second presidential visions Johnnie had were of Kennedy—his election and assassination. The Spirit told her when Johnson was going to resign. "I told my husband, and he said, 'Oh Lady, no man would leave his party hanging like that!'

"I said, 'He's going to tell it tonight when he gives his State of the Union message. So just be ready!'

"We were listening for it. Johnson got through with his State of the Union message, but he did not give that resignation message! I was devastated! My husband said, 'Well, you didn't make it that time.'

"I said, 'It's true! It's true!'

"And he did give his resignation in the next two or three days. He said he intended to do it at the State of the Union address, but he changed suits at the last minute and left his speech in the other suit pocket.

"I said, 'I know my spirits wouldn't do me that way!' "

Johnnie began to relate to her spirit guides outside of dreams and visions around 1975. At a Friday night message meeting, conducted by Dr. James Thomas of the School of Guiding Light in Los Angeles, she was chosen to do the reading. She was astonished, but consented. She had never worked with a group. "People asked the questions, they were put in a bottle. The first question I drew, I began to talk. I don't know where the things came from. It looked like I began to be someone else and was taking charge. I did it that night and everybody was amazed. Things started to happen that I wasn't conscious of. I called the names, the places. I wasn't conscious then of that. After that Dr. Thomas took me under his wing. We became very good friends. He taught me discipline. He had all kinds of classes and I was involved.

"Nothing told me how I knew. I became conscious of me. Looks like something came, and I became conscious of me.

"I thought it was just something that everybody had. When I would tell somebody something, they would just look at me and say, 'Ahhh!' I would think, 'Do they think I'm crazy?' I thought maybe I talked too much. That everybody else knew it but they just didn't say it."

Johnnie has two spirit guides. "Sometimes it will be Michael, the Guardian Angel. I love him. It seemed like I claimed him. And sometimes I have a happy-go-lucky Japanese. He came to me through a dream."

In working with individuals, Johnnie says, "I use a person's birthpath. I am clairvoyantly in tune with that person. I can call places, times, and names. Also while I am talking with that person, I can tell if the birthdate is correct, a forgery, or when they really don't know it. There is something about the true birthdate. It comes so spontaneously. It just flows out. When it is forged—I seem to feel the insecurity about it.

"Sometimes, when I am talking with a person, I see it like a movie screen. Sometimes I get voices and then sometimes the two will be together. It is never always a set pattern."

Johnnie enjoys explaining her metaphysical philosophy. "I believe that God made a purpose for all things He creates. He gave talent to all, and those who did use it He multiplied. Those who did not use it, He took it away.

"I also know that my God has given me the knowledge of knowing the difference between right and wrong," she asserts. "I believe that we are responsible for us."

"Tom sings beautifully, and he doesn't have to learn any tunes. He knows them all. As soon as we begin to sing, he sings right along with us!"[3]

In these words a slaveholder's child wonderingly described one of the abilities of Thomas Greene Bethune. Born as a slave on May 25, 1849 in the vicinity of Columbus, Georgia, he has been considered a "musical medium" in metaphysical circles. Blind from birth, he is generally known as "Blind Tom."

George P. Rawick recorded in *The American Slave: A Composite Autobiography* that Blind Tom's talent for music was evident before he was two years old. A piano was brought into the household when he was not quite four, and Tom quickly mastered it. Upon hearing lengthy pieces of music he was able to reproduce them note for note. At five years he composed "Rainstorm," revealing what he felt the rain, wind, and thunder had said to him.

Rawick noted other abilities. "He could hear a sermon, political speech, or lecture of any kind, and quote it word for word ... Another thing Tom could do was feel a piece of cloth and tell the color, or smell a house, and tell what was in it."

Tom became an acclaimed composer and pianist, performing throughout America and Europe.

In dreams, James Thomas receives ideas of what he might sculpture in clay. Dreams bring solutions to art problems, as well. He needed teeth for his clay figures: he dreamed of using corn. It proved to be a good material.

James' uncle, Joe, showed him how to work with clay; and as early as six years old, he was selling his sculptures around the neighborhood. He bought school supplies, which his family could not afford, with the money earned from his clay squirrels, mules, and rabbits.

James Thomas' sculpture has been exhibited at the Mississippi Historical Museum, in national folk art exhibits, and at folk art events around the United States.

He is also a blues guitarist. One of the last Mississippi Delta bluesmen of the old tradition. "I was always around music, because my grandfather played, and also my uncle," James explains.

"My uncle taught me how to make a note on the guitar. That was all. From then, I played by ear." He sings, and composes music for the guitar. Sometimes, ideas for lyrics come through dreams.

From cloud formations, and ice, he has spontaneously seen the future. "There would be an array of big clouds; you know how the clouds boil up. In them, I can see the future of people coming. I don't tell about it, I just bear out that it is true.

"When I was flying out of Oslo, I could see the future on that ice. You can't look at it too long, unless you have shades, because the sun hurts your eyes."

Born in October, 1926 in Yazoo County, James has lived in Mississippi all his life. But as a musician and artist he travels over the United States, and goes on tours to Europe.

"I've done logging, caterpillar driving, tractor driving, digging graves, hauling furniture. I've had hard work. I've picked cotton." But James emphasizes, "On the weekend, after all that work, that still didn't stop me from going on with my music on Saturday night."

"One night in New York, a big black fellow over six feet tall with muscles just felt like beating someone up. He pushed me in the face. I was rolling with the punches. Blood was all over.

"The next morning, I could not see that this had happened to me because there was not one mark. The funny thing is I saw that big black fist coming toward my face, but I couldn't feel anything. It never landed. What was he hitting? It was as if I had a shield. An invisible shield between my face and that fist. There was an invisible something taking the blows—but not my face!"

It is with other incidents like this that Pasadena resident Richmond Barthe begins his account of some of the miracles from his lifetime. An octogenarian, the famed sculptor speaks of a spiritual presence that acts as his guardian.

"I think my Guardian Angel takes care of me," he explains. "It gives you a sense of security to know you are not alone, but taken care of. I was once in New York, and I had to pick up photographs. I was rushing along the side of a building.

"Suddenly I felt a tug, and a voice said, 'Come away from the wall!'

"So I pulled away from the wall, and there was an explosion. A potted plant had fallen. I looked up and a man was looking down from the fifth floor window to see if it had hit anyone. I was just pulled out of the way in time! There was no one on the sidewalk but me.

"Another time I went to get on a train to New York. A voice said (there was no one there), 'Don't get on the train!'

"Usually I listen, but this time I tried to argue. I said, 'I don't want to spend the night in Chicago!'

"The voice said, 'Don't get on the train!'

"So I said okay. I called a hotel, went there, got in bed, and stayed there until 4:00 the next day. When I got on the train this time, the voice didn't tell me not to get on.

"We were at Dunkirk, Ohio when the porter said to me, 'In a couple of minutes, we'll be coming to the wreckage.'

"I said, 'What wreckage?'

"He said, 'Yesterday's train.'

"I looked down in the valley. There was the wrecked train I was told not to get on. I was trembling so I had to sit down."

Earlier in Barthe's life, his brother, confused over Barthe's mystical perspectives, had him committed for a seven-month period in a New York mental hospital. It was there Barthe experienced what he associates with the "loaves and fishes," the New Testament account of Jesus of Nazareth feeding the multitudes with a loaf of bread and a few fish.

"There were boys in the hospital. No one came to see them or brought them anything. I had various friends who would send me cartons of Lucky Strikes, and also my brother would bring them to me.

"Those kids all smoked! They were young teenagers. All day long, until we went to bed, I was issuing out cigarettes to those boys.

"One day my brother called to say he couldn't come down the next day to bring the cigarettes. The next day I woke up and I had one package left. It would be enough for me, but not for them. So I thought, the only thing to do is to give them out as long as they last.

"That day, the boys and I smoked as many as we did any other day. The next day my brother came with more cigarettes. The package of the day before still had three cigarettes left in it. Where did the cigarettes come from? I'm sure that wouldn't have happened if I refused to give them away. There was no bottom to that package, because I was giving them to others.

"When I looked at that, I said, 'Now I understand the loaves and fishes!' That's what happened."

He alludes to the miracle of his monetary support. "Why should I save up for rain or sickness? Our Father supplies me with all I need. All I have to do is go into my bedroom, sit down and meditate and ask for it. I come out of the room, knowing that has been taken care of, and I don't have to worry about that anymore!

"Sometimes it's material things I ask for, like money. I let go of my problem. I don't worry about it—never worry! Several days later, I go to the mailbox, and there's money I need from someone I never heard of. They claim they saw my picture in a paper or magazine and they were sending me a gift!

"I think those are my miracles. This has been going on all my life," Barthe reflects. I'm in my eighties and never have had to bother about a nickel!

"I went to Jamaica for two weeks and stayed for twenty years," he smiles. "I left Jamaica when it got too civilized.

"I was out of the United States thirty years altogether. I left Jamaica, and went to Switzerland. I stayed there from November until the following April. Then I went down to Florence and stayed there until I came here.

"The time I spent in Jamaica was one of the most wonderful things that happened to me because I got close to nature. I began to understand nature. People say it is amazing that I can communicate with animals, insects, and birds, and things like that. I think it would be amazing if I couldn't.

"When you stop to think, that little body is made of matter from the earth—so is mine! Now the only spirit that there is—there is only one Spirit, and we call that Spirit God—now if those growing things, animals, flowers, trees, did not have the Spirit in them, they would be dead. Any person without that Spirit is dead, too.

"If our bodies are made of the same matter, and the Spirit inside of us is of the same Spirit—wouldn't it be amazing if we could not communicate?

"I have had a good life, a very exciting one," Barthe comments. "In looking over my life, if I had a chance to relive it, I would choose everything that happened—including the bad things!"

"She was a woman of strong character and unusual intelligence."[4] So said Booker T. Washington, in his biography of Frederick Douglass, about Douglass' maternal grandmother, Betsey Bailey.

"There were many things she could do uncommonly well, such as gardening, and her good luck at fishing was proverbial.

"She was also famed as a fortune-teller and as such was sought far and wide by all classes of people."

Will Johnson predicted the weather by looking at the sky and making up his mind. Called "Weather Prophet" by a reporter from *Ebony* in September, 1947, Johnson had a rate of error in prediction which ranged from once a month to once every ten days.

At the time he was interviewed, the Georgia resident, sixty-two years of age, had been giving daily forecasts on his radio program for two years to a loyal audience, predominantly farmers.

Blanche Collins picks up people's thoughts. Her youngest daughter, when a toddler, made her realize that. She wouldn't talk, but chose to persevere in silence until her mother read her mind.

"I read vibrations. People automatically feel better when they come to me. I am a trouble-shooter. If something is wrong, I bring it up. Sometimes I write or just talk to the person. The Lord will break down my language so I can talk to a professor or to a moron."

As she detects confusions of energy around an individual, she identifies the discord, thus allowing the process of healing to start. While doing readings, she writes down thoughts received from the person's vibrations. She may have the individual meditate on "The Lord's Prayer," or she may read from the Bible. She uses spiritual counseling, dream interpretation, automatic writing, and psychometry in her work. The method varies in accordance with the individual's personality.

Claiming no special powers of her own, Blanche explains, "It's God's work. God does it all. I do really feel we are all endowed by God with gifts."

Blanche comes from a strong Catholic background, having attended Catholic schools. She relates a personal "baptism of spirit" between 1964 and 1967 during which she overcame the loss of a child and a broken marriage. "I learned lessons and wanted to show them to the people. I drove up and down the coast evangelizing—in bars and grocery stores.

"I learned my mind was a house, and I cleaned house. I forcibly pulled negative thoughts out of my mind and replaced them with positive.

"The day I gave myself to God, He gave me the peace and the power to do what I needed to do." She reflects, "I have been through difficult trials, trials I must pass to go higher" (in spirit).

Blanche Slaughter Collins, born in Arizona, moved with her family to the San Francisco Bay area when she was ten years old. She is still a resident of that area, giving consultations and lectures. She has also been a guest on radio programs where she is introduced as a prophetess. "My gift of faith healing, teaching, and counseling are strong. I'm getting into lecturing now.

"My purpose is to help teachers and leaders, who are now coming to me."

Blanche advises, "Clean up oneself. Don't look into other people's negativism and complain about it. Get one's own mind clear."

In looking back on her spiritual progression in this lifetime, Blanche asserts, "I see the most important thing was finding peace within myself."

Exiting from work one day in 1954, Wilda Mays, a long-time San Francisco Bay area resident, arrived at the elevator coincidentally with a middle-aged white man. He stood with the ease of one confident and familiar with the setting. But she could not recognize him as among her coworkers. Many early evenings after that, as she was leaving for home, he appeared. They were always the only ones waiting for the elevator. Others passed them, seeming to choose to leave by the stairs, not noticing.

Neither physical speech nor physical gesture was ever exchanged. From the beginning his presence caused Wilda's problems to dissipate.

Thoughts were transferred. He apprised her of the exact headlines of the next day's newspaper, of future events at work and home. These things then happened as he had indicated.

Under his tutelage, she knew the truth of things beyond the scope of earth, things she had long forgotten. She reclaimed that which was her own from among these spiritual truths, and integrated them into her being, and she felt a growing calm and integrity.

In that year after they met, she began speaking in a learned way about metaphysical subjects of which she had never thought, or read about. She could also sense people's thoughts, their failings, and feel their pain. She became aware of her abilities to see through walls and go places without her body.

With sudden insight, one day Wilda realized the man by the elevator had never been in a physical form at all, but was of spirit! It was revealed that he was an ascended Master who had chosen to work with her to revitalize her spirituality.

Through her astral travels Wilda has become acquainted with other aware beings in varied parts of the world. She is especially aware of alliances with beings in Cairo and in Washington, and has been recognized as appearing by people who live there.

"In 1968, three o'clock in the morning, July the fifth, the Spirit woke me up and said, 'Carve wood!' "[5]

Needing work and over seventy years old, Jesse Aaron had prayed that God might reveal a new trade to him.

"I got up three o'clock in the morning, got me a box of oak wood and went to work on it. The next day or two I finished it."

Aaron, born in 1887 in Lake City, Florida, was selected for a Visual Artists Fellowship in 1975 by the National Endowment for the Arts. His sculpture now has been presented widely in folk art exhibits. It is exhibited at the art gallery at the University of Florida in the town of Gainsville, where he made his home.

He most often carved from cedar and cypress because those woods naturally suggested human and animal forms to him.

Aaron once professed, "God put faces in the wood."

David Butler cuts and folds metal into flying elephants, lizards, fish, dogs, and trains, which he then paints. Biblical scenes are one of his sculpturing themes. His yard in Patterson, Louisiana is filled with his creations.

"He says he usually receives his ideas fully formed in dreams," write Jane Livingston and John Beardsley in *Black Folk Art in America 1930-1980*.[6]

Born in 1898, Butler was in his forties when he began sculpturing.

Kim McMillion says she was introduced to metaphysics by her father after his military stay in Korea. "My father came home a Buddhist. I was about eight years old. He came home believing in reincarnation, and saying he wouldn't eat any meat. This was Texas, and everybody had steaks! He said we were going to meditate. This was also 1967; we couldn't talk about it to people!"

"It was real important for him to find some kind of spiritual awakening. He was a Rosicrucian, and had been a Rosicrucian by then for a couple of years. And it was just so important for him to develop his soul.

"When I was six years old, I was really afraid of death. I was scared that I was going to die and leave my family. And it was very hard on me. After my father came back from Korea, he said:

" 'You don't die. We don't call death, death anymore. It's merely transition. You don't die, one door closes and another one opens! When you are a little older, I'll explain reincarnation to you. Meanwhile, just believe that death doesn't happen to you!' "

Kim recounts, "My worst experience was around eight years old. I remember going to bed at night, and all these people in white robes came. They said, 'We're taking you home, now.' And they would start taking me toward this planet. And I just started screaming, 'I don't want to go!' They would say, 'This is home.'

"My father always told me, 'If you get in a situation you don't understand, you just say, 'I'm a child of God, I'm a child of God!' So I started saying that and they disappeared, and they never came back again."

Kim McMillion is the author of *Voyages*, a play about reincarnation, which she produced and directed two times in the San Francisco Bay area. "I got interested in the whole writer role about the age of eleven. I told my mother I was going to become a famous writer.

"I mostly write about theatre and my experiences in theatre, and my experiences in human relationships. I love writing about relationships. How people interact with each other. How they develop through those interactions. I love working with words. Not so much words, but the communication, the subtlety of communication that goes on. I guess that's why I decided to be a playwright. I think I'm good at language, and communicating at an easy flow.

"I'm not a poet, but *Voyages* is mostly poetry. I never studied poetry. I wanted to write quickly what I felt, and so I wrote what I felt, and it came out like poetry. I also wrote about relationships because I find that from my past I'm feeling like I'm not part of anything, but more an observer. I go toward relationships as an observer. And I want to be loved. I think we are all searching for love."

The playbill's synopsis describes the production.

> *Voyages* is a series of vignettes composed of poems, monologues, and dialogues on reincarnation, chronicling a soul's journey. The dancers and actors are the soul's past lives. A painter is on-stage during the entire show and through art documents their universe. Everything the characters have ever done in or out of the human form is being painted by him. The musicians give rhythm to this universe. The theme of re-

birth is being explored through the creative tools of mixed
media, allowing the characters to go through their pain in order to come out whole, through the rebirth process.

"Basically a lot of what *Voyages* is, is my voyage. It is my voyage
because it has things which can happen to anyone, which could happen to me.

"I got real scared. I couldn't believe I did it. People came by af-
ter the show telling me how seeing the show changed their lives.
One lady came to see the show every night. She was in a wheelchair.
She said seeing the show for her was just like going to church."

A later project was Kim's writing of a screen play on Atlantis,
whose main character is an "intergalactic space traveler" named
Persephone.

"She heals different universes. She goes around with a pet lion
called Eon. He can dematerialize whenever he wants to. And he's a
healer to the animal kingdom.

"I was talking about Persephone, and she became so real that
one night when I was writing about her, I fell asleep; and the next
thing I knew I thought I was awake, but there was this lion in bed
with me. He thought I was his best friend. He was curled up against
me. I was sleeping in a loft. I don't know how I got in a loft! I got out
of the loft and quickly got in the middle of the floor, wondering what
to do about this lion. He seemed pretty safe. He seemed like a nice
lion. I realized when I woke up that I had been concentrating so
much on Persephone that I had materialized her pet lion in my
dream.

"Persephone seems like she has always been around. She really
cares about the universe and the world. She had a fall from Grace.
She is not from this planet. When she first came down here, she was a
vapor, and then she turned into a human being because of what she
did. It's a real detailed screen play. She is the favorite of all my characters. I feel really close to her."

Writing a play about racial problems around a reincarnational
theme is among Kim's plans. For this work, she describes a spiritual
being who, over a succession of lifetimes, experiences life as an African American, and then as a white person. Each lifetime having its
own problems and pains related to racial issues.

"A lot of my stuff comes in dreams. I use dreams, and I meditate, and ask myself questions. I feel I have a high degree of intuition.
Dreams help me a lot. I figure out things from dreams, and then I fig-

ure out things from my meditation. I ask myself a question about what is happening.

"I have always felt metaphysics and my life kind of went hand in hand." Kim pauses a moment, then continues. "What I want to educate people on is a sense of letting go. Such as letting go a sense of myself as stuck in little me, this body, this color, this person, towards more of a universal attitude towards life. More of a loving attitude which people should have towards themselves and the whole universe."

The Gift of Teaching

"I looked to September each year when my students entered my classroom. I was able to discern many things about them. I would look into the eyes of each student. I could tell what their talents, interests and disabilities were."

Retired teacher Elizabeth Toles describes aspects of her psychic abilities which she applied to education. Having discerned the nature of each student, she worked with them toward gaining competence and confidence in themselves. She assigned classwork on an individual basis according to what the student was capable of doing in that subject.

"I taught the fourth grade," she relates. "I could tell what the problem was with a child. I helped other teachers in telling where a child had talent. The children in my classes all made high grades, so supervisors were sent to my classes to observe me.

"I knew what the children were doing when I was out of the room," she smiles. On these occasions, much to the students' chagrin, Elizabeth would return and designate what rules were broken and who were the offenders! Another of her techniques she shares: "I always told kids to pray before a test."

With this ability to be in psychic attunement with individuals and situations, enhancing her teaching mission, Elizabeth taught elementary school for more than thirty-two years. After retiring from teaching in 1975, she worked as a counselor for the Vocational Educational Department of the State of Tennessee. A majority of her work consisted of holding workshops for teachers. Her educational assistance later extended to colleges and universities. "I talked to students there and would help them discover what to major in." Among other local honors, her educational career culminated in her receiving the Outstanding Teacher of America award.

"I was raised by an aunt," Elizabeth continues, "and later a stepmother. Finally my aunt realized there was something there different about me. In college I was conscious of using my gift all the time in school, but I wasn't aware of what it was.

"I had a friend—Thelma Green, who was a teacher. She encouraged me to use my gift openly while I was in college."

Elizabeth's services have not been limited to education alone. She has counseled individuals regarding their personal lives and businesses since 1945. She also is known as a prophet.

Participating in educational and community projects as a volunteer has been a high priority. She works with senior citizens. She helped organize a law-and-order club in South Memphis, and served as its first president. One of the club's activities was in providing anti-drug information and counseling.

In 1969 she donated half of a commercial building to the city of Memphis to be used as a community service center in a South Memphis neighborhood with a high crime rate. The center's programs have included a library, tutorial services, a junior police club, an office for the Youth Employment Service, a public assistance service program, and a sports program.

Elizabeth Toles continues to live in Memphis, where she has been the recipient of several citations from the mayor. Governor Wallace of Alabama made her an Honorary Lieutenant Governor in 1974 in recognition of her community contributions.

As a child, Elizabeth lost her sight for several years. She believes she may have developed other senses to compensate for blindness, such as her psychic abilities.

"I thank God for the gifts I have," she says. "And I am unable to explain how my God-given gifts work."

Seriously ill, in her early thirties, Terrell decided to risk surgery rather than spend her life as an invalid. "I was lying in the bed of the private hospital ... waiting to be taken to the operating room. I was praying fervently to live. I did not want to die. I promised God that if my life was spared I would devote it to the service of those who needed it most. Suddenly I felt a presence near my bed. I opened my eyes and literally saw the Saviour standing beside it, separated from me only by a small table ... I looked at Him just as I would have looked at a human being. It seemed perfectly natural for Him to be standing there. He assured me that all would be well with me. He smiled at me as a father would smile at a child in the grip of a terrible fear whose terror he wished to dispel. From that moment I felt perfectly sure I would recover from the operation and get well."[7]

In her 1940 autobiography, *A Colored Woman in a White World*, teacher and early civil rights leader, Mary Church Terrell wrote of being aware of the psychic constituent in her life.

Terrell was born in 1863 in Memphis, Tennessee. She taught at Wilberforce University in Ohio between 1885 and 1887. In 1895, she was twice appointed to the Board of Education in Washington, D.C., probably the first African American woman to hold such a post. She taught in that district from 1887, serving a total of twelve years.

She was active in the Women's Rights Movement, and the first president of the National Association of Colored Women, founded in 1886. She was an energetic supporter of the NAACP, helping to organize and participate in demonstrations and litigation for racial equality. What may be her greatest achievement was her leadership in desegregating Washington, D.C. restaurants, which occurred by court decision in 1953.

"All my life I have been conscious of something within me which enables me to feel things which were coming to pass. At times, without knowing why, I have been very wretched, and after a while I would discover that something deleterious to my family or myself had occurred during that period. Once when I was a girl about thirteen years old I cried all day one Saturday without knowing why. No girl in town was gayer than I, as a rule. I ran and played and climbed trees and sang whenever I had a chance. On this particular Saturday I had intended to spend the afternoon with one of my friends. But I felt too unhappy to go anywhere. Some time afterward I learned that my dear mother had been in serious trouble and had been treated very badly that day."

A talented artist, George Washington Carver gave up his art career to follow his destiny—becoming a teacher to his race.

"In St. John, the eighth chapter and 32nd verse, we have this remarkable statement: 'And ye shall know the truth and the truth shall make you free.'

"Were I permitted to paraphrase it," Carver added, "I would put it thus; And you shall know science and science shall set you free, because science is truth. . . .

"We get closer to God as we get more intimately and understandingly acquainted with the things He has created. I know of nothing more inspiring than that of making discoveries for one's self."[8]

From Gary Kremer's book, *George Washington Carver: In His Own Words*, come further extracts from Carver's writings which illuminate the philosophical principles which Carver used in teaching.

> The study of nature is not only entertaining but instructive and the only true method that leads up to the development of a creative mind and a clear understanding of the great natural principles which surround every branch of business in which we may engage. Aside from this it encourages investigation, stimulates and develops originality in a way that helps the student to find himself more quickly and accurately than any plan yet worked out . . .
>
> More and more, as we come closer and closer in touch with nature and its teachings are we able to see the Divine and are therefore fitted to interpret correctly the various languages spoken by all forms of nature about us. . . . Nature in its varied forms are the little windows through which God permits me to commune with Him, and to see much of His glory, majesty, and power by simply lifting the curtain and looking in . . .

Director of Agriculture and an instructor, Carver taught at Tuskegee Institute in Alabama. Born towards the end of the Civil War, in Diamond Grove, Missouri, Carver was never certain about his birthdate, but estimated it about 1864.

Carver taught, "To those who have as yet not learned the secret of true happiness, which is the joy of coming into the closest relationship with the Maker and Preserver of all things: begin now to study the little things in your own door yard, going from the known to the nearest related unknown, for indeed each new truth brings one nearer to God."

"I want to teach people how to help themselves, and to train people to use spiritual power." Mother Neal in this way describes her motivation. "I believe each and every man has to develop his own potential."

Mother Neal reads mind images, picking up vibrations through personal contact or letters. "Sometimes I get symbols, inner visions of fish, flowers. Sometimes I hear. When I open up my consciousness, I get whatever is there for that person.

"I don't see that much, but hear." She explains, "My greatest development is listening to the small voice which is 95% right."

Mother Neal was born in Quitman, Georgia in August, 1911. The fourth of thirteen children of a minister, both he and her mother encouraged their young to assert themselves. They taught them God was not at a distance but was within each one of them. "I was raised in the Holiness Church. I studied and searched, myself. I was not born with powers. I learned from Mother Miller. I joined her Temple in 1944. She taught me how to call out with water. How to work with candles."

Now a resident of Miami, Mother Neal declares, "A person has to develop the knowledge that God is not behind one, He's with you. The greatest thing is for man to find God."

"We have a way of attributing our failures to outside influences and forces. We cannot ever make another human being responsible for our own happiness. The fact of the matter is that we are the ones, the only ones, who can make ourselves a success or failure," teaches Henry Rucker. "We create our own reality," is his definitive epitomization.

Using metaphysical principles about changing attitudes, he instructs students and workshop participants on handling negative emotions and building on personal creativity.

Henry, a healer, palmist, and clairvoyant, has been aware of his psychic abilities since childhood. He lectures at colleges, organizations, and conventions throughout the United States, and he travels abroad in his work.

The Psychic Research Foundation was set up by him in Chicago in 1969. Henry's goal in establishing his Chicago foundation is a

broad one: "to bridge the gap between metaphysics, science, and religion."

"Music vibrates on all the chakras, turns thoughts inward."

Singing is the special tool of Ella Eaton. It allows the Universal
Spirit to flow through her, assisting in healing individuals and
groups, and in restoring harmony. "Singing goes into the heart of
each person."

A soprano with the New York Metropolitan Opera Company
for twelve years, Ella left in 1975 to devote herself fully to metaphysical counseling and teaching. Her work as a healer began earlier, in the 1960s. Her initial interest in metaphysics came from trying to help her daughter overcome problems with learning disabilities.

Methods she uses to raise consciousness in her teaching, counseling, and healing: meditation, prayer, visualization, techniques of
breathing, and laying-on-of-hands.

A North Carolina native, Ella lives in New York City. She is an
ordained minister in metaphysics, and a Reiki healer. Reiki is an ancient system of healing touch in which the healer directs energy toward a person to promote physical, mental, and spiritual well-
being.

She works with hospice programs at local hospitals. At the
Hospice Center at St. Luke's Hospital in New York, she served as director.

"I try to open myself to be free of judgment," she concludes. "I
consider myself a channel for communication about love for all. I
provide myself as a channel so the one Universal Spirit can work
through me."

"The goal in life is to find God." These words changed Allen
Young's life. They were spoken one day in a seminary class discussion by his teacher, Howard Thurman. "There is no need for books,
seminary, or anything but the search," Thurman had said.

"Not that I didn't know that, but those simple words were

enough for me to drop out of seminary," Allen explains. By the time Allen was twenty-nine years old, he had a degree in math and engineering, and a doctorate in education.

Fully world-minded, he was immersed in two business ventures, a greeting card firm and a consultancy business. He was associate dean in the business school at a State University campus and was also running for office in the city government. And he was married.

All these things suddenly fell apart at the same time!

"Everything that I had been attached to, that I identified myself with, just went for a big turn. If it had only been one or two, that wouldn't have been enough. Because it was so many things, I just thought, 'Something in my life is not right, I don't know what it is, but I have got to find an answer. This many things don't go wrong without a reason.'

"My first goal was to learn to understand people, so I would come to understand myself." The process of self-discovery began. After a psychic reading, he took meditation classes. Then for a year, Allen studied with a psychic organization. This led him to religion, and to seminary. He was there twelve months before he left, inspired by Howard Thurman's statement.

"Then I started pursuing Jungian psychology ... I did dream work. That really put me in touch with the language of symbols."

Two years after his "downfall," Allen reached a turning point. He gives this description:

"I had an experience in mid '77 of me really wanting to find the Truth. I had been asking that question so much that I had this lucid dream on it. I was awake, but drifting. This figure sort of curled around my body and said, 'Are you ready to follow your true spirit, your true guide?'

"I saw myself looking at my body (it was all like a dream!) and saying, 'Yes, I am ready to do this.' "

He was then asked if he was ready to give up all that he had, including his lifestyle. "As soon as that was said, I did see in the mind's eye in the dream state everything that I had been attached to—my car, my house, my education, my degrees, different people, and even the program of developing psychic ability."

The final question presented to him: "Are you ready to cut the cord?"

"The silver cord that connects you to the body, everything that I read about it, said you don't do that except when you are dying ... I said, 'No!" he recalls clearly.

Days after his experience Allen underwent change. "There was a tangible concrete shift ... I felt more awareness in my nervous system to look at the difference between good and evil in the following of the spiritual realm versus my world and its values."

Some months after another vision in 1983, Allen became aware of a new ability. "I found I could create oracles in my mind without having to use physical devices. One of them was in sitting down, asking questions, and using imagery."

He affirms that his strongest ability is in the interpreting of mental imagery. One of his main interests is in teaching what mental imagery is, how to interpret and apply it for personal benefit and in business. He implements the principles about mental imagery into the business world. "Because of my business experience up to 1975, it seems I am definitely to apply (myself) to the business world ... and to somehow blend spirit and matter together."

Born in Berkeley, California, Allen is co-founder of the Aquarian Institute which was created in the San Francisco Bay area during the years of 1978 and 1979.

Summarizing the potential in his mental imagery techniques, Allen remarks, "Whatever there is to be known (people) can get it. For people who want it totally for materiality, it won't work. But if they want to find the Truth, they will receive the answer."

As a child, Queen Ann Prince told her family what was going to happen. She saw things she knew family members hadn't seen, and could feel things coming along. "I was born a seer."

"Shut your mouth! Shut this foolishness up!" was often the family response.

"When I was fourteen, I got so mad at my mother because she always wanted to whip me. I said, 'You won't hit me anymore!' I went to the well to jump in. She said, 'Oh, no!' I have been on my own ever since," she says firmly.

"I once went totally blind for three days. But that was uncovering the spiritual. It was to wake me up from the material life to the spiritual line of life.

"My mother always rejected it because I think at that time she did not understand it. Then when I got to be thirty-five years old I said, 'Mother, one day you will appreciate me before you leave this life.' Then she began to understand and give me credit for my seeing."

Born in Martin, South Carolina in 1916, the oldest of thirteen children, Queen Ann moved to Boston in 1944 to begin her studies in Spiritualism, metaphysics, and occultism. "I had a rough time getting established because all my family turned against me—the idea of being a Spiritualist minister, and a spiritual leader."

Queen Ann has premonitions, and describes a psychic awareness and discernment. "I read directly from the mind. Mine comes from within."

She works within the school system around Boston. She has a teaching permit as an outreach teacher. Directing children and young adults toward realizing the Truth within themselves is how she explains her commitment. "When you find yourself, you have nothing on earth to worry about. You will be rooted in God. You don't have to worry about anything," she proclaims.

She is the founding Spiritualist minister of "Lily of the Valley," a nondenominational church established in 1955 in Malden, Massachusetts where she is a resident.

"That means all nations can come, anybody."

She lectures, gives readings, and teaches metaphysical and occult principles to individuals and groups. She performs healings and exorcisms.

One of the exorcisms she describes as being among the worst matters to which she has ever attended. "But when you know yourself and what to do, you don't have to worry about what kind of danger is coming up, because you are rooted and grounded."

Her spiritual gifts helped her "learn to love the world," and taught her to accomplish widely through their use. She loves doing spiritual work. "I am a happy soul in my life," Queen Ann claims. "Your life has to be balanced. The material has to have its food, and the spiritual has to have its food."

"I try to motivate people to realize that whatever they need is internal. You must come from the inside and then go out. Most people, I say, are outside all the time. I try to help them get inside. Everything you need is inside of you. That is my master goal, to help people to have their own personal realization of that, and to be aware of how we are spiritual."

These are goals which Delilah Grayer has for students attending her workshops on intuitive perception. She blends clinical psychology with non-traditional techniques.

More than fifteen years ago, Delilah was given the name "Soyini" (which means "greatly endowed") by a priest who teaches African philosophy.

Soyini knew of her psychic attributes in childhood and used them, encouraged by her family which strongly acknowledges intuitivity. Her daughter, Bakara Oni, whose name in Yoruba means "of noble promise, born at a special place and in a special time," shares in the endowment.

From an informational pamphlet of her "Celebrating Yourself" workshop series, Delilah's approach is further amplified.

> In her practice, Soyini considers the pluralistic nature of interpersonal behaviors, looking at the physical, psychological, social and spiritual aspects, culminating them into a holistic therapeutic approach. Soyini utilizes palmistry, basic astrology, and numerology in her counseling and consulting.

In one of her workshops, titled "Back to Our Roots," participants are taught to use traditional African healing rituals in the treatment of modern-day mental health problems.

Delilah, a resident of Cleveland, Ohio has a Master's degree in clinical psychology, and has completed doctoral coursework in that discipline. An independent consultant, she also works with stock brokerage and business firms.

"People must learn to shift their perception," she teaches. "It took me years to understand the phrase 'everything works together for the good.' It only works for the good if you see it as good—no matter what your experience is. If it is negative, you have to reverse it, shift your perception and make something positive out of it. So I have people shift their perceptions. That is what I do."

"When I was 10 years old, I got up one night to go to the bathroom. When I returned, my father, who had died a year earlier, was standing in the door!

"I had no one to talk to about this experience. I could feel things—I had clairsentience. I gave people warnings about things. But I couldn't talk with my mother. She didn't understand, and my uncle was a Methodist minister, so my abilities then were not recognized."

When Eleanor Walker studied metaphysics in adulthood, and came upon the concept of free will, it liberated her. She made immediate changes in her life. She could then acknowledge her psychic gifts. "I was a visionary, clairvoyant, and then became clairaudient. We are all here to grow. Each person comes with an opportunity to work out his karma."

A certified metaphysical teacher, Eleanor holds church services in her home in Washington, D.C. "Man has to know himself, who he is and why he is. The thing is, not to become obsessed by material things. My purpose is to teach and serve in whatever way I can. My students all learn to help people to become aware of beauty within. I teach that as children of God we are all one." Her students come from varied religious backgrounds, and after training, return to their own congregations to share. Her courses include the study of telepathy, vibrations, and how to heal through energy adjustments.

"Mankind is not really aware of what it is and what it has to offer. Few realize that God is not up in the sky but within. Everything lies within oneself. You don't seek it outside of oneself.

"Mankind," she emphasizes, "has to realize what Jesus died for is to show us the way. Mankind needs to dwell on life the way it is now, and not life way back there."

Eleanor is a native of Washington, D.C. Both her husband and son have psychic abilities. "This is the Spiritual Age," Eleanor states. "Some people don't believe it, but this is the time for people to get into awareness of their spiritual selves."

Being able to materialize physical-world events, and effect solidifications and conditions from consciously created pictures in her mind are abilities Beverly Moore has had since childhood. "But in childhood, I didn't know if I was creating it or if I was just foreseeing it. I am one with very much faith. When I ask God for something, I know without a shadow of a doubt that it is going to happen.

"There is no lack in the Universe. I have problems like everybody else, but I only give energy for it to work out for the highest good."

Beverly is clear-hearing and clear-seeing, with abilities in creative visualization, automatic writing, and card-reading. A resident of Stamford, Connecticut, she teaches courses in psychic and spiritual development through local adult education programs, and provides individual counseling.

Beverly recalls her abrupt leaving of her family when she was 17. She had only $25 when she left college in North Carolina to go to Atlantic City, and only $10 left after paying her bus fare. She knew with some certainty that she was going to get a job upon arrival—it was an intuitive knowing. As the bus approached Atlantic City, she fell asleep. In dreamstate she saw a motel and the unclear image of a man. She saw he would give her work, a place to stay, and meals as well as wages.

"About five minutes after I saw that vision, I awoke and pulled the bus cord for the bus to stop. Outside I had seen that same motel from my vision." The motel manager said his chamber maid had just quit. Would she be interested in taking over the job, with salary, board, and room?

Beverly remarks that she has sometimes suppressed her clear-seeing ability, because of incidents relating to it. "After I suppress it, it takes time to get it back. I can see, but there for a time is kind of a fear there.

"For example," she reflects, "at two in the afternoon one day I was quiet—not meditating, just quiet. Every time I closed my eyes I would see something. I saw a man. What I saw wasn't frightful, but there was a part of me that got upset. The man was close to me. He had a bald head and I could even see the wrinkles in his scalp!

"I said: 'Ohh!' I wasn't asleep and I wasn't dreaming! I'd seen other things like that—but he was a little too close! Most of the other real things had been at a distance, as if I'm looking through a telescope. It's like a light, and it opens up and then the images are there.

It's just like I'm peeping through a peephole and I can see you on the other side in the flesh. That was fine with me, as long as it was at a distance!

"There was a time I was meditating, and I astroplaned. But I didn't do it voluntarily. I said to myself:

" 'Dear heavenly Father, I'm not ready yet!'

"I could feel the altitude change. I could see so many beautiful things but I didn't want it. But I did want it!"

Changing the subject, Beverly says, "I do past life regressions. I do know that in a past life I was very clear-seeing, and exactly what it is I haven't tried to find out. I do know for 17 years in a past life I was blind with the physical eyes, and that made me develop clear-seeing more. There is a block, a missing link for why in this life I'm having trouble accepting it. What I think it is, it just reminds me of when I was blind so part of me doesn't want clear-seeing."

Asked how she implements her gifts, Beverly replies, "I teach. There seems to be a yearning or an urge to develop people's sensitivity." She tells her students they can handle their own problems, and proceeds to show them what to do. "It is not that you are born with a veil over the face or something like that; everyone has a gift. I like to bring it out."

One of Beverly's projects is in teaching self-awareness to children. Using a technique of meditation and breathing exercises, she teaches them self-attunement. "They find they can do it. It doesn't take days. They can do it the same day I show them."

Recalling an experience with her husband, Beverly notes: "Over a period of a month and one-half, I felt something was wrong. I knew somebody was going to pass. Somebody close to me. I thought it was maybe someone in North Carolina. I did my automatic writing my meditation.

"Automatic writing said, 'Leave it alone! There is a meaning and a purpose!' The automatic writing would not let me find out and now I'm glad. The information which comes through me is for my highest good.

"I left it alone, and then about a week later, I began feeling really, really eerie. It was so strange. I felt the separation. I noticed even the children did. It was like my husband wasn't even here. It was like he was here in the physical, but he wasn't. There was a block between us. The feeling was like there was no need for us to be married. I started thinking about a divorce." Beverly's husband died unexpectedly soon after from heart stoppage during a tracheotomy.

Earlier, Beverly had done a card-reading which revealed he was sick, that a physical problem was not being handled. The cards pointed to a separation, and a new beginning for him and her. She told him about it. For the first time, her husband listened to her and went to a doctor. "When he came back, it was like a new lifetime for us. It was beautiful. He was more loving. We had the best time. That one week was like a lifetime. I never saw him pray, but I knew he prayed and listened to me that day." Within a week, however, he authenticated the message Beverly received from the cards.

To explain how she has used creative visualization in resolving conflicts, Beverly says, "No matter what they have said to me or done to me, I separate myself from the personality of Beverly Moore or ego. I lift myself to a higher state of consciousness, a more divine state of consciousness. I visualize I am looking back down on Earth, and I am sending them a lot of love. I see them hugging me and I am hugging them.

"What happens is that the person either calls me, comes to my door, and sometimes I come to them. I don't worry. I just allow myself to be led. If I am led to do something, I do it. It doesn't matter who comes to who. When the meeting is there, you can tell that something divine has happened . . . When you want someone else to win, you are winning yourself.

"Suppose a negative thought comes to my mind; I know how to strike it out . . . how to release negativity from my mind. I teach people how to do that. It is part of loving yourself, you make sure you don't feed on that negativity. Whether it's a courtroom situation, a job—send that love in.

Beverly advises earnestly, "Love is the highest vibration. Visualize love coming from the God sources, through the chakras, and loop it into that courtroom. I don't worry how it's done. It works out!"

"I'll bring you up on the marquee!" This is the favorite expression Claude Perry uses to signal his intention to psychically read the individual before him. In this way the Livingston, New Jersey high school guidance counselor and psychic receives information about another person's future or hidden troubles. Before his inner eye a marquee flashes with messages about people and events, and he reads from this psychic sign-board.

Claude has a Master's degree in education and is working on a doctorate. His wife, Mable, also a guidance counselor, already has her doctorate in education.

In his guidance counselor role he reads the high school student's auras as he counsels them. "I can tell the student what's on his mind," he imparts. One student planning a technical career admitted with relief that he really wanted to go to college, after Claude told him of his inhibited desire. Claude has often prepared a student for a crisis which he foresaw for that student. His efforts are towards awakening the potential of each individual he counsels. "I pick up their auras, but I don't tell them I'm psychic.

"As a child," Claude comments, "I would dream a lot and I would have understanding of my dreams. I would send telepathic messages to my mother."

His auric sense arrived in a spontaneous manner. The electromagnetic energy fields surrounding people and objects, in varied colors, densities, and vibrations, suddenly became visible to him. Placing his hands on an object, he knows through vibrations the owner's concerns.

Not until college did Claude give much credence to his abilities. His gift of prediction was emerging. He predicted three years before it happened the resignation from the presidency by Richard Nixon.

During a trip to Japan he became interested in Buddhism. He has learned to appreciate the cultures of all people. One of his enjoyments is reading the Psalms. He feels religiously attuned with the Biblical hero, David.

Along with his gifts came the knowledge that he could not use them for lotteries, or any material gain for himself or others. "My gift is spiritual and may not be put to use that way," he stresses.

"I think I extend myself to people on the basis I perceive their needs. I can reach to people and help them prepare for situations."

Claude gives attention to getting the right nutrients into his body. "I can tell when my body needs certain vitamins." He feels African Americans should make greater effort to keep themselves healthy.

His advice to youngsters: "There is a whole big world out there. Get an armful of it! Get out there and contribute!"

A group of discorporate spiritual beings, in accord with her, and availing themselves for Universal good, work with Latifu Munirah. Different ones share in the readings. They respond based on the specific knowledge needed. There is no single guide which consistently manifests to Latifu when she reads or teaches—nor even when she requests direction for her own growth. Through her own voice that she hears in her head, and through her feelings, they communicate with her.

"I don't really see them. I ask them to come and I know they are there," she says. "They are very gracious. Their personalities come out quite a bit when I start communicating and asking questions in my head when I do readings. They have a wonderful sense of humor. And it takes people off guard. They give jokes. And it's not that the guides aren't serious!

"I'm not a trance medium. I'm totally in control. I will give messages but not yield my body."

Latifu teaches psychic development in the San Francisco Bay area to individuals and groups. "I feel a large part of my calling is to be a teacher. And to teach a variety of things," she explains. "I taught social work for many years. I felt very comfortable with that.

"I think I'll always teach and get involved in training, because I feel I'm doing something worthwhile when I work with people in assisting them in developing their own skills and encouraging them to expand themselves. I like being a catalyst for people."

After accepting a teaching position at Atlanta University, she lived in Atlanta, Georgia for three years. She went on to teach social work at the University of Iowa for two and a half years. She was also a graduate student there. She taught practice classes on racism and discrimination, and did academic advising.

It was not until Latifu settled in the San Francisco Bay area that she took classes in psychic development. She studied at the Aquarian Institute for two years, and taught beginning classes there for a while before starting her own metaphysical study groups. "I'm coming out of a period where I've not wanted to be involved with other people. Spirit has made it such that I have not been involved with other people, in terms of teaching. I have been going through some personal transformations.

"I am preparing to teach again, and I also am preparing to learn. Now I've requested that Spirit send me a teacher, and I'm awaiting the teacher's arrival. I also said that I'm prepared to teach again, and so have scheduled a class in psychic development.

"I just decided that it is important for me to go ahead and develop, because I have a tendency to do more work on the psychic plane, through the use of the voice. Probably because I am a social worker by training, and it's part of that training I have."

Latifu elaborates on types of psychic healing, explaining that there are two types. One has to do with the adjusting of the aura and laying on of hands. The other is mental or psychic healing which is done on a psychic plane without any movement of the hands.

"Basically what I do centers around the gift of healing, and to some extent the gift of discerning, to a little precognition of what's going to happen. To me, discernment is getting at the truth of what's happening." Latifu reflects for a long moment. "I feel like I'm still at the beginning of all this, and there is so much more for me to learn. And I just opened myself up to that. "I'm really interested in what women have done," she proclaims. "I'm really serving as a catalyst for women to regain power over themselves and their own destinies, not over others."

Latifu revealed her own philosophy, "I will encourage my students with everything I have to develop their own skills, and be dependent upon themselves. And to have a healthy interdependency with other human beings. And to use relationships differently than perhaps they have before.

"Because to me, when people are dependent upon other people, and yield seniority, or yield their powers, there is no way on Earth they can fulfill their own potential."

Laura Edwards was going through a troublesome time. Her four children were very young. Her grandmother admonished Laura on how she was relating to them. "You don't know these people. They are people! Individually!" She then gave Laura a little book on astrology. It was the older woman's intent that her great-grandchildren be raised differently than most people, that her granddaughter know her children and herself on a deeper level.

"In my family all my children are naturally spiritual beings. It was a unique experience learning from the children what being psychic was all about, what being spiritual was all about."

Laura regards her grandmother as her true friend and teacher. She recalls being most impressed by her grandmother's capacity to love and forgive. When Laura sought to be instructed in those qualities she was told, "You just do these things." Her grandmother's forte was in the Tarot cards which she used to make predictions.

"My grandmother pushed a button in me, and I unfolded. I guess, like I was supposed to. Before that, there was nothing, except being fascinated by people. My awareness of being psychic was never there until my grandmother pushed that button!" That Laura was benefiting from the studies became evident, so her grandmother introduced her to cards and palmistry as well.

"I developed my psychic self from those avenues. Things started to happen to me as I started to raise my consciousness to a different level. All of a sudden it wasn't just my children or my grandmother. They became different to me. I studied them with a passion!"

A teacher of metaphysical and psychic subjects, Laura Edwards has lived in Cleveland, Ohio all of her life.

Laura moved into the study of meditation, metaphysics, and everything she could find of the positive aspects of the spiritual world. She studied philosophy, yoga, Eastern and Indian thought. "I was never in anything negative," she relates. "I've always had this intuition which would say to me, 'This is not a good thing!' Over the years this intuition developed more and more as I became further interested in God and people.

"Someone would ask me, 'Have you heard of this?' And something within me would say, "Leave it alone!"

Her perceptions awakened. Laura could now see auric pictures which had audible qualities.

"It is strange to see a picture when you are looking at a person. I didn't have my eyes closed. It was never like that for me. I am looking at you, and I can see something, and I am hearing something, and I am experiencing something else at the same time." It was in this manner, at first, that information and conditions of the future came to Laura.

Asked about the difficulties arising from practicing psychism as a service to the public, Laura concedes that for a while she withdrew from her practice. "You can get caught up in the glamour of it. When I was in the public a lot, I found it was intimidating to my own spiritual growth. When you start looking at yourself as 'somebody' you've automatically lost yourself. You've just slammed a door in your own face. The pull on you is enormous. When you get out there, people start giving you attention. You feel wonderful. We are like children. Your pendulum will swing from loving it to running from it."

Laura teaches meditation as a way to find answers within the self. She helps people to tap their own potential of knowing, encouraging their consciousness of spirit to flow through them. "There is a stream that is constant between us as human beings," she assures. "What we are dealing with is our search for this truth that unites us. I think we are looking for that connection on every level. I believe that the people who are involved in the spiritual world, for the most part, understand that oneness more, and are trying to do something about making everybody aware of it. We feel kinship. We are working on trying to overcome ourselves."

"My purpose? Teaching, so that people can find their way. We are all here for a reason, and the reason for any lifetime is growth. If you don't grow, you rot!"

So asserts Delores O'Bryant, director of the Uranian Agency, Center for New Age Sciences in Cleveland. The Uranian Agency is a holistic health and education establishment.

"I have been aware all my life. In childhood, I heard voices, felt an intuitiveness, and there were feelings."

Delores' profession was real estate, which she gave up to teach astrology and other metaphysical disciplines. In a pamphlet issued by Astro-Logic-ally Speaking, an Ohio metaphysical network of which Delores is the executive director, she writes:

> It seems to me that astrology and the ancient teachings are experiencing a renaissance. I would suggest, so as not to become caught up in chaotic, unrealistic conditions caused by

the ruthless tactics of those in authority, that we make use of our own personal, natural resources on a collective level. I would suggest that we choose not to participate in the nega- tive. Choose to accept changes, offered now, in the way you relate to conditions and situations around you. Choose to be willing to be a part of the group through positive reinforce- ment of our imaging faculties, and to gain control of and direct this illusion of which we have chosen to be a part.

Since first studying astrology in 1969, she has written newspa- per columns and has been featured on radio and television pro- grams. From an outline of one of her talks given in 1984, Delores is described as coming "to realize that everything and everybody is part of one whole ... And an idea or dream, which is a goal set for yourself, is also something which you have to do. You are supposed to do!" She emphasizes, "Once you are excited about something, you are getting in touch with your mission, and then every door opens to make that dream come true."

"My life's purpose? Teaching in all of its forms. I consider my- self teaching through my storytelling and the artistic stuff that I do.

"And then there is teaching through being. If you do work on yourself, you start to embody certain qualities. I often say when I see something that I view to be good, I say not only let me know it, but let me be it. Because we accept each other in several ways, as well as very clear-cut deliberate ways. "We need to keep going compassion- ately, not in denial. It's not my nature to go hide on the mountain when there are things that need to be done on Earth, of a physical and material level."

Luisah Teish of the San Francisco Bay area is author of the book *Jambalaya*. In her role as teacher-lecturer, she travels the country giv- ing workshops and classes on African goddesses, feminist spiritual- ity and shamanism. She has been doing this work since 1980. A friend of Luisah's attending the first workshop said to her, "Teish, you really think you're being generous by sitting here and giving us this information. Think about that sister in Mississippi who is sitting in her cabin and crying, depressed with no one to talk to. By not writ- ing a book—you're being stingy with her."

"That made it real for me," Luisah says. "Suddenly I could see that woman a thousand times over. I let myself agree that a book should be done and more widely distributed."

Luisah gained support from "sisters" who burned candles and sent her energy as she wrote. Once when she was stuck, she corresponded with a woman who had sent her a letter from somewhere in the Northwest. The woman wrote her back, saying she had gone into meditation, during which a goddess appeared to her as a three-legged hen. She told the woman to send a message to Luisah that everything would be all right, that she would finish the book.

"I think about that and start to recognize that the book is the product of a number of people. Not just me." Luisah credits, "She-Who-Whispers, Yemaya, and all the ancestors from Africa on through. They pumped the information into me. She-Who-Whispers brought me the inspiration, and the women of my community kept the motivation going."

Luisah speaks of other assistance from another plane. "Shortly after we had an eclipse of the moon, I came into this house. The lights went out on the block for an hour, we had candles lit all over the house. I laid down and I got the message real clear of all of my ancestors sitting around a table. They were shuffling the papers of my destiny. They were looking at the contract of my life. They were saying, 'We have to make some amendments here and look at something there.'

"I don't know what areas they are talking about. But I do know on a spiritual level, me and my ancestors are renegotiating. Right now I feel eclipsed. I go from one day to the next. I don't know what's going to come on the next wave of vision. But I do know that if it is true to pattern, it will be hard work and exciting!

"Almost every religion in the world tells us to listen to the still small voice," Luisah relates. "But when that voice really starts to talk to you—you cannot say that publicly. At times when I was working on that section (a story in *Jambalaya* entitled 'The Needy Winter') I could see the blue-suited psychologist standing by his desk saying, 'We clearly have a case of disassociative personality!'

"That's a problem because unfortunately psychology and psychiatry forget that they are the grandchildren—not the forebearers. They create a mode where the only time they have anything to say about hearing voices—it's that someone is crazy. So it is projected that if you hear voices at all, you're sick. This instills fear. So that as soon as your guiding voice speaks—you add fear to it and ruin it.

"I felt to say clearly to people, 'I've been crazy, and have come out the other side, and it's wonderful over here!' "

Conceding that sometimes her heightened perception makes day-to-day living somewhat difficult, Luisah still opts for the importance of gaining knowledge. "For me, ignorance is not bliss. Yes, it is painful sometimes to be so very tuned in to the pains of so many people. But a reward is knowing that sometimes you can do something about it. The reward is that people's joy is also contagious. The biggest reward for me is that I am never bored. I don't know what bored feels like. I'm able to say that I love my life, and I know there was a time that I couldn't say that. I am infinitely richer because I'm willing to be, open to be. I can find the joy in the very simple things. Like a lot of people, I like material things. But we get trapped into thinking we can only be happy if we are wearing Calvin Klein's.

"We're beyond the age of tribalism," Luisah reminds us. "I am fortunate in that I can walk outside and look at the roses, and birds and children playing down the street and I can be really happy. I can really count myself fortunate, for the treasure is in recognizing interconnection with other people. Of not being blinded by overbearing ethnocentrism."

Prior to founding the Crenshaw Metaphysics Institute in Los Angeles, Cora Keeton and Jessica Marshall studied together at a metaphysical university to earn their doctorates. "I met Jessica in 1970 through my deceased husband," Cora recalls. "We shared similar interests and studied together at the university. Now, we meet to work together for each other and with other black psychics in the area."

As far back as seven years old, Cora remembers her dreams came true, and that she saw disembodied souls. Information came to her before it was actualized in the physical world. "But I ran away from it," she says. Her mother opposed her gifts, but the real blow came while she was in her teens. A friend's boyfriend disapproved of her gifts so strongly she tried to shut them off.

In her mid-twenties, Cora decided to understand her attributes through study, and to learn to use them as tools for the spiritual betterment of herself and others. "I started reading professionally after

I got my doctorate. I had more certainty and structure. I asked guidance from God. I started teaching classes to those wanting to develop and also giving psychic treatments. I am better because of my psychic gifts. There is meaning in my life. I feel more fulfilled than ever before. Studying, and opening the Center have been very rewarding." She counsels, and teaches through psychic readings, metaphysical consultations, voodoo, past life regression therapy, exorcisms, and meditation. "I let people know they have control when they come to me."

Cora's deep interest lies in helping African Americans to develop and use their intuition. "I do psychic work—negatively called voodoo. I want to enlighten black people to use their psychic abilities and to bring those abilities out of fear and superstition." Only five African Americans studied at the university when Cora attended. There, she resolved to open a center in her community. "When I started in 1976, all my clientele was white—now, it's 50-50!"

Cora's associate, Jessica, aware at ten that she could predict, purposefully and confidently, directed mental energy to influence people's thoughts and to get her way.

Her studies of metaphysics began in 1975, and in 1977 she received her doctorate.

She refers people to the Bible, not for religious doctrine, but for spiritual Truth. "Sharing a deeper meaning of the Truth in the Bible," and teaching people how to apply those Truths to everyday living are her goals. The Bible, meditation, the alchemy of herbs, candles, oils, incense, and regular playing cards are some of the ways through which Jessica implements consultations and psychic healing.

Of her own directions, Jessica confides, "Being psychic lets me develop my life to make it more harmonious, peaceful and closer to God. To be one with, and be aware of my oneness with God. To be able to share the understanding and wisdom with all people. Regardless of where or who we are—we are all on the path to God. We sometimes need physical tools to remind us that our purpose is to serve God and humanity."

Jessica evaluates, "I feel that I have helped people to understand themselves better and how they fit into the universal scheme of life. That even though we are individuals, we are in this together. I have shared a lot with people. I intend to continue sharing my understanding of life with other people. Whenever someone comes with a personal problem, I let them know they need God with them. I use counseling to get them back into the Bible—not for religious dogma, but for spiritual growth."

Jessica, born in Louisiana, raised in Oakland and Los Angeles, is a long-time Los Angeles resident.

Cora and Jessica speak of growing together, and inspiring each other in their relationship, which goes back to 1970. They travel nationwide to co-teach seminars. Since the last decade, they have brought African American psychics together to work on "directing light into the collective thought forms of the black community."

When I was a little boy, I gave a declamation as part of the "Children's Day" exercise of our Sunday school. When the program was over, "Old Lady Murray" came up to me, placed her hand on my head, looked down into my upturned face, and said: "Howard, God's spirit has surely touched you. You must ask Him not to pour more of His spirit upon you than you can manage."[9]

This is a personal recollection from Howard Thurman's autobiography, *With Head and Heart*. A writer of religious composition and poetry, he authored more than twenty books; a minister, philosopher, and teacher, he educated about spirituality.

Self-love is the kind of activity having as its purpose the maintenance and furtherance of one's own qualitative self-regard and is in essence the exercise of that which is spiritual. If we accept the basic proposition that all life is one, arising out of a common center—God, all expressions of love are acts of God.[10]

It is the solitariness of life that makes it move with such ruggedness. All life is one, and yet life moves in such intimate circles of awful individuality. The power of life perhaps is its aloneness ... Each soul must learn to stand up in its own right and live ... Ultimately, I am alone, so vastly alone that in my aloneness is all the life of the universe. Stripped to the life literal substance of myself, there is nothing left but a naked soul, the irreducible ground of individual being, which becomes at once the quickening throb of God. At such moments of profound awareness I seem to be all that there is in the world, and all that there is in the world seems to be myself.[11]

But there is loneliness in another key. There is the loneliness of the truth-seeker whose search swings him out beyond all frontiers and all boundaries until there bursts upon his view a fleeting moment of utter awareness and he *knows* beyond all doubt, all contradictions.... There is the loneliness of those who walk with God until the path takes them out beyond all creeds and all faiths and they know the wholeness of communion and the bliss of finally being understood.[12]

Providing perspective on Thurman's teachings, these are writings by him drawn from Luther E. Smith, Jr.'s book, *Howard Thurman: The Mystic as a Prophet*. Smith gives this interpretation of Thurman's theme:

The individual personality has ultimate significance. The person is a "child of God," and this status has no superior. The welfare of each member of God's creation is important to the welfare of the whole creation. Containing the *imago dei*, the individual personality is able to express love throughout creation, and bring the universe to its proper state of harmony.[13]

Thurman's approach as a teacher and minister is conveyed in the Publisher's Preface to *God and Human Freedom*, edited by Henry James Young. "Howard Thurman's response to 'first-hand experience' was to share—in the classroom, in the pulpit, and in print—the oneness he felt with God and creation. His writing and speaking drew us beyond ourselves toward our divine possibilities."[14]

Having earned a doctorate in theology, during his teaching career Dr. Thurman taught at Morehouse and Spellman Colleges in Atlanta, also serving as religious advisor to students and faculty at both institutions. At Howard University in Washington, D.C. he was on the faculty for twelve years, and a professorship at Boston University followed. He retired from his academic career in 1965. Then his focus shifted to working within the Howard Thurman Educational Trust, a non-profit organization, with offices in San Francisco. Established in 1965, the activities of the Trust continue today and its purposes are described in *With Head and Heart*.

The Trust was dedicated to the education of black youth in colleges all over the country, but primarily in the Deep South; it was also dedicated to the enrichment of the religious and spiritual commitment of individuals who would be helped by the collection and classification of my written and taped messages and materials that were the distilled essence of my spiritual discoveries—what I had gleaned from the collative fruits of more than forty years.[15]

Melvin Watson, professor emeritus of philosophy and religion at Morehouse College, reflected about his former teacher in *God and Human Freedom*. "For Dr. Thurman, education was not considered to be a pouring-in process but a leading-out, the development of the innate powers of the student's mind. He threw himself enthusiastically into this process."[16]

In the same publication appear the comments of Benjamin Mays, former dean of Howard University, and former president of Morehouse College, on his former student's qualities as a teacher. "Many times he would spend hours with a single student engaging in the search for religious truths. Students became so overwhelmed with the intellectual genius and effective teaching style of Thurman that his popularity began to emerge at the national level. He attracted students to Atlanta from all over the nation."[17]

Author Luther E. Smith, Jr. reminisces about his association with Dr. Thurman, and shares some of his personal impressions about his teacher. "There was a freedom one felt in his presence. But Thurman was well aware that life had to be disciplined. And he could be funny—at times. I resonated with what Thurman was saying," Luther goes on in memory. "Thurman brought me to a legitimacy of my own path. He added depth to my path. My spiritual heritage was confirmed. My contact with Dr. Thurman provided depth and clarity to my spiritual development. This included fully embracing the rational and embracing the intuitive aspects.

"There was something about Thurman's presence. It was not just in the way he spoke. Thurman created experience and it elevated one. He opened a door.

"You felt love in his presence," Luther explains. "He cared and you felt love."

Having received an invitation to be a visiting lecturer at a university in Nigeria, in 1963, Thurman wrote of his anticipation in *With Head and Heart*:

> I longed to discover the sources of indigenous African religions, to explore the underground spiritual springs that ran deep, long before the coming of Islam or early Christianity. I hoped to find a common ground between Christian religious experience and the religious experience in the back-

ground and in the heart of the African people. If such a common ground could be located and defined, it seemed to me that the finest insights of Christianity could be energized by the cumulative, boundless energy of hundreds of years of the brooding spirit of God as it expressed itself in many forms in the life of a great people.

It seemed to me . . . in Africa were still preserved perhaps the oldest religious memories of mankind.[18]

"We are in search. Everybody is in search, whether they know it or not." These words of Alfred Ligon applied in his lifetime. In his own search, he was inspired by his reading of *The Aquarian Gospel of Jesus The Christ*, which communicated to him the idea of the coming of the Aquarian Age. In 1941, Ligon wound up his activities in Chicago and New York, and headed to Los Angeles, where he started a bookstore called "The Aquarian Library and Bookshop."

Before long, lectures, forums, and workshops were being held on the premises. Leading local metaphysicians and occultists came to speak. Ligon and his wife, Bernice, lectured, conducted series of study groups, and held metaphysical events in the bookshop and in their home over the years.

Regarding his own studies in metaphysics and occultism, Ligon said, "From 1936 to 1945, I was studying, preparing myself. I was interested in being an occultist and a doctor of metaphysics."

His astrological interest began in the 1930s when he read and took courses on the subject. "I was actually looking for answers in terms of my life."

Disappointment over being unable to establish himself in dance in the theatre started his personal search. "Prior to that time, I had followed, since I was a small child, the theatre. I was working in the dance field and the singing field in the theatre in Chicago for a number of years. A circuit went from New York, Chicago, Philadelphia, Detroit, and Kansas City. I was working with that. All black companies. When they put in the 'talkies,' they stopped the stage productions."

While in their early forties, the Ligons embarked upon a twenty-year occult philosophy course which they completed within the designated period of time. It was called a laboratory workshop, and was also known as the Sabaen Assembly. During the 1940s when the Ligons started the course, founder and occult philosopher Marc Edmund Jones was offering it for the second twenty-year cycle.

There were very few African Americans besides the Ligons participating in the metaphysical and occult programs the couple attended or organized in the Los Angeles area in the "early days." In 1965, most of the Caucasians who were engaged in metaphysical studies or programs through the Aquarian Spiritual Center, an expansion of the Aquarian Library and bookshop, left because these were located in the general area of the Watts riots. "They wanted me to come with them, but I had a purpose here. Some of the work we endeavor to do is in helping people to establish the 'Beloved Community.' The Beloved Community is also the background of what we would define as the fellowship or the brotherhood of Aquarius where the group would get together and live in peace and harmony.

"I continued with the work at the Center. I began to have small classes in astrology. I began to call the classes Studies in Black Gnosticism. I can't tell you what motivated me to take that particular name." With the advent of Black Gnostic Studies, an interest in the bookstore and Center was sparked in the African American community. "The young ones started coming into the bookstore. In our lessons we defined that the word 'black' was also used by the Sufis, the esoteric group which is related to Islam. They used the word 'black' to mean 'wise'. They used it in that particular sense: if you are black, you are wise. That was the early part of the background we studied.

"The witch doctors were actually highly evolved in their spiritual orientation. They were clairvoyant or mediumistic. Albert Churchward (author of *Arcana of Freemasonry*) speaks of how at the time of one's death those witch doctors (masters) could see the energy coming out of the body in the form of what the body was. They knew that something existed outside the physical body. So they would try to make contact with those energies."

The Aquarian Spiritual Center has become a national organization with seven lodges located across the country. As printed in one of its publications, *Studies in Black Gnosticism*, The Aquarian Spiritual Center offers aspirants knowledge from black gnosticism which is based upon the teachings of the Mystery Schools of ancient Egypt and Africa. Helping members to discover who they are, and the means by which to put this knowledge into practical application, are the ultimate goals of the Center.

From the archaeological findings and other records that have been passed down through the ages, we find proof that the human race began in Africa. Moreover, not only are the origins of humanity to be found in Africa, but the origins of religion and freemasonry are to be found there as well. This spiritual evolution of mankind out of Africa is based on three main points:

1) A belief in the powers or spirit forces in the elements of nature: Earth, Air, Fire and Water. Recognizing that the continuation and health of human life was dependent upon these forces, the early Africans had greater fear and respect for the powers of nature than we have today . . .

2) Psychic ability. It is well known that many early Africans had highly developed abilities in what we now call parapsychological powers (e.g., clairvoyance, clairaudience, and psychometry) ... Because the early Africans had such good psychic communications between the visible and invisible worlds, they developed a different attitude toward life and death than that which we have today. They realized that life and death are unending cycles.

3) The existence of a Great Spirit in the Universe. The early Africans gave this Great Spirit no name for they described it as the nameless, formless, unknowable, unseeable, untouchable indestructible force. It had no beginning or ending and did not concern itself with the everyday problems and lives of humans.[19]

Born in Atlanta, Georgia in 1906, Alfred M. Ligon, a doctor of metaphysics, is a resident of Los Angeles.

Dr. Ligon says that "In the field of work of what we have to do is to bring the soul of man out, and help him to utilize his soul energy instead of just being a physical person. We try to take the young ones and give the proper kind of training; not education, because that is already in them and has to be drawn out. But finding the soul that can relate to the work and be trained in that particular sense."

He pauses to encapsulate his thoughts. "We have to go forward and understand what those things were all about. We have to go forward and prepare the younger generation for what we would define as the Aquarian Age."

A plane crash shifted the direction of James Moye's life in the early 1970s. A crash which left him two years in a wheelchair.

Before the accident his training and goals were in music. A pianist, James had earned a Master's degree at the Juilliard School of Music in New York. "After being involved in the air crash, I resolved my musical career, and went on to further my works and studies in the spiritual realm." He was still very much in the world of music and theatrics after beginning his spiritual preparation.

James perceives through voices, vibrations, and visions. "I was born with the gift. I was first aware of having abilities at an early age." Among his gifts from childhood are prophesy, telepathy, and healing through prayer.

Several years before the air accident he went to Nigeria to become a Yoruba priest, one who ministers through ancient African religious traditions. "I came home for a short stay. I stayed home for about six months to prepare myself to go back to Nigeria. I went back with the intention of staying for only another two weeks, and I stayed for four years!"

In that time he was initiated into the priesthood. In his training as a priest, the channels of communication with the realms of the Yoruba deities opened to James. He became mediator between the Yoruba divinity in the etheric world and humankind in the world of concrete realities. "In each ceremony, when the person takes the saints, he is given the Orisha, the saints in his head. Then he has given him a name which the Spirit of the Saint gives to him, in an initiation ceremony." In his Yoruba initiation ceremony, James was given a name, which in the Nigerian language means "King of the Fountain of Knowledge and Youth."

A teacher and a priest, James interprets the ways of the African deities for Western minds unfamiliar with African spirituality, discoursing on the spiritual powers and the divine wisdom of the African Gods, the Orisha, describing their relationship with humankind. They come to the aid of humans, giving guidance in the adjusting and balancing of events as mortals progress toward fulfilling their individual destinies on Earth, and in gaining completely the understanding of their spiritual nature and divine origin.

James is a priest of Shango Ife Divination. "Shango is represented by Santa Barbara. Santa Barbara is my ruling saint. Santa Barbara is represented by the sword which represents thunder and lightning. The more powerful of the Orisha is Shango."

The identities, which the individual Orisha assumed upon their entry to the New World, correspond with those of various

Catholic saints. The major Orisha, including Shango, are: Oruna, Ogun, Ellegua, Obatala, Yemaya and Oshun. Obatala is the father of the Gods. Ellegua is represented by Saint Martin de Pourres.

A ceremonial sword was given to James in Nigeria. He has an obi stick which is a tribute to call the Orisha. "Any of the saints can heal, can cure, or they can run death. The positive and the negative. In working with the Orisha, many things are possible," he states.

In his priestly duties, James performs rituals, ceremonies, does Ibos, and prays to the Orisha in behalf of humankind. "I go to the ocean, to Ibo, to Oshun and Yemaya, and take the sword to the ocean."

He counsels with a variety of individuals. "Some people were involved in some very serious crimes, but it wasn't that I sat in judgment. I prayed and asked the Spirit that a way would be opened that they would see their wrong-doing and would be given another opportunity to come to justice. And It did.

"You have to be very much in tune to receive the warmth and the blessing that the Spirit has. The Spirit sees sometimes you need money, they give you money; they see you need knowledge, they give you knowledge. With the knowledge, you can always get the money. Sometimes you've got the money, and you don't know what you want. But most of the times, you have to give up, to get. Sometimes you have to suffer. When you do without, then sometimes, when the blessing comes, it comes in greater proportions."

Higher states of consciousness exist with more proof than most people have been allowed to believe, he explains. James enables students to become aware of these spiritual realms. "My goal in life is to try to touch as many souls as I possibly can, to help them."

He is often a guest lecturer at educational and cultural institutions. He has been invited on numerous occasions to speak on the campus of Florida State University at Tallahassee. He lectures at the Museum of Natural History in New York, giving workshops and seminars.

To give students insight on how divine intelligence touches upon lives, he provides them with personalized illustrations. "The Spirit gives, I have no way of knowing. The night before I went to a class, I went to the lake, and the Spirit brought the information from the lake." He was shown a young woman, her physical identity. "I saw where there was going to be an injury to the foot. I could see a piece of glass."

The next day James talked to the gathering of students in Dr. N'aim Akbar's psychology class. In giving the student what had been revealed the previous night, he told her she was going to have trouble with her foot. She responded, "Not me, Dr. Moye!"

"I said, 'You have to be very careful, young lady.' Three days after the class, the girl cut her foot with a piece of glass, and she had to get fifteen stitches." She came to tell him of it. "I was profoundly shocked that she came. I said, 'That was prophesied for you!' She said she was getting out of the car and some glass cut the side of her shoe, it cut the shoe and her foot, and blood was all she could see."

He singled out a young man, revealing he knew the digestive problems that troubled the student's father. Then he spoke of the herbs that could help cure the condition. In speaking with a different student, he imparted she would be successful with her hands. He stresses to students to continue their education, and to search to know themselves as well.

About his vocation, he explains, "I am an herbalist. I do plant some Ibo plants dealing with the Orisha, the spirit. The cactus is used for many things. It could be used for a court case, it could be used for a person having difficulty on the job, it could be used for a person having a deep cold in the chest which will not heal. It could be used for burns and sores that will not heal.

"My Ibo ('offering') to the Spirit could be something very minute, such as a handful of pecans. I have saved many people's jobs with pecans and coconuts by going to the ocean and praying to the Spirit to bless them, and scattering the rind of the coconut and the pecans.

"I love to work with the herbs of Ellegua. He is the ruler. He is the ruler of the herb kingdom. He and Oshun. They give the plant, oche, which is Yoruba for 'power'. They give the sustenance of those things, all the good things Earth has to offer."

James Moye, born in New Jersey, now lives in Tallahassee, Florida. From experiences in childhood and in attending a Holiness Church, and his further experiences among the Yoruba people in Nigeria, James makes his own evaluations.

Of the Holiness Church he says, "Each person when they shout, they have a different shout. That means a different Spirit. Some hop, that is like the spirit of Shango. Some people go like mirenda (a dance); that is like the spirit of the sea, Yemaya. You have some people who dance from side to side; that is like Oshun dances with the skirt. They have the instruments, the drum, tambourine, the horn, string instruments, the organ and all that. The Spirit was really positive and a very strong force.

"Many things were revealed to our minds in the midst of a service. The way the Holiness people react was the way that the African people react. That is the closest religion to the Yoruba in Africa."

A soprano, Kathleen Carter at one time worked with Pearl Bailey, Nat King Cole, Dorothy Dandridge, and other entertainers as a background singer. She also had a singing career with the New York Metropolitan Opera Company. Now, as a psychic consultant and advisor, Kathleen works with artists like these.

"A lot of people in the entertainment world come to me. Entertainers are always in a contract, and they want to know where they are going with the manager and the contract. Whether the contract is proper, or not. That is true with those in the Metropolitan Opera. I work with some of the outstanding singers in the Met, and some of the great performers in the theatre. I have also worked with congressmen. I have read across the board."

Kathleen, a New Yorker, born in Omaha, Nebraska, explains how she accomplished this transition from singer to psychic. "I stopped singing around 1970. By 1972 or 1973, I had gone into this work. I had been studying all that time and was doing this work around 1972, on a part-time basis, and by 1973 I began doing it more full-time. It was actually 1974 that it was a full thrust."

Kathleen designs study programs for individuals on specific areas relating to psychic and spiritual growth. She makes referrals to organizations, such as holistic health services. Through classes she additionally instructs in the development of intuitivity and in the study of metaphysics. "My purpose is to guide, to direct. That is a combination of psychic readings and of getting some metaphysical principles out. I am a resource person. All these things I am about, and I feel it is my purpose to do." Kathleen counsels toward turning negative signs and conditions into positive ones. "When I predict, I have a tendency to say, 'Okay, I see this particular thing is off, but think positively about it. Let's try to stop it—ward it off.' The mind is energetic. The mind can travel through the ether and ward off things. There are some things which will come to pass, regardless. Other things can be warded off."

The information she receives comes directly from her super-consciousness, Kathleen confides. "There are three ways I get my messages: clairvoyantly, clairaudiently, and through impressions.

"I might feel a certain thing, and feel it is coming. The majority of it is seeing through picture form and sound. I can hear music. I can hear cars. I can hear most of what anybody might hear in everyday life. A statement might come, clairaudiently. I might hear a person speaking in his own tone a certain way. Sometimes it is just my own mind hearing it. It is psychic and prophetic."

She shares her thoughts about the Aquarian Age. "I feel as we move more into the Aquarian Age, people are becoming more aware of what they can do. They are more sensitive to the intelligence that is around us in the atmosphere, the inner world which is the spiritual plane. Hierarchy people or hierarchy beings are here to guide us, to guide mankind in a certain way. I feel we are more open to these energies as we move into the Aquarian Age. People are more open to psychic things, more so than ever before. And I say to young people, study all you can about nature and its laws in the metaphysical world."

Kathleen reflects, "I have black people, as well as all ethnic groups. I have a United Nations here!

"Of course, my first concern is with black people. I have to say that. We as a people, at times, do not feel that we can attain in certain areas. I feel that I am able to peer into that and see sometimes where they cannot see. And I feel that I've done something wonderful when I've done that. And that's my concern with black folk. With other people, other ethnic groups I feel the same thing, but my first concern is with our people.

"I am very much into our (African American) culture as a people and what we have come from, in regards to this work," Kathleen continues slowly. "We have come from very powerful things, from the Dogen in Africa who are the star watchers and who are very metaphysical.

"Our people had old ancient societies that were equivalent to what we might want to call the Rosicrucians of today. Rosicrucianism is based on Mystery School teaching, which the Greeks call Greek philosophy. There is no such thing told us, as we know, if we read history," Kathleen complains. "I am about educating our people to that, and letting them understand we come from something great. The scholars know this, and whites are very aware of this.

"Our nature is spiritual. That is our basis. We are a healing group of people, and we can only do that from a spiritual point of view. Once we get back to our basic selves, we will begin to expand, by developing our intuition, and developing ourselves on a holistic basis: that is, eating properly, meditating, exercising, and positive mind-thinking. Once we understand, through studying these things, we can align ourselves with the laws of nature. That is what we came from. All of our religions were based on natural law.

"We all have genetic memory," Kathleen concludes with emphasis. "Once the black man has tapped the genetic resource, he will be a god again, as he was in the beginning."

The influence of African religion which James Moye observed in his childhood church gives evidence to how spiritual legacy passes from ancestors to descendants. Kathleen Carter, Alfred Ligon, Luisah Teish, and Howard Thurman have similar perceptions.

By way of the slaves from Africa, as early as the 1600s, ancient religious and mystical beliefs, practices, and observances of Africa were carried to the New World. The spiritual heritage of African Americans is in this way founded in the Group Spirit of ancestors whose religious precepts predate Western ones. Some metaphysicians see the roots of the planet's religions as beginning in Africa and India. African Americans thus reflect, to varying degrees in their beliefs and practices, the earliest religious and spiritual heritages of Earth's prerecorded history.

The individuals presented in Company of Prophets: African American Psychics, Healers and Visionaries, *of course, share in the blessings, in their very singular ways, of that ancient spiritual inheritance.*

Some day an Aquarian spiritual ecumenical will be created among African Americans. The gathering will exist outside of all earthly religions, exterior to groups holding to restrictive belief systems, and beyond bodily, socio-economic, and political orientations. This African American spiritual interconnectiveness would materialize for the purpose of building a reservoir of positive energy to clear away the suspended age-old negative energies of racial invalidation accumulated from the African American people's tragic history. The refocusing of positive energy, composed of the unified spiritual awareness of African Americans, would then thoroughly cleanse the hurt, the hostility, the hate and despair, and the wounds of minimization, dehumanization, and despiritualization.

In that spirit-cleansing, the collective consciousness of Black America will be heightened and subsequently revitalized. And so will each individual spiritual being, who has chosen to incarnate as an African American, be rehabilitated, in that time of transformation, through the agency of group spirit and the positive mass consciousness of the race.

Bibliography, Notes, & Credits

Chapter One

1. Ruth Montgomery, *Threshold to Tomorrow* (New York: A Fawcett Crest Book published by Ballantine Books, 1982), pp. 2, 181, 183, 185.

2. Count Carnette, *Psychic Piano Music from the Masters* (Seattle, Washington: Carnette Archive Recordings, 1977).

3. Zora Neale Hurston, *Dust Tracks on a Road* (New York: Arno Press and *New York Times*, 1969), pp. 56-60.

4. Edmund L. Fuller, *Visions in Stone* (Pittsburgh, Pennsylvania: University of Pittsburgh Press, 1973), pp. 3, 6, 8, 12, 14, 20, 22, 24, 26.

5. Gary R. Kremer, *George Washington Carver: In His Own Words* (Columbia, Missouri: University of Missouri Press, 1987), pp. 20, 142-143.

6. Allie Light and Irving Saraf, *The Angel That Stands by Me* (San Francisco: Light-Saraf Films, 1984), documentary film transcript.

Chapter Two

1. The National Colored Spiritualist Association, U.S.A., *The National Spiritualist Reporter* (Detroit, Michigan: April, 1984), Vol. 46, No. 738.

2. Ruth Montgomery, *Threshold to Tomorrow* (New York: A Fawcett Crest Book published by Ballantine Books, 1982), p. 185.

3. Count Carnette, *Psychic Piano Music from the Masters* (Seattle, Washington: Carnette Archive Recordings, 1977).

4. Emma Hardinge Britten, *Modern American Spiritualism* (New Hyde Park, New York: University Books, Inc., 1970), p. 205.

5. Michael P. Smith, *Spirit World: Pattern in the Expressive Folk Culture of Afro-American New Orleans* (New Orleans: New Orleans Folklife Society, 1984), pp. 12, 13-16.

6. Jean McMahon Humez, editor, *Gifts of Power: The Writings of Rebecca Jackson, Black Visionary, Shaker Eldress* (Amherst, Massachussetts: University of Massachussetts Press, 1981), pp. 222, 241, 254-255, 303.

Chapter Three

1. Master Yogi Thomas, *Divine Light Meditation* (Chicago: Divine Light Temple, 1986), pp. 9, 74, 77.

2. Master Walter N. Thomas, *Spiritual Meditation* (Chicago: CFS Healing Temple, 1983), p. 17.

3. Jean McMahon Humez, editor, *Gifts of Power: The Writings of Rebecca Jackson, Black Visionary, Shaker Eldress* (Amherst, Massachusetts: University of Massachusetts Press, 1981), pp. 72-73, 87-88, 92-93, 96, 107-108, 128, 142, 144-145, 147, 174, 185-186.

4. Edmund L. Fuller, *Visions in Stone* (Pittsburgh, Pennsylvania: University of Pittsburgh Press, 1973), pp. 3, 6, 8, 12, 14, 20, 22, 24, 26.

5. Robert Bartlett Haas, editor, *William Grant Still and the Fusion of Cultures in American Music* (Los Angeles: Black Sparrow Press, 1972), pp. 107, 113, 118.

6. Verna Arvey, *In One Lifetime* (Fayetteville, Arkansas: University of

Arkansas Press, 1974), p. 181.

7. Robert Bartlett Haas, editor, *William Grant Still and the Fusion of Cultures in American Music* (Los Angeles: Black Sparrow Press, 1972), p. 113.

8. Verna Arvey, *In One Lifetime* (Fayetteville, Arkansas: University of Arkansas Press, 1974), pp. 72, 103.

9. Sarah Bradford, *Harriet Tubman: The Moses of Her People* (New York: Corinth Books, Inc., 1961), pp. 23, 61, 83-87, 92-93.

10. Darwin T. Turner, editor, *The Wayward and the Seeking: A Collection of Writings by Jean Toomer* (Washington, D.C.: Howard University Press, 1980), pp. 130-131.

11. Jean Toomer, *Exile into Being* (The Yale Collection of American Literature, Beinecke Rare Books and Manuscript Library, Yale University).

12. Jean Toomer, *The Life and Death of Nathan Jean Toomer: An Autobiography* (The James Weldon Johnson Collection, Beinecke Rare Books and Manuscript Library, Yale University).

13. Cynthia Earl Kerman and Richard Eldridge, *The Lives of Jean Toomer: A Hunger for Wholeness* (Baton Rouge and London: Louisiana State University Press, 1987), pp. 154-155.

14. Jean Toomer, *Exile into Being* (The Yale Collection of American Literature, Beinecke Rare Books and Manuscript Library, Yale University).

15. Amanda Smith, *An Autobiography, Amanda Smith* (Chicago: Meyer & Brother, Publishers, 1893), pp. 42-43, 104, 107, 110-111, 132, 133, 158-159, 174, 200, 308, 383, 429-430.

16. Allie Light and Irving Saraf, *The Angel That Stands by Me* (San Francisco: Light-Saraf Films, 1984), documentary film transcript.

17. Zilpha Elaw, *Memoirs of the Life, Religious Experience, Ministerial*

Travels and Labours of Mrs. Zilpha Elaw, an American Female of Colour: Together with Some Account of the Great Religious Revivals in America (London: Published by the author and sold by T. Dudley, 1846), pp. 22, 23, 36, 39, 47, 55, 60, 73, 74.

18. William Loren Katz, editor, *Narrative of Sojourner Truth, a Bondswoman of Olden Time* (New York: Arno Press and the *New York Times*, 1968), pp. 27, 64, 156-159.

19. Toby Thompson, "The Throne of the Third Heaven," *The Washington Post Magazine* (Washington, D.C.: *Washington Post*, August 9, 1981), p. 32.

20. Jane Livingston and John Beardsley, *Black Folk Art in America, 1930-1980* (Jackson, Mississippi: University Press of Mississippi and Center for the Study of Southern Culture, published for Corcoran Gallery of Art, 1982), p. 44.

21. Garland Anderson, *From Newsboy and Bellhop to Playwright* (San Francisco: Published by the author, 1925), pp. 11-13.

22. Jane Livingston and John Beardsley, *Black Folk Art in America, 1930-1980* (Jackson, Mississippi: University Press of Mississippi and Center for the Study of Southern Culture, published for Corcoran Gallery of Art, 1982), pp. 47, 97.

23. Sandi Donnelly, "The Red Light Came On," *The Times-Picayune* (New Orleans: *The Times-Picayune*, December 12, 1972), section 2, p. 2.

24. Howard Thurman, *Meditations of the Heart* (Richmond, Indiana: Friends United Press, 1979), p. 117.

25. Howard Thurman, *Disciplines of the Spirit* (Richmond, Indiana: Friends United Press, 1963), p. 96.

26. Howard Thurman, *The Inward Journey* (New York: Harper & Brothers, 1961), p. 51.

27. Howard Thurman, *With Head and Heart* (San Diego, New York,

and London: Harcourt Brace Jovanovich, 1979), p. 252.

28. Howard Thurman, *The Growing Edge* (New York: Harper & Brothers, 1956), p. 75.

29. Howard Thurman, *The Inward Journey* (New York: Harper & Brothers, 1961), pp. 51-52.

30. Bert James Lowenberg and Ruth Bogin, *Black Women in Nineteenth-Century American Life* (University Park and London: The Pennsylvania State University Press, 1976), p. 130.

31. Mary McLeod Bethune, "God Leads the Way, Mary," *The Christian Century* (Chicago: Christian Century Foundation, July 23, 1952), pp. 851-852.

32. Glenn Clark, *The Man Who Talks with the Flowers* (St. Paul, Minnesota: Macalester Park Publishing Company, 1939), pp. 17, 18, 21.

33. Linda O. McMurry, *George Washington Carver: Scientist and Symbol* (New York: Oxford University Press, 1981), pp. 43, 179, 285, 286, 287.

Chapter Four

1. Ruth Montgomery, *Threshold to Tomorrow* (New York: A Fawcett Crest Book published by Ballantine Books, 1982), pp. 182-183, 186.

Chapter Five

1. Neil Irvin Painter, "Henry Adams," *Dictionary of American Negro Biography*, edited by Rayford W. Logan and Michael R. Winston (New York and London: W. W. Norton & Co., 1982), p. 4.

2. Jean McMahon Humez, editor, *Gifts of Power: The Writings of Rebecca Jackson, Black Visionary, Shaker Eldress* (Amherst, Massachussetts: University of Massachussetts Press, 1981), pp. 89-90, 133-134,

163-164, 273.

3. Michael P. Smith, *Spirit World: Pattern in the Expressive Folk Culture of Afro-American New Orleans* (New Orleans: New Orleans Folklife Society, 1984), pp. 12, 14, 15.

4. William Ferris and Judy Peisner, *Fannie Bell Chapman: Gospel Singer* (Memphis, Tennessee: Center for Southern Folklore, Southern Culture Records, 1983).

5. Bill Shaw, "Where the Needy Come To Be Healed with Faith," *The Arizona Daily Star* (Tuscon, Arizona: October 12, 1978).

6. Amanda Smith, *An Autobiography, Amanda Smith* (Chicago: Meyer & Brother, Publishers, 1893), pp. 42-43, 99-101, 104-107, 110-111, 132-134, 158-159, 174, 199-200, 308, 382, 429-430.

7. Michael P. Smith, *Spirit World: Pattern in the Expressive Folk Culture of Afro-American New Orleans* (New Orleans: New Orleans Folklife Society, 1984), pp. 16.

8. Paul Neimark, "The Incredible Pain Killer Psychic," *Sepia Magazine* (Ft. Worth, Texas: March, 1976), pp. 72-79.

9. Clara Phillips, "Psychic Sees Reincarnation as a Reality," *Everett Herald* (Everett, Washington: August 11, 1979), p. 10c.

10. "World's Most Unusual Psychic Relieves Suffering," *Modern People* (Franklin Park, Illinois: February 8, 1976), Vol. 8, No. 6.

11. Brad Steiger, *Psychic City: Chicago* (Garden City, New York: Doubleday & Co., 1976), p. 85.

12. Sandra Parlin, "Psychic with X-ray Eyes Astounds Doctors," *Globe* (Boca Raton, Florida: Globe Communications, Inc., July 21, 1981), Vol. 28, No. 29.

Chapter Six

1. "World's Most Unusual Psychic Relieves Suffering," *Modern People* (Franklin Park, Illinois: February 8, 1976), Vol. 8., No. 6.

2. Paul Neimark, "The Incredible Pain Killer Psychic," *Sepia Magazine* (Ft. Worth, Texas: March, 1976), pp. 72-79.

Chapter Seven

1. Luisah Teish, *Jambalaya: The Natural Woman's Book of Personal Charms and Practical Rituals* (San Francisco: Harper & Row, Publishers, Inc., 1985), pp. 8, 38, 39, 81, 82.

2. Jean McMahon Humez, editor, *Gifts of Power: The Writings of Rebecca Jackson, Black Visionary, Shaker Eldress* (Amherst, Massachussetts: University of Massachussetts Press, 1981), pp. 111-112.

3. Cynthia Earl Kerman and Richard Eldridge, *The Lives of Jean Toomer: A Hunger for Wholeness* (Baton Rouge and London: Louisiana State University Press, 1987), pp. 153-155.

4. Jean Toomer, *Exile into Being* (The Yale Collection of American Literature, Beinecke Rare Books and Manuscript Library, Yale University).

Chapter Eight

1. Paschel B. Randolph, *The Wonderful Story of Ravalette, also Tom Clark and His Wife* (New York: Sinclair Tousey, 1863), pp. 83, 214.

2. F. Roy Johnson, *The Fabled Doctor Jim Jordan* (Murfreesboro, North Carolina: Johnson Publishing Company, 1963).

Chapter Nine

1. Howard Thurman, *With Head and Heart* (San Diego, New York,

and London: Harcourt Brace Jovanovich, 1979), p. 254.

2. Luisah Teish, *Jambalaya: The Natural Woman's Book of Personal Charms and Practical Rituals* (San Francisco: Harper & Row, Publishers, Inc., 1985), pp. 8, 81.

3. Lloyd Strayhorn, "Numbers & You," the *New York Amsterdam News* (New York: Amsterdam News Publishing Company, September 18, 1982), p. 48.

4. Sarah Bradford, *Harriet Tubman: The Moses of Her People* (New York: Corinth Books, Inc., 1961), p. 115.

Chapter Ten

1. Reverend C.C. White and Ada Morehead Holland, *No Quittin' Sense* (Austin, Texas: University of Texas Press, 1969), pp. 5, 134, 167, 169.

2. Jay Hall, "Calestine Williams: All in the Mind," *The Commercial Appeal Mid-South Magazine* (Memphis, Tennessee: April 15, 1979), p. 19.

3. George Rawick, editor, *The American Slave: A Composite Autobiography Vol. 3* (Westport, Connecticut: Greenwood Publishing Group, Inc., 1977), Series 1, Vol. 3.

4. Booker T. Washington, *Frederick Douglass* (Philadelphia and London: G.W. Jacobs and Company, 1907).

5. Jane Livingston and John Beardsley, *Black Folk Art in America, 1930-1980* (Jackson, Mississippi: University Press of Mississippi and Center for the Study of Southern Culture, published for Corcoran Gallery of Art, 1982), p. 55.

6. Ibid., pp. 65-66.

7. Mary Church Terrell, *A Colored Woman in a White World* (New York: Arno Press, A New York Times Company, 1980), pp. 285-286.

8. Gary R. Kremer, *George Washington Carver: In His Own Words* (Columbia, Missouri: University of Missouri Press, 1987), pp. 142-143.

9. Howard Thurman, *With Head and Heart* (San Diego, New York, and London: Harcourt Brace Jovanovich, 1979), p. 265.

10. Howard Thurman, *Deep Is the Hunger* (New York: Harper & Brothers, Publishers, 1951), p. 109.

11. Ibid., pp. 169-170.

12. Howard Thurman, *The Inward Journey* (New York: Harper & Brothers, 1961), p. 131.

13. Luther E. Smith, Jr., *Howard Thurman: The Mystic as Prophet* (Lanham, Maryland: University Press of America, 1982), p. 55.

14. Henry James Young, editor, *God and Human Freedom: A Festschrift in Honor of Howard Thurman* (Richmond, Indiana: Friends United Press, 1983), p. XII.

15. Howard Thurman, *With Head and Heart* (San Diego, New York, and London: Harcourt Brace Jovanovich, 1979), p. 259-260.

16. Henry James Young, editor, *God and Human Freedom: A Festschrift in Honor of Howard Thurman* (Richmond, Indiana: Friends United Press, 1983), p. 163.

17. Ibid., p. XIV.

18. Howard Thurman, *With Head and Heart* (San Diego, New York, and London: Harcourt Brace Jovanovich, 1979), p. 259-260.

19. *Studies in Black Gnosticism* (Los Angeles: The Aquarian Spiritual Center, 1978).

PUBLICATION CREDITS

Excerpts from *Sepia Magazine* reprinted by permission of the African American Life and Culture Museum (Dallas, Texas).

Excerpts from *Modern American Spiritualism* distributed by Ayer Company Publishers, Inc. (Salem, New Hampshire).

Excerpts from *Fannie Bell Chapman: Gospel Singer* reprinted by permission of the Center for Southern Folklore (Memphis, Tennessee).

Excerpts from the July 23, 1952 issue of *The Christian Century* reprinted by permission of the Christian Century Foundation (Chicago, Illinois), copyright © 1952.

Excerpts from *The Commercial Appeal Mid-South Magazine* reprinted by permission of The Commercial Appeal (Memphis, Tennessee).

Excerpts from *Black Folk Art in America, 1930-1980* by Jane Livingston and John Beardsley reprinted by permission of The Corcoran Gallery of Art (Washington, D.C.).

Excerpts from *Psychic Piano Music from the Masters* reprinted by permission of Carnette Archive Recordings (Seattle, Washington).

Excerpts from *Divine Light Meditation* and *Spiritual Meditation* reprinted by permission of Master Walter Thomas (Chicago, Illinois).

Excerpts from *Psychic City: Chicago* by Brad Steiger reprinted by permission of Doubleday Dell Publishing Group, Inc. (New York, New York).

Excerpts from *The Everett Herald* reprinted by permission of The Everett Herald Publishing Company, Inc. (Everett, Washington).

Excerpts from *God and Human Freedom: A Festschrift in Honor of*

Excerpts from *The Times-Picayune* reprinted by permission of The Times-Picayune Publishing Corporation (New Orleans, Louisiana).

Excerpts from *Howard Thurman: The Mystic as Prophet* by Luther E. Smith, Jr. reprinted by permission of University Press of America (Lanham, Maryland).

Excerpts from *Studies in Black Gnosticism* reprinted by permission of Alfred Ligon (Los Angeles, California).

Excerpts from the playbill of *Voyages* reprinted by permission of Kim McMillion.

PHOTO CREDITS

The author wishes to acknowledge the following individuals for granting permission to reprint their photographs:

Eddie Cabral, Los Angeles, California. His artwork, "Buddha on My Mind."

Noelle Hoeppe, New York, New York. Photograph of Alpha Omega.

Allie Light and Irving Saraf, San Francisco, California. Photographs of Minnie Evans and of her paintings from their private collection.

STAY IN TOUCH

On the following pages you will find listed, with their current prices, some of the books and tapes now available on related subjects. Your book dealer stocks most of these, and will stock new titles in the Llewellyn series as they become available. We urge your patronage.

However, to obtain our full catalog, to keep informed of new titles as they are released and to benefit from informative articles and helpful news, you are invited to write for our bi-monthly news magazine/catalog. A sample copy is free, and it will continue coming to you at no cost as long as you are an active mail customer. Or you may keep it coming for a full year with a donation of just $7.00 in U.S.A. and Canada ($20.00 overseas, first class mail). Many bookstores also have *The Llewellyn New Times* available to their customers. Ask for it.

Stay in touch! In *The Llewellyn New Times'* pages you will find news and reviews of new books, tapes and services, announcements of meetings and seminars, articles helpful to our readers, news of authors, advertising of products and services, special money-making opportunities, and much more.

The Llewellyn New Times
P.O. Box 64383-Dept. 583, St. Paul, MN 55164-0383, U.S.A.
• • •
TO ORDER BOOKS AND TAPES

If your book dealer does not have the books and tapes described on the following pages readily available, you may order them directly from the publisher by sending full price in U.S. funds, plus $3.00 for postage and handling for orders *under* $10.00; $4.00 for orders *over* $10.00. There are no postage and handling charges for orders over $50.00. UPS Delivery: We ship UPS whenever possible. Delivery guaranteed. Provide your street address as UPS does not deliver to P.O. Boxes. UPS to Canada requires a $50.00 minimum order. Allow 4-6 weeks for delivery. Orders outside the U.S.A. and Canada: Airmail—add retail price of book; add $5.00 for each non-book item (tapes, etc.); add $1.00 per item for surface mail.

FOR GROUP STUDY AND PURCHASE

Because there is a great deal of interest in group discussion and study of the subject matter of this book, we feel that we should encourage the adoption and use of this particular book by such groups by offering a special "quantity" price to group leaders or "agents."

Our Special Quantity Price for a minimum order of five copies of *Company of Prophets* is $38.85 cash-with-order. This price includes postage and handling within the United States. Minnesota residents must add 6.5% sales tax. For additional quantities, please order in multiples of five. For Canadian and foreign orders, add postage and handling charges as above. Credit card (VISA, Master Card, American Express) orders are accepted. Charge card orders only may be phoned free ($15.00 minimum order) within the U.S.A. or Canada by dialing 1-800-THE-MOON. Customer service calls dial 1-612-291-1970. Mail orders to:

LLEWELLYN PUBLICATIONS
P.O. Box 64383-Dept. 583 / St. Paul, MN 55164-0383, U.S.A.

Prices subject to change without notice.

THE LLEWELLYN PRACTICAL GUIDE TO
THE DEVELOPMENT OF PSYCHIC POWERS
by Denning & Phillips

You may not realize it, but you already have the ability to use ESP, Astral Vision and Clairvoyance, Divination, Dowsing, Prophecy, Communication with Spirits, to exercise (as with any talent) and develop them.

Written by two of the most knowledgeable experts in the world of Magick today, this book is a complete course—teaching you, step-by-step, how to develop these powers that actually have been yours since birth. Using the techniques they teach, you will soon be able to move objects at a distance, see into the future, know the thoughts and feelings of another person, find lost objects, locate water and even people using your own no-longer latent talents.

Psychic powers are as much a natural ability as any other talent. You'll learn to play with these new skills, work with groups of friends to accomplish things you never would have believed possible before reading this book. The text shows you how to make the equipment you can use, the exercises you can do—many of them at anytime, anywhere—and how to use your abilities to change your life and the lives of those close to you. Many of the exercises are presented in forms that can be adapted as games for pleasure and fun, as well as development.

0-87542-191-1, 256 pgs., 5 1/4 x 8, illus.   **$7.95**

A PRACTICAL GUIDE TO PAST LIFE REGRESSION
by Florence Wagner McClain

Have you ever felt that there had to be more to life than this? Have you ever met someone and felt an immediate kinship? Have you ever visited a strange place and felt that you had been there before? Have you struggled with frustrations and fears which seem to have no basis in your present life? Are you afraid of death? Have you ever been curious about reincarnation or maybe just interested enough to be skeptical?

This book presents a simple technique which you can use to obtain past life information TODAY. There are no mysterious preparations, no groups to join, no philosophy to which you must adhere. You don't even have to believe in reincarnation. The tools are provided for you to make your own investigations, find your own answers and make your own judgements as to the validity of the information and its usefulness to you.

Whether or not you believe in reincarnation, past life regression remains a powerful and valid tool for self-exploration. Information procured through this procedure can be invaluable for personal growth and inner healing, no matter what its source. Florence McClain's guidebook is an eminently sane and capable guide for those who wish to explore their possible past lives or conduct regressions themselves.

0-87542-510-0, 160 pages, 5 1/4 x 8   **$6.95**

Prices subject to change without notice.